LEGACY OF A

ANGEL WARS TRILOGY
VOLUME THREE

LEGACY

OF

ANGELS

KELVIN CHILVERS

LEGACY OF ANGELS

Copyright 2023:   KELVIN CHILVERS

Cover illustration: No copyright infringement is intended.

Publication of this book is by: AMAZON KDP

Available in soft cover and eBook.

LEGACY OF ANGELS

I wish to thank family, friends, and all beautiful souls who are following my author's journey. Your support is inspirational and a source of encouragement.

I reserve special thanks to Katie Kavanagh whose selfless, kind-hearted and spiritual nature, gave me guidance and focus to make my dreams a reality.

With Katie's permission, it was an honour for me to portray her as an integral character in the Angel Wars Trilogy, as First Angel and daughter to the universe, Abigail.

It is my fervent hope I have created a character which does the greatest service to Katie, to me and others.

As with my collection of crystals, their energy as a source of comfort, and in the belief I am receiving the support of the universe, my guardian angel and spirit guide, I continue my beautiful journey with passion.

All of you are a part of me; embedded in my soul.

Bless you all: LOVE AND LIGHT!

Previous publications by author: KELVIN CHILVERS

DREAMING ANGELS: Volume One ANGEL WARS TRILOGY

FIRST ANGEL: THE PREQUEL Volume Two ANGEL WARS TRILOGY

HOLDING ON TO HOPE

5

LEGACY OF ANGELS

Author's Biography:

Born October 1954, my passion for writing began aged seven. I was basically a shy individual who would often lock himself away in his room and write. It was a way

of letting my fantasies carte blanche to roam the pages and tell a story. Suffice to say, my imagination never went away over the years. I never lost the passion to create and tell a story, as I have always wanted the reader to be given an opportunity to expand their own mind and question, what is real and what is not.

PART ONE

UTOPIAN

CHAPTER 1

A NEW WORLD...

Imagine, waking up to a new world,

A world without travel or communications

Essentially.

No TV or mobile phones,

No public events.

With a scarcity of food and water.

Imagine, waking up to a world in chaos,

Wondering, if waking up is your curse.

It will change.

In time.

So, for those of you who survived,

Look to your neighbour,

And those who are less fortunate,

And help them rise.

For it is the meek who have inherited

LEGACY OF ANGELS

What remains, of our world.

* * * *

Imagine, waking up to a new world,

A utopian existence,

Where energy of the universe

Is mankind's lifeforce,

And nature's heartbeat.

Imagine, waking up smiling each day,

Imbued with positive energy,

And feeling blessed with love and light.

Imagine a life, where children

Are free to roam,

Safe from harm.

A life without crime or fear,

A life without disease

And where the only illness

Is age, and the allotted time given to us.

Imagine, a world where religion,

Does not conflict with another's belief,

Where nirvana

Is the drug of life.

LEGACY OF ANGELS

* * * *

How do we react then,

When dark energy insinuates

Its evil intent?

Seeking vengeance,

Beginning as an insidious parasitic influence

On all, which is sublimely perfect?

When beauty, becomes ugly.

When those barriers erected as a shield

Against discord,

Falter, crack, and crumble.

And darkness

Threatens to extinguish,

The light?

A new world begins with chaos. It will not always be this way.

For those who survived 'world's end,' they are fortunate, as they have the time to witness its rebirth. Not that the majority believed, they were blessed.

LEGACY OF ANGELS

Byron Jones woke up each day, and he was content on the surface. He felt differently on the inside, where there existed an empty void within his heart, as memories were slow to dissipate and grant him solace. It had to be the same for everyone who had survived the holocaust, or so he believed.

He had no conception of time, yet he supposed two weeks had elapsed since the world, as he knew it, became hell on earth.

Byron had witnessed more than he cared to experience, and even now, wondered why he had been spared a similar fate to most everyone.

With each new day, he felt himself growing stronger, positive, and more determined. It was with relief the air around the peaks of Snowdonia in Wales was refreshing and seemed to be energised. He didn't think it was from radiation, as the world had collapsed, not from a war created by men. What he perceived, was a world's end from natural causes. Or, as he was inclined to assimilate, a world destroyed by unnatural forces.

He'd left the chaos and destruction of his home city of Cardiff, having lost everything which meant something. He believed, he hoped, by taking a sojourn to Snowdonia would help alleviate the pain of having lost so much which breathed life to his mind and body, his spirit and soul.

As with so many, his efforts had been insignificant, as unprecedented earthquakes ripped across the landscape and reduced cities to rubble. As if the heatwaves, and plummeting temperatures, the relentless floods, hadn't been enough to test one's resolve for a time.

His wife, his beautiful Ellen and three young children, were unable to escape their home as it crashed down around them.

Byron had been outside when the catastrophe struck, going to assist a couple who had been in a car accident trying to flee the frenetic destruction to their city and a vast area around it. Their CRV, crammed with possessions, foodstuff and crates of water had nose-dived into an immense crater which had opened on the road beneath them.

They didn't make it.

Neither did his family.

The grief endured, having dug for hours amongst the carnage wrought by a series of quakes to recover the bodies of his wife and children, was worse than all the days of suffering prior to that moment; the fear of the unknown. They had been unified, as a family. He was their rock, as they were his. A combined love, as with faith, was their source of hope and kept them going.

Having to say farewell to those he cherished above everything, was his reason to leave. He imagined; his own existence was perhaps measured in days, or weeks.

Byron recovered what supplies he was able to; a two-man ridge tent, some items of food, and he purloined as many bottles of water from the wrecked CRV as his 650cc Suzuki would carry.

He supposed, it was the only mode of transport equipped to traverse the piles of debris, abandoned vehicles and hellish fissures along the roads.

And there were the corpses. Those who didn't make it, or were blessed, and he must have passed hundreds, even thousands. He had to pull a veil over his thoughts as the motorbike weaved a precarious path around these obstacles. He needed to be away from the stench of decay, all the chaos; those memories which stabbed incessantly at his heart.

On his journey, he became witness to others who had survived, trundling around lost and bereft of spirit. They were few to the many who lay dead.

14

LEGACY OF ANGELS

It was with a monumental effort, but somehow, his faithful machine got him to where he needed to be.

He'd chosen a trail most tourists once used and set up camp at a midway point. It afforded him a view of the peak on one side, and a breath-taking view of what was once a landscape of sheer beauty.

That no longer existed, as everywhere, as far as the eye could see, was a panoramic vista which looked like a battlefield. Sat atop a ridge, he often pondered as to whether the world could recover, or whether remaining life had a short time limit left to them.

Byron would spend frequent moments in meditation, and there came episodes when he was convinced his wife Ellen and the children were reaching out to him, as he recalled having a heartfelt conversation. He was certain it was simply an outpouring of grief where his subconscious would have him believe there was an afterlife.

There were moments when he wished he had a dog for company.

He missed his guitar, one of those possessions as with so much, which did not survive the house collapsing.

When he wasn't meditating, or reflecting on all he'd lost, his attention would be drawn to the monument in the distance, of a large pyramid; not of quarried stone of any description he surmised, but appeared smooth and was of a dull black colour and composition.

Before the world came under attack from extremes of climactic and geological change, the pyramid had not existed. Beneath a warming sun and atmospheric haze, the pyramid was otherworldly, an imposing structure to have come from space or to have emerged from its tomb beneath the ground.

Byron would wonder, as to its purpose in the new world, as to whether its purpose for being, was either benign or hostile.

From his position he felt a rhythmic pattern of subtle energy emanating off the structure, and it was possible, this was a reason the air around felt clean and revitalised and served to make him feel hopeful.

Not that he himself felt overly energised or motivated, as here on the fourth day since leaving the ruins of his home, he was choosing the time to lay ghosts to rest.

On the fifth day, Byron was to receive visitors.

He woke up surprisingly refreshed, as the subject matter of his dreams were once again of moments spent with his family. He went for an early morning bathe in a freshwater spring, which he felt certain, had not existed until recent times. He would have known, as he came with his family on regular jaunts to Snowdonia, when all was good and wonderful in his world. Breakfast was to consist of sausage and beans from a can and French toast crisp breads. He was able to heat water on a small camping stove as he loved his black coffee. He still had some sugar sachets, so he was all set for the day.

Feeling more determined, and greatly invigorated since the day he arrived, and having done his laundry, he could face the remainder of the day in a positive frame of mind. Even formulate a plan of action, as it would soon be necessary to do so to keep supplies replenished.

It was while meditating, and singularly entranced by the first bird song he'd encountered for quite some time, he detected a shift in the pattern of air currents. Just briefly, he imagined his skin was to be flayed off his bones before all became incredibly calm. Peaceful.

It had him wondering if it was a direct result of an intense meditation and he'd transcended to another plane. As to where, and why, and how; he had no idea.

He was compelled to look over his shoulder and was surprised to receive the company of a gracious and beautiful woman of indeterminate age, alongside a tall muscular man whose skin gleamed the colour of seasoned patinaed mahogany.

Byron dutifully nodded and was again surprised he should receive a greeting via a telepathic connection. Fortunately for him, the message was delivered in the only language he knew.

'We apologise for the intrusion,' the woman said, in a musical tone which caressed the walls of his mind soporifically. *'My name is Georgina, and my companion here is Mazouma.'*

'Pleased to meet you,' Byron answered, and not quite believing he was able to fashion a response with his own mind. *'I'm Byron, and you're the first living souls I have encountered in days.'*

Georgina was first to approach and she sat beside him on the ledge, crossing her legs, and gazing imperiously out at the view afforded them, seeing not the destruction wrought by adverse inclement weather and geographical shifts, but the beauty encapsulated by a clear sky, a resplendent sun and clean invigorating air.

'Where have the two of you come from?' Byron enquired, aware the one called Mazouma maintained a position at their rear.

'For your information, young man,' Georgina answered, *'We are emissaries of hope, and there are many like us scattered across the globe, given the task of assisting mankind and nature in embracing a new world without fear. It is for us to instil courage and a sense of wellbeing in the hearts of those who survived, to prosper and evolve, and become united.'*

'*Emissaries of hope, you say?*' he remarked without quipping or denigrating the ethereal person's faith all could be different, and for the best.

Byron's attention was again on the pyramid in the distance.

'*Being a witness to something which at no time existed until recent times, should I not be disconcerted?*' he asked. '*As with the mystical appearance suddenly of two elementals who are more than they seem. In that we can converse telepathically. Just saying, as I have never experienced it before, and at no time presumed I had this gift. There were occasions when I would anticipate things my late wife was thinking and would speak of them before she was able to. We laughed about it, found it in no way invasive or weird. Just accepted and concluded it was a reason why we were so close and bonded. My Ellen laughed a lot, as I recall. She loved life, doted on our kids; made me complete.*'

'*We know of your great loss,*' said Georgina, and let a hand drift to his arm to quell the tide of remorse threatening to resurface. '*As with so many. This is a new world, and all will be granted special gifts to help them evolve from this moment, as with their ancestors at another time.*'

'*You and your companion; who or what exactly are you?*'

'*We are celestial elementals, my friend; messengers of hope.*'

'*I see.*'

'*We have lived many lives, as and when required.*'

Byron was given brief pause to ponder the semantics of Georgina's statement.

'*Do you know the meaning or purpose of the pyramid, standing proud and glorious in the distance? I know that it has recently appeared; but from where? What is the purpose of such a thing? I thought, maybe, it was an alien craft. What I'm asking is;*'

should survivors of the holocaust have a reason to fear its presence, or embrace it?'

'It is one part of the future,' said Georgina, 'a monument *created by universal design billions of years ago, that which has remained dormant, hidden in secret, until this moment. The pyramid is an ancient source of natural power and will replace all the fuels and energy the world once relied upon.'*

'Impressive,' he quietly ruminated. 'And quite beautiful.'

'You have a part to play also,' Georgina intimated, and giving his arm a gentle squeeze of affection, preparing him.

'I wish that I knew my purpose,' he said, deep in thought. 'I have lost everything which meant something to me. My wife and children were my world. A reason to exist.'

'You have not lost everything,' she said in placating and sincere tones to soothe his conscience. 'You have compassion, and a heart of purity others can benefit from. You have hidden strengths you may not be aware of. You are a leader, fair-minded, and have a natural desire to help those in need.'

'None of which I am remotely feeling, if I'm honest.'

'You will; in time.'

Mazouma approached silently and sat on his left, closed his eyes, and breathed in the clean energised air. From a pocket of his colourful smock-coat, he handed Byron a gift of a palm-sized natural quartz crystal in its raw state.

Byron could only stare at it as he pondered the significance of the object presented to him. He became aware instantly the crystal possessed extraordinary energy and imagined it was seeping into his pores. He felt light-headed and had to close his eyes, as whorls of contrasting colours swam hypnotically in his mind's eye.

LEGACY OF ANGELS

The crystal had appeared quite heavy when it was first placed in his hand, and within moments, had become light as a feather. Its energy became a spiralling blossom within his head, chest, and lower abdomen, and he was shown a possible future he was meant to participate in. That, of assisting others in rebuilding their lives, their homes, while inspiring hope.

When he eventually opened his eyes and exhaled it was to find the two strangers had departed. He'd not known or sensed them leave, as if they had simply evaporated into the ether.

Byron knew his purpose, and he was enthralled. He closed his eyes again, the crystal trembling in his palm as he held a conversation with his belated wife. She gave her blessing before an image of her dissipated, and he wept inconsolably for a time.

Not from sadness, but from elation, knowing in his heart he had been granted a reason to continue.

To live!

CHAPTER 2

BLESSED...

> There was once delivered a prophecy,
>
> Of hope to mankind beyond 'THE RAPTURE.'
>
> I deliver God's work to those who cling to faith,
>
> Even as I witness,
>
> Those who believe in something else entirely.
>
> Something miraculous...

Cardinal Rossini took a moment's respite following afternoon prayer.

Six weeks had elapsed since the world became a living and dying hell. And of those who had survived he had witnessed a remarkable change. For a torrid time, he had observed broken hearts and withered spirits, of souls cleaved. He was subjected to grief on a scale he had never encountered. The tears of the damned could have filled a reservoir.

Following those six weeks of confusion and uncertainty, his prayers were to receive an answer, as his dwindling flock endured mass emblazoned with genuine smiles. Even when his people were not in prayer, most would sing to pass the day.

Not hymns, as he'd hoped.

But that was okay, he confessed, if the mood of people was joyous.

Aside from the change in the psyche of people, the Cardinal had observed other miracles, of those who had suffered appalling injuries. Many of whom were left maimed, suddenly recovered, and became mobile and stronger. This was not achieved by getting medical assistance or having received depleted medicinal resources.

There came harmony, focus and balance in the thriving communities scattered around the ruins of his beloved country. He'd acquired knowledge there existed a governing body, as such. Not like before. Nothing was like it was before. It was the ruling powers edict to implement plans, whereby everybody was expected to concentrate their resources creating a sustainable life every person could benefit from.

Miraculously, there was no profit to be gained, as there was no currency circulating. All which existed had no monetary value, it appeared.

Cardinal Rossini was intrigued by this, as there has always been a reason to barter and to garner acquisitions of wealth and power; a reason to trade. He believed it was a temporary measure only until the economy was established, yet it had him wondering if it was the same the world over, supposing there existed a world outside of his country.

He'd received reports, sketchy at best, the southern provinces no longer existed, as with areas along the eastern seaboard. Some were adamant, the island of Sicily and Venice were lost to the tsunamis. It was not a subject Cardinal Rossini wished to ponder. He prayed, and it would have to suffice, until he was able to witness the devastation for himself.

As of the present, his duty had been to his beloved city and Rome; what was left of it. His presence helped at the beginning. The power of faith was instilled in the psyche of every individual. It was changing though. His flock were not so dependent on spiritual enlightenment, it seemed; at least, not from the Church and all it had given to them in the past.

Cardinal Rossini reflected on the time he was visited by a celestial being, an angel no less, for she had been the designated Chosen One to wage a war against evil and prevailed.

At a great cost, he surmised; yet all is not without hope for those lost souls who survived the 'Rapture.' As it was decreed, his was a powerful voice, and was called upon frequently to administer prophetic words to placate those who were struggling with change, confronting a new order, in a new world.

He became witness to the miracle of positive changes daily, that which filled his heart with joy, as all was progressing at a formidable pace. He saw the benefits of progress, as man worked alongside man harmoniously, to further the advancement of hope and well-being. They did so, not for praise or gain, but because their hearts were a vessel of love and light for their neighbour.

Everyone, it seemed, was blessed with glorious light.

On the following day, having had an epiphany, he was to venture beyond the ramshackle ruins of the Vatican. A voice in his head had cajoled him into leaving his post for a time.

As to the purpose for his proposed sojourn, he was given no sign, only in that he was to travel the wasteland of his once beautiful country and observe the changes. There was progress, undeniably, yet few understood the ramifications of the changes in position since the aftermath of war.

Rossini was of the belief, not everyone had been 'touched' by the divine goodness afforded them, and there would be those in need of guidance in order to achieve enlightenment. In a utopian world, there was still the propensity for evil; as it was once written, or so he'd been led to believe.

He left the confines of his home in capable hands; with the knowledge he was to embark on a journey without additional company. Outside, and wearing simple clerical apparel, the Cardinal breathed in the air suffused with an energy which flowed within his veins.

He was no longer seeing mounds of rubble and decay, instead, had an insight of all that was meant to be.

Rossini walked perhaps a kilometre, no more, and was amazed at the progress already prevalent. The debris of fallen monuments had been removed in places, even as areas existed still of Rome's history lying in despairing piles, having survived centuries and countless bloody wars. It had come to this; and it was with great effort he should not have this affect his calm persona and make him morose.

Casting his gaze across the ruins which remained, it was as if God had stamped his feet in a moment of petulance and fervour, to teach his subjects a valuable lesson in humility, to his way of thinking.

As he progressed along a precarious road the Cardinal became intrigued, and at the same time, surprised and gratified to witness groups of survivors actively toiling to rebuild his beloved city.

Close to the skeletal hub of the Parthenon monument were a line of marquees, and it was these and the people gathered around them which became an enticement.

LEGACY OF ANGELS

Gone, were the once bustling restaurants, cafes and designer shops, the congested roads and vast groups of tourists. He supposed, it all began at the start of the pandemic. An imposed lockdown at the time, had changed the face of everything, and it was only the beginning.

Then came the Rapture, and it was a memory which still haunted him. How could it not? It was the same for everyone yet, as a witness to the resplendent joy all around him, it had him wondering if most everyone had overcome the horror to have affected their lives.

As with the Cardinal, they were survivors of bedlam and the wrath of evil.

He paused as a motorcycle puttered along the broken road; the man riding it, waving and smiling to him. It had Rossini wondering if there were fuel supplies readily available, to benefit transport and machinery. Should it be so, then there was an opportunity to get the world's electricity back on grid, with doors opening to greater advancement.

As he approached the first of the marquees, he felt a tide of resplendent energy wash over him and seep into his pores.

A young woman, in her thirties; he surmised, stepped forward to confront him. She appeared to glow, the radiance to touch her eyes and vivacious smile, drawing him into her aura. Once again, he was reminded of the time an elemental had entered his chambers, purporting to be the Chosen One and messenger of hope.

Was this then, to be her legacy to all who survived? He reflected on the preposterous notion the angel of light had succoured, in that it was her dream to have mankind live an existence of purity and forgiveness; 'to love thy neighbour'.

'Your eminence,' the woman greeted him, 'My name is Maria, and it is my wish you take on your journey a talisman for personal guidance. Please, come, let me show you my collection.'

As he was led into the smallish marquee, he was further surprised by the young woman's candour, as she was to steer his passage by holding his arm. It was normal etiquette, for a person not to display physical or intimate contact with a man of the cloth, as it was once seen as anathema and disrespectful, and frowned upon.

Rossini forgave her, as he was content this woman should feel joyous and not afflicted with grief.

'May I ask, how it is, you should know I am to embark on a great journey?' he enquired.

Still smiling, Maria answered him. 'The crystals; they let me into your thoughts.'

'The crystals?' He was momentarily stupefied by her comment, more so, as he became confronted by an array of crystals and minerals displayed on three trestle tables.

It instantly had him remembering the moment he had witnessed an angel's feather along with a gleaming black stone the size of his palm which had revealed magical and mystical properties beyond his simple understanding at that time.

'Forgive my ignorance of such matters, but what is the nature and purpose of crystals?' he asked, becoming light-headed as the energy within the tent seemed to engulf him and insinuate a path into his brain. 'Members of my flock speak of such things, with reverence.'

'The crystals,' said Maria, while continuing to hang on to his arm, 'are the future. They are the source of all energy in the new world. They give light to a darkened room, as an example, for they have replaced a requirement for fossil fuels and electricity. They retain other properties, as the energy of these crystals inspire people to be positive in their outlook. They heal the sick; it's true. Once, we were in the grip of a killer virus; now, it is believed, the virus which killed millions no longer poses a threat.'

'How can that be?' he wished to know and would have slumped to his knees in prayer had Maria not supported him, with a strength which belied her size. 'You are telling me; the energy of these crystals can operate machinery, even create a source of light? At the same time, this energy insinuates a path to a person's mind and body, which in effect, suggests that they have a controlling influence on a person and their actions?'

'I suppose; the answer is yes. But in a good way, your eminence. Imagine for a moment; the beneficial effects of a positive mind and a sense of euphoria, where goodness replaces negative thoughts and impulses, where there exists only love and light; is it not a Godly thing? Are you not feeling this? We are all blessed. We have little and want for nothing. Women and children can walk the streets freely, safe from predators. Crime is non-existent. People's penchant for greed, lust and power has been eliminated.'

'A utopian world, as I suggested,' he casually remarked. 'I met someone briefly, before our planet was to endure the Rapture. She saw the future, and predicted such a world, should the forces of light overcome darkest evil.'

'She had to have been one of the earth angels,' said Maria coquettishly, and flouncing her body with a mischievous sway of her hips, that which encapsulated her joy and freedom. 'One of many.'

'My dear; she was so much more. As with our saviour, the Lord Jesus Christ, she came to deliver a message of hope, to a chosen few.'

'It will always remain beyond our comprehension, as to why so many have perished who were innocent, yet some of us have survived to help rebuild our communities. Please, let me choose a crystal for you,' she insisted suddenly, her smile at no time dwindling, and it was a smile to captivate her eclectic audience of one.

She moved around the tables, her hands passing over the energy each crystal and mineral transmitted to her, and became drawn to one, that which was in its natural raw state. She lifted it away from its nest of tissue paper and as it settled in the palm of one hand, the crystal was seen to glow. Taking the Cardinal's right hand, she placed it on his own palm and enclosed it with his long tapering fingers.

'Dear Lord!' he exclaimed, and the energy he derived from its source, had his eyes fluttering and closing, briefly. Yet all became transparent in his mind's eye, for he was another to receive a glimpse of the progress occurring in the surviving regions of his beloved country as of that moment.

'The crystals,' said Maria in soft tones, have been blessed by those earth angels I have mentioned. This will guide you on your travail. Your prayers, sir, have been answered.'

Rossini was aware of tears squeezing beyond his closed lids, and dared to hope, mankind and the planet was saved. He would play his part, as was expected of him. The celestial queen, Seraphina, had placed her trust in him. As with another, who came to his rescue at a fortuitous time, when he was faced with two entities who had strayed from the path of righteousness, whose purpose was to continue the spread of evil against those who meant to deliver hope.

Rossini forgot his position of clerical importance at that time, as he swept the diminutive figure into an embrace, laughing raucously to feel the freedom and joy Maria and others were imbued with.

CHAPTER 3

LEANDRA...

A dark soul can be tamed.

It will not last,

As evil will always find a way.

For it is never content.

Never more so, than when it craves,

The sustenance

Of CHAOS...

Leandra had chosen to stay on Azinor's country estate with her young son, despite the winged beasts who had acted as guardians, having fled. They must have sensed what was to come or had been called to war.

Leandra supposed the resultant devastation to the rural regions around her home, culminated from her one-time friend Seraphina and her role as the Chosen One. Considering everything to have occurred in the past two months, with dramatic climate changes and unrelenting quakes, Leandra had to wonder if Seraphina had failed in the war against evil.

The fact remained, Leandra was a survivor as with her beautiful son, Mateo. She kept a reclusive vigil without the courage to venture beyond the gates since before it all began. She'd not seen another person all those times she stood looking out at the desolation around her, and it served to exacerbate her loneliness. Not that she had been one to mingle with the village folk at any time. Her life, for a time, was to exist in Azinor's shadow and do his bidding. The man she loved had been taken from her, yet his legacy remained. She was mother to his son.

Considering the unbelievable trauma to have struck and the carnage caused, she supposed it was a miracle the house still stood, only the outbuildings suffering superficial damage to the roof and supports. There was a generator, and it was next to useless, as there was no more fuel to feed it.

As for her Explorer 4X4, it was going nowhere, as a felled tree crushed the bonnet and engine. Other trees in the dense copse had been pushed out of the ground and toppled, and it was miraculous none were close enough to cause damage to the Georgian mansion.

The perimeter wall was reduced to rubble in several places, even though the gates remained standing, untouched, like true and loyal sentinels to the memory of the mighty Azinor whose realm it once was.

Leandra was no slouch, and knew she had to formulate a plan of action, as even her food and water supplies were dwindling, would only last another two weeks at most.

She had to consider her son's needs; not so much with regards to baby food or milk as he was unique and could exist on whatever Leandra fed him. The greatest and most important source of sustenance was having him suckle on her breast still, not that he was seeking her milk. It was her energy he feasted on and following every feed she would have to rest for an hour or more, to replenish all he had succoured from her teat.

He still required nappies, or it was going to get messy. It was a random thought to make her smile.

While she was pondering their fate, she cradled him in her arms as they took a casual stroll around the ruins of the estate. As it was not only the fate of the world and the position they found themselves in which played on her mind. There was one person who seemed to take up residence in her thoughts. Whenever she dwelled about Abigail Armitage, she would catch Mateo staring at her with his bewildering dark eyes, aware he was gifted and could access a trail to all that she was thinking, for the most part.

He would be attuned to memories of his father, and know it was the immortal, Abigail, who it was took him from her son; murdered him.

It was Leandra's fervent hope Abigail had fallen in the war of angels and was even now a chattel of the Dark Lord and serving her penance in Hell. She had to be sure though, if Abigail was alive, or not. She saw it as her destiny to avenge the man who was father to her son, the guardian lover she stole from them.

Leandra had attempted on numerous occasions to reach within herself and glean from those powers she once possessed and became frequently frustrated as she was unable to project a simple scan or even to astral project.

It had her wondering if her gifts had been transposed to her son while he suckled and felt her essence flowing into him. This had her constantly worrying as to their fate, as without those powers once invested in her; how was she supposed to protect her son?

She was desperately alone.

Groundless.

Despairing.

And Abigail was the reason. How she hated her one-time friend, and it was an anger to manifest itself into a hideous montage of thoughts, of all she wanted to do to exact revenge.

On their quiet amble around the strewn trees to have fallen and where the roots had churned up the ground and mulch, Leandra arrived at a gaping rent in the perimeter wall several metres to one side of the sturdy wrought iron gates.

Baby Mateo was becoming quite animated in her arms, his coal-black eyes brightening and widening to receive an image of the devastation beyond as he pointed off to the distance. Leandra tried to visualise what her son was seeing and had to hold him more firmly as he began to bounce up and down.

Despite his excitement, he became quickly frustrated, making Leandra gasp as a hand clawed at her shirt and spread it, so that he could affix his greedy mouth to one exposed breast.

One important gift she had retained, was that she could communicate with her baby telepathically. Leandra went to one of the gnarly felled trunks and sat, closed her eyes for a moment and gave a gasp as she felt her energy being drawn into the baby's mouth.

He was hungry, she was thinking, and knew she would grow tired and listless quickly. When she again opened her eyes to smooth back his dark wavy hair, she became alert to a shift in the molecules and atoms of the ether around them.

She became anxious, as beyond the perimeter wall, a roiling grey mist had descended which completely obscured a view of the desolation to the countryside. From the mist stepped a tall willowy and shadowy form; a man who was dressed in a hessian weave smock the colour of ochre. Even at distance, Leandra thought the stranger handsome, whose long light brown hair fanned around his shoulders like a cowl. Beneath a salt and pepper beard his teeth gleamed, as he telegraphed a friendly smile. She even saw that his eyes were a vivid mix of blue and green, and these too reflected warmth.

As he approached the ruined wall. Leandra felt trails of energy probing around her thoughts, those to put her at ease and not make her fearful.

She raised an eyebrow as the stranger levitated to navigate the piles of stone barring his path and floated across to her position, bare feet several centimetres above the mulch.

'You're one of them,' she said, as Mateo released his prize and became transfixed on the man towering over their position. 'One of the celestials.'

The man growled without answering as he placed one hand on the crown of her head, the other drifting to Mateo's wavy mop. The baby chuckled and continued suckling with increased fervour, having Leandra bare her teeth in a grimace and close her eyes.

'Hungry little bastard isn't he?' the man gruffly answered.

'Who are you?' she asked him, the moment she overcame the pain and pleasure given to her breast. 'What is your purpose for coming here specifically? Are you hungry? I have food, but not much. Not much of anything, as it happens. There's just myself, and my son. Are there others out there? I have no idea what's happening in the world beyond the wall. I've heard nothing and seen no other person. You're the first.'

'For your information, the world survives,' he said, withdrawing his hands and clasping them against his stomach. 'It is a new world, where mankind and nature have been delivered hope. It will not last.'

'I worry about my son, as I'm not sure of all I should do, or whether it's safe to leave the estate. I wish that I knew my purpose, as I feel trapped; alone.'

'I can give you a purpose. I can restore certain of your powers. But, there is one who remains constant in your thoughts, and I ask that you forget ideas of revenge at this point.'

'There is one,' she blustered, and letting her angst show. 'She took from me, my lover and father to my son. I would see her in Hell for the suffering she has caused.'

'The one you are referring to, this Abigail, is the same celestial body I seek. Let her be my concern, not yours. Concentrate your energy on giving strength and sustenance to your son, for I may have a use for him later.'

'Will you be staying for a while?' she asked hopefully and was surprised by the lascivious train of thoughts to have revealed themselves. 'I wouldn't mind the company.'

The man sneered, and then chuckled.

'A tantalising morsel you are, and pleasing to the eye, but you are not the whore I seek.'

Leandra was momentarily shocked and hurt by the cruel barb delivered to her, even as she was compelled not to speak out in her own defence.

'One will come, and soon, and he will be your guide to security and longevity. I ask that you remain patient, just for a time. A new world beckons, and you will come to know your purpose.'

He placed a palm against her forehead and Leandra's posture became rigid. She trembled, as the stranger poured dark energy into her soul.

'Use your gifts wisely,' he added. 'And be ready for what is to come.'

'What of Seraphina; the Chosen One?' she blabbered and was horrified as he slotted fingers into her mouth.

'You ask too many questions,' he said, and his tone had grown deep and menacing. 'Should I rip out your tongue?'

Leandra relented, and telegraphed a response of subservience, as it once was with the mighty Azinor. The man released her.

He looked from her upturned face, which had become instantly mollified, to the dark eyes of the child studying him.

'The little bastard has potential.'

Leandra blinked as her son went to continue suckling and was saddened as the stranger turned and floated away in the direction of the awaiting shroud of grey mist. He became swallowed up instantly, and he along with the mist, faded away and was gone.

Leandra kissed her baby's crown and supported the back of his head and let go a keening cry as she felt the inexorable tide of energy flowing in her veins.

CHAPTER 4

ON CALM WATERS...

Serenity is often a misconception,

An illusion to all which

Lurks beneath its mantle.

Shadows loiter where,

No light exists.

It's what lies in the shadow,

One must fear...

Zanula, husband Cole, and their two-year-old son Luka were taking respite from the frenetic celestial duties to have governed their time since the great war of angels. They and their kind had been called upon to establish an environment of blessed hope to those who survived the tumultuous devastation to the planet.

They were also custodians of the pyramids and their secrets. Following the Universal battle, their services were employed distributing the vast hordes of crystals to those surviving domains of a vastly depleted planet.

Their home, as with their country of Ghana, was no more. During a difficult two weeks when there came Hell on Earth, they along with others of their kind, instigated emergency evacuation measures. They saved thousands, even as millions more perished to the quakes and floods and extremes of temperature.

Temporary homes were established, primitive in their concept, regressing mankind millions of years. Most were dwellings fashioned as caves and simple niches in rock faces, and even hollows dug into the ground. Later, discarded material from the destruction in and around the cities and townships, were used to create houses.

Zanula was deeply sensitive, more so perhaps than Cole, and as witness to the widescale loss of life to humans and animals, it was a formidable wrench to her heart. At times, she questioned the morality and edict of a universe which on the surface, preached hope and kindness, love and light; only to allow the mindless suffering and slaughter of innocents.

As it has always been, her husband Cole would solemnly declare; and will always be. The universe, he would say, is the architect of continuous conflict, that which is reflected on the face of the planet. Man, nature, and the climate are the product of the disruptive flow of energy.

Now though, in the new world, a utopian existence has been forged. The energy of light has harvested true balance, serenity; manufactured hope and transmuted negative influences into positive ideals.

Zanula was eternally thankful, all the suffering endured over a period of weeks was, but a faded memory in the minds of those who had survived the aftermath of Armageddon. No one person wished to dwell on all they had been witness to, of individual loss, as all knew the importance of what it meant to have survived and be content with what they had. For they were blessed and were granted a second chance.

The celestial bodies had led a community of people from her neighbourhood, acquiring others as they trekked laboriously across countries to reach Chad situated in a central part of the new Africa. No one complained of tiredness, as all became imbued with the energy of crystals they carried with them.

Despite the horrific scenes of carnage, they became witness to on their journey, hearts remained strong, as with the spirit. Most spent the time gathering provisions along the way, and everyone found their voice and sang.

Cole worked tirelessly alongside the refugees who started the journey with them, and of the stragglers even now arriving, farming swaths of fertile land close to a river which fed a large freshwater pool. There was a waterfall, several hundred metres tall, where another tributary meandered around broken boulders and felled trees.

Crops of maize and squash were predominant, along with a selection of hardy vegetables and potatoes.

Trees which had been uprooted were specifically used for the building of huts, the branches of which were a source of fuel for fires.

Freshwater was constant.

It became a township without a name over a period of a few months, where every person happily toiled to create an existence, where abundance was in the self-satisfaction and utter joy, their labour returned to the growing community.

All the people were supremely energised; of mind, spirit and body, a by-product of the crystals brought with them.

Other than Zanula and Cole, there were a score and more of their kind; celestial elementals whose purpose was to continue the evolving of humanity and nature.

Zanula had befriended one of the beautiful souls, an imperious and beautiful woman who went by the name, Layla. She arrived with two companions, Peter and Homer, and they let it be known they were sent by a mutual acquaintance, someone of huge importance, despite remaining an enigma to many.

Layla became instantly enamoured with Zanula and Cole's son, Luka, and despite the fact she could erect a shield over her thoughts, Zanula had quickly established a sadly worrying aspect with the celestial she had befriended.

Layla had admitted she once had a daughter who had become a victim to the dark energy. What she omitted to say yet was slow in smothering her thoughts on the topic, was wondering why Zanula and Cole had been granted the miracle of having their child reborn; the son who they had also lost to dark forces and was returned to them. Especially, as there was not a day passed, without Layla remembering how it had once been, to be a loving mother to a radiantly beautiful and special daughter for a short time.

Zanula was unable to give a satisfactory answer or placate her friend with the right consoling words to help make sense of her situation. Whatever the universal design decreed, was often enigmatic, even to the ancients.

Zanula watched her young son playing with another child and smiled vivaciously as her handsome husband approached. She was overtly admiring his toned shirtless torso, and he would know she was doing so,

Cole swept his son up from the ground, spun him around to get him squealing and kissed him, before lowering him to the grass and sand to continue whatever he was doing. Cole loped across to Zanula's position, slumped down, and eased her into an embrace.

When the lingering kiss ended he lay back, with the soporific sound of the waterfall, excitable chatter and laughter, and high-pitched squeals of all the children in the vicinity, playing a symphony of joy to his ears.

With his eyes closed he sensed Zanula pressing closer, the invigorating warmth of her aura washing over his skin as she sought more of his kisses, despite the numbers all around the rock pool enjoying time away from chores.

The kiss was slow, deep, and delivering promise, as with the way she explored his lean frame with tremulous digits.

'Are you to relax now and spend some quality time with your family?' she asked him around a smile, teeth gleaming in the light of day.

'That is the plan, my darling,' he remarked, while delighting in the feel of her skin beneath the flouncy bright orange blouse she was wearing. 'We received more than two hundred new arrivals today. All have been given a place in people's dwellings, until such time as a home has been established for each of them.'

'It's a miracle,' she said wistfully. 'Just listen; everyone is so happy to be alive. No one person complains of hardship. All are blessed and grateful to receive what is available to them, and not the luxuries they were perhaps once used to.'

'Life in the new world,' he said succinctly. 'One of hope.'

'And to love one another, and mother nature.'

Checking their son was okay, Cole pulled her down and taut to his body, cradling her head against his chest. He soothed her with subtle caresses and telegraphed his intent for later when they could settle in their crib undisturbed. His proposals had her chuckling, clawing, and nibbling his flesh, just as a strident scream cut high and across the wall of chatter and jubilation in the vicinity.

There came another scream, and it appeared a child was crying. There came anxious shouting, that which had Cole and Zanula getting to their feet. As Zanula lifted their son into the security of her arms and aura, Cole was already perceiving elements of discord from an area of the pool.

Zanula sent out a scan also, trying herself to determine the cause of the continuous stream of screeches. This was not from over-exuberance, she ascertained, as she was sensing despair, pain and fear.

Cole ran to the water's edge and waded in, as a woman in her twenties and carrying a young girl not much older than Luka, staggered towards him where the water was shallow. It was the mother doing the screaming, her daughter sobbing against her neck.

Cole caught up with them just as the young woman seemed to momentarily deflate and collapse into his arms. He bodily lifted them up and carried both to shore where others were wading in to assist.

Some of the celestial guardians had been alerted and were positioned at strategic points around the perimeter of the rock pool, each one trying to establish a reason for the mother and child's obvious distress.

Zanula placed Luka in the care of a neighbour and went to join Cole, who had lowered the woman still clutching the child to her chest. She was no longer animated and Cole was gently prising the lids of her eyes back, saw how the pupils had receded away to reveal only the whites flecked with blood.

Her body suddenly went into convulsions as Zanula stooped to lift the child away from her embrace. Zanula became horrified at sight of the little girl's shredded shirt along her back and the angry red weal's criss-crossing her flesh.

Layla appeared and knelt, placing a hand to the woman's forehead, the other splaying her stomach. The distressed woman ceased to have a seizure and settled, even though her breathing remained ragged and raspy.

Layla looked up at the child Zanula was supporting and rose to her feet, laying a hand to each of the wounds where they became less angry and vivid and gradually faded.

She knelt again, and telegraphed a message to Cole, to ease the woman over onto her front. Cole was appalled at sight of the open rents streaking the woman's back. It was almost as if she'd been flayed several times, with a whip.

Layla once again lay her hand over the ugly suppurating welts and willed her energy to close them and repair the tissue. It took a few minutes, yet eventually the flesh began to fuse, the lividity of her wounds quick to fade to insignificance.

'What do you suppose caused this?' Zanula requested. 'Is mother and child going to be okay?'

Layla looked to Cole and then to his wife.

'I sense much darkness,' she telegraphed solemnly.

'How can that be?' Cole asked. 'Are you certain? I mean; is it not possible they strayed too close to the waterfall and became thrown against the rocks?'

'This has to be reported,' Layla informed them and getting to her feet. 'As of this moment, mother and child are sleeping, but I can tell you this; dark energy has found a path into their veins.'

'The crystals can help,' Zanula pleaded, and was thinking back to the moment their eighteen-year-old son had been touched by dark energy, and how it corrupted his personality over time.

The young woman and her daughter were mortals and could not hope to fight the insidious evil they were afflicted with, not without help.

Cole jumped to his feet, went to kiss Zanula, and was then running towards the water's edge passing groups of worried men and women who had gathered to witness scenes they failed to understand the meaning of. Zanula cried out as Cole waded to where the shelf dipped away to deeper water, and then he dived; swimming beneath the clear blue and green water towards the deluge striking the surface some distance away.

All those gathered at the shore were watching an area around the base of the waterfall, most of whom were wondering why their gallant warrior and saviour was swimming to the location the woman and child had fled from, and what he hoped to achieve by doing so.

Zanula paced as she telegraphed her unease and anguish to her husband, urging him to give up his mission and return. She placed the child alongside her mother and left them to sleep, before moving closer to the shoreline. She projected a scan and saw all that Cole was able to visualise, as he cut through a miasma of tiny bubbles. It was her fervent hope, mother and child had met with an accident, their injuries having been caused by being dragged across the rocks on the water bed, and not as Layla perceived; with the emergence of dark energy after all this time.

Layla had to be mistaken, she repeated to herself. The atmosphere was positively charged, with no elements of a threat to discern from this.

Her attention was deflected away from her husband's progress, saw the way he was swimming in tight circles where the cascade struck the surface of the pool with relentless force, as the victim gave a moan. Layla went to the woman and knelt, keeping vigil, as she soothed the woman's subconscious torment using her formidable healing powers. Layla hoped it was enough to dispel the grey shadow she saw formulating within the woman's mind.

It was the moment Layla was able to peel back the barriers on the woman's thoughts and received a montage of flashing images which made no viable sense; not immediately.

Expectations mixed with uncertainty hung as a shroud over those who could only watch and wait. Anticipation rendered everyone mute.

There came gasps of wonder and dismay, as a huge geyser shot out of the water at the base of the waterfall. An intense light of golden yellow tinged with the hue of violet exploded from within and coruscated around the fringes of the water spout. It dropped heavily, causing ripples to fan outward towards the shore, inducing those people to have waded into the shallow areas, to quickly retreat.

Zanula clutched her chest the moment Cole leapt several feet clear and dropped again, but not before she had witnessed the energised sword extending from his right wrist. She caught the other guardians around the perimeter watching her closely, as each was aware her husband was locked in a frenetic battle; despite not knowing what Cole was fighting.

The water began to churn and belch and change colour, and then all became calm instantly. Zanula was prepared to go to Cole's rescue until the moment she saw his head bobbing along as he swam the short distance to the shoreline.

People began to point, as it appeared their 'hero' was dragging something behind him, and it was monstrous; its length surpassing one hundred metres.

Cole raised himself and staggered through the shallow water towards the amassing crowds awaiting.

Zanula was unable to make sense of the 'thing' he was clutching in his right hand, as it appeared not to be solid, was gelatinous. It was also transparent.

Only Zanula, along with the celestials Peter and Homer, waded in to assist Cole, none of them wishing to touch the grotesque Cole was dragging.

People stepped away and kept at a discreet distance as Cole revealed his prize to everyone.

'What is that?' Zanula cried, aware everyone was again speechless.

'This,' said Cole, and releasing the dead creature to hit the ground hard with an audible squelch, 'Is a jellyfish. Probably a Portuguese Man o war or a hybrid relative, and a long way from home. As you can see, this is no ordinary specimen.'

'It is a mutation,' interrupted Peter, 'And I daresay, very deadly.'

'But what's it doing here?' Zanula pleaded, 'In a freshwater pool hundreds of miles from the nearest coast and salt water? It's natural habitat.'

'I think we all know,' said Cole, 'Nature is evolving rapidly and adapting to change. As for why it has found its way along the tributaries to this location, I have no idea.'

He turned his attention to Layla, who had left the woman and child to join them. She'd cast a wary gaze over the immense glutinous dome and the extraordinary cluster of deadly tentacles streaming away from its damaged core. She knew of such things, but only regarding its natural form, before the world became different. It could deliver powerful electric shocks with its tendrils, and there was once several reported cases of fatalities.

The creature at her feet, she knew, could inflict so much more, and worse.

Reiterating all the questions Zanula had asked, Layla wanted desperately to know how it was something could mutate into a monster, in a short time, and why it chose to travel hundreds of miles from its natural habitat to arrive at a smallish rockpool, where food resources were minimal to sustain it. Unless, she pondered, the creature perceived humans as next in the food chain.

Zanula gave Cole a hug and turned him, so that she could inspect his torso for wounds.

'Babe, you would tell me if you were hurt,' she said in tones to soothe his conscience. 'I was certain you were in trouble out there. I saw the weapon you summoned.'

'I'm not hurt, sweetheart,' he answered her, tugging her close and kissing her temple. 'This thing; it's like nothing I've seen, not since the war of angels. The creature attacked, and I was fortunate, was ready for anything.'

'It reminds me, of our time spent in the Sea of Crete, when you battled dark energy's guardian creature. Is this the same; do you think? Was this monster a sentinel to something we may have overlooked. Have we all grown complacent, believing the world is truly safe from evil?'

'There's enough of our kind, powerful ancients, who would have known if a source of dark energy was close. It's my belief, the creature became drawn into a different habitat and went with the currents, unable to find its way back.'

'If it is a creation of dark energy, we should have been aware of its presence. We let our guard down, believing the new world was safe.'

LEGACY OF ANGELS

'If so, then it is a clear warning.' To the guardian, Layla, Cole asked; 'What's to become of this monster? Are we to bury it?'

'It has to be sent away,' she said to him, while still immersed in troubling thought. 'So that an autopsy can be done to determine its origins. I propose to relay a message to the universe and report back the moment I receive a sign. In the meantime, I suggest this beast is removed and placed undercover, somewhere remote, until we have our answer.'

Cole nodded, and turning to Zanula, kissed her again, as she looked like she needed assurance from him.

'Take our son home, honey. I'll organise the removal and internment of the creature. I'll be with you soon; a promise.'

He felt it was necessary to kiss her once more, as he secretly shared her anxiety; knowing their perfect idyll had been compromised.

At the back of his mind, he had to wonder, if there were others like the monster laying at his feet.

CHAPTER 5

THE ENEMY...REVEALED.

Evil will find a way,

As it is relentless.

That, which must be contained,

Before it spreads

And is set to undo,

All the good, which has been done…

The First Angel, Abigail, was another granted a time of respite. She chose to take this on her home estate 'Spiritual Lodge,' a stable complex, cottages, and grazing fields, which was comfortably nestled in the heart of despoiled countryside.

She was the architect in co-ordinating a structural plan as set down by universal design, to revive a beleaguered planet. Following a span of two years and more, all was going smoothly, and moving along at a rapid pace.

She had earned the right to rest, as it was imperative in the grand scheme of things, to spend quality time with her son Luke and the prodigal child of the Chosen One, Seraphina. Daniel was approaching his third birthday, although many who came and went on the estate, believed he was older.

The influx of refugees dwindled as order across the counties was restored, as it was in most countries and across continents. Progress was rapid with the emergence of pyramids and widescale distribution of crystals as a source of energy. There was something more profound and beneficial, as in the overall wellbeing of those fortunate to have survived the holocaust.

Everyone had a purpose, and laboured with a positive attitude, as the mysterious and magical properties of light energy encouraged communities to follow a dream to completion.

The meek inherited a desolate Earth, and as a result, became stronger, determined; and all believed there was genuine hope for the future.

The fields around the stable complex on the estate was home to a scant few temporary dwellings of marquees and tents. Those who had arrived at the beginning, lost souls in search of enlightenment, had moved on to rebuild a life for themselves.

Spiritual Lodge had been their haven for a time, having given them an opportunity to repair physically and psychologically, and to believe all would be better in the new world. They had found salvation.

Only six makeshift dwellings remained in one of the fields; of families and of those who had survived alone at a difficult time in the aftermath of the storms and quakes. Of those to have arrived in recent times, personal healing was to take longer, as they had endured two years of personal torment, creating a reclusive lifestyle for themselves, as trusting others was an issue.

49

Now, was different, and they had an opportunity to be a part of a utopian society, where fear of the unknown was practically non-existent.

Abigail had devoted time to playing with the children in the back garden, the spiritual guardian Celestine as company and ward to the boys in her absence. Abigail's mother, Aisha, along with the twin souls residing in the same host body, Gillian, and Margaret O'Shaughnessy, were on a sojourn visiting new townships around the country and were constantly sending reports on progress being made and as to whether all was going according to the universal design and edict served to the new world.

The other guardians of the estate were continually establishing the protective shields around the perimeter remained strong at all times; as nothing could be taken for granted, even at a time of peace and calm. They were also responsible for the welfare of the horses and other animals on the farm.

The celestial, Joshu, had remained for a time after the war of angels was concluded, until his services were required elsewhere on the planet, and had been absent for more than a twelve months.

Abigail's stalwart companion, Chan Li, guardian to herself and the children, and she supposed had become a lover, was on a mission which had taken him to China.

Abigail was always on her guard, knowing there was an affiliation with another supreme celestial body, one who was set to engineer repercussions later.

She was the First Angel; daughter of the universe, and Luke was a son to the universe. She and her son were a product of universal light energy, property and chattel to the overlord of the universe. Abigail was aware she had challenged the might which ruled, as to consort with another was considered anathema and a breach of universal rules.

Genesis, the name given to the victorious universal energy breathing life to the new world, was aware his daughter had strayed from the path she'd been set. As to those reprisals she feared would come, so far, there were none.

Abigail was in consultation with Genesis daily, and the Lord of the Universe kept her diligently updated with world news.

HE kept conversations professional.

There was a job to be done.

Abigail had been informed she was to receive proof Dark Energy continued to exist and was seeking deviant ways to dismantle the utopian values granted to man and nature.

She was intrigued, as the message delivered to her, had been cryptic and vague.

As First Angel, she was perhaps the only entity to foresee episodic glimpses of the future, and these had the propensity to veer off course and change, as the future was not constant or definite.

Abigail had been the architect of a visionary tome scribed in energy, neither with ink nor dye, portraying a possible future leading up to the universal war of angels. She had not been assigned a similar task, and avenues normally opened to her for receiving images via Genesis, were not as prevalent at this time.

Abigail's role, as she saw it, was mentoring the children to an age when they would themselves take on specific responsibilities as guardians of the new world. Until such time, the onus was on her and dispatching her edict to all the earth angels across the globe.

Genesis was responsible for balancing the energy flow, using pyramids as a conduit; and maintaining a temperate climate for nature to flourish. As in the past, there was to be no dramatic and destructive weather fronts. Hurricanes and tornadoes were a byword. Rainfall was in moderation to prevent flooding and further catastrophe. Every aspect of the planet was to enjoy prolonged periods of sunshine without excessive heat.

The vastly depleted polar caps of the Arctic and Antarctic regions were able to grow and develop once again and not suffer extremes of temperatures, so that even life could flourish.

Despite the planet having significantly tilted on its axis, Genesis controlled the rotation and propulsion, and ensured there was no lasting effects.

This was a Utopian world created to bring an everlasting peace and stability, as decreed by Universal design across a span of billions of years.

Abigail explained to Celestine she had been called to investigate a minor development, while not submitting details. She hugged the children and departed the home, fuelled by intrigue, even as an undercurrent of concern was to play on her mind.

Her valiant mare and kindred soul, Free Spirit, was standing vigil at the gate to the first field as if anticipating an appearance from her mistress and gave a snicker of excitement and contentment to see Abigail approach.

Abigail spoke to her charge and soothed her in the coded ancient tongue they had devised stating, she would return to ride her later, on her return.

Abigail's destination was the circle of five ancient oak trees in the field at the rear, sentinels to a universal portal and the heart of light energy. Stepping within the circle of concentrated energy, Abigail was teleported inside the secret pyramid below ground.

On the occasions she visited the portal, it never ceased to amaze her, just how resplendent was the giant crystal obelisk which jutted out of the soil. It constantly pulsated with the energy of the universe, that which sustained the estate and a vast area around.

Abigail's cascade of light brown hair tinged with blue on the one side, became instantly static, swelling into a glorious fan around her frame. Her attention was drawn to the suspended monster which had been passed to her for inspection and analysis.

She recognised it immediately as a creature she, along with Chan Li, had confronted on a travail into a possible future. One of these hybrid mutated creatures had followed them to her home and became trapped within an energised fortress of crystal prisms and obsidian stones.

Abigail levitated, to better inspect the abnormal specimen whose immense tentacles floated on currents of energy around the huge body of the crystal obelisk, giving the otherworldly impression it was alive and swimming.

She saw how its colourful domed hood had been cleaved at its core, and by scanning the circuitry which had mobilised the monster, was able to perceive images and establish from where it had come from.

She was witness to the celestial, Cole, waging a ferocious battle with the giant and it had her inwardly smiling. As First Angel, it was she who invested Cole and his wife Zanula, with the mantle of guardians and keyholders to all the pyramids on the Earth's surface and of those hidden, in preparation for the aftermath of war. One of their duties was to locate the source of dark energy at specific locations and have it contained.

On the second occasion she met with them, it was to save their son from the grip of dark energy to have infected his host body. When next she was called to visit, it was to repair the damage done by an evil ancient entity and restore to life the son they had lost. Abigail was unable to comprehend at the time, the extraordinary courage and sacrifice Zanula had shown when confronting the might of evil, for as a loving and devoted mother, she was the one who had cast the dark energy within her son to oblivion and by doing so, his physical host body was lost to them, his beautiful soul once again reunited with the universe.

Abigail had also witnessed the valiant part they played in the war of angels.

As it was now, in the task set for them and others of their kind, uniting pockets of humanity into communities once again, so that people could enjoy and benefit from a second chance.

Abigail reached into the mind of the dead creature so that she was able to access its memory, believing it must have a brain and had not operated purely on instinct.

She flinched away as the frenetic currents of energy caused the tentacles of the creature to become increasingly animated, as they weaved a mesmeric dance around the crystal. She extended her auric field and as one of the smooth tendrils slithered across it, she felt its extraordinary power.

The tendril whipped and retracted, not the reaction she'd expected from something purported to be dead. Abigail assumed the beast could feel her, not that she thought it was conceivable.

Even though the power ensnaring the monstrous jellyfish was adequate, Abigail resorted to strengthening her own defences. Intuition told her not presume all was okay, when it was apparent; all was not.

Synchronising her mind with the creature's DNA and instinctual habits, she had it divulge to her a passage of time from its creation until the moment it revealed itself at a rockpool in an area of Central Africa.

As she'd anticipated, Dark Energy would find a way. It was only ever going to be a matter of time, even as she recognised the scale of the threat while unable to predict the extent to which it could employ itself. She supposed it was enough, knowing the monstrosity had evolved to its present form in only a span of two years. Once, in its natural form, it was seen as an amphibious predator and known to be deadly. Assuming the specimen before her was a generic example of its species, just one of these creatures posed a serious problem.

What confounded Abigail; was that she failed to understand precisely why it had not killed the young woman and child, when it clearly had the propensity to do so. Ordinarily, it would only require someone to receive contact from one of the tentacles for it to be fatal.

She supposed this creature and those like it were conditioned to infect as many of the population as was possible, but it was only conceivable should the world's surviving populace all went for a swim.

Abigail saw this as a weak strategy, which meant she was overlooking important factors attributing to a greater threat.

She scanned the depths of the monstrous psyche where residual data remained; as a taunt, or so she believed.

There was one, she knew existed, who had to be the arbitrator of evil discord re-emerging, just as the new world was establishing itself as a utopian society.

She knew her adversary as Nemo, who was not a mortal; was a celestial force like no other of his kind.

And was perhaps, Abigail's equal.

As daughter to one part of the universe, Nemo was first angel and son to the Dark Lord. He was dark energy's Chosen One and was to be the architect of world destruction in the future if his father and mentor failed.

Their spiritual paths had connected, briefly, and it was a moment Abigail often pondered. A secret she had kept concealed for billions of years was revealed and it was her fervent belief, her opposition was set on a course to meet with her, when he could be assured his powers and strategy were enough to defeat her.

Until the designated and unavoidable confrontation; as guardian to her son and Daniel, her purpose was to mentor and prepare them for an unpredictable future.

And face the might of evil.

CHAPTER 6

A WORLD BENEATH THE ICE...PART ONE

For those who choose isolation

They are perhaps, more alone,

And vulnerable,

In the belief, solitude makes them safe,

From all the evil they have witnessed,

Unaware,

Evil will follow.

Is everywhere,

Waiting…

The Antarctic region of the South Pole had suffered great geological trauma and transformation yet fared better than many of the more civilised and populated countries and continents of the world.

The shift in the Earth's axis was responsible for the upheaval; ice mountains and bergs collapsing to create a new landscape, one of serene beauty. It even had its own energy source; that which was provided by a smallish pyramid to have risen from the depths of the ice plains. As with so many scattered across the globe, it was composed of obsidian. After more than two years, it stood as a unique monument, a deep and glorious shadow against the brilliantine white canvas around it. It controlled the climate so that it remained constant at night and during daylight hours.

Its energy fed life and hope to the small communities of indigenous folk, and refugees fleeing the holocaust and had sought the southern-most region for sanctuary.

Only one guardian Earth Angel watched over them, and he was known as Pandea.

Even as these small communities were scattered across the region, all thrived and became self-sufficient. Everyone worked together, to ensure survival. Despite the primitive lifestyle they were to endure, all were content and feeling blessed.

There was to be an unexpected newcomer, a young woman who brought with her a dark secret, having fled her native Moscow following the inexplicable carnage and destruction wrought by the severity of the weather and unprecedented earthquakes.

At the beginning there had been seven others in her group, all fleeing the perils of collapsing buildings and the earth erupting beneath them. The other six perished along the way before they had even reached the Baltic region.

Katerina had been the only female in the group and ordinarily, would have been considered the weaker sex, yet her spirit and determination was indomitable. Intuition and astuteness were her saving grace. She made her own decisions and could not be led astray. The others failed to see the frequent warning signs when confronting them, and one by one, their decision-making cost them dearly.

Katerina alone endured the hardships they encountered, as the forces of nature were relentless. The scale of destruction was cataclysmic, but Katerina survived it. Along the way she befriended a German Shepherd, and it was a union which came at a time when loneliness was to become a burden, that which would have drained her spirit.

She gave the name Lexor to her companion, as it was without a collar and nametag. It was full-grown and surprisingly friendly; something to do with the fact Katerina encouraged a genial and trusting disposition by feeding him.

Having rested for a time, and foraged for supplies, she overcame the debilitating inertia and continued her journey; not that she had an idea where she was going. She only wanted to escape the Hell her country and of those around had suffered, and Lexor chose to follow. The moment a bond had been forged, he no longer chose to drag himself behind and at a safe distance and would walk alongside Katerina.

They eventually reached the Black Sea, and it was here Katerina felt more energised, focussed, and was even able to smile. Not that she understood why she should feel suddenly positive and hopeful. Even Lexor was beginning to lope beside her with greater purpose, and no longer walked with its tail between its legs. He even found his voice, barking at birds and snapping at an array of dragonfly.

The Black Sea was as a behemoth, perfectly calm and sun-dappled; beautiful and mysterious. She was unable to ascertain why; but she felt drawn, enticed, to feel a light tapping within her mind. She had to get across somehow, no matter the scale of her task, or how daunting it seemed.

She was compelled to keep going forward, not backward, or even to put down roots. As to where she needed to go she had no idea. Momentum was important and crucial, she believed, as deep down, she feared to stay too long in one place.

More than anything, she craved peace within her mind and heart, and a chance to exorcise the ghost of horrific memories; of the hell she'd left behind, and a brutal life she'd turned her back on.

She had no recollection of a genuinely happy and contented past. Her stepfather was an evil man, (had been an evil man), who began a reign of terror and torrid abuse on her body and mind at an early age. Had her mother been aware, not once did she step forward and confront the beast with her claims. Katerina suspected her mother was just as afraid as she had been.

She did make it to university where she hoped to better herself and seek freedom from tyranny. She mixed with the wrong crowd, who in effect, had a hidden agenda for someone like Katerina. These people were no different to her abusive stepfather. Katerina was beautiful, sexy, yet vulnerable. When she confided her story to someone she wanted to trust, she unwittingly started a chain of events she was unable to escape from. Petrov was involved with some hard-hitting individuals. He made the stepfather disappear, and ensured he suffered for the things he did.

Following which, Katerina became the property of this dangerous group of individuals and became once again trapped in a life she despised and was unable to escape. She was to become a prostitute, and chasing a degree became history. Whatever identity Katerina had crafted for herself had been stripped away, along with any vestige trace of self-esteem.

The moment the world came under attack from the forces of nature, Katerina saw an opportunity to flee, or perish. She had to try, at least. Beginning her journey was fraught with peril, and the six men she banded together with, were equally set on self-preservation, and not interested in the fact there was a young woman among their group.

LEGACY OF ANGELS

With Lexor for company, and feeling surprisingly upbeat and invigorated, Katerina was beginning to feel at peace. More importantly, she had a reason to live. Once, her thoughts leaned to the negative, now she was able to face each day with optimism. The earth no longer quaked and the climate had settled.

The journey she'd embarked on had been hazardous and grim, with cities, towns, and countryside in ruins. On the shore of the Black Sea, it was like stepping over the threshold into a new world.

She took the time to bathe in the cool, clean refreshing sea. It stripped away layers of grime, but also, it removed the façade of misery she'd worn for an interminable time, it seemed. Following a refreshing swim Katerina prepared food for herself and a contented Lexor.

And she couldn't stop herself smiling.

She was a survivor, and all the beasts who had dogged her life had perished.

A decision was made to continue her journey when she stumbled upon a small fishing boat tethered to a leaning wooden stump further along the shoreline. It had an outboard and oars, and importantly, it was in good order having not suffered damage to its hull. There was fuel in the tank, not much, and she supposed it would get her and her companion so far.

It was a start. Before she set off on the next leg of her jaunt, she spent a further day foraging for food and other provisions she felt would be useful. Food with a long shelf-life and unspoiled had been plentiful and would keep her sustained.

She'd been fortunate in her choice, as she was in good health. She had in her swag-bag a selection of medical supplies; painkillers, tablets to battle dysentery, antiseptic, bandages and plasters. It was something, at least.

LEGACY OF ANGELS

While she was foraging with Lexor who wanted to help, she'd become suddenly drawn to an area where, on first inspection, was just an expanse of fallow ground and a few rocks, and the occasional felled tree. Something pulled her toward a depression around the exposed roots of a beech. There was an object concealed within a section of folded velvet and curiosity had her revealing the unexpected and beautiful surprise. It was a crystal cluster which comfortably nestled in the palm of one hand, and Katerina spent a considerable time simply staring at its mesmeric beauty. There was something else which she found fascinating, as the stone seemed to vibrate and thrum. It was either reacting with her own energy, or possessed its own source, and she instantly felt it seeping into her pores, to flow in her veins.

That was the moment she realised she'd been given a reason to smile.

The crystal in her grasp instilled hope. Not wanting to leave it behind, she secreted it away in a section of the backpack and continued her search for essentials to take with her on their journey.

Lexor yipped constantly. He might have been singing.

Her companion was happy; and this she saw reflected in his eyes. Lexor was another laying a few ghosts to rest.

On the second day of crossing the tranquil sea, enjoying temperate weather, a vista of blue sky and warming sun, the outboard gave a cough, spluttered noisily before it died. Only to miraculously start up again on its own accord, propelling the small wooden craft without the necessity of fuel.

Katerina questioned as to how this could be possible, while understating her gratitude, knowing she had been given a reprieve from having to row the boat to get to where she needed to be.

Lexor didn't seem to mind the boat ride and for the most part, sat on his haunches surveying the never-ending expanse of water.

Katerina became mesmerised at sight of a dull black pyramid a long way off in the distance, and she supposed it had to be on land and not jutting out of the sea. This was the fourth such monument she'd seen on her travels since leaving Russia.

Even though it appeared as a dark blot on the horizon, it filled her with peace. It was beautiful, she'd be thinking. Untouched in all its majestic simplicity. It was also ethereal and otherworldly.

As it was, with the miracle of fish jumping out of the water to land in the boat. It became a source of sustenance, and even Lexor became partial to something else which was edible and offered variety in their scant diet.

Katerina was in possession of a flick-knife, and she used this to gut the plentiful fish and remove the skin, scales, fins, and bone to get to the raw flesh. She didn't think it would harm them, as she was aware sushi was a delicacy all over the world having originated in Japan. It was the same with Scandinavians, and possibly the Inuit's who endured the hardships of the polar regions.

Thinking simply about the source of food finding gastronomic acceptance across the globe, had her wondering how much of the world had survived. From what she'd witnessed since leaving Moscow and Russia, and of the few survivors she'd encountered, she was inclined to think the worst. And of those who had survived the holocaust, many would continue to suffer and die. Humanity had been decimated, food becoming rapidly depleted, as with fuel and other sources of energy. The cities and countryside had become a dangerous wasteland. Millions, perhaps billions of corpses lay rotting on the ground. Disease would be rife, and Katerina suspected, there would exist few hospitals to care for the injured and of those who fell ill.

There was no transport left, and if there existed some which had survived, there were no roads to travel on, and no way of replenishing fuel supplies. The future was bleaker than she'd first imagined.

And what of the governments to have controlled the world? Had they survived? Did anyone have a contingency plan in the aftermath of such a widescale disaster. Without a system of communications, how would they know who to reach and what to do to establish order from chaos?

Without order, people would exist without purpose, and it was a thought which terrified her, and believed it was a reason out of necessity to escape and get as far away as it was possible. She would know her sanctuary and haven once she reached it, believing such a place existed.

On the third day, Katerina saw land stretching all the way along the horizon, despite a heat-haze distorting her view and focus. It could have been Greece, or even the Northern fringes of Africa. Not that it mattered either way, as her bearings were askew from having puttered slowly across open sea for three days having only seen the pyramid and nothing else. No other boats, large or small, were committed to escaping as she was doing.

It was prudent to assume she had left the Black Sea, and had ventured into the Mediterranean, where the land in between and the island of the Crimea was probably submerged under water.

She saw another of the pyramids (not the same one, she didn't think) as this lay to the West and was smaller, whereas the other she'd spotted in the East.

While reclining across a bench seat, bare feet thrilling to the splash of water where she draped her legs over the side, she gave a sudden squawk, brought both legs in quickly, and wondering if she'd been bitten or stung. Inspecting the sole of her right foot her eyes widened at sight of the livid red weal cutting obliquely across from toes to heel. The pain was excruciating, seemed to flow into her ankles and calf muscle, then as quickly subsided having massaged the injury for a time.

It was at that moment the outboard suddenly spluttered and died, the boat slowing to a lazy crawl. Katerina cursed her luck as she shuffled across and leaned against the bench at back, giving the motor a slap, a reaction borne of frustration, in the vain hope brute force would cajole the machine to life. The small craft was jostled and she lost her balance momentarily, just as Lexor became agitated and began barking and snarling.

Propping herself on the gun whale she leaned over the stern and pulled back sharply, having seen the wide gelatinous fleshy disc clinging to the outboard motor. It's what she saw trailing down from beneath the giant translucent hood which had repulsed her more, to see a cluster of immense tendrils dipping away into the murk below.

Blowing out her cheeks, she calmly retrieved the flick-knife from a pocket of her jeans and released the blade. She rummaged in a bag and found a leather glove she'd picked up on one of her foraging expeditions, for no reason, other than she liked the studs sewn into the knuckle section. She slipped it on, gripped the haft of the knife and launched her upper torso over the end of the boat, slashing and hacking at the thick glutinous hood of the jelly fish.

It reacted instantly to the onslaught yet was unable to unravel itself from the propeller mechanism. The hood fluctuated and it was conceivable the creature reacted from pain as the knife blade sliced open the flesh.

Katerina plunged the hand deep and slashed at the thick group of tentacles trailing away from beneath the hood, and almost toppled overboard as the small boat pitched and lurched violently.

Lexor was going crazy, jumping and pacing and turning in circles, his relentless barking echoing across the surface of water.

LEGACY OF ANGELS

Katerina dragged herself to the port side and saw a score and more of the creatures throwing themselves at the hull. All along the starboard side was the same. The boat was surrounded.

She gave a scream as she felt something whipping across her back, her flesh on fire, her shirt in rents. One of the giant jelly fish had hurled itself from the port side, its enormous tendrils flailing the air, and it was these which had struck her as the monster plunged into the sea again.

Katerina clung to the gun whale, barely able to breathe, and believing the agony she endured was worse than the beatings she'd regularly received as a prostitute.

Lexor had ceased barking and was whining pitifully, and Katerina had not the strength to go to him and give comfort. She watched, weakened and thankful, as the hoard of jellyfish submerged and were gone from sight.

It was the moment the outboard gave a stutter and once again purred into life, the boat chugging forward to cut a swath through the gently undulating waves. The motion made her vomit and when she was done, lay out on the floor of the boat beneath the central bench, unable to muster the strength to do anything.

Lexor had become quiet as he shuffled across to lay beside her. She screwed her face up at sight of the ugly welts along the dog's flank and hindquarters. She was thankful he was still breathing, and when she closed her eyes, she slept.

And dreamt.

And her dreams were darkly unpleasant.

When she recovered consciousness eventually she felt re-energised. It was daytime, with some scudding cloud in the sky. The sea was calm around the boat, lapping peacefully against a wide ridge of rock shards where it had gone aground.

Lexor was another who had recovered and was skipping on his paws and yipping at something which had gained his attention. Katerina rubbed her eyes, sat up, and was witness to a vast irregular shoreline of sand and jagged boulders. It could have been just about any place on the planet. There were no discernible landmarks, only a view epitomising a bleak and devastating epitaph to what was once an area which had thrived.

Katerina raised herself as she saw the reason for Lexor's reaction. Balanced on a promontory of rock stood a lone figure. From distance, she supposed the person was male, with long scraggly dark hair. He wore shorts and nothing else. His back was to the dark mouth of a smallish cave or hollow created from where giant boulders and slabs leaned together.

Katerina didn't react, not immediately. That was, until the enticing pull towards stepping onto terra firma once again after a few days on the sea, was too much of an invitation. She checked the water for jellyfish, not that she expected they could exist in the shallows and seeing no sign of a threat made her feel upbeat; safer.

The lone figure in the distance had still to move or react, and Katerina hoped the person would not be a problem.

Katerina stepped over the prow and approached a golden spit of unspoilt sand. Lexor jumped out the boat and followed, his tail wagging furiously as he was another grateful to be on land. She'd noticed his wounds were not as angry as she remembered, following the attack of a monster jellyfish. They didn't appear to be infected either. She was unable to inspect her own, yet it made perfect sense she was healing, having not suffered any side-effects. She was feeling stronger and energised, something she'd experienced since leaving the Baltic shores and travelled the sea by boat. She supposed and believed, the crystal in her possession had something to do with her sense of wellbeing.

She squatted on the sand and tried to recall her dreams, only to realise her mind had become a blank canvas with regards to that experience. Looking off to the side she was aware the person had left his position and was nowhere to be seen.

She gave Lexor a vigorous petting before leaping to her feet joyously and removed her shirt and jeans, wanting only to slip back into the water and wash the grime from her skin. Once her ablutions were done, she would organise a meal for herself and her companion, while considering a course of action, as to whether to stay or continue their journey.

She was too excited to feel pangs of hunger but supposed they should at least have something to sustain them. Their last meal of raw fish seemed like days away, when she supposed it was perhaps one or two at most.

As she paddled around the shallow waters and delighting in the cool refreshing cascade she scooped over her skin, she became alert to Lexor's warning growl. She looked back over her shoulder and confronted the stranger watching her a short distance away. He was Caucasian, of a similar age, tanned and toned. His shorts were slung low as if he'd lost weight, or he'd come across them on a foraging trip and they were a size too big.

He simply stared, and Katerina supposed it was because she hadn't tried to cover her modesty. She let Lexor continue growling a warning to the young man, not to approach, believing her loyal companion would leap to her defence should it be necessary. She went to where she'd discarded her clothes and put them on, all the while, studying the stranger as he was apt to do. It surprised her, in that not once did his gaze drift to the dog and let her know he was not afraid.

Katerina introduced herself in the only language she was fluent in and was pleasantly surprised the stranger was able to answer in her native tongue.

'I'm Christov. You; from Mother Russia?'

'Yes.'

'Small fucking world.'

He turned as if to leave and hesitated, cast his gaze back.

'I have food, some water. You're welcome to join me. As with the mutt, if he doesn't try any funny business.'

Katerina thanked him, skipped across to the boat to retrieve her own meagre possessions and hurried after the stranger before he got too far away. Lexor kept to her side, no longer snarling a warning at the young man. Katerina realised she was smiling as she observed the young man's exposed back, while wondering how he'd come across the faded network of scars from the nape down to the crack of his taut buttocks.

It had her wondering several things.

CHAPTER 7

A WORLD BENEATH THE ICE...PART TWO

A powerful source of energy

Can generate solace, on the one hand,

And deliver a legacy of torment,

In the other.

As it will always be…

Christov had taken up residence within the confines of a large shadowy hollow. Much of the floor space was taken up with clutter, all of which were the spoils he'd salvaged on his frequent foraging expeditions, that which he believed had a useful purpose.

He'd fashioned a bed from a section of foam and a faux-fur throw added to its comfort. Not that the nauseating aroma of sweat and grime within the gloomy interior was welcoming.

Katerina contented herself Christov was not someone who posed a threat and was able to quickly settle and relax in his company. It took time and effort to get him to lower barriers and open-up to her, as he was a young man of few words. Conversation didn't come easy to someone who appeared to carry the weight of his past on his shoulders. Katerina was able to relate to this, considering her own experiences, believing Christov had seen and endured great hardship, and was coming to terms with it, slowly.

Over a meal of beans and potato, she asked how he'd acquired the scars criss-crossing his torso. He didn't answer, not immediately, so she gave him the time to consider. It was agreed, they would share the one crib, or she'd have to endure lying on the hard unyielding rock floor.

She issued a stern warning, setting out parameters not to take advantage. He simply nodded; basically, saying he understood, or he was not interested in her. Not in the way she imagined he might. She had her knife, not that she admitted having a weapon about her person, should it become necessary to defend herself.

It took two further sunrises and following three claustrophobic nights, cramped together, before Christov found the courage and trust to reveal a portion of his life-history. He'd been a political dissident and activist in his home city, St Petersburg, gaining attention from government officials and security forces. His movements and actions were constantly monitored, regarding his public rants and subversive viewpoints. He was eventually issued a stern warning, to desist, or answer to his crimes against the state.

He had been fortunate, he'd said, as his father was KGB and his only son was an embarrassment. He supposed he was lucky, in that he had been warned-off, as countless others who created ripples in the political cesspool would mysteriously disappear, never to be seen again.

His situation became dire, and moments before the world was 'turned on its head', Christov had been forced to take a vacation. Along with two friends, they came to Morocco, and it was there he received a cryptic communique from his father, suggesting the world was on the verge of an unprecedented climactic and geological upheaval. That, which could not be subverted, even avoided. He was not talking weeks, months, or years. The planet was facing possible extinction, and the timescale was merely a day, possibly two.

Christov pondered this with scepticism at first, yet kept a wary eye on news reports, and even tried to study the changing weather patterns for himself. When animal and bird chatter suddenly ceased and there came an eerie quiet, only punctuated by piped local music through banks of loudspeakers, Christov took his father's plea seriously; perhaps, for the first time in his life. Without having any answers to hand, Christov believed it was imperative he and his friends fled the coastal resort, while there was still time to do so.

As with others, Christov became alert to atmospheric change, the lull before the storm.

Christov admitted, he'd tried exhaustively to persuade his friends to leave with him, and they simply scoffed at him; called him an 'old woman' and asked him why he should believe his father now, after all this time. His father was the enemy, should he forget.

Christov's father was a lot of things, he could admit. Yet something was telling him, this was not a fabrication of events to come, in that this was the real deal. His father was reaching out to him, trying to save him. As with the warning he'd received, to not pursue his public rantings to the media. Powerful circles within government and the military were losing patience.

Christov's friends were having a great time, and it would be foolish to leave, as beautiful willing girls were plentiful. They were not inclined to follow the words of an estranged father or submit to Christov's spiritual transcendency. Christov was hurt, he admitted, but not once did he question those feelings he was having.

He was given no choice, as he saw it, and made his mind up to abandon his friends to fate. He put clothes and bottled water into a backpack and departed the resort, travelling inland by taxi, not having a destination in mind at the time. Saying his farewells had been a terrible wrench, and he almost relented and have the cab turn around and return.

Then came the moment his father's predictions were to come true, and there came Hell on Earth. The taxi suffered a head-on collision, the driver killed outright. Christov admitted lady luck was on his side as he was unhurt, not even a scratch, he'd said. With the searing heat blistering the ground and causing fires to break out everywhere, he kept going. On foot.

He saw terrible things, great suffering. And he was powerless to help.

He remembered the snow, not that he was a stranger to it. The people of Africa probably had never seen such a thing in their lifetime. Christov sought shelter, and warmth; in his mind, safety, as it became apparent the snowfall was deadly and burned the flesh.

There followed a period of the worst earthquakes imaginable, and if that hadn't been enough, there was the floods.

He was one of the lucky ones, he'd admitted, supposing the existence he had could be construed as fortunate. He made do.

He tried to make Katerina understand, that their location would ordinarily have been several hundred miles inland. A great swath of the western fringes had been swallowed up by the tsunami to have struck with relentless speed and ferocity and had not retreated as one would have expected. Many cities and thousands upon thousands of luckless individuals were now in a watery grave. He made mention of the mythical Atlantis and chuckled, not that it was borne of humour.

He had Katerina looking south where debris of boulders and the skeletal remains of buildings obscured the view he was attempting to explain. He let her know there lay something beyond, hidden from view, which made no sense.

He spoke of a pyramid, which was unlike any he'd known to exist prior to this time, as it was not the usual, crafted and built from sandstone and granite. This was metallic, he said; completely black. It was his belief the world had faced an alien attack.

Then he made a comment as to Katerina's obsession with a rock he caught her handling and staring at on occasion.

'Not just a rock,' she'd remark. 'A crystal. Sometimes it speaks to me; hard to explain. It has energy, and when I'm holding it, I feel it vibrating. It makes me feel good. Hopeful.'

He scoffed at her words.

'It's a fucking rock!' and she caught him sneering at her.

That was the moment Katerina became aware of a change in his personality. He wasn't as convivial and could no longer keep a mask over a darker element which was a part of his psyche.

If she had to sleep on the rough ground, she would, as trust was to become an issue and contentious.

During a moment when he became withdrawn and chose not to speak, she continued to study his profile, and once again, prompted him to speak of those scars on his torso.

He squatted in front of her, seemed to glare, but what she saw in his eyes she'd seen on numerous occasions. There was fear, uncertainty, humiliation. She perhaps saw it as a reminder of all those times she'd stared at her own reflection in a mirror.

Christov confessed he'd been attacked by a giant jellyfish while swimming in the sea to catch fish. He went on to say, the pain from being stung a 'million' times over was unlike anything he'd ever experienced. He supposed he was lucky to have survived. Now, he admitted, he was afraid to go into the water beyond a certain depth which meant, a sustainable income of edible fish, sea urchin and other marine life was no longer a part of his diet.

Katerina believed it was his fear that which conflicted with his machismo ego, which made him bitter and at times angry. He didn't want her to think he was a coward.

She left him to compute his own tired thoughts, of the memories he'd committed to, and went to stretch out on the crib.

Despite his fluctuating behaviour, Katerina did not perceive him to be a threat. He was just another dealing with all he'd lost and having to face an uncertain future without guidance. Katerina was different, and stronger emotionally, as she was positive in her outlook. She was someone who didn't let her past spoil the present or encumber her goals for what lay ahead of her.

She was secretly wondering, whether to stay with Christov, or continue her journey. His shadow blotted out the glare of a morning sun as he stepped close to tower over her recumbent form. She opened her eyes and looked up, to catch him leering at her. She'd seen that expression on the faces of men countless times, and she didn't like it; not then, and certainly not at this time.

'I wish to fuck!' he said bluntly. 'I ask that you feel the same. I don't want to take you by force. I am not like that. Do you want to fuck? You miss fucking?'

Katerina sat up, her mind in disarray, and aware Lexor had taken himself off to explore the area around. He was not at her side to protect her. She steeled herself, scrambled to her feet without meeting his gaze, and pushed past him.

'No, I don't want to fuck!' she rasped. 'I'm going for a walk. I suggest you take the time to cool-off while I'm gone.'

She didn't wait for a response, ducked away to one side and quickly, agilely, clambered across the outcrop of rock where it shelved down towards the flat surface of sand and shale. She inhaled deeply, held a breath, and let it go, before going to explore the area beyond their shelter and the shoreline.

She took the time to compose her thoughts and overcome her discomfort, and realised she wasn't unduly surprised Christov should exhibit feelings of desire and lust, given their situation. They had slept together for three nights, as close and intimate as it could get. At the beginning, she'd slept little, as she was unable to trust him implicitly. She'd didn't really know him.

The second night was better, and more relaxing. Christov had been more relaxed. The previous night she'd witnessed subtle changes, in the way he pressed himself close to her while believing she was asleep on her side facing away from him. It became a little more physical, and his behaviour had her not relaxing, so that she was prepared for a confrontation if the situation got out of hand.

Katerina stopped ambling around the moment she was afforded a view of the pyramid Christov had spoken of, found a small boulder to sit on, and took time to gaze across at the strangely beautiful monument. It seemed out-of-place and surreal against a bleak and ugly canvas.

She held her crystal cluster and felt extraordinary energy pulsating within it. She wondered if the crystal was connected to the subtle source of energy she felt emanating off the pyramid in the distance. What she was able to establish, was the way it increasingly invigorated her, both mentally and physically.

During that time of contemplation, Katerina arrived at the decision to stay a further day and continue her journey the following morning.

She had her knife, and there was Lexor, to protect her in the night should Christov let his frustrations get the better of him and tried to force himself on her.

Katerina returned to the shelter as the sun was set to dip and melt into the sea. She approached the entrance from a different direction, and where she clung and pawed the rock wall she was suddenly assailed by a mouth-watering aroma of food cooking.

Christov was using the firepit he'd created using a depression of small stones and a metal grate covering the wood he was burning.

He flashed a sullen smile as she stepped down onto where the surface levelled out.

'I cook us a stew,' he rasped. 'Fucking good stew. You will like.'

She didn't much care what he was doing for her, his efforts to ingratiate her, except it smelled delicious and she became aware just how hungry she was.

Katerina went to the crib and sat, devising an explanation as to why she was going to leave. She grasped her crystal, as it not only placated her, but she also had to wonder if its mystical properties would grant her easy passage and avoid an unpleasant confrontation. Lexor was nowhere to be seen and felt sure her the appetising aroma of food cooking would have enticed wonderful companion. She would make certain there was some left over, even if it meant sharing her own spoils.

Christov had made it apparent he had no liking for Lexor, was perhaps as wary of him as he was the sea, and of the creatures which dwelt there.

While they sat in silence with the stew served in artisan wooden bowls, Katerina had to admit it was good and tasty, despite the chunks of meat being tough and chewy. Christov was a good cook when he put his mind to it. On this occasion he'd boiled up some kelp and other forms of seaweed he'd gathered where it hugged a shelf of smaller rocks further along the shoreline.

She saved some and set her bowl to one side, leaning back and stretching, to better digest the food.

'Fucking good, yes?' Christov barked and laughed and belched crudely.

'Have you seen Lexor?' she asked, without commenting on the meal he'd cooked and served for them.

He merely shrugged. 'You enjoy exploring? Do you see the pyramid? What did you make of it?'

Katerina's mind was in disarray as she caught him leering at her once again. She was thinking of Lexor and thought it odd he should stay away the best part of a day.

'Lexor?' she prompted again, 'Have you seen him since this morning? He wouldn't stay away this long. He could be hurt.'

'Lexor! Lexor! Lexor!' and he jumped to his feet, his posture exuding menace. 'You think more of the dog than you do me.'

'Where is he?' she asked calmly, becoming uneasy, not from his tone or the craziness to have touched his eyes, but in the feeling something bad had happened.

'In your belly, ungrateful bitch. There's your fucking Lexor. The fucking bastard tried to take a chunk out of me, so I fucked him up. Didn't want to waste good meat, so I make stew. You liked it, so quit complaining.'

Katerina had jumped to her feet, neither angry nor horrified. She supposed his confession had shocked her, sufficient to nullify her senses, so that for a moment she didn't know what to feel or how to react.

Christov approached.

'It's okay,' he said. 'It's just you and me now. How it should be.'

He dared to reach up and fondle a breast, slip a hand into the opening at front of her shirt. That was the moment she swept the blade of the knife she'd extracted from her seat pocket across his exposed throat. He staggered away, as both hands tried feebly to smother the gaping rent across his windpipe, blood gushing between his fingers.

He spluttered, wept, and loosened his bladder, before dropping to his knees and crashing to the hard ground face-down.

Katerina could only stare at the corpse, and several minutes elapsed before she became galvanised again.

She didn't want to spend another night in their hellhole, so she gathered up all the essentials she felt she would need for her journey and made several hazardous trips to the boat with her haul.

The moment she set-off, she was filled with remorse, and grieving for her lost companion had her sob. She couldn't remember the last time she'd shed tears for anyone or anything. Lexor had been the first and only companion to have filled a gap in her deplorable existence and made her life rewarding and joyous for a short time.

Now though, she was to face an uncertain future, alone.

When the tears ceased, she felt a solid weight enclose her heart. She'd weep no more. Her past life up to the present had immured her within a hard, unforgiving and unyielding shell. She could no longer feel anything. The compassion she had felt for a time, had been wrenched out of her. Just as it had in the past.

As with Christov, she came to believe a dark shadow had crawled over her heart, where it had potentially snuffed-out the flame of goodness she was coming to embrace.

CHAPTER 8

A WORLD BENEATH THE ICE...PART THREE

I AM THE FUTURE,

I AM WRATH.

I AM, A SERVANT TO DARK DEEDS...

Several days passed, and Katerina was still feeling despondent and lethargic. She seemed to have acquired less focus since leaving the shores of Western Africa.

Initially, her journey had begun at a laborious and tedious pace, as she had to exhaustively row the boat with oars. It was as she was passing the location of the black pyramid the outboard miraculously puttered into life once again, and she was able to make steady progress without exerting herself.

The small craft hugged the coastline for a considerable time, and it was only after she slept and she no longer steered the rudder, did the boat begin to veer away into open waters.

LEGACY OF ANGELS

When Katerina eventually awoke, she recognised the fact the lethargy she'd experienced had gone and seemed to have acquired greater vigour. She could exercise, but her attempts were limited by the cramped quarters within the vessel. The open sea was not as daunting as she imagined it might have been, especially as she no longer shared the company of her loyal and faithful companion.

She felt as if she was not the one governing her own fate and wherever the boat was to take her, that was okay with her. Katerina began to believe in miracles, as fish continued to jump out of the sea to land at her feet. She never went without, even as she became aware her water rations were becoming depleted, despite being frugal and taking the occasional sips whenever she felt the need.

It was her hope she would reach land soon, even though the open sea was a tranquil source of contentment to her. The gentle rocking motion made her giddy at times, and once again she craved to be on land. What baffled her most was the climate, in the way it remained balanced at all times of the day and night. Not once since leaving Mother Russia had she endured storms. Even the waves were calm.

Her journey continued, her spirits becoming uplifted at sight of land in the distance, the boat having steered her back to the Southern fringes of the African continent.

Once aground, she was to discover life had learned to thrive in a short time. Food was plentiful, and the people she was to meet, were friendly and accommodating. These survivors of catastrophic world events had formed communities, where happiness ruled; and not the fearful uncertainty of a government, dictatorship or rebels taking control of the lifestyle they should lead. It was difficult to imagine, yet she was fortunate to experience the concept of a utopian existence, and it assisted her in forgetting the past she'd left behind.

Every person, no matter their age, were happy to toil the land, to grow and harvest crops. There was an abundance of fruit trees, the first she'd seen since her journey began. Just as important, fresh water was plentiful, as numerous springs had emerged when mountains had shifted and settled after the quakes.

Katerina found a home for a time and stayed for months, basking in the goodness where a new society preached well-being and togetherness, and not to live constantly in the shadow of fear, as she had done.

She had acquired a new wardrobe, was given a roof over her head, and when it was required she had her freedom. Every night, the people of each township gathered to sing and dance. Some stringed instruments and bongo drums had survived, and competent musicians made use of these. Craftsmen were still plying their gifted trade to carve additional instruments, along with toys for the children, and even furniture for the dwellings.

Then came the day she received her calling, in the form of a distinctive tugging at her thoughts, and she felt destined to continue her journey by boat. She no longer questioned her need for a nomadic lifestyle, as she believed still, Fate was taking her to where she was meant to be.

All those friends she'd cultivated since landing were saddened to see her leave, and all wished her a safe voyage and an abundance of happiness wherever she went. Several score of well-wishers lined the beach to wave their farewells. As Katerina set out to sea, she waved back, and refused to let despondency ruin the moment.

Those who had ventured to watch her leave stayed vigil on the shore, until the small boat became an insignificant speck in the distance.

The outboard puttered its rhythmic tune as the boat slipped easily across the surface of the ocean, as to where; Katerina was still none the wiser.

She supposed she'd slept for hours as day was now night, and when she opened her eyes it was to witness another spectacle, of a plethora of coruscating stars and a full moon.

Katerina retrieved the crystal cluster she kept secreted away inside the pocket of the native African smock she was wearing. She lay with it cradled against her bosom and hoped it might speak to her, of assurance, and to grant her hope she might discover her purpose soon.

Beneath the lunar effulgence, the tiny prisms flickered an array of colour, yet not with the same intensity of brilliance she'd come to expect. Its lustre had become dulled over time. She leaned over the side and trailed the stone in the water to cleanse it, and became distracted, as her concentration was on a wider area to ascertain whether a threat existed. It was at that moment she relaxed her grip and cried out, as the precious stone slipped away from her grasp and became lost to her.

Within minutes of this calamity, the outboard gave a familiar cough and splutter, and died; the small boat slowing to a crawl.

Katerina became fearful, as now she would have to row the boat or let the currents steer her path. With no sight of land on the horizon she had to wonder if Fate had doomed her. She lay back and screamed her frustration.

She missed Lexor.

Already she missed the comforting influence of her crystal and cursed her stupidity.

Mentally and emotionally exhausted, she closed her eyes and slept some more.

It was while she was sleeping, and dreaming, the boat gave a little lurch and settled again.

A gigantic gelatinous tentacle burst out of the water, whipping, and flailing the air above the recumbent form, before taking a purchase on the portside gun whale. Other tentacles appeared and drew sinuous patterns in the ether, and they too gripped the boat on all sides. The monstrous hooded head of a jellyfish emerged and hovered over its prey for a time, giving the impression it was studying her, the glutinous folds pulsating and fluctuating in time to Katerina's breathing.

The hood darted forward to completely enmesh her face and scalp, the tentacles recoiling to ensnare her body. Katerina went into convulsions as the powerful grip on her frame was exacerbated. The creature throbbed, insinuating itself into every orifice, the human it embraced, bucking, and heaving beneath it.

Katerina was lifted and she and the beast were launched overboard into the murk of the ocean, being dragged to a greater depth, as the creature became absorbed into the body it was clutching.

Katerina believed she'd been in the merciless throes of a particularly nasty nightmare, when finally, she recovered her senses and consciousness, only to discover she'd fallen into the sea and was sinking. She was remarkably composed and didn't panic, as she kicked and swept her arms forward and outward, propelling herself to the surface. The moment her head broke water she ejected a thick spout, seeing the boat a short distance away and swam towards it. She hauled herself over the side and stretched out along the bottom beneath the bench seat, letting her ragged breathing settle and become steady.

Touching herself tentatively revealed she was naked, having lost her colourful smock dress. Between her legs was smooth, and when she instinctively caressed her scalp with both hands, discovered all the hair on her head was gone.

Katerina drew in deep breaths and kept herself composed, while trying to make sense of the situation she found herself in. She tried to recall the dream she'd had, and it took only a moment for her subconscious to unravel the mystery.

Jesus! her mind screamed, just as she imagined she'd been attacked by one of the giant jellyfish.

She chuckled to herself, knowing if she had been, she would be scarred head to toe; worse. She would be dead!

There was still the fact she'd fallen out of the boat, had lost her dress, along with all the hair on her body.

It made no logical sense, and considering she was alive and feeling happily relieved, she supposed it didn't matter.

She caressed her scalp again, as if to confirm she wasn't still dreaming, and when she lowered her hands to the gentle rise and fall of her small breasts, she gave a hissing gasp through gritted teeth. Pressing a hand between her thighs had her buttocks lifting off the concave planks as each of her actions reawakened desire; that which had remained dormant for many years.

She raised herself and shuffled on knees to the defunct outboard, willing it to acquire a magical source of life once again. Only when she hugged it, did she feel tremors from within the metal casing, and gave a gasp as the machine purred into life in answer to her prayers.

The rudder tapped her hip as the boat found impetus and cut steadily through the gentle swell. Katerina cried out, jubilant, the sound of her voice resonating high and wide, and then she was straddling the smooth wooden column as it vibrated between her thighs. She moaned and screamed again and thrilled to the steady rhythmic beats along her pubis.

When eventually she slipped back, she gave a shriek of exultant pleasure, and cackled. She thought it sounded demented and didn't care. And then she slept, and on this occasion she was untroubled by nightmarish dreams.

CHAPTER 9

A WORLD BENEATH THE ICE…PART FOUR

And goodness will fear the shadow,

And all will come to know,

A utopian existence

Is, but a fanciful dream…

Katerina awoke to a glorious clear blue sky, and seagulls. She supposed it was a sign, that she was approaching land once again.

She wouldn't mind vacating the boat for a time once more, no matter where it was taking her; just so that she had an opportunity to stretch her legs.

And she was ravenous.

Even as she was thinking about food, the sky was suddenly and miraculously, raining a variety of fish. Several landed within the boat, jiggling and dancing, and it was the moment Katerina understood the meaning of true happiness and contentment as her wishes had been answered.

Instead of laboriously cutting away the scales, fins and paring away the skin, Katerina gorged on her hoard; devouring head, tail, and bones until none of the fish remained.

She lay back for a time, completely satiated, and following a deserved rest crawled to the outboard motor just to straddle the rudder once again.

She was unable to stop herself cackling, it seemed, until the pleasure she derived from the pulsating vibrations had her grunting and moaning.

Life was just so fucking good! her mind screamed.

She must have slept, following several exhaustive orgasms, and when she awoke on this occasion, it was to discover the environment had changed considerably.

The air was crisp and she searched through her canvas bag for jeans and sweat top, all the while unable to take her gaze off a blinding white vista of ice floes all around the boat. Up ahead lay a raised promontory of snow and ice, and beyond that and way-off in the distance was a chain of mountainous peaks.

The object to capture her interest was of one ice-encrusted mountain, in the familiar shape of a pyramid, and perhaps it was she was thinking.

She was further surprised the intensity of the freezing cold hadn't seeped into her bones, as suffering from hypothermia would have been an insurmountable problem. She had no coat, not that it mattered, as her jeans and sweat top were sufficient to keep her body temperature even.

Katerina crawled to the prow and marvelled at sight of all the fantastical bergs rising out of the frozen sea, like ice sculptures at a sumptuous wedding.

The view took her breath away, all around cloaked in heavenly silence, except where the hull of the boat scraped ice floes and the outboard chirred a steady rhythm.

She saw King Penguins inhabiting a few of the plateaus, which were becoming steadily denser and more compact as she approached a solid stretch of landmass. Their antics and incessant chatter had her chuckling. She saw babies, and it made her smile even more.

It had her reflecting on all those possibilities and lost opportunities, as she didn't suppose she would ever have children. Not that she was maternal in any way and wondered if it was something to do with the fact she'd lost some of her focus since the world went to hell and back. Her journey since leaving the motherland proved she was no longer a person who could settle in one place for any length of time; and children needed stability, and love.

She didn't think she was capable of either; should she be honest.

No big deal, she'd tell herself. She was content, despite everything she'd witnessed and endured.

She had taken her knife and committed murder, and amazingly, she was not left with any lasting trauma. She had a cold heart, and it suited the climate and environment she'd arrived at. She was okay with that, and supposed she had to be. She was taught a hard lesson in life, in that no one could be trusted.

She flinched and steadied herself as the hull of the boat screeched out a warning it was scraping against the compacted ice where the sea had become a narrow inlet, and even this was soon to be swallowed up as her journey juddered to a halt.

She had no idea what she was meant to do, now that she had landed, in what appeared to be a bleak, unforgiving landscape. She even wondered whether it was prudent to turn the boat around and head out to the open sea again, that was, until she was alerted to a person calling out to her. She had a sense of *déjà vu.*

She saw him then, standing on a promontory of ice further along the cap, waving frantically. He didn't look that young, at distance, and didn't appear to be in his dotage either. The stranger appeared to be happy to see her, as he was quite animated and exuberant, and seeking a way down from his position onto the flat bed of ice she was stranded on.

She gave a light-hearted chuckle the moment he began to scramble down the ledge, lost his purchase, and slid the rest of the way on his posterior. She didn't approach, believing it was prudent to remain where she was and let him come to her. She had her knife, should she have a need to defend herself once again. She'd killed before and knew she could do so a second time should it become necessary.

Struggling to keep his balance, despite wearing sturdy boots, he was still waving. He was even laughing, ridiculing his own clumsiness.

Katerina felt comfortable and sensed there was to be no threat from the stranger.

He slowed as he closed the gap, and she noticed the way he studied her, in much the same way she overtly appraised him. At least he was not staring in a lascivious way. He appeared more intrigued, to find someone who had appeared out of nowhere, or maybe it was the shaved head to have sparked his curiosity.

He was wearing a fur-skin coat over trousers which had been patched together from a variety of clothes, she suspected.

The man was quick to prompt a conversation, seeing as the young woman he was confronting appeared reticent and wary of him.

'My word,' he spluttered, before mustering composure. 'Where on this Earth have you come from? You're alone; I can see that. But how did you make it here?'

Katerina was unable to understand how she came to know what the man was asking, as he spoke English and she knew so little of the language.

'I've been at sea for months,' she said.

'Months, you say?'

She'd answered in her native language and it was apparent he understood her also.

'You survived, that's the important thing. My, my, I can only imagine how difficult it must have been. I have food and beverages, warm blankets. Are you hungry, my dear?'

She nodded a response, her gaze drifting to the barren wilderness.

'It's not far,' he added. 'Less than a kilometre. There are others in the village, our community numbering forty-seven. Other survivors have set up home in other areas. There are military installations, not that they're operable anymore, and the residents are friendly and been a great service to the many hundreds who arrived here escaping the chaos in the world. It's not that bad here. Food and water is plentiful, if you like fish. We make do with what we need, and we're content. Forgive me; let me introduce myself. My name is Richard and I've been a resident since the outbreak of disaster.

Anyway, we can talk more later. Will you join me? I can help with your possessions as I have a sled on the ridge up yonder.'

He waited eagerly for Katerina to accept his invitation, and had she declined it would have played on his conscience. He didn't want to abandon her and leave her stranded in this bleak haven he'd chosen for himself, as had many others.

Katerina finally gave a nod of assent, and formerly introduced herself. There was no handshake or hug, as she turned away and approached the boat.

Richard was like an ebullient puppy, and still had trouble keeping his balance on the ice, as he stepped up to help retrieve the bags in her possession.

Katerina was more sure-footed, even without shoes or boots. She had trainers yet was comfortable without. It further surprised her the freezing temperature had no effect.

She got to ride on the motorised sled, and was enamoured at the thought, a simple crystal was the source of energy and the sled's propulsion.

Richard rode from the rear, a small rudder to steer the long sleek mode of transport. He declined making further conversation until sight of a cluster of igloos and icehouses forming a wide circle, appeared in the distance.

'That is my home,' he shouted. 'Your home too if you wish. You're more than welcome.'

Richard's dwelling was a good-sized block-built house with a domed roof and having a vent. The interior was surprisingly homely, and not cold as Katerina imagined it might be. Richard was a neat and orderly person, as everything he possessed had its place, without clutter. He led a simple, Bohemian lifestyle, and supposed others of the community were content with having little.

Once he had brought in her bags from the sled and Katerina was settled, he insisted she ate and drank something before giving her a guided tour, and perhaps to meet with others in the community.

He spoke of one with undisguised reverence. There was a man, who was not mortal; he'd said, and it was obvious he was waiting for a response and gauge his guest's reaction.

He referred to this person as Panea, and all believed and accepted he was an Earth Angel, one who was blessed with incredible powers which defied the imagination at times. He was guardian of all who inhabited the Antarctic region, and it was he who had taught them survival skills and life-sustainability.

Richard admitted keeping a haul of fish outside, set into a depression under a thick coating of snow. Everyone shared their spoils; he went on to say.

He led her outside and exposed his latest catch and had her choose whatever she needed.

While he prepared a small firepit, Katerina could no longer control the pangs of hunger she felt, grabbed up a large cod and began gorging.

'Really? I mean, you like your fish raw?' he stammered, unsure how to proceed, as he watched her devour huge chunks at a time, with relish, and not finding the tough skin a problem or, for that matter, the rough scales, and bones 'I never imagined for a moment, one is able to find satisfaction demolishing a fish in its raw state.'

Eventually, he had to look away, and gave up on the firepit he'd put together. Witnessing Katerina ripping and gutting the big fish with her teeth stole his appetite. After, he made up a separate cot, lining it with fur and pelts which had been given to him by those who inhabited the foreign outposts. There were four in total; American, British, Russian and French.

The work they were doing before the advent of the holocaust remained a secret, but since the world underwent a cataclysmic change with the loss of communications, their work had become obsolete. They were stranded in the Antarctic wasteland, along with the newcomers; not that anyone complained. In a short time, and with the arrival of Panea, everyone became upbeat and content, and all learned to trust and work together.

All of those who served different countries and governments no longer had to spy or suspect hostility from their neighbours. It was a matter of survival and making the most of a dire situation.

Life could be worse; was the mantra of solidarity. As all recognised the fact, they were survivors and had been granted a second chance, and to learn from past mistakes.

Having set up a second cot, Katerina was quick to thank Richard for his kindness and generosity and wanted to test her bed for comfort. Richard surreptitiously appraised the newcomer as she stretched out and gleefully stamped her feet. From his position on his own cot, the questions as to where she had heralded from and how she made the daunting journey, played heavily and eagerly on his mind.

'I have to ask,' he said in soft tones, becoming enamoured with her movements as she seemed to nestle into the fur covering and sinuously writhe; just to embrace the softness and texture it afforded her. 'Do you possess telepathic powers? I ask, as you seem to understand my language, as I appear to be able to decipher Russian.'

He paused to deliver a message to her mind, as a test of her abilities.

'Are you comfortable?' was the question he posed. *'I need you to know, that you are quite safe here.'*

'Yes, and thank you,' she answered, without reverting to natural speech.

'Splendid,' he answered her in his voice. 'Just so that you know, I have informed our guardian, Panea, we have a new arrival. He will visit shortly and become acquainted with you. As of this moment, he is overseeing another new arrival. One of our fortunate ladies is giving birth to a daughter. This will be number five among our community within the past two years. Tomorrow, there will be a gathering, and all will give thanks and blessings to the new born.'

He wanted to ask if she'd had children of her own and was surprised and embarrassed she'd picked up on the threads of his thoughts so easily and readily.

'To your question; no, I had no children of my own. I suppose, even though I'm not quite sure, but I must be twenty-three or four. It appears, I have no conception of time, days, weeks, months. It's of no consequence, as each day I wake up, I find a reason to be happy and thankful I am alive. As before the holocaust, I was dead.'

'Dear me, and perhaps I shouldn't delve into personal issues, but what do you mean by; *you were dead?'*

'Yes, there are some things you should not ask about.'

She closed her eyes and steadied her breathing, emptying her mind of clutter. She didn't want Richard accessing data she wanted kept secret. She sensed he was content to watch and study her from his cot and found his scrutiny stimulating. She imagined herself swimming within the depths of the ocean, could feel the cool embrace of the water on her skin. She felt completely free, not that she understood why her instincts became predatory, as if she were hunting for something to satisfy a deep craving.

The 'one' who was known as Panea appeared to them one hour later, and he was not how she imagined him to be.

She hoped he was not reading her mind, as she thought him to be ancient in appearance, even though his movements were sprightly and convivial. He had a permanent twinkle in his eye, and always it seemed, he had a reason to smile.

Richard had earlier stated; Panea was considered an Earth Angel *(whatever that meant)* and was known to possess specific powers. What those powers were, in relation to mortal men, Katerina hoped to understand in time. She was still marvelling at the idea she was telepathic.

On arrival Panea greeted the newcomer with an affectionate embrace, and Katerina was quick to assess this otherworldly person was a source of energy, transmitting itself much in the same way her crystal did. The thing which didn't sit well with her thoughts, was in that he travelled from one homestead to another in bleak icy conditions, dressed in a suit the colour of deepest sapphire. He looked as if he was selling something, not pertaining to be an elemental guardian.

She was also instantly attuned to the manner of him probing delicately around her thoughts, something she found invasive, not that she gave anything away. She kept her mind free and imagined she'd erected a powerful barrier, and from the querulous look he gave her, he would know her strength.

Katerina was requested to sit, while Panea paced and sometimes hovered over his audience. He displayed obvious signs he was both intrigued and wary of her.

'I imagine your journey was an arduous one, my dear,' he stated calmly. 'Let us give thanks you arrived here unharmed and appear to be in good health and spirits.'

'I had a crystal for a time,' she admitted. 'It was a source of comfort and energy. Sadly, I lost it.'

'Not to worry, my child, for there are many such crystals to be distributed. As with you for a time, everyone in residence, are in possession of crystals. They not only present a sense of well-being; they are a source of light and heat.'

He pointed to a corner where a small geode was aglow and illuminated the interior of Richard's dwelling.

'The energy derived from each crystal comes from the universe, as with every living person and animal, bird and insect, and aquatic life,' he added, 'an energy which is fed from a contained source which lies within a monument not too far from here.'

'A pyramid,' Katerina interpolated quietly, musing at the thought of such a magical force governing all of life on Earth along with the energy to sustain it.

'Yes, yes; a pyramid. I suspect you saw others on your incredible passage from the motherland to here.'

'You are right. I saw these amazing structures from time to time and believed then they were a reason why the outboard on my boat was propelled without the need of natural fuel.'

'Exactly, my dear; as with your personal crystal, the one you discarded.'

'What do you mean? I lost it. It fell out of my hands into the sea.'

'This source of energy from the universe,' he went on to explain, while abruptly dismissing her reasons, 'Is mankind's future hope in a new world. All is going according to plan, with civilisations coming together in harmony. This, child, is a utopian existence where all have an opportunity to grow rich; not, as it once was, by acquiring personal wealth or possessions. All are equal, and content with their new regime.'

'It's my understanding,' said Katerina carefully, 'The source of energy you speak of, controls everything; the climate, nature's evolving, and how people behave and think.'

'Precisely.'

'So, by your own admission, we have all become puppets. Robots.'

'Is this how you perceive the ways of the new world, child? Evil has been eradicated, all have gendered humility and kindness. It is now safe for children and women, especially, to walk the streets safely and not live in the shadow of fear. All are prepared to toil for what they have and to share. Greed has been abolished. Crime is a byword. The climate, indeed, is governed so as not to inflict destructive influences on our planet, as it once was. The crystals I have mentioned, promote health, and are attributed to the healing of injuries, and debilitating ailments. Do you understand? All have been given a life of promise, to live in the light and not the shadow. To be free to express joy, not sadness. To not have them cower in fear, as it was prevalent all over the world before the change. There are countries, where once, the innocent suffered during long periods of political and religious warfare. Terrorism was rife, and millions perished as a result of evil extremist philosophy. This no longer exists. There are no weapons of mass destruction, they have become obsolete and useless. There are knives, bows and arrows, spears, and clubs; all of which are merely used for a sustainable income. There is no trade in tusks and furs. People take only what they need or use. Would it surprise you, if I were to say, there is no governing currency acceptable on the planet? Without the need for money, there is no propensity for greed or power. The true currency lies within us, and within the crystals. Universal energy, my dear.'

'You paint a beautiful and idyllic picture,' Katerina remarked. 'Can you categorically claim, all of evil has been removed, or is it merely wishful thinking? Or perhaps, the dream of utopia has blinded all to reality.'

Panea seemed to hesitate as he gave himself a moment to consider the newcomer, feeling surprisingly, an undercurrent of unease. Why he should feel a necessity for caution defied an explanation at that point, as it was anathema to his new way of thinking, and of all the positive results he'd witnessed since the world's rebirth.

'I will say this,' he continued, in tones which had become strained. 'As I have explained, evil has no place in the new world. Those, who once laboured with dark thoughts and committed to dark deeds, have climbed from the self-imposed abyss they were once immersed in, and have discovered their true and real vocation. They have learned the value of life and to assist in preserving it, not remove it.'

Katerina refrained giving her answer on the edict the guardian, Panea, had served to her.

'Welcome, child, to our haven of hope and salvation,' Panea continued. 'Following tomorrow's festival of thanksgiving in blessing the child born this day, a dwelling will be constructed at a place of your choosing. Everyone will want to help make your home and stay a comfortable and happy one. If it is your wish, dark memories stored within your mind will be expunged, as new and joyous ones are forged. You were brought here for a reason, and in time, you will come to understand the meaning of this.'

'And should I decide to continue on my journey?' she queried and becoming oddly fatigued and felt unexpectedly drained of energy. She suspected Panea was the reason, if not the guardian, she had to wonder if the crystals were absorbing her essence. It was a consideration, believing it was the reason why people had become robots. She still had questions to ask. 'You stated that the people who survived are free of dark thoughts explicitly. What if; should a person commit a crime under the new regime, and it's perceived as a criminal act, who presides over judgement on that person or persons, and ultimately decides on a justifiable sentence? What would that entail, I wonder, in our perfect new world? This utopia created by the universe, by your admission. Sorry, if my question is perceived as a negative response. But I have seen the face of cruelty and evil, still. That which took my best friend and loyal companion. So, forgive me, if I have my misgivings. To trust, is weakness. I trusted Lexor, my canine companion, and he was taken from me. I have tasted the sadness to have blighted my joy. I tell you; it is always wise not to view life through rose-tinted lenses, and to trust our instincts.'

'I am truly sorry for your loss,' said Panea succinctly. 'These feelings and negative emotions will fade with time, I swear.'

'Thank you; the both of you, for taking me to your bosom. You are both genuinely kind-hearted.'

It became an effort to speak or even to coordinate her thoughts, and she fell instantly asleep. Richard went to cover her.

Panea spoke to him within his mind.

'Watch her closely this night, Richard. The child is much troubled; and for one purported to be mortal, she possesses extraordinary powers. She revealed little by way of her past, and even her immediate thoughts are sporadic and difficult to decipher. Following tomorrow's festival, we will have the newcomer open her eyes to the splendour of our new world. Let her have a good night's sleep, and have the crystals work their magic. I will take my leave now. Thank you, Richard. Let tomorrow be a new day of wonder.'

He shook Richard's hand warmly and departed, and Richard would know the guardian angel would have used his special powers to take him to where he needed to be.

Richard was carefully digesting the conversation between the guardian and the stranger as he lowered himself to the edge of his cot. His gaze was transfixed on the recumbent form, a beautiful young woman with a shaven head, whose mind continued to remain

100

troubled, even after all this time. He saw the way her eyes moved behind closed lids and wondered as to the content of her dream. Fingers scrabbled at the folds of the fur coverlet, pulling it tight to her frame one moment, and pushing it lower the next.

He turned away, as the way she sinuously moved her hips made him uncomfortable. Yet he couldn't help himself, as her movements were suggestive and reawakened feelings he'd not felt for many years. It had him wondering why he should be experiencing a mix of emotions, and as to whether it was considered wrong.

He raised himself and began to pace, going to the crystal glowing on a wooden stand, in the hope he could find the answer. He was thinking about the argument she'd posed to the guardian, as to whether evil had been completely eradicated, and if not, could a person's soul still be afflicted. All of faith was in the belief, the energy of the universe could control this and eradicate those instincts once prevalent and a reason for hate, warfare, and bloodshed.

He had to wonder her reasons for doubting, even as he'd come to accept the world was evolving and all was harmonious and perfectly balanced. With nothing to fear.

She'd once possessed a crystal, as all did, and couldn't understand why it had not filled her with hope as it had with everyone he'd met.

He turned away from the geode, his frame diffusing the lambent glow it gave, and casting the form writhing seductively on the fur covered cot in shadow.

Her behaviour disturbed him, as did the train of his thoughts.

He had a few spirit cubes remaining, a gift from one of the Russian scientists inhabiting one of the international outposts on the ice and decided to make himself a green tea. It was while he stood mesmerised at sight of the bubbles boiling to the surface of the water in a small pan, he became alert to movement creating distorted shadows on the smooth ice walls.

He felt the subtle heat on his face as he immersed one of the pyramidal tea bags into the water and looped the thin twine around the handle. He supposed the tea had expired it's 'best before' date; not that it deterred him, as the leaves still retained their subtle flavour and evoked wonderful memories to mind.

He fervently hoped, once she'd rested, Katerina would benefit as all have and willingly become a part of the community and settle.

It would be nice to have a companion, he was thinking.

As if his mind had been read, and dreams were to come true, he gave a gasp of surprise and froze as arms snaked around his waist and held firm. Uncertainty incapacitated him as he was unsure how to react, especially as hands moved beneath his sweater top and lightly caressed him. Finger tips teased his nipples and it had him holding a breath.

'Smells delicious,' Katerina telegraphed to his mind.

'I thought you were sleeping,' he answered her, and gave a whine of capitulation as a hand slipped lower and pushed down front of his trousers.

'Why are you doing this?' he asked, aware his thoughts were in disarray.

He gave an audible grunt, as dormant memories and residual urges of desire were reawakened.

Katerina gave a little chortle and stepped away.

'Where do you people shit and piss?' she asked crudely.

Richard turned to face her, feeling colour creeping into his cheeks.

'I prefer the term; defecate, not shit,' he said, averting his gaze. 'Come with me, I will show you.'

It was night outside, yet the moon reflecting off the snow and ice was an ethereal shroud of luminosity.

'As you can see, there is no need for light, as the moon is our ally in the darkness,' he said, and led the way a short distance in an easterly direction away from his domicile.

Katerina followed, her gaze flitting off to the side where other homes in the distance were lit up by moonlight. There were no signs of life, so supposed all the residents within the small community were tucked up in their beds. She wondered what they did for entertainment within their icehouses. What was there to do? There was no television or a means to play recorded music. She imagined reading and writing matter was scarce. There may exist board games, but doubted they made it this far.

Katerina came to the conclusion the residents toiled at making clothes when not fishing or hunting or sat around actually conversing. Or fucking.

'It's like a fucking ghost town,' Katerina sniped and had Richard hesitating.

'Why do you say that?'

'I mean; is this it? Is this your new life in a supposed new world? Toil by day and sleep all night? And it makes you content?'

'Most nights, the residents gather around camp fires; sing, dance, laugh, tell stories and forge dreams together. It is relatively quiet this night, as everyone is preparing for tomorrow's festival of thanksgiving to celebrate a birth. You will come to understand the meaning of unquestionable joy, to be a part of this. You will feel such love and be empowered by gratitude; I swear. Tomorrow, you will think differently.'

LEGACY OF ANGELS

Richard pointed to a hole in the ice, where a shaft bore down for a mile and more, to where the sea flowed beneath the plateau they were on.

'You may be thinking our ways are primitive,' he stated, 'And I suppose they are, if one compares our new life to the one we once took for granted. All of us who survived world's end, have been granted an opportunity to start afresh. Material wealth comes from within our hearts. It is for us to make do, as we again evolve. It is hoped, mankind will have learned a valuable lesson from this.'

Katerina merely shrugged and sneered.

'So, I get to shit in a hole. Always, I'm shitting in a hole when I haven't got my arse hanging over the side of a boat.'

'Defecate,' he admonished her lightly.

'You defecate; I'll shit, if you don't mind.'

He turned sharply away as she tugged down her jeans and went to squat over the hole. She stopped herself as her gaze peered into the abyss, which was like a dark mouth. Her senses became heightened so that she was able to see deeper than she believed was possible. She saw the ocean beneath the ice; shoals of small fish, and something else. The creature she witnessed bobbed and weaved with hypnotic deadly grace, and it was a sight which was familiar.

Jellyfish.

She gave a surreptitious smile, feeling neither intimidated or fearful, as she proceeded to do her toilet.

'We use the snow to ablute ourselves,' he said in a curt tone, as his attention was drawn to a recent anomaly he was perhaps the first to witness. 'Naturally, we do not have the luxury of soft toilet tissue. Paper is scarce, as you can imagine. Any books to have survived are to be preserved, not abused or destroyed. As I have said, we make do.'

He stepped away from his position, boots crunching noisily in the deep snow, to better inspect the fissure he'd noticed. Seeing a significant crack in the ice made him uneasy and he followed its progress for several metres. It wasn't very wide, but it appeared to stretch to infinity. There was no way to determine how deep the fracture went.

What unsettled him, was knowing the ice plateau may have become unstable. He would have to alert the guardian.

His train of thought was compromised as once again the stranger crept up behind him, making no sound in the snow, her arms going around him and hugging his waist.

'This fissure is recent,' he said, 'otherwise someone would have sounded the alarm. No way of telling if it's life-threatening, or not. Once I have telegraphed a message to the guardian, he will know.'

'Ice is bound to crack,' Katerina answered. 'The ocean flows beneath us, the currents creating pressure on the ice floe. It's perfectly natural, and I imagine we're quite safe. Remember, this is utopia. The energy of the universe controls everything.'

'You're right. Yet it should be reported, just in case the area has become unstable.'

He gave an effeminate whinny as fingers pushed down inside his trousers, enclosed and stroked him.

'I want to fuck,' she whispered close to his ear. 'When was the last time you got to fuck?'

'I prefer to say; make love, not fuck. Fuck, makes the sex act sound vulgar.'

'Whatever you say. Thing is I have gone without a fuck for a long time.'

'But why me?'

'Because, you have proven yourself to be truthful, kind and generous; and gentle, which is a rare commodity in any man. I should know, as I have never known the compassion you have shown to me.'

'Never?'

'That's right. I've had a hard life, and I mean for it to change.'

He cried out the moment she gripped him more firmly and worried the sound he made might carry.

Katerina released him, chuckling coquettishly, as she took one of his hands and led him back to the cosy icehouse. It was her aim to take his mind off the fissure. There were others, all around; and she had no idea how she knew this or why this event was occurring now.

Whether it was a premonition, or something else entirely, she felt certain there was more to come.

Richard was nervous and skittish as she undressed him and removed her own clothes. She cooed soothing words into his mind to placate him, marvelling at how easy it was to use her telepathic powers. She had him lay down on his cot and straddled him, seeing that he was completely caught under the spell she'd woven.

He moaned and whimpered and beseeched a higher power for mercy on his soul. Katerina was of the opinion religion had no place in the scheme of things, especially in the new order governed by the universe, and supposed some ingrained ideology was difficult to dismiss altogether.

She rode him slowly to begin with and only quickened her rhythm when she felt a glorious tide of elation and desire melt within her loins. Her flesh began to palpate and she became delirious to feel something squirming and flowing just beneath the surface of her skin.

Katerina opened her eyes and caught Richard's horrified expression, as he was witness to her body continuing to ripple and undulate in the lambent light, that which had faded significantly, as if the sex act was expending the crystal's source of energy.

He grabbed her arms and was repulsed, threw himself back. He wanted her to stop assaulting his body, yet something formidable and inexplicable kept him pinned to the cot. He went limp suddenly, his mind unable to comprehend all he was to become witness to.

Katerina's flesh appeared to erupt, circular lesions leaking blood and pus all over her torso and legs. Sinuous, gelatinous tentacles emerged from each wound, whipping and flailing the air around them. He went to scream, and this was cut off as the barbed tendrils stabbed and penetrated his frame. His stomach and chest was punctured, as were his thighs. Another slammed into his open mouth and forged a path down his throat.

Katerina's face developed a rent from her crown down past her chin, the flesh separating and peeling away to the side, transforming her features into the fluctuating hood of a jellyfish. She leaned low and the wide dome enclosed Richard's demented grimace, the tentacles cocooning him so that the mutant creature could feed on his liquidised organs, tissue and bone.

When she'd finished gorging, and was again of human form, Katerina staggered away from the dark stain gleaming on the fur coverlet and crawled out into the cold invigorating night air. She inspected her body and saw an array of pale contusions. Fingers traced her features and was satisfied the rent had fused and healed, even though a faint raised line of puckered tissue remained as a reminder.

Naked, and feeling her strength returning, Katerina trudged through the snow away from the icehouse. She was in a stupor and not believing all she was seeing. Giant jellyfish were emerging out of the scattered bore holes in the ice and were able to incongruously walk on their spindly tentacles in the direction of the other dwellings.

They found ways in; open doorways and vents, attacking the unsuspecting residents shut away in their domiciles, that which had been perceived as their haven.

Katerina smiled as the creatures ignored her to get at their prey. She was kindred now; she was a part of the insidious influence to have been unleashed.

Evil will find a way.

It always does.

And Katerina had become evil.

CHAPTER 10

LOST LEGACY...

>**The joy of many**
>
>**Is, but a mask,**
>
>**As an insidious darkness**
>
>**Still seeps in the veins,**
>
>**Of those who are lost,**
>
>**And wish,**
>
>**To remain so...**

The China Provinces were developing at a speed and progress Chan Li had not anticipated. Everywhere he was to visit in the interim of his journey, he was witness to the fortunate survivors of the great war of angels and there remained vast numbers, using the materials and resources lying in great piles of rubble to rebuild sectarian homes.

Many of the shops, bars and restaurants to have survived devastation had been transformed into domiciles. Many homes had been rebuilt, were of minimal structure, yet served a purpose.

Chinese philosophy continued.

In every direction one travelled there was at least one pyramid visible on the skyline. Improvements to lifestyle, health and well-being were predominantly promoted by the distribution of crystals having received the energy of the universe stored in the pyramids throughout time.

It was what he perceived as lying beneath the façade he was shown which concerned Chan. On his travels, he was to meet with other guardian Earth Angels, and most spoke of surreptitious activity occurring sporadically in remote areas.

It was Chan's duty to confront the problem, to understand and report his findings. Where possible, to terminate acts of dissidence so that the Universal plan decreed to the planet could continue unchallenged.

Chan saw the task set for him as a monumental undertaking, as reports were being relayed from other areas across the globe, those to keep him separated from the Spiritual Lodge Estate which had become his home. He suspected; certain isolated incidents could have been engineered to keep him from Abigail's side. He hoped he was wrong, but intuition had him thinking he was being played.

After more than two years, Chan was thankful, his beloved country of inception had progressed beyond his expectations. Much of the country had escaped the destructive and deadly forces of tsunamis, created by the Earth tilting.

As with the entire planet, the geographical landscape had dramatically changed with devastating earthquakes razing cities and towns to the ground.

Chan could only imagine the terror and grief each of the survivors had suffered at that time. Yet, wherever he journeyed, he saw hope on the faces of the thousands to have risen from despair. He was a witness to joy, gratitude; and most were idealistically content with their new way of life.

On the fringes of the utopian society, among the sparse villages where inhabitants were less educated, Chan was aware of negative attitudes which evidently stole the natural joy which existed in the majority of people.

There seemed to be a code of silence, but Chan used his powers to reach into the minds of the few who remained confused and saddened and were unable to rise from the gloom as others had.

His findings were disturbing, and the source required careful and cautious investigation. It was while travelling around the outlying regions and assessing the cause of people's mistrust and fear, Chan became aware also his movements were being monitored. He had no visual proof, relying on his intuitive ability to sense a disruptive influence truly existed.

It had him wondering if darker elements had emerged, as it had always been his belief the seeds of true evil would never be completely eradicated. Dark energy had been defeated and repelled following the war of angels, and it was always suspected, it would return to seek vengeance. All believed it would happen millions of years in the future.

Chan stored huge faith in the power of the universe, that which was generated by two conflicting sources of energy and gave life on Earth. It could subsequently remove all forms of life at whim, as he had witnessed throughout time.

Chan argued; that where a core of evil once existed, and every city the world over had criminal and evil influences as part of their culture, it was conceivable some would not embrace the positive light all could glean from the crystals and the pyramids. The

111

Universal Design was specific, in flooding the planet with a positive atmosphere, while negating any influence Dark Energy once had. It would be a monumental achievement to maintain if it were conceivable.

Chan Li was of the opinion, evil would continue to exist on the periphery, finding new ways to chip away at the very fabric of goodness until it found a chink in that armour, where it could once again insinuate its presence as a disruptive force.

He'd been instructed to visit a region of the North Western provinces, and in particular Changchun which was now a shadow of its former majesty. It was there he was to meet with one of the Earth Angels presiding over events in the region. He introduced himself as Kao.

Kao was a survivor of the recent war of angels, and throughout his many lifetimes, had fought numerous bloody battles in the name of justice against adversity.

Chan was able to pick away at his thoughts even though conversation to begin with was conservatively used to expound on the progress being made in the region. Kao was reluctant to speak of the underlying currents of unease settling in a few of the communities on the borders.

They conducted their initial meeting on the newly developed shores of the Yellow Sea, that which had been extended several hundred miles inland because of the tsunamis, and where the Earth's tilt had prevented the flood waters retreating.

As if able to read Chan's mind Kao gave an explanation to the geographical change, informing Chan most of Korea had been engulfed as with the mythical Atlantis where entire civilisations were swallowed up by the oceans.

LEGACY OF ANGELS

Chan Li felt a great sadness, in that it had come to this. There was a time when he believed it could have been prevented. Throughout history, the planet had suffered change, and at great cost.

As at this present time, mankind and nature to have survived the debacle had to rebuild. It was different, in that the combined forces of the Universe and its emissaries, could establish growth in a matter of decades, not centuries or millennia, as before.

The problem, as Chan saw it, was if evil remained a presence, it was conceivable the Overlord of the Universe he knew as Genesis would know his perfect dream was being challenged.

Kao led Chan to a simple dwelling fashioned from bamboo. It was Kao's home when he was not called to assist the people of surrounding communities, and simply furnished, having a crude cot, a mat and a table for an array of crystals and incense.

The host served up fresh water flavoured with lychee and gave an account of his time in the provinces. He went on to explain the stories he'd been told, even though he'd not witnessed events described to him.

Kao believed there existed small groups still living the old ways, preferring a shadowy existence rather than walking in the light as with the majority. Kao failed to understand how it could be so, with the atmosphere positively charged and changing everyone's perception. He hoped, someone of Chan's stature, would uncover the answers and eliminate the seeds of fear which had been sown and free to sprout.

Kao gave a personal account, which would have Chan Li pondering in the future. He'd said, *'We were the victors of a great battle, but was it for nothing? Evil cannot be defeated in its entirety. The concept of such does not exist. Evil, as with goodness and light are inextricably linked, as with the Ying and Yang; opposites to make a whole. It is a matter of time only as, even though I have not witnessed its emerging presence, I can feel its detestable and ugly*

113

caress wherever I travel. I have tried, without success, to infiltrate the source, but always it remains on the periphery; unchallenged, provocative, waiting for the moment to reveal itself.'

Chan Li was eager to get to the bottom of the situation causing concern, as all the while he was seeking the answers to growing dissent, the problems were keeping him away from his new home and of those he loved and swore to protect. He requested Lao travel with him to the great pyramid North of Beijing, or what remained of the once bustling city. He was aware a wide area was under water and had been desolated by violent quakes and unrelenting fires, its tallest structures toppling as a house of cards as strong winds fanned the spread of flames. The impact was horrific, yet resilience and fortitude was evident in those who had survived. The inscrutable ideology and single-mindedness of the native Chinese people had them rise from the ashes of despair and were doggedly rebuilding a new China.

Following his short interlude, Chan Li and Kao teleported to an area close to the base of the great pyramid dominating the skyline to the North. The energy emanating off its smooth sloping walls could be felt. Others were scattered across the provinces, generating power and hope to the people.

Chan surveyed the area all around with the remains of the once great city at his back. As far as the naked eye could see stretched flat plains of paddy fields, with separate cultivated areas for the growing of bamboo and water chestnuts. It was natural, with so much of the landscape under water, edible marine life was plentiful. There was no shortage of food, at least.

Kao informed Chan he'd received reports of an 'illegal' trade, that which was organised by small bands of individuals, who bartered wares not for currency, which was meaningless in the present society. They exchanged food and clothing for crystals and were not adverse to using threats to get what they wanted. These spurious gangs of dissidents controlled numerous plantations and it

114

is said, should anyone not trade with them, they would terrorise families into submission, specifically the daughters who were seen as ripe for breeding.

Chan Li was appalled this could be happening, when he'd believed the Universal Overlord had everything under control. It appears, not all was going to the Grand Design set out to encourage a utopian environment. Harmony existed, yet there were escalating inconsistencies. The proof lie with small groups who shunned a harmonious world, and preferred the old ways; that of discord, and spreading the darkness in the souls of man to encourage the growth of evil once again.

Chan Li needed to understand why these renegades resisted the flow of positive energy, and why it was necessary for them to trade for those crystals which were mankind's source of hope and spiritual healing.

He didn't think the pyramid had been compromised, considering the flow of energy emanating from its heart. Chan Li approached the black behemoth, that which was created from blocks of obsidian, and it reminded him of a time long ago, as energy swept over and through him to exacerbate those memories.

He was remembering a great battle to have been fought not too far from their location, at a time when the Great Wall of China had withstood an otherworldly army of beasts during the reign of Qin Shi Huang.

It had been an occasion when destiny would have him cross paths and connect with the amazing and beautiful First Angel, Abigail. It was a period in the calendar, despite events having been recorded differently by historians of the time, where light had prevailed over darkness. As with so many wars, thousands died needlessly, and it was a war like no other. The First Angel had encouraged Chan to reach deep within his soul, to the angel residing there. It was the first occasion he was able to flex his wings, out of necessity, as terror was to descend from the skies. Had it not been for his own ancient heritage and that of the First Angel, the battle would have been lost on that day, the future re-written.

Victory was salvaged from bloody chaos as the enemy of darkness sought a great secret, a powerful source of energy and of hope, that which had to remain hidden away until the present day. Following the battle, the emperor had the giant crystal entombed beneath a monument he had erected, except the monument was an area of deep trenches, that which immortalised the fallen warriors and of those who survived. Thousands of artisan stone masons created what was known as the terracotta army, as a landmark tribute and to continue in the afterlife as guardians of the crystal.

That source of energy resided now within the great pyramid, serving the purpose it was always meant to.

Chan approached, himself in awe of the giant monolith rising to a point where the sun seemed to sit atop the apex. He lay a hand flat to one of the walls and felt the slide of energy moving beneath his skin.

Stepping back, Chan Li instructed Kao to take him to where he believed the heart of dissident operations existed, so that he could meet with these people and dissuade them from embracing the darkness.

Kao bowed, even as his expression relayed a reluctance to pursue the course Chan Li wished to take.

'The people you seek, hide themselves away underground,' he explained. 'Others and I have tried to approach them and have been repelled. Powerful fields of energy protect them. I felt, personally, it was prudent not to engage them in the physical sense, merely to observe and relay the stories to have been passed on to the Universe. As I'm sure, others will have done, should the problem of discourse not be an isolated incident confined to the China provinces. If, it is the same the world over, then we are facing once again, the rise of evil.'

'It is a reason I have answered the call from the Universe. I wish to meet with these people who have strayed from the path of light and goodness and put an end to it.'

At the forefront of his mind, he wanted to know why emissaries of dark energy were amassing hordes of crystals which are harmful to them. Unless and it was a worrying thought, should these people be seeking a means of acquiring immunity against the powerful energy stored within the crystals.

Not all in the world was flowing smoothly as it was hoped.

Chan sensed also, if the problem existed throughout the world, it needed to be addressed swiftly; the canker removed permanently.

CHAPTER 11

SCENT OF EVIL...

> **Drink the poison,**
>
> **Flowing in the veins of evil,**
>
> **And walk the path**
>
> **Of darkness and discontent...**

Chan and Kao teleported to Guiyang, close to the Vietnamese border and situated on the fringes of Tibet and a landscape of mountains.

From their position they were afforded a panoramic view of paddy fields, where sunlight dappled along the shallow troughs of water. Another area, separate from the rice fields, was a plantation for cultivating bamboo. No one was working in the vicinity, which surprised Chan, as much of the produce on display was ripe for harvesting.

Glancing to the west he observed a low-level range of mountains, those which bordered Tibet, and he noticed several apertures or cave entrances in the rock. Some were relatively small and were probably used for storage purposes. The larger caves, he suspected, were the habitat of the people he was seeking.

Kao gave an audible gasp as Chan himself, was alerted to the sudden strains of music in the air around them, that which was discordant and harmonious at the same time. The blend of rock and opera was distinctly European in taste, and not indigenous to Chinese culture.

Chan was intrigued, as it had been quite some time since he had heard music being played, and wondered how it was possible, without electricity or batteries to power a transmitting device.

The source came from beyond where a smattering of reeds and trees became a gateway to dense jungle.

Chan projected a scan and came up against a powerful barrier. Suddenly alert, his gaze swept side to side, the emptiness and tranquillity, ominous and eerily haunting. He probed beyond the cavernous maws which resembled hungry mouths dotted around the base of the mountains, expecting to see others observing them. Other than the musical beats and angelic strains of a female singer, there was no one around. No birds or animals, almost insinuating they were in a forbidden zone.

'I have to be leaving,' said Kao, a tremor in his voice, wariness within the dark pupils of his eyes. 'I am called elsewhere.'

Chan would have known if there was truth to the frightened man's words, not that he understood why the guardian was fearful of this place. Chan perceived no threat, as he'd anticipated there might be before arriving.

'Go,' said Chan, 'I would not have you at my side, or at my back, if there is no valour in your soul.'

'I am sorry,' said Kao, bowing to conceal his shame. 'This is not a place touched by the light, as I'm aware you know. It would be wise if you were to leave here. You are one against many.'

'I mean to stay, until I have those answers I seek; with, or without your assistance.

With that, Kao was gone.

Unperturbed, Chan was once again drawn to the guttural growl of guitars, a frenetic drum beat, and symphonic keyboard. The female lead singer was chanting an aria, so sweet as to be angelic.

Chan determined the source was coming from a depression where the paddy fields met with a raised bank of earth.

Remaining alert to a surprise confrontation while erecting a protective barrier around his aura, Chan levitated and skimmed along one of the water channels towards the source of the music.

Around the deep depression and surrounded by tropical ferns, he came across a man draped in a grey robe cinched with cord at the waist. He had in his hand a portable CD player, the other hand resting along its aperture. He was of indeterminate age, having a long smoky-grey beard he was stroking in meditative contemplation. His eyes were of a vivid sapphire, his hair – more dark than grey – floating in scraggly waves past his shoulders.

Chan sensed a formidable power within the stranger, something the man kept restrained.

Without appearing to acknowledge Chan's sudden appearance, indicating he'd been aware all along, the man spoke. His tone was friendly, on the surface.

'What do you make of this little miracle? To think; it is possible in these dark times, to resurrect recorded music from a bygone area with little effort. I happen to like this, a lot. That pounding heavy rock beat, the constant changes in tempo, and then; the sweetest voice, like that of an angel. What we have here is a live recording going back more than ten years. Listen to the crowd, singing enmasse, unaware of the change to come. You should listen closely to the lyrics, for she sings of love, lost love, of grief and of hope. Fitting, as the majority of those who survived the war, loved at some point, only to lose it.'

The stranger became quiet, maudlin, and as he removed his hand from the device he was holding, the music and singing abruptly ceased.

'You have come here specifically, to fulfil a purpose, and a thankless one I should add,' the stranger quietly continued, as he stared into the gloom of the jungle. 'That which keeps you from someone who has grown dear to your heart.

Chan interposed, as he sought to protect his private thoughts from the stranger's powerfully invasive tactics and scrutiny. 'May I ask; who you are, and why is it you labour at this location?'

'To meet with you, naturally; mighty Chan Li,' the man answered, adding an inflection of humour as he favoured Chan a wry smile. 'That surprises you, I can tell. As for who I am; perhaps you should ask the one you consort with from time to time. She has the answer.'

'You are, Nemo?'

'Ah, very good, and very astute of you.'

'Other than wishing to speak of musical influences from the past, you wanted to meet with me in person; and it intrigues me. One as to how you would know. And secondly, are you the one to have instigated I come on this journey?'

'You ask several questions, and I detect a measure of doubt in regards to the forces you supposedly trust. As for why I wanted to meet with you in person, so to speak, I wanted to ask you; how is the subject of our mutual interest? Abigail? See, I'm intrigued also, as to why someone of her pedigree and higher standing, would risk all consorting with someone who – shall we say – is just not on the same

LEGACY OF ANGELS

level. I know Abigail, probably better than you do, as First Angel and daughter to one part universe. I imagine, her fall from grace by demeaning herself with someone as lowly as you, has caused more than a few ripples of dissent.'

'I have nothing to say on the subject of Abigail,' said Chan, bridling at the man's goading. 'I was asked to come here as it is common knowledge groups of people have been trading illegally and are not averse to using threats.'

'There has always been trade, illegal or not,' said Nemo, whose disarming smile revealed rows of gleaming teeth in the gloom.

'Not in the new world,' countered Chan. 'It's my considered opinion, you perhaps, are influential in the spread of discord. Naturally, you wish for evil to grow in stature, as it once was. The power of light is too strong.'

'Is it? What do you know, pray tell me? I would hazard a guess, you along with others of your kind, are woefully ignorant of events taking place at this time in your precious new world. Sweet Abigail, she knows; as daughter to the universe, it would make sense she has been made aware things are not what they seem or were hoped for. Regardless of the fact, you desire not to speak about the one entity who inspires me and is the subject of my interest, I would ask, after her welfare. Does she speak of me? I know that I am constantly in her thoughts, as she is in mine. There will come a time, and soon it is hoped, when our paths will cross. I look forward to meeting with your First Angel, as admittedly, the idea excites me. Abigail is perhaps the only one who can challenge me as I rise to claim the throne I am destined for.'

'You propose to threaten all that has been achieved, and all that is meant to be? Your arrogance will be your downfall, as it was with your father and all the other minions who believed they were the greater power.'

Nemo raised his head to the sky and chuckled, and it was a chilling sound, which served to antagonise his adversary.

'Alas, mighty Chan, a confrontation with your First Angel and fuckbuddy, is unavoidable. As it is being written. All you can think about, is getting your dick wet and playing happy families with the children. They, you clueless love-struck fool, are your Achilles Heel. Take it from someone who knows; abandon them, while you can, and save yourself. Would it surprise you if I was to say, I have observed you along the passage of time? You have more than proved your courage and loyalty to the cause you were set. But is it enough? Personally, I don't think it is.'

Chan refused to rise to the bait, knowing the one called Nemo was testing him. Instead, he reverted to the tactics he began with.

'Why are the rebels trading food for crystals?' he asked. 'Is it not inviting the enemy into their camp?'

'Why should I demean myself by giving an answer to that which is obvious. Perhaps, and it's just a thought; their purpose is to remove hope from those who are seeking it.'

'And you are the perpetrator of these recent acts of terror against innocent folk?' Chan queried.

'You think, acquiring a few pretty stones is my game? Let me assure you, Chan Li, when it is time for me to rise and claim what is rightfully mine, I will do so and in a way which will be felt in every person, mortal and celestial. You will know, when that moment has arrived.'

'We were prepared before; and of necessity, we will be ready again.'

'Life,' interposed Nemo, 'Is merely a game of chess. An ancient game of strategy, where pieces are carefully manoeuvred into a commanding position, until such time as one of the opposing forces is set to strike.'

Nemo raised himself up and enjoyed seeing his adversary become wary of him, taking consideration of the defensive stance Chan had employed, even sensing his foe's latent power waiting to be unleashed should it be necessary.

'Relax, my good man,' Nemo jeered contemptuously. 'Now is not the moment to rattle sabres. A time will invariably arrive, when I can look forward to bringing you to your knees, so that you may know humility. I only wanted to meet with you on this occasion, for you to deliver a message to the First Angel. Let her know; she has an admirer, who seeks an audience with her.'

'And what if I was to intervene, and keep you from meeting with Abigail; make the problem go away?'

'You are welcome to try. As I mentioned before; Abigail and the children will be your downfall. As much as I have enjoyed talking with you, I must leave now, as I have more pressing engagements to attend. One other thing though, for you to consider, Chan Li. The First Angel's father, ruler of his universal empire at this present moment, is probably toying with you, and perhaps instigating your dismissal. You have probably considered this yourself, but why do you suppose you are getting to see less and less of that sweet little pussy you crave? Hard to say; but who can you trust in these difficult uncertain times? Once again, it's been a pleasure, Chan Li.'

Nemo took two long strides to close the gap and passed Chan the CD player he'd been grasping.

'Consider this a gift,' Nemo growled, as he stepped away once again to afford some distance between them. With a wink and a smile, his form evaporated, and he appeared to achieve this without any effort or having to compose his equilibrium before teleporting.

Chan could only glower at the dull silvered object he'd been handed, as if the thought of something he was holding had once been in Nemo's possession, disgusted and appalled him. He almost disposed of it in anger, instead, secreted it away inside a pocket of his tunic.

CHAPTER 12

CHANGELING…

> **Sleep with angels,**
>
> **Walk the dark path to oblivion.**
>
> **Stray from the light,**
>
> **Into the shadow.**
>
> **Become lost and alone,**
>
> **For eternity…**

Chan levitated and approached one of the larger cave entrances. At the periphery of the dark yawning mouth, he projected a scan into the throat of the wide tunnel. He went so far before surprisingly coming up against a wall of resistance.

Undeterred, he was drawn towards it, as his mission dictated. He'd been sent to accumulate information, acquire answers, and determine the extent of dark energy's influence in the region.

He had the unexpected confrontation with Nemo playing on his mind, and they were thoughts to unsettle him as Nemo had clarified his intent, to continue a quest and induce a meeting with Abigail.

Once his work was completed in the provinces, Chan would return to his new home in the United Kingdom, speak with Abigail and ensure maximum defences were employed around the children. It was Chan's belief all three were targets of the re-emerging force of dark energy, and he saw it as his divine purpose and destiny, to continue as guardian and protect them.

Assuming he was not too late, and Chan's quest was a ruse to keep him from the estate and his charges.

Wanting to get the matter over with swiftly, Chan entered the cave, while erecting a strong barrier of protection around himself.

There was an eerie tranquillity around the cave complex, his keen senses detecting small rhythmic sonar echoes in the walls and ceiling. It came as no surprise to find its source several hundred metres beyond the entrance yet marvelled at sight of a wide pool which ambled laboriously from one hollow beneath the right wall and flowed into another opposite. He wondered if the water swept down from the mountains and sought a natural passage to the sea, or a river nearby.

Chan stepped close to the edge and peered down, his aura cutting a deep swath, without reaching the bottom of the channel.

If the community of dissident rebels used the caves for cover and made it their home, it had Chan wondering how someone could achieve the feat of crossing the wide stretch of water. It was conceivable they could swim. There were no small boats to be seen. As he looked side to side, he was given a plausible explanation, having witnessed a narrow ledge and a series of small hollows which could assist someone to scale the wall and get across.

Chan chose levitation to cross the channel, the moment he sensed a faint pull on his thoughts urging him on. Instinct had him hesitating at a midway point, as he sent a scan down into the deep waters beneath him. He saw a fluctuating shadow in the murk, which could have been a large boulder or something animate. It was illusory, as there came a ripple of movement and several small air bubbles found their way to the surface, all of which remained on the periphery of his luminescent aura.

Chan continued levitating across the expanse until he was settled on the opposite side, and it was then he concentrated amassing his energy as a flaming sword which served as an extension of his right arm.

The gloom ahead seemed to balk and shift, and he imagined there was someone observing him from afar. He maintained a defensive stance, should a threat appear from ahead or behind. He even expanded his mind to encompass the ceiling and walls. He felt something pressing around him, even as he was unable to determine a source or its intent.

Chan tensed the moment he saw a greyish figure hovering on the periphery of his aura ahead of his position. Unperturbed by his presence the figure took a step forward and became illuminated, a dark canvas at the person's back. The person was dressed as Chan was, in a black tunic with a sash cinched at the waist and with a hood and lower veil to obscure the person's features. Only the eyes showed, and they failed to gleam in the light.

The person spoke, the voice deep and husky enough to establish the male sex.

'You are either, quite foolish or very courageous to venture here without an army at your back,' the man's voice echoed within the confines of the cave. 'Which is it, I wonder? Are you a fool?'

Chan refused to respond to the taunt initially as he felt a sinuous energy trickling around the barrier of protection he'd erected.

'It seems, you have come prepared for a fight,' the stranger continued in mocking tones, 'And there was I thinking hostility between men, even angels of the universe, was dispensed with in our coveted new world.'

'Who are you?' asked Chan curtly. 'And supposing you are head of a band of rebels who, it has been said, are terrorising village and town-folk, I ask that you give me your reasons. Why would you barter food for crystals, when crystals are plentiful. Or, do you perceive the crystals to be a natural currency?'

'For your information, we trade in keeping with past traditions, that which has always been our heritage. As for my name? Well, it is only a name. You can call me Yaoguai.'

'A name derivative of a Chinese demon from cultural mythology, that which purports to be a harbinger of dark energy. I sense you have great power, are perhaps an ancient; an angel who survived the great war of our kind.'

'Let us agree; for I am more than I appear, as you are. Chan Li: I know of you. All on the side of darkness and light know of the mighty Chan and his valour. All know, in recent times, he has ventured along a path he should not have.'

The way in which Yaoguai's eyes crinkled at the corners, suggested he was smiling as he delivered his taunt. Chan's attempts to inveigle himself into Yaoguai's thoughts were easily rebuffed, almost nonchalantly. It had Chan studying the man's eyes in greater depth, and instinct told him to leave.

'Have I satisfied your curiosity, Chan Li,' Yaoguai continued in a conciliatory tone. 'Whatever you believe to be happening in the provinces, I can assure you, the stories about us are taken out of context. We trade honestly, and do not consort to making threats. We are simply preserving the old ways and cultural traditions, in preparation for when they return. Not everyone in this new world desires to be controlled or manipulated, how to think and act. It is what the crystals do, along with the power source generating from the pyramids. It has removed free-thinking, conditioning the majority to act against natural impulses.'

'You cannot dismiss the fact; people of the new world have been granted hope and to live a life of harmony. They no longer despair or have a reason to be fearful and are content to work for each other. Is that so bad, and difficult to digest?'

'Only, when you have the choice taken away,' said Yaoguai, and Chan noticed the way his eyes had a habit of flitting to other areas of the cave.

Chan did not hesitate to determine the reason, teleported himself across the pool to stand at the entrance. The man, whose name epitomised the mythical Chinese demon, was literally walking across the water, where the surface erupted sporadically in large bubbles. Yaoguai paused, a short distance from Chan's position, his eyes having further darkened to pools of tar.

'Won't you stay a little while longer?' Yaoguai teased, 'Or has your courage failed you?'

'Whatever name you choose for yourself, is of no consequence. You know it is inevitable, in that we will meet again,' said Chan, and retracting the sword of energy in a display meant to show he was unafraid.

'I do not recall saying we will meet again,' said Yaoguai, his own stance relaxing. 'Unless you mean to return. Whether you are alone or with an army at your back, that is your choice. I am only a threat if you make me one.'

'If you do not seek me, then I shall return, and I will not need a guard at my back.'

'And here was I foolishly thinking, the crystals so prevalent in the world, were meant to negate hostility. Despite your outward show of bravado, I sense undercurrents of uncertainty within the context of your simple mind. What's it like; to fear the unknown, as never before? Perhaps, when we next meet you will tell me how it feels, to lose someone you truly care about? To not have love reciprocated as you hoped and dreamed of? For it is written; from the light, darkness will flourish and consume all of hope. The one who is the subject of your desire, will one day change her allegiance, and turn her back on you and others. I know this to be true, as I have seen the future. Now, does that surprise you, and make you fearful, mighty Chan Li?'

'I should point out; the future is neither certain nor constant. If you have nothing more to say, I will take my leave,' said Chan without his customary bow of respect.

'I would just like to add, that it has been a most welcome diversion meeting with you,' said Yaoguai, the first to turn away, while making a salient point doing so.

As the mysterious elemental walked back across the channel of water, luminous columns rose from the depths, those of creatures he recognised; giant jellyfish with hooded domed heads and scores of tentacles extending down and out of sight.

'Enjoy the music, my friend!' Yaoguai called back and waving nonchalantly at his receding foe.

Chan held his breath, believing he'd witnessed sinewy tentacles erupting out of the man's frame just before the darkness beyond swallowed him up. The other creatures left the sanctity of water and waddled ungainly after the man, using their tendrils as limbs to support their cumbersome bulk.

'Will you join us?' a voice spoke within Chan's mind. *'We are the future, and all will come to know us intimately.'*

There followed a cacophony of voices, varying in pitch and tone, each one deceptively seductive as it was hoped, Chan could be enticed.

'AS IT IS WRITTEN.'

Before the grip on his thoughts became an untenable one, Chan willed himself away from the location and source of evil which had breached his defences briefly.

Chan respectfully acknowledged the Dark Angel he'd confronted, was supremely powerful, and was of necessity he send his report to the universe.

In the time it took him to teleport across dimensions, Chan could only think about Abigail, knowing she was again to face the might of dark energy.

Whether Yaoguai or Nemo, dark energy had returned, and the son of evil was preparing to extend his wings.

He was biding his time and was quietly confident he would be victorious in a confrontation, where his father had failed. Chan didn't believe dark energy's First Angel bristled with arrogance as lesser ancient angels had done. He had a plan and was implementing it, and it seemed, no one was prepared.

If anyone could stop him, it was Abigail, even as unreasonable doubts gnawed at his resolve.

Chan returned to *Spiritual Lodge Estate,* having deviated course, and establish he had not been followed, and materialised outside the stable complex. He sent out a scan of the environs to ascertain whether a presence existed to cause him concern.

A few of the horses were in their stalls, the others enjoying the freedom of the fields. Chan located the position of each guardian and went to them in turn. He was informed, Abigail had been called away on a secret mission. Their purpose was to fortify defences, and to constantly alternate routines. No person was allowed entry onto the estate, no matter their reason for calling. No one was to be treated as an innocent.

These were dark times, the glow of universal light having diminished.

Chan let them know, dark energy was re-emerging once again, and could change guise; appear as an angel of light, while masking the truth. Whether animal, child, woman, or man, all should be treated the same, using caution.

Abigail and the children were the targets, Chan iterated firmly.

Chan left the field, only when he was satisfied defences in the form of a dome were satisfactory. The power thrumming from the underground pyramid beneath the circle of ancient oak continued to pulse a rhythmic pattern.

Being content, all was as it should be, Chan next called on the children. He politely knocked and Celestine, it was, granted him entrance. The children were playing in the back garden where a high wall trapped the heat of the sun and encouraged tropical blooms to flourish.

The moment he saw him at the entrance to the conservatory and patio, Luke abandoned Daniel on the grass and charged across to be swept up by Chan in a formidable embrace. Luke understood the importance of the role Chan was given, notwithstanding the intimacy he shared with his mother.

As Daniel approached, Chan asked Luke if everything was okay. Supporting Luke with one arm, Chan hoisted Daniel to his chest and kissed his temple.

'I miss mummy,' said Luke pensively, the moment he caught Daniel studying the despairing Chan Li and realised the younger boy was scanning his inscrutable friend.

'As I have missed you all,' said Chan.

Celestine stepped up to join their circle of warmth, as Daniel touched Chan's forehead with a digit and sighed.

'Sad man,' he said. 'Chan be sad.'

Celestine cut in with an explanation as to why Abigail was absent, stating the First Angel was on another of her missions. She confided also; despite Abigail not giving specifics as to where she was to go or her reasons for doing so, it was apparent the news she'd been given was causing her concern.

'Bless you both,' said Celestine with genuine warmth, 'you are each being pulled in all directions, when you should be spending quality time with the boys. There is something amiss in our wonderful new world. I'm able to feel it deeply. They are emotions I hoped never to embrace ever again. Not all in the world is as it should be or was hoped for.'

Chan was surprised when Daniel spoke next; prophetic words telegraphed to his mind. *'Dark Energy is here! It is growing, will continue to grow.'*

Chan locked gaze with eyes of a vivid blue and dropped a lingering kiss to his blond curls. He didn't have to answer, as he intuitively felt the escalating pull of evil in the world. He set Daniel down and Luke led him back to the garden play area.

To Celestine, Chan asked if she had any idea where Abigail's mission had taken her. He wanted to know if her high level of intuition had received a clue to the location Abigail had travelled to. Celestine gave a rueful shake of the head.

'You are aware, Abigail is secretive when it comes to receiving messages from the universe. She must be certain; the information has substance before she can act.'

'I sense, you are feeling something which is unsettling to you. Your words express a measure of doubt. Am I right to assume as much?'

'Dark Energy has returned, and will know its enemy, and will find ways to infiltrate the source; is the feeling I get.'

Chan turned away, frustrated, opening his mind to telegraph a beseeching plea to the First Angel. Chan bowed, and stated he was to leave again, if only for a brief time. He waved to the children and was gone, with the intention of going into the fields to be with the herd of horses. He wanted, more than anything, to establish a spiritual bond with Abigail's personal mare, Free Spirit. It was a belief; the mare might know where her mistress had travelled to and was always maintaining a psychic connection with Abigail.

Chan was aware also, the loyalty shared between horse and mistress, was a bond of loyalty which could not be broken.

It was imperative he try.

As evil was coming.

He went by the name, Nemo.

First Angel to Dark Energy.

And his time; WAS NOW.

CHAPTER 13

FACE OF EVIL...

It has come to this,

Darkness eclipsing a glorious light.

When evil chortles in the corridors of power

Where once, not so long ago,

Evil was evicted...

Abigail circumnavigated the lesser travelled spiritual highways, as it was pertinent to establish which elemental bodies crossed dimensions and their purpose for doing so.

Had she expected opposing energies to have emerged from a short period of dormancy, it was a relief to her she encountered none on her journey. There was a smattering of light energies on some of the channels, and Abigail ascertained their intentions were genuine.

Her own journey was to take her to the southernmost region, of Antarctica, having received a cryptic message from the universe of an urgent matter needing attention, not that specific details were submitted to her.

She reached her destination as daylight was on the wane, and shadows oozed down from the mountains onto the plateau basin and the small, deserted township which raised initial concerns.

She telegraphed her arrival to the guardian, Panea, who had been the architect of the distress signal sent to the universe. Without waiting for a response, Abigail swept across the huge swath of snow in the direction of the nearest dwelling, projecting a scan to ascertain any possibility of a threat. She took mental note of the meandering fissures criss-crossing the ice, believing them to be recent fractures which ultimately created a hazardous environment for the residents and their homes.

Abigail paused at the low entry point, her powers of perception receiving memory traces of recent events to have transpired in the locale.

Her form faded as she teleported beyond the walls of compacted ice blocks to the interior. Her gaze became instantly drawn to the wide cot with the congealed stain of dried blood matting the fibres of a fur coverlet, images revealing themselves in garish detail within her mind.

She was made to witness a couple having sex, where the act culminated in the face of evil revealing itself. She had seen too much in her many lifetimes to be appalled by this latest mutation created by Dark Energy. The creature spawned from within the host female form was like that which had been delivered to the underground pyramid on the estate back home.

Similarly, having witnessed its initial emergence, having travelled to the future with Chan. One of the creatures had followed them back, using their energy trail as a beacon.

LEGACY OF ANGELS

This was something else entirely; a marine creature with the propensity to exist out of water and was able to absorb itself into the human body.

Having witnessed enough to concern her, Abigail teleported outside, wondering if evil had discovered a means to infect even the earth angels and by doing so, find ways around their bodily and spiritual defences. Should it be possible, Abigail was convinced there would come another war, supposing the army of light had not been sufficiently depleted by this insidious infection.

Already, in her mind, Abigail was contemplating reaching out to the source of evil and initialising a personal confrontation, in the hope she alone could defeat the source before it spread.

Abigail continued and approached the other domiciles and was to witness a similar pattern of events in each. No physical evidence of the victims remained, only blood-stained silhouettes on walls, cots and floor space. The monstrous incarnations had absorbed them, liquidising flesh, organs and bone as sustenance to a ravenous appetite. It appeared, none of the victims were deemed worthy of becoming human generators of their evil intent.

From the small township, Abigail continued next to the nearest outpost, a clutter of prefabricated buildings all flying the French flag. Even as she approached, a scan detected no signs of life within. It was the same at the other localised villages nearby and the other military and scientific outposts.

The inhabitants were gone, slaughtered; by creatures who attacked with stealth, made no sound, and easily overwhelmed their victims before they could react. As no one was prepared for the face of evil to come visiting in a supposedly utopian world.

Abigail again attempted to establish a link with the guardian Panea and received a flutter of vibrations which were ominously faint. She was drawn to them, anyway. She needed to acquire answers, beyond all she had witnessed in her mind's eye, if indeed answers could be gleaned.

She had to find the infected young woman.

Abigail sensed the woman had not fled the barren wilderness. She was also of the belief this young woman was chosen specifically to become host to this new evil. Why the remote region of Antarctica had been chosen to express its intent, Abigail was still to determine.

The girl was the source; and invariably had the answers.

Abigail followed the elemental trace to a line of snow-drenched mountains looming off to the west of her position. She had noticed an opening a hundred metres or so above the plateau, and it was there she was to go. As she appeared at the entrance, so the signal she was receiving gained strength and substance.

She discovered Panea deep within the confines of the narrow cave aperture, clawing at one wall which shimmered in ice beneath the faint glow of his aura. He initially kept his back to the new arrival, as Abigail's own brilliant aura illuminated a wider area around them.

Panea felt her power along his spine where it crept unchallenged into his mind, and it almost had him recoil into a tight ball.

He shuffled round then, looking small and insignificant where he crouched and hugged his knees. A hand automatically came up to cover his empty gnarled eye-sockets, as if he were able to still see the vision confronting him. His mouth began to open and close, the machinations of which encouraged guttural groans and clicks, for his tongue was no more.

'Help me!' he telegraphed with his mind.

Abigail refrained at that time submitting a response, as she was carefully and diligently untangling the confused pattern of

139

thoughts she encountered. She was seeking the path to memories leading up to the present moment.

'You are an ancient,' Panea continued, scrabbling around the base of the wall on hands and knees as if the Angel's potent energy were scalding him. *'More powerful than I, I would think. Can you help me? My sight has been taken from me; the third eye cloaked in mist.'*

Abigail observed the pathetic creature bobbing up and down and wondering why his flouncy shirt and trousers were pockmarked with holes, their frayed edges fused as black-tarred rings.

She remained alert to aggression without the need of summoning a weapon of protection, believing she had the situation under control. She felt subtle waves of dark energy emanating off the walls and ceiling, and where it seeped out of the ground.

A collage of images assailed her mind, and she became aggrieved by their content.

There are those who wear a shadow on their heart and wish to dispense with the harmonious optimism in others. It is their aim, to make others sad, as they are. To bring them to their knees; and not content, will stoop to push them lower. It's what gives them a sense of power. It is the only joy they know and feel, to witness others fall as they once did. Never again to rise and be resplendent. It has become their nature; to wallow in the abyss of gloom and discord.

It's all they know.

'Everyone is gone!' Panea gabbled dementedly. *'Struck down by an evil elemental, and others of her kind. There is something the child-woman seeks. It is here. Can you not feel its power? It speaks to me; calls to me. What am I to do?'*

Abigail levitated and steadily rotated, her formidable aura stretching to the entrance where she perceived an approaching presence.

She was drawn again to the pathetic creature cowering by the wall, who was becoming evidently more agitated and began whipping his head side to side. He became still and raised his head up from his chest, and Abigail would swear she saw movement within the deep cauterised sockets.

'Evil is coming! She is not afraid of you, as Dark Energy has a home here.'

Despite his warning, Abigail did not sense an imminent threat, only the continuing seductive and lilting pull of the energy oozing out of the rock.

Panea was correct to assume evil had a home within the bowels of the mountain, as Abigail was of the belief there existed a hoard of dark crystals; those which had either been overlooked or had been transported to this location in recent times. She doubted as to the significance of this one source changing anything to have been created since the aftermath of war and could easily be contained: as with all the other nests.

Abigail prepared herself as Panea attempted to stand, his movements erratic, legs unsteady.

'Why won't you help me?' he pleaded, the telepathic retort having an edge of petulance and contempt. *'Am I not worthy? Do you believe, I failed in my mission to protect my flock? Will you restore my sight; give back to me my voice? Or am I to serve penance for surviving, where others did not?'*

Abigail retreated a short distance as there came the first glimmer of a threat, not that she was instantly able to define the source. It could have been the guardian Panea, or the other entity skulking in the shadows.

She felt the strengthening pressure at her back as another approached, traversing spiritual gridlines by attaching itself to her elemental trail. The celestial visitor was benign, she'd assessed, even as her concentration was on Panea and his movements. His posture had changed, as someone resembling a marionette whose strings had become entangled.

Abigail still refrained summoning protection in the form of a weapon, knowing she could send out pulses of destructive energy from her hands and eyes, should it be necessary.

'You will be tested,' came a taunt within her mind. *'The great one has his allies; and they are legion. They are watching you.'*

Abigail held her position as gelatinous tentacles burst from his body, his mouth and both sockets, flailing the heavy air between them. She gave a gasp as a formidable power was projected past her shield to punch a searing hole in the creature's chest. Its tentacles thrashed in a frenzy, just as Panea's head separated down the middle to reveal a widening domed mantle, that of a jellyfish.

Another surge of power struck and obliterated the exposed hood, the tentacles becoming absorbed within the host body as Panea slumped to the ground. It continued to writhe for a time as the exultant energy spread and devoured the source of evil.

Abigail didn't move; could only stare in amazement and despair at the pathetic husk heaped against the wall, as Chan stepped up to join her.

'There's another close by,' he spoke within her mind. *'I don't think it will show itself, remains cautious, while assessing the extent of the power it faces.'*

Abigail seemed to snap out of her stupor and turned to face him, fire blazing in the tawny hue of her eyes.

'Why have you come here?' she demanded to know, incensed, and not adverse to showing her displeasure.

'I sensed there was a problem,' Chan answered meekly. 'You were being threatened.'

'And you suppose, this creature is the worst I have had to confront throughout time?'

'Evil has been resurrected and is spreading. I believed you to be in danger, as dark energy is using cunning and guile, and seems unaffected by the energy of the pyramids and crystals.'

'The one source I had hoped to engage with, is now lost to me; will not now reveal herself having witnessed your power. I purposely played down my own so that I could entice her into the open and engineer a confrontation on my terms.'

'My apologies. I wanted only to protect you,' said Chan with an ingratiating bow.

'You were given your own mission to complete,' Abigail sniped bitterly. 'So, what did you learn, from your meeting with Nemo?'

Chan gave her a querulous look.

'Does it surprise you; I should know what transpired in the conversations you had with Nemo?' she asked. 'He was testing you; goading you, while seeking ways to exploit your weaknesses.'

'You presume I have weaknesses?' he asked, trying to cover his pain from Abigail's remark.

'I am your Achilles Heel, and Nemo is aware of this,' she said. 'As are the children.'

'What would you have me do? I am sworn to protect you and act as guardian to the children, an edict passed down by your universal father; Genesis.'

143

LEGACY OF ANGELS

'Not only am I daughter to the great power who presides over our new world, he is lover and father to Luke. Nemo is but one enemy. My father, is another, if you test him.'

'He is aware of us, our love for one another.'

'As is Nemo.'

'I ask again; what would you have me do?'

'Do all you are asked to do,' Abigail answered with cool ambivalence. 'Our duty is to the planet, and the life which serves it. We can never be as you hoped it might. We are celestial angels who should not enlist the emotions of mortals. We can lust, we can love; and as First Angel, I, perhaps, have not the freedom to indulge certain desires I may exhibit time to time. It is what it is.'

Chan cast his gaze to the crumpled heap on the cave floor, while sending out another scan to discern the location of the other entity Abigail was seeking. He was aware of dark energy drifting on pulsating waves in the claustrophobic air around them.

'What do you suggest we do now?' he asked, wanting to believe the rift between them was shored.

'My duties take me elsewhere, and I forbid you to follow,' she stated firmly. 'Return home and continue your role as guardian or remain here and find the creature which haunts this place and put an end to it.'

'How long will you be gone?'

'For as long as it takes. You will be aware now; evil has found a way back, and Nemo is the key. Take my advice, Chan, even though I have no reason to doubt your courage or prowess in a fight, under no circumstances should you invite a confrontation with the Dark Angel. If you are to meet again, even if he provokes you; walk away, and not feel shame doing so. I want you alive, for we are again at war, and would have you at my side.'

144

She raised herself up and kissed his cheek and was then gone; a gentle fading and then her aura was sucked into a candescent orb which sped out the cave entrance.

Chan felt the weight of remorse settle on his heart and was instantly alert to a mocking chuckle within his mind.

He made the decision, not to return home.

He needed to make amends, face the evil presence to have decimated the small communities of the Antarctic wasteland, and terminate its reign.

In doing so, he would be sending a clear message to the enemy.

CHAPTER 14

EXISTENTIAL...

We see only that,

Which we wish to see

On the surface.

The fearmongers

Will have it so...

Cole was restless, had been since his recent battle with a mutant jellyfish, as it went against everything Universal Design had set out for a utopian society. It was not only the people within his community which were his concern, he had to ensure his wife and son remained safe and all of this weighed heavily on his mind.

It had him wondering, as to how a creature with the propensity to kill had not. The woman and the child, victims of the unexpected attack, were recovering steadily from the injuries they had received, neither one professing to have any knowledge of what happened.

Along with others of celestial heritage, all shared a similar opinion; in that dark energy was again emerging as a potent force.

No one was prepared or had expected the possibility of evil showing its face again, so soon after the war of angels when it was believed, the formidable enemy had been ostensibly defeated.

Cole was someone who needed to be appeased with answers and be prepared for any eventuality.

The creature's carcase had been sent away for examination as all awaited a response.

The waiting was the problem, as Cole was steadily growing impatient. To his way of thinking, the mutant could in effect, be an isolated entity. Cole was of the opinion it was unlikely and there would be more. Establishing their numbers was a priority; their location and habitat, as he believed the threat from these creatures could be widespread and not an isolated occurrence.

Zanula was beside him, sleeping peacefully, their son beside them on a separate cot where light from one of the crystals bathed him in a swath of muted light. He too was sleeping and seemed not to have been affected by the negative attitude among the frightened community folk.

Cole leaned over his wife and felt a surge of love clamp around his heart. He lay back down, not wishing to disturb her with his thoughts, closed his eyes and induced a passive state of mind, so that he was able to teleport from the home in the physical sense, rather than journey on the spiritual plane in astral form.

In seeking answers to the dilemma, they faced, he hoped to put an end to the latest evil insurgence.

He materialised on the fringes of a jungle and where the ocean lapped serenely over gentle folds of golden sand beneath a three-quarter moon. His open shirt flapped nonchalantly, as with a large bird preparing to take flight, as with an angel.

He sent out a scan, trying to determine if there lay a threat in the ocean depths. Cole levitated and threw around himself an aura of protection, and then he was skimming across the surface of gently undulating waves whose deep blue had turned a sinister black beneath his bare feet. As he moved further away from the shoreline, one would think he meant to embrace the moon settling just above the crest of the horizon.

His scan went deep, without reaching the ocean bed, and saw numerous species of marine life, but not the giant jellyfish he'd anticipated seeing.

He kept going and meant to continue until he was completely satisfied a threat did not exist.

As Cole was searching for signs the enemy existed in the waters on the eastern coast of Africa, Chan had felt compelled to venture deeper into the cave complex, following the enigmatic trail of energy which had become a taunt to his senses. If dark energy had a home in the cave, he needed to know, and remove the source before it could spread.

The hollowed-out fabric of the mountain meandered left and right, and gradually dipped away as it led him deeper into the bowels of the cave. The further he progressed, the ice within clung snugly to the walls and created stalactites from the ceiling. There came an echoing sonar sound, and he perceived this as ocean currents flowing beneath him.

The floor shelved away more steeply, and after a mile he almost gave up on his quest. The pull on his senses became more enticing, not that Chan could pinpoint the location of its source. The atmospherics within the tunnel along with the sonar reverberations created a deviating pattern in the signals he was receiving.

As he approached where the floor ended as a shelf and a wide channel of water flowed across into another tunnel, Chan became steadily more cautious, as here the signal was stronger. He encouraged a broader texture to the defences he'd erected, and believed it was prudent to summon a flaming sword of energy to extend away from his right wrist.

As he stepped closer to the edge where the seawater gurgled and churned as it swept along the channel he became aware there was a ledge against the ice encrusted wall veering off to his left. Huddled over upraised knees was a naked young woman. She was rocking herself, and moaning softly, and it was apparent to Chan she was very distressed.

As he approached, intuition told him all may not be as it seemed.

'Child,' he spoke and awaited a response, his gaze flitting off to the side at the fast-flowing gulley of the ocean. 'Are you a survivor of all that went down in this region? Are you hurt in any way?'

The girl stopped moaning and rocking, and she turned to face him, his aura stabbing the hood around her eyes. She flinched away at sight of the weapon in his hand, and where licks of flame seemed to flare off it. She quickly buried her face in the gap between her knees as she inwardly fought the dark impulses threatening to resurface once again.

Chan retracted his power and stepped closer, and wished he had something to cover her, as he was aware she was trembling. He had it all wrong, as it was not from the cold or from fear which caused her to tremble. Having dropped his defences, he continued to scan the area around them for a possible threat, aware of the energy waves dabbing at his thoughts.

Keeping her face averted so as not to reveal a metamorphic change, Katerina raised an arm and spread her palm, beseeching the angel of light to save her.

149

LEGACY OF ANGELS

Chan reached out, and with his auric defences obsolete, he felt a white heat snap around the lower part of his right leg, just above the heel. Sudden pressure had him scream, as he was wrenched off his feet and dragged into the roiling waters.

As Cole was levitating across the surface of a calm sea, he was another concentrating his defensive resources in anticipation of a surprise attack.

In his mind, all appeared too calm, and his own intuition let him know he was being observed. As to the direction, he was unable to determine, as the vibrational pattern he was receiving drifted on a distortion of etheric currents.

When he glanced back the shoreline was a silvery sliver, the stretch of jungle cast in a shadowy pall without definition.

He cast his gaze downward again where a source of energy seemed to emanate from and projected his aura into the depths without reaching the bed. The luminescence of his aura stirred the curiosity of small shoals of fish, and then he saw something which moved and saddened him instantly.

Beneath him lay the ruins of a town or city, one of many he didn't doubt. He refused to allow negative thoughts incapacitate him, aware of the thousands upon thousands of lives reduced to bleached white bones haunting the depths, having perished at the time of the great floods.

He became distracted as a dark smudge crept across the moon, strengthening the shadows around his aura. Looking down was the same, as all around the periphery of the aura he projected was like an inky black stain.

It reminded him briefly, of the great battle, when all substance became swallowed by the irrepressible darkness of the encroaching enemy; that which was the Dark Lord.

Cole remained static, locked within a stupor, the moment he saw a shape cut across the swath of light forging a luminescent pit in the water's depths; and then another joined it, this one smaller.

When they slowed and swam gracefully in concentric circles, Cole recognised the forms as the mother Naomi and her daughter, who were attacked by the incarnate creature at the rockpool.

It had him wondering how they had managed to venture so far from the compound, and why they would choose to swim beneath the waters of the ocean, considering the trauma they'd experienced together. He was not mistaken, knew it to be them, swimming free and naked beneath his hovering feet.

It further surprised him they were able to hold their breath for an interminable length of time, without the need to surface for air; considering they were mortals and not of celestial heritage.

Cole attempted to reach into the mind of the mother and made no sense of the pattern of thoughts transmitted to him.

The child was first to react, suddenly stopping and paddling water, improbable large eyes imploring him.

The child's smile became a disarming distraction. Cole was unable to comprehend the next, as a long sinuous tentacle erupted from the mother's gaping mouth, streaking upward, and lashing itself around one protected ankle. He was sharply tugged downward to join them beneath the surface of the water.

Pain filled his mind as he willed the power within him to ignite, just as other tentacles burst out of the bodies of both forms, flailing against his protective shield to gain a purchase. The taut grip around his leg weakened and he kicked free, a sword of energy he'd summoned lashing side to side as he became embroiled in a dance of death.

Chan hauled himself onto the narrow ledge, the sword thrumming in his right hand as he continued to parry and thrust and slice, believing there were more of the creatures to fend off. His mind began to labour as pain and confusion and dark shadow made a home in his mind, squeezing as with a tourniquet.

Rolling onto his back he looked up and saw the naked young woman peering down at him, a wry smile curling the corners of a cruel mouth. He had his weapon primed should he need to defend himself, as his focus slipped to the swelling pain in the lower part of his right leg. He realised, in one horrific moment, the foot had been severed, his host blood pumping into a spreading pool over the ice-encrusted rock floor.

The girl crouched and he had not the strength to react, even as she swiftly clamped both hands around the bleeding stump. A searing white heat slammed through his leg and torso as he gasped through gritted teeth, fighting the agony with his own reserves of power.

When the pain subsided he looked down, the girl stepping away, and saw that the wound had been cauterised. He raised a weary gaze to the young woman who made no attempt to cover her modesty, who seemed not to be afraid, almost as if the world beneath the mountain was natural as with the evil which festooned the waters flowing through it.

Chan tried to understand how he'd not recognised her as an ancient with extraordinary healing powers. Perhaps, it was the reason she'd survived, and was unafraid of the creatures lurking in the water's depths.

He fought to unscramble the fog oozing around his thoughts, as his focus became drawn once again to his missing foot, where a darkened stump seemed surreal to someone like Chan. Had he not dropped his defences, he was thinking, as he tried to make sense of his predicament, he would not have suffered the indignity of losing part of a limb.

He lifted his gaze to the girl again, and couldn't quite believe what he was witnessing, as her flesh seemed to palpate and ripple, giving the impression a nest of eels had been disturbed within her. Instinctively, he went to summon his powers, just as a tentacle exploded from her slight frame, the girl's face splitting and separating transforming her features into a hooded jellyfish.

Chan threw himself back and launched a powerful orb of energy at the mutating creature bearing down on him, saw the way his energy smothered the form and seemed to wrestle with its counterpart.

The creature staggered and dropped into the channel, the seawater boiling and throwing up geysers of steam.

The light energy enshrouding it sank into the depths, fading quickly, until nothing but an oily gloom remained.

Chan stretched out, his breathing ragged, and summoned all his remaining energy to telegraph a plea for help to the universe. When he next tried to teleport away from the bowels of the mountain, it was to find his own source of energy was so severely depleted it prevented him doing so.

He felt trapped and powerless and didn't think he had the strength left to defend himself should other mutant monsters attack him.

He even had to wonder if his call for help would be received, even ignored, leaving him to fate.

Chan felt an unfamiliar human response; that of fatigue and desperation, and this was a frailty to heighten concern.

His attention was on the flow of water chugging past his position as he wondered if he'd done enough to defeat the evil masquerading as a young woman. There had to be others, as he'd been dragged into the channel and had his foot severed.

It took all his willpower to stand and lean precariously against the rock wall, until he was able to compose himself and feel a glimmer of energy re-emerge. As adrenalin began to flow he found he was able to levitate, and he was able to glide away from his vulnerable position alongside the channel and enter the cave tunnel which would take him to the exit.

The portable CD player he'd been given by his nemesis and was kept secreted away inside a pocket of his tunic, suddenly burst into life and began playing a song.

He became enthralled by the lyrics seeping into his tired brain, saw them as a taunt, while wondering how it was possible for the device to become activated. He stopped and dragged it out of his pocket, wanting only to make the echoing tune stop. He gave up trying as he became increasingly drawn to the beautiful, classically trained operatic lead. The lyrics were poignant and had him spellbound. They spoke of unrequited love and its consequences. There would follow suffering in the wake of folly. Those committed to the madness of a love never meant, are doomed to lose everything. Only memories to remain, until such time as even memories fade to dust.

Chan's response was to launch the portable player against the opposite wall, the sound of it shattering, reverberating eerily around the interior of the cave.

More determined, he persevered with his quest to reach the outside, the crisp air, and be given an opportunity to redefine the situation he found himself in. It was with a sense of relief when he eventually reached the cave entrance and drifted down to the iridescent plain of virgin snow. Up above, an almost full moon lit up a star-spangled canvas, and gave the false impression all was perfect and beautiful in the world.

Chan felt greatly invigorated since emerging from the cave and travelled in an easterly direction, knowing the geological terrain, and location of one of the military and scientific outposts. He hoped it would provide him shelter and a haven until help arrived; supposing his earlier message had been received and given attention to.

Chan needed a period to recharge. It would have been prudent to have travelled to the pyramid and its formidable source of energy within. Either he was being drawn to the outpost, or he was receiving an instinctive warning not to venture to the pyramid.

Chan believed; if he could summon the powers which had been sapped out of him from having dark energy attack while he was defenceless, he could teleport to the pyramid's location and determine if the enemy had compromised it.

He even stopped at a midway point across the plateau, just to try and summon his angel wings. He quickly became frustrated and gave up trying, knowing his injuries went beyond the physical.

At this time, some distance from the eastern coast of Africa, Cole was still embroiled in a frenzied battle beneath the churning waters of the ocean. For every one of the tentacles he demolished, there came others to snap at his defences, seeking to penetrate his shield and impale him.

He was loathe to enlist his full potential, as his conscience played on the fact the creatures attacking him were once friends before they had become infected.

The mother, Naomi was using cunning and guile to get past his protective aura, whereas the child, Cassandra, was uncontrollably aggressive.

Cole even thought about teleporting away from their clutches, knowing to attempt it would leave him vulnerable, as there was every likelihood they could follow on his trail and ambush him before he was able to prepare.

His lower leg ached where he'd been gripped and dragged underwater. He supposed it could have been worse, only his powerful aura of protection saving him. The fact remained, the creature had managed to breach the shield, sufficient to gain a purchase without injuring itself. Cole didn't want to think about the alternative.

The assault seemed to have waned as severed sections of the deadly tentacles floated away on the water's currents. Still, Cole had to pivot and parry, slash, and thrust as he was constantly tested. He lost cohesion and focus as the water became an inky black shroud from the fluid extracted from the creatures, swallowing up the intensity of his aura.

He gasped as a white heat streaked past his position and saw Naomi's decapitated head sail past him. The child, Cassandra, reacted quickly by kicking away, the remaining tendrils retracting into the host body. He watched as she grimaced, snarled, and managed to slalom away from another projectile of energy, and then she was gone, the dark waters beyond the scope of his aura devouring her sleek slight form.

Cole saw a figure approach from distance, and his size was immense, a powerful aura boiling the currents of the ocean. Before he could react, Cole was grabbed and lifted, and at a relentless speed both were launched out of the water like a missile. He was carried to shore and released, the giant of a man stepping away and pacing, himself in an agitated state of mind it appeared.

156

LEGACY OF ANGELS

Cole threw himself down on the sand so that he could better inspect his lower limb for signs of injury. His ankle was undamaged and it gave him a reason to smile and then chuckle light-heartedly.

'Thank you,' he said to the person who had come to his rescue. 'I fear, my conscience got the better of me, as I wanted to kill the creatures without harming the woman and child host forms. I knew them, you see; before dark energy infected their souls and made them into monsters. But how can that be; I keep asking myself? What the fuck is happening? And how far has the evil spread?'

He caught the big man appraising him, having stopped pacing, a gnarly hand stroking his long, saturated beard before lifting to caress the smooth crown of his barrel head.

'You were very fortunate I received a plea for help from the universe and I was on a mission nearby,' the man answered in a rich gruff voice. 'Your reluctance to remove the host bodies of those creatures could have been your ultimate undoing. I think it's important to understand, there is no place for complacency, as it is fact; our new world and utopian existence is not all it seems. Nothing, it appears, is going according to plan.'

'The child, Cassandra, she is still out there. She is most likely grieving for her mother, and she will be angry and spiteful and will no doubt seek revenge.'

'She is no longer the child you once knew,' the man answered. 'She has become an emissary of dark energy. There will be others. It would be unwise to think differently.'

'Once again, thank you. My name is Cole. I owe you. I must ask; you said, you received a message from the universe I was in trouble. Who was it sent the call for help?'

'Your dear wife, as it happens. The call went to a mutual friend who instantly relayed the distress call to me. From your home

I was able to follow your trail and spiritual signature. Let me introduce myself; I am Joshu.'

'I know of you; thought that I recognised you the moment you swam towards me. I was a witness to your great courage in the war of angels. You were alongside the Chosen One, as I recall.'

'Yes; sad times indeed. So many sacrifices made to further the growth and survival of mankind and nature.'

'Give me a moment, as I wish to telegraph a message to my wife and let her know I'm okay.'

'She will know, but please, go ahead if it will put your mind at ease.'

Cole had already closed his eyes in preparation to send his message and was not a witness to the way in which the big man stumbled back and had to steady himself, his features screwed into a grimace of pain and anguish as his flesh began to palpate. Snake like protuberances swam back and forth beneath the surface.

Smiling to the response he'd received from Zanula, Cole opened his eyes and raised himself up, saw the giant Joshu hugging the shoreline and blotting out a view of the moon. He was gazing out to sea, not that Cole was able to intrude on his thoughts.

It was something to do with the man's ungainly posture, the way in which he began to stagger, and there came an unearthly growl which had Cole on his guard and summoning an aura of protection. He threw out a scan and became momentarily disconcerted at sight of his beloved wife and one of the guardians, Homer, who materialised on the shore a short distance from his position.

Zanula ran to him, throwing her arms around his neck as he lifted and kissed her deeply and passionately. Out the corner of his eye he saw Homer approach the giant, Joshu.

Zanula grabbed his face to get his attention.

'Why did you not wake me and tell me you were coming here?' she berated him in soft tones. 'Had I not awoken when I did and sensed you were in trouble...'

She kissed him then, with a desperate soulful yearning. 'Don't ever leave me like that again,' she admonished him. 'We're a team; we stick together, for the sake of our son.'

Cole ended the embrace the moment he sensed two other celestial bodies had materialised on the shore, and he recognised Homer's companions, Layla and Peter immediately.

He had a feeling he'd come to recognise over time, all was not as it should be.

Joshu and Homer joined the new arrivals, the four of them facing Cole and Zanula. It was Layla who spoke for them.

'Are you hurt, Cole?' she asked. 'You must tell us, if you have been infected.'

'You think, I would endanger my wife if I believed dark energy had touched my soul?' Cole answered, in a manner which was stern, as he was coming to terms with a mix of signals. Zanula would know what he was feeling. 'As it is, I'm good.'

He felt Zanula tensing, even as she kept her thoughts behind a shield. He knew she was sharing his concern and relayed her disquiet by digging nails into the palm of his hand.

Joshu took several steps towards them as moonlight glinted off his dark skin, white teeth, and a crazed look in his eyes.

Cole threw Zanula to the sand and summoned his formidable power, preparing to unleash it against one of their kind as Joshu bore down on them. The inexplicable happened, and as with Naomi and her daughter, giant sinewy tentacles erupted out of the big man's frame; just as there came a blinding flash from the heavens above, where the brilliant white light threw down columns of lightning bolts. One of the darts of energy struck the giant on the head and Cole was mesmerised at sight of the celestial melting away to insignificance.

The other angels of light were returning immense flares of energy at the sky as Cole leapt several feet in the air and lashed out with the weapon he grasped, having the advantage as all their attention was fending-off the aerial assault.

The venom Cole displayed cut through the defences the trio of angels had erected around themselves, as did several searing darts of energy from above, until only a spiralling vapour trail of their depleted energy remained, and this too quickly evaporated.

Cole retracted his armoury and looked skyward as Zanula moved quickly to join him, both becoming witness to the descent of a glorious, winged angel. Despite all the horrors Cole had endured and having to come to terms with losing comrades to the energy of darkness, he was able to smile when he recognised Abigail behind the mask and costume of small white feathers.

Abigail settled on the sand nearby, the lunar light reflecting off the skimpy armour covering her upper and lower torso.

'We meet again,' said Abigail wryly, 'and it is with the greatest regret. These are circumstances no one had anticipated.'

'I fail to understand,' said Cole, exasperated. 'They were angels of light, celestial ancients; how is this possible? And Joshu it was, came to my rescue. He killed one of the creatures, only to turn into one himself. Can this get any worse?'

'As you are aware, evil has found a way back, and I have much to discuss with you.'

'Will you come with us to our home?' asked Zanula. 'It is comfortable, and you will have an opportunity to see our son.'

'How is Luka?' Abigail asked.

'Beautiful, wonderful; he is our little angel reborn. I would ask this; do you believe the darkness will again try to reclaim his soul?'

'No, my lovely. It's my belief Dark Energy has an alternate agenda, and that is to corrupt the pure spirits of light and their souls for an eternity. I must prevent this happening and will do whatever it takes to ensure the safety of the children in our new world. I wish to prepare you for what is to come, as you are both candidates for dark energy to attack. My concerns are also on my Luke and the Chosen One's son, Daniel. I will miss my friend Joshu, yet cannot allow the sadness of losing him, as with the others, make me lose focus. I have to find the solution to our problem and need the courage of yourselves and others to remain strong.'

Zanula nodded, feeling the grip of her own despair, knowing their idyllic world was in ruins. Once again, they were at war with evil.

Cole sensed her sadness and pulled her taut to his body, raising his other arm to invite Abigail to join their tight intimate circle. Abigail accepted his invitation, as deep down, she was feeling pangs of remorse and even a little vulnerable. They were emotions she'd not experienced since saying her farewells to her soul sister, Seraphina.

She hoped Seraphina's sacrifice was not in vain.

LEGACY
OF
ANGELS

PART TWO

DYSTOPIAN

CHAPTER 1

UNSETTLING TRUTHS...

The hearts of men

Are fickle.

Those of angels

Are a force,

To be broken. . .

Cole and Zanula were given the unenviable task of visiting those locations scattered across the globe which were known nests to dark crystals. They had to ensure the potent force of dark energy was contained.

With the geographical change affecting the planet, many of the sites were now under water, whether the oceans, seas, rivers, or lakes. It was feasible the earth's tilt may have damaged the defences around these sites, and Cole and Zanula needed to establish if dark energy had leaked and infected the waters and marine life. It was the task of every angel of light, to commit and stem the tide of evil and always protect themselves from infection.

Many beautiful souls had already fallen under the spell of dark energy, and evil had to be eradicated at any cost and without compunction, before its power became overwhelming.

Zanula hated being separated from Luka, despite the fact he was taken into care by none other than Abigail, even as she understood, it was Abigail's sworn duty to help the world continue in harmony and at peace. By defeating the source of evil, the children of the new world had a chance. Failure was not an option.

Cole and Zanula were to travel to specified locations once they received coded messages delivered to them from the universe.

It came as no surprise to Cole when told they were to visit the site situated beneath the waters of the old Sea of Crete, at the location their teenaged son at the time had been touched by dark energy.

When they reached their intended destination through teleporting, they remained in a state of levitation just above the surface of the calm blue-green waters of the sea. Gentle undulating waves beneath their feet gave the impression all was tranquil and with nothing to pose a threat.

Zanula reached for her husband's hand and squeezed, as both erected a powerful protective shield.

'Can we be certain this is the same place?' she asked, just as she sent out a peripheral scan of their surroundings. 'Without a landmark, this could be just about any place.'

'The signals we received were very precise, so I'm inclined to think, this is where it all began. When Abigail came to our rescue and sank the atoll and its hoard of evil energy. Oddly enough, I'm not picking vibrations, positive or negative, which makes no sense. It all appears calm, but we both know, appearances can be deceptive, with people and with nature.'

'What are we to do, now that we're here?' she asked, a note of trepidation creeping into her voice.'

'We dive to the site,' he said succinctly. 'It's the only way to determine if the source of evil remains contained.'

'I fail to understand how it is we're not getting any impressions. I was sure we'd be able to pick up vibrations from the combined energy.'

'The way I see it, with a global shift following the war, water levels have risen across the planet, swallowing up huge sections of coastline on every continent. It's possible, the atoll is at a depth where even the signals are weak. We'll know more when we swim down to the rock.'

'Do you suppose it's safe to investigate the source? What if those jellyfish creatures are the new guardians?.

'Considering everything to have happened in recent days, let's not leave anything to chance. Wherever we go, whoever we meet, we always exercise caution. I got your back baby.'

'I have your back, sweetheart. Just when I thought, all the evil in the world had vanished, it has now come to this.'

'Let's get this over with baby. If Abigail believes we can stem the tide of dark energy, it will help save thousands of lives; perhaps millions. After what happened to Joshu, Layla and her companions, I don't wish to see it take other beautiful souls from our army of light.'

He tapped his head as a reminder.

LEGACY OF ANGELS

'Telegraph everything,' he insisted. 'What you see; what you sense. When we hit the water, arm yourself, and be prepared for anything. So far, we know the enemy cloaks itself as jellyfish, and they have the power to absorb themselves into a host body. Should the oceans and the seas be contaminated, all marine life could be infected, even the plants.'

'Don't say that, please. Fish is a staple diet in our home country and is perhaps the same the world over. Does that mean; we are ingesting the source of evil in our diet.'

'Jesus Christ! I sincerely hope not.'

She glided closer and kissed him.

'I bloody love you, Cole.'

'Love you too, baby.'

As one, they dropped heavily into the water and swiftly kicked away from the sun-dappled surface.

Chan was unusually tired having done a complete and thorough reconnaissance of the military and scientific compound. He was not surprised there was no living soul around. The base had been attacked, as was evident in the congealed blood stains, on floors, up the walls, and even where arterial sprays had splattered the ceiling and furniture. Every room gave up their sordid secrets. In the mess room, spoiled food still sat on plates. Mugs contained the dregs of a beverage the inhabitants were drinking.

If the people had weapons, they were given no time to use them. The assault was swift and brutal.

Chan levitated himself to the recreational area, which had a pool table and a dart board, several chairs, and a card table. He threw himself down in one of the worn comfy arm chairs and shut his eyes, just to settle the rambling path his thoughts had taken him on.

When he could focus, he lifted the leg of his tunic so that he could inspect his injury. The stump was blackened where the girl creature had gripped and cauterised the open wound. He'd seen worse in his many life times, but never an injury to himself.

He felt both repulsed and saddened, and unbearably alone. He was remembering the way Abigail had spoken to him and the way she'd looked contemptuously at him. He'd never before witnessed that look or suffered her ire.

He felt desperately alone, abandoned even.

Nemo's words returned to haunt him in the claustrophobic gloom within the room, as he recalled each of his taunts, and in the way he'd suggested Chan was being punished for daring to consort with a higher being. Abigail was the coveted First Angel, daughter to the universe. Luke was the exalted son of the universe.

Chan could accept his punishment, if indeed it was the case. His ultimate fear was for Abigail and the boys, should they have to suffer for his primary indiscretion. Would the Universal Lord absolve Abigail of her sins, or was she too, to be abandoned to fate?

It had Chan wondering if any of his distress calls had been received on the outside, or if the signals had been deflected or quashed. If that were the case he would have to face his fate, alone and adrift in the Antarctic wasteland.

He didn't want to believe the mighty Genesis could exhibit destructive human emotions; such as jealousy, disappointment and malice.

Should it happen, it would make the source of universal light a cruel and vengeful entity, no different to its sibling rival.

It had him thinking further; that perhaps he and Abigail had doomed the world by committing to love and a physical and spiritual union of souls.

Chan lay his head back and closed his eyes again, wanting only for despair to dissipate. He made up his mind; come the morning and if he had sufficient strength remaining, he'd attempt teleporting away from the glacial region, even to unfurl his wings and fly.

Where would he go? Was a question causing him angst. He didn't think it would be prudent to return home. Somehow, he'd get a message to Abigail, one way or another, giving an explanation and his reasons for staying away. It was imperative, his presence was in no way a potential threat to them. It was a thought steeped in irony, by showing the power of the universe he was prepared to sacrifice love in the hope the master puppeteer was mollified.

Having lost a foot to the darkness, along with his powers, he had so little to give, and would commit to his sacrifice out of love and compassion.

It was another fervent hope, he would find answers once he visited the pyramid.

Cole and Zanula's combined luminescent auras cut a huge swath in the underwater wilderness as propulsion had them swim to a greater depth.

Zanula used the weapon sizzling in her grasp to point out the looming shadowy structure of the submerged atoll beneath them.

They communicated telepathically, remaining alert to marine life attempting to breach the barriers they'd erected for protection.

Some of the larger varieties of fish were naturally inquisitive but quickly veered away from the charged impulses of the shield.

Cole and Zanula settled on the rough, cumbersome surface of the craggy atoll, Cole dropping to a crouch to ascertain whether there were vibrations emanating from within.

'I'm not getting anything,' he relayed to her.

'That's not possible, sweetheart. There is something deeply unsettling with this. So, what do you propose we do?'

'The signals could be severely weakened by the pressure of the water. I must find the opening, if it still exists, and make certain.'

'Baby, there is nothing we can do here. We should leave and move to the next site.'

'Sorry, honey, I must know. Once I'm inside I need you to remain vigilant and report anything which might pose a threat.'

'I don't want you to go in there. What if those creatures have made a home inside?'

Cole smiled ruefully. *'I'll get my cute arse out of there in a hurry; or fight it out. We don't have a choice, babe. It's our mission. Abigail has put her faith in us, and I have no intention of letting her down.'*

'It sucks!' she stated, exasperated.

'Yes, it does.'

He kissed her, had a quick look around, before kicking away to find the aperture which would give him entrance into the atoll. Zanula followed on his heels. It wasn't long before he found the opening he recognised, even though it was smaller than he remembered., and it instantly brought back memories he hoped not to have to dwell on ever again.

Pulling Zanula taut to his body once again as he was in dire need of physical comfort and to feel her love, he tapped his forehead and slipped with the grace of an eel into the yawning mouth in the rock.

Zanula was conscious of everything he was able to feel and to see, not that it put her at ease. She was another noticing certain landmarks and remembering their previous visit to the atoll, visiting with their then teenaged son, before the adventure took a terrible turn.

The chamber with the ledge around it was filled with water, but Cole was not hanging around to take in any of the sights as he propelled himself at speed along a narrower tunnel to get where he needed to be. Zanula felt the intensity of his emotions knowing, he hated being apart from her as they were stronger together.

Zanula continued to scan the undersea world they were in and became a witness to murky shapes fading in an out of focus beyond the boundary of her defences. They could have been a species of shark, dolphins, or small shoals of fish. She hoped they were not the jellyfish monsters to have attacked Naomi and her daughter; infecting them and changing them into monsters. As with the beautiful Layla and the other guardians. They were facing a formidable power, surpassing anything that went before.

Zanula thought she understood how Abigail must be feeling, having come to their rescue and by doing so, using her powers to defeat the evil which had possessed her friends. It was not so long ago, when Zanula was compelled to draw a weapon against her own son, to free his soul from the cruel clutches of dark energy.

It was barely conceivable, their utopian existence just three years after the war of angels, was falling apart and reverting to dark uncertain times. Evil had once again pried open avenues into the hearts of men and angels, seeking to sow its hunger and wrath, and promote discord and misery.

Keeping attention on activity beyond the scope of her aura, Zanula was still able to follow her husband Cole's progress. She felt his increasing angst as he entered the opening where a nest of dark crystals originated. She saw nothing of the evil hoard, and adding to her concern, was knowing Abigail's incredible powers to contain the threat were no longer evident.

She sensed Cole's shock as they were witness to the cavernous maw depleted entirely of its nest. She inwardly sighed with relief the moment Cole decided he'd seen enough and kicked away to return to her. His tension was palpable as he slalomed through the channel and within a minute he emerged. Without saying anything he grabbed her hand and propelled them both away from the rock. Before they reached the surface Cole intimated his intentions and she quietly submitted to his control, her breath taken away as they teleported away from the cool ethereal calm of the waters and travelled the luminous highways of another dimension.

They materialised on a stretch of coastline, and she didn't think they'd returned to Africa. Cole let her know he was being pulled to this location, and he believed it was somewhere on the western fringes of what remained of Italy. They were close to a shore bereft of sand and where the ocean lapped against a sloping gradient of rock. In the distance, out to sea, was the exposed upper peak of the volcano Etna. More than half its bulk had been swallowed by the ocean.

At the present time, it was thankfully inactive.

Cole stood facing out to sea initially, puffing out his cheeks, and trying with difficulty to co-ordinate his thoughts into a pattern he could understand.

Zanula caressed his bicep, feeling his confusion deeply, having it add to her own.

'Darling,' she spoke in soft tones. 'Talk to me. Why do you suppose the crystals are missing at the other site? And where do you suppose they have gone? Aside from which, they were contained by a powerful shield. That protection was not evident. Would Abigail know this?'

'So many questions, sweetheart. The fact is I don't have the answers. Just maybe, that is our mission; to determine a reason dark energy has emerged and has grown increasingly powerful in a short time. I'm still of the opinion, the sudden Earth's tilt was a primary reason for the energy around the nest to have ruptured, and for dark energy to be released. It's a concern, that much I can say.'

She would know he was sending out a scan to the volcano, where another supposed nest was to be located.

'Are you feeling anything?' he queried.

'I am getting faint signals, not that I can say for sure if they are vibrations from either a negative or positive source.'

'It's my opinion, this is another nest which has been compromised. The crystals have been removed. When Etna erupted, it's feasible the incredible force of nature fractured the shield around the nest. What I fail to understand, is how the crystals were removed and by whom or what? It would have been no easy feat as up until recently, the world was bathed in universal light energy. The great power would have known this, and perhaps, could have stopped it before the evil spread. Now, that is a worrying thought.'

'What now?' Zanula asked him, wanting very much to take him home, once they'd collected their son, and snuggle up with her husband on their cot.

'We continue with the search. There are hundreds of sites scattered across the globe, as you know, and each one must be investigated before sending our report to the universe.'

He felt her tensing suddenly and the grip on his arm was powerful.

'Baby are you receiving those signals?' she asked him softly.

Cole swept his scan further afield.

'There's a trail of energy,' he said, 'and I think we should follow it. It seems to have culminated further along the coastline, perhaps a mile or so North of here. I think it would be prudent not to reveal ourselves initially, not until we can be certain a threat does not exist.'

He took her hand, kissed her, managed even to smile. 'I love the idea; you taking me to our cot and making our problems go away for a time. We need to stay focussed though. Are you ready?'

'One more kiss, my handsome husband.'

CHAPTER 2

A SOUL, OF TWO HALVES...

When the mighty fall

And the abyss greets with its greedy maw,

One is given a choice.

To concede

Or to fight,

To remain

Or to rise.

What if; choosing to stay,

Abandoning hope

To an existence in Hell,

Is the right choice?

When, to rise

And cling to hope

Is to further the destruction,

Of those you love. . .

Chan awoke in confusion, an impenetrable wall of darkness removing definition from within the room he was in. Despite the fact he was weakened, his aura ignited and became suffused by the dense gloom,

Levitating so that he was able to rise took a monumental effort, yet it saved him from having to hobble on the one remaining foot. His attention was drawn to a large crystal balanced on a tripod fashioned from wood and it had him pondering as to why it was not illuminating the room as he expected it to. Its energy was non-existent and had him believing it had been drained at source. Not that he understood how it was conceivable.

He was thinking about the pyramid he hoped to visit come daylight where, if he could gain entrance to its core, he just might succeed in strengthening his powers.

With his aura dimming fractionally, Chan glided through to the mess room and adjoining kitchen. Having the need for sustenance suddenly, he hoped he might find something edible to satisfy his craving.

A large upright refrigerator revealed a tray consisting of a variety of fish, of cod, herring, and sardines. Closer inspection let him know they were fresh and was perhaps part of a bigger catch the previous day, just before Hell came to visit the occupants of the outpost. Chan saw the irony, in that marine life were seeking humans for their own sustenance, in deference to the staple diet mortal men depended on.

Chan had no desire to gut the fish and prepare them instead, grabbed them up and gorged on them, devouring each of the fish in its entirety.

He didn't consider his behaviour unnatural at that time and once his appetite was satiated, he admitted to himself he felt invigorated, sharper. Even his aura had gained vitality and was able to penetrate the darkness all the way to each wall.

His damaged leg no longer throbbed.

Chan saw the positives in all these things as he returned to the recreational area and sat again, wanting only to conserve his energy and not expend it unnecessarily. He closed his eyes, composed himself, and telegraphed another distress signal to the universe. Abigail and himself had devised a specific coded sequence of vibrations, as he knew she had with her mare Free Spirit, along with her son Luke and Seraphina's miracle child, Daniel. It was a universal code unique to its creator, except perhaps for one, who lauded it over the universe. He would know.

It was imperative he informed Abigail of his situation and to be prepared for an emerging dystopian new world threatening to replace the old. Mankind and nature had been given temporary immunity from evil, to evolve and develop in harmony, and dark energy had emerged to remove all the beauty in the world, sever hope and instil fear once again.

Chan came alert suddenly to a vibrational shift in the atmosphere, and pushed with his aura, at the same time directing a scan in and around the vicinity he was in.

He kept thinking about the pyramid and the source of energy contained within its walls and how, if it were possible, to absorb its power and make it his own. With his own powers depleted, he was wallowing in territory he'd never experienced before, and it made him vulnerable, anxious, and indecisive.

Chan allowed his mind to travel beyond the boundaries of the outpost and received images of bleached coruscating snow stretching beneath the face of a huge moon. Stars lit up the black canvas of night as fresh flurries began to fall. The compound had a fence around it, having suffered neglect over time, with glaring gaps evident at several locations.

There was a smattering of outbuildings, some of which were used for stores, living accommodation, and there was even a nonfunctioning laboratory. Along with defunct tractors, a dozer and several snow mobiles lying as corpses beneath tattered tarpaulin covers, there were numerous shadowy areas which added to the ominous and ethereal quality around the outpost.

Despite Chan being able to leave his body in astral form and journey short distances, his keen senses were able to establish the strength of wind currents swirling the heavy fall of snow.

He was alert to the wind howling around the skeletal equipment left abandoned and unused for a time, even the crack and snap of a loose sheet of corrugated roof panel on one of the buildings.

Just as he was about to pull back from his scan he had the eerie feeling he was being observed, yet he saw or perceived nothing which posed a threat or to stir his curiosity.

From his relaxed position in the armchair, he went to scan beyond the room he was in, just to be sure, and instantly came up against a powerful net of energy. The vibrational patterns he felt were ominous and cloaked in dark energy.

He went to rise, and found that he couldn't, almost as if he had been shackled to the arms of the chair with invisible cuffs.

'What are you waiting for?' he called out. 'Show yourself!'

A vaporous form gained substance in a far corner, the apparition hovering without advancing. Instead of lashing out with the weakened powers at his disposal, Chan fought those impulses and composed himself, to allow his energy to feed and grow.

The apparition approached eventually and stopped a short distance from where Chan was locked to his seat. Chan observed it acquiring definition as it metamorphosed in the form of a man. Chan was certain he recognised some of the features of the being confronting him, most notably the man's hair colouring and salt and pepper beard. The grey smock coat was another to spur his imagination.

He was witness to eyes which were the colour of jet, the dark intensity fading away to reveal a glacial blue which appeared to exert filaments of flame; such was the person's power.

Chan saw the sneer on the man's face quickly evaporate and became a taunting smile lacking warmth and compassion.

Chan smiled and dutifully bowed his head, granting acknowledgement of his desperate situation, and perhaps knowing in his heart he would have only one opportunity to salvage pride over his existence.

One chance was all he required; or so he hoped.

'Once again, I am to have an audience with the not-so-mighty Chan Li,' remarked Nemo gruffly, and pacing side to side, with the stance of a college professor preparing a private tutorial for his pupil. 'It has come to this, as I foretold.'

'What do you propose for me, now that you have me at your mercy?' Chan asked, with an air of defiance and mettle in his tone.

Nemo ceased pacing and confronted his foe, his big frame casting a shadow much darker than the furniture around them, despite the intensity of his flaring aura falling across Chan's profile as he bore down on him.

'You are to be given a choice, Chan Li; to live, or to die.'

'Do whatever you feel is necessary, I will not submit to your will. My pure heart and spirit will preserve me beyond this moment.'

'Oh, but I guarantee you will think differently when this is finished; I promise you.'

Nemo raised his left hand, palm hovering on a level with Chan's heart, fingers splayed. The hand suddenly glowed with a concentration of energy and this was expelled to punch Chan further back in the chair. Chan was unable to react, sensing Nemo meant to exert his will to get him to grovel, and not slam a hole through his chest as he would have liked to do.

Chan's gaze lifted to the ceiling as he fought the pressure increasing around his heart and visibly flinched at sight of the young girl monster he'd confronted in the cave, crawling across the space directly above him, defying the laws of gravity.

She stopped scurrying across the smooth paintwork, her head turned down and mouth agape, as tentacles whipped free of her flesh and each orifice to flail the air.

Nemo stepped back as the creature dropped and landed effortless on her feet.

Chan held his breath through gritted teeth as the sinewy stalks danced hypnotically in front of him, taunting and teasing him. The girl's mangled face attempted a grotesque smile, just before it split, separated, and peeled back around a skull which became transformed into the hood of a jellyfish.

Chan released all his pent-up energy in one desperate surge, slamming the creature back against Nemo who was taken by surprise. Keeping the flow streaming at his adversary, Chan felt the shackles of power releasing him and leapt to his one good foot and swiftly levitated to the outer door, flinging it open and propelling himself into the blizzard conditions on the exterior.

Without pausing, even as he felt his strength waning, Chan's goal was to reach the pyramid in the hope its inimitable power would grant him salvation.

Midway across the plateau his power ebbed away and he slumped dejected to his knees. He wanted to believe he'd claimed a pyrrhic victory over his nemesis. He was confident the girl creature, receiving the brunt of the full force of his power, was perhaps defeated this time.

It gave him some satisfaction, knowing he'd faced evil and overcame the odds.

His gaze lifted wearily to the sky and mantle of coruscating stars, gateway to the universe; where the master puppeteer played his games and was manipulating the grand design he had initially created.

Compelled to glance back over his shoulder, he saw what he hoped not to see; Nemo, ahead of a small army of ungainly giant creatures gambolling across the snow towards him. All around, others of the one-hundred-foot monsters were slithering out of fissures in the ice, encircling his position.

Chan closed his eyes and sought the core of spiritual energy from within his heart; wanting to believe there existed still, a flicker of hope.

CHAPTER 3

EVEN THE MIGHTY, WILL FALL . . .

I have had my faith exalted,

And shown magical proof,

There exists a greater power,

I will refer to as my Lord and Master.

As with all things,

One has its opposite.

Yet who can say for sure,

The intended path

One is supposed to follow.

There has always existed dark times.

A canker at the heart of goodness and glory.

Those dark times have returned,

And all the light I was once witness to,

Has dimmed.

Made insignificant.

As I have become . . .

Rossini

Cole and Zanula remained at a discreet distance, observing activity on a renovated stretch of highway. Twelve trucks with canvas covered trailers attached were parked alongside a stretch of coastline. Almost two hundred people of both sexes had formed a chain where crates were being unloaded and passed down to four large rowing boats. The crates had to be heavy as the process was slow and needed three people at a time to connect the cargo to the next trio.

Anchored a short way out to sea was a trawler and Cole supposed whatever was being hauled onto the smaller boats would then be taken to the awaiting ship.

Along with his wife they sent out a tentative scan of the surrounding area, wary of negative energy existing in the close environs, and not wishing to alert anyone to their position.

Cole pulled his wife back so that the large rock concealed them, just as he caught sight of a distinguished looking man in a smock coat shifting his gaze from the proceedings he was clearly supervising, to where the boulder concealed a view of them. Cole probed carefully and visualised everything without seeing. If the man in charge of the shipment had been alerted, he gave nothing away and seemed unconcerned.

The transfer of the cargo went smoothly and was well co-ordinated, without commands having to be issued.

Zanula diverted her husband's attention momentarily as she reached up to stroke his cheek.

'*They have mobile transport,*' she telegraphed to his mind. '*That is a sign of advanced progress, not something I have witnessed since the war and its aftermath.*'

'*The power of the crystals; is my guess,*' he answered her. '*I had wondered if their energy had the propensity to replace fossil fuels and nuclear energy. I imagine next, we will witness working wind turbines to create a natural flow of energy. You would think, all is progressing rapidly and favourably for the new world, but we both know there is dark energy prevalent. It's our task to establish just how big a threat the enemy poses, and whether it can be contained before it spreads out of control.*'

'*The signals are unclear to me, my darling, but what do you suppose they are carrying to the boats?*'

'*It may be all quite innocent, on the surface. Provisions, maybe, to be delivered to areas of the world where populations continue to struggle.*'

'*I sense that you believe otherwise. There are elements of negative energy in the air around us. Are you feeling it too?*'

'*Regrettably; yes. Did you notice the man standing off to the side, who was not toiling as the others do? I get the impression; he is the one in charge and organising the exchange. We should concentrate our resources on him provisionally, and hope to understand what's occurring on the shore. I'm sure he is not a celestial, is in fact a mortal like the others. Knowing dark energy resides somewhere close, we must exercise caution. I suggest this; while I'm probing around the man's thoughts you maintain a scan on the area.*'

'*You think we are in danger?*' she remarked, her message conveying growing unease.

'I'm not prepared to take chances, honey,' he said, and smiled to put her at ease. *'If the odds are against us, we're out of here.'*

'Yes. Having witnessed the presence of evil back home, I wish only to be with our son. I always believed dark energy would find a way back to our world. It is a virulent disease and will continue to spread unless it can be stopped.'

Cole stooped to kiss her before turning away to concentrate his efforts on discovering the answers they were seeking. Zanula sent out a scan to ensure their location remained undiscovered and safe from a potential threat.

After a short duration, Cole turned back, dropped to a crouch, and pulled Zanula close. He felt the need to thread his arms around her, relaying his love with a simple act of intimacy.

In his natural voice, he spoke in quiet soft tones. 'As I feared might be the case, not all appears innocent on the surface. Those crates being passed down to the boats; they contain dark crystals, not provisions as I was hoping.'

'Jesus, Cole, so that is the reason for all the negative energy around us? They mean to load the smaller boats and take the shipment to the trawler. Why would they be relocating the source of evil to other parts of the world, when it should be contained? It makes no sense. We must stop this, Cole. Even if they mean to dispose of the cargo out to sea; without casting a net of protection around it, the energy will pollute the waters and we already know what that can mean. As with the jellyfish we have encountered. What of all the other marine life? The oceans provide much of the food people eat. Admittedly, there are crops being cultivated, fresh fruit in abundance, but this is taking time. Marine life is a staple diet and has been for a few years. And what if all marine life is contaminated?'

'I hear you, and it really is a concern. Our mission is to locate each source and report the stability of the nests. So far, I think it's fair to say, the stability is non-existent.'

Zanula shuffled to the one edge of the boulder

'They have finished loading the boats,' she said, 'and are filing back to the trucks. What do you suggest we do, baby?''

Cole wondered if the people called upon to distribute the cargo to the rowing boats were aware of the content, or whether they were to disperse now to their humble homes or be taken to another location, and another source.

Cole watched as the boats laboured under the weight of their precious cargo, six men to each vessel, each straining on the oars as the gap to the awaiting trawler narrowed. He became alert to the trucks pulling away and when he chanced a look, saw the only person to have remained behind, was the man he presumed was overseeing operations and ensuring the transfer went smoothly.

The distinguished looking man wandered away from his position on the roadside, not teleporting or levitating or having wanted to join the crew on one of the trucks. He was a nomad, who had served his purpose for a time, and was moving on. As to where he meant to go Cole had no idea, but his signature trail would be a guide to the man's intended location.

Cole turned and held Zanula's face with tenderness, kissing her softly, while telegraphing the need to remain alert and be ready. They teleported from their position and materialised some distance from the shoreline, beneath the erratic swell of the ocean and in the wake of the trawler chugging smoothly ahead of them.

They didn't swim as mortals did, could propel themselves as a torpedo of necessity, closing the distance on the hull of the boat swiftly until they came alongside the weathered boards. They used telepathy to communicate.

'The power within is strong,' Zanula relayed to her husband as they kept pace with the large vessel.

'I'm going to swim under the hull to the other side,' Cole explained. *'When I give the signal, punch a fucking great hole in the boat. This vessel is going nowhere, and its cargo can sink into oblivion for all I care.'*

'The crew will drown,' she practically pleaded with him.

'This is war, baby, and I dare say the crew know what's in the crates.'

'Okay but be careful.'

'Remember, to keep scanning, sweetheart. There is every likelihood, those mutant jellyfish will be close by. Just a feeling.'

He kissed her swiftly and kicked away, ducking sharply beneath the deep hull. Zanula kept pace, her aura extending outward, just to discern whether one or more of the monstrous incarnations had arrived to oversee the passage of the trawler and its precious cargo of evil. She allowed her inimitable powers to build as she pushed away, just as the command came abruptly to her mind. She launched a concentrated stream of energy at the hull and blasted a huge hole in the planks and strutted framework, just as another hit the vessel on the opposite side.

The boat juddered and listed instantly, as water poured into the two gaping rents.

Zanula kicked away from the sinking bulk as the water's displaced currents threatened to suck her towards it in its final death throes. She gave a gasp as an enormous tentacle whipped out of the murk and was deflected harmlessly away by her powerful auric shield.

Zanula summoned a weapon of energy, turned, and trod water as her aura illuminated a score and more of the monstrous incarnations she and her husband had hoped to avoid. They were gathering as a tight group, sharing an intelligence, believing they could penetrate Zanula's defences with a concerted assault.

It came as a relief Cole should appear alongside her and grab her hand.

'As much as I would like to stay and fight, I suggest we get the fuck out of here.'

He teleported them both away from the deadly waters, Zanula sharing her surprise when they next materialised, not on the shoreline by the boulder they had vacated, but at the heart of a bustling area of a newly renovated city of Rome.

Most of the architecture had been transformed, as one would expect, but even Cole was surprised by the industry and artistry to have been employed rebuilding monuments, dwellings and shops using the materials and masonry from the ruins of ancient monuments.

'I have to ask,' said Zanula, equally in awe of all she was seeing, 'But why have you brought us here, my husband?'

She was momentarily mesmerised by the sheer scale of beauty and cleanliness all around them, and the sheer numbers of people in the vicinity.

'The reason, my darling,' said Cole, 'I was following the signature of the man overseeing the cargo onto the boats. He is here, ahead of us. How he made it as a mortal, I fail to understand. We're talking hundreds of miles. He had to have teleported, not that it should be possible. I feel like I'm overlooking something; a vital piece of the puzzle.'

Cole was the one telegraphing a scan of the area, to determine the quality of vibrations in the atmosphere, and was duly surprised there should exist a mix of positive and negative energy.

'So, you mean to engage with this person, is that the plan?'

'I would have him explain, before I commit to saving his soul.'

'I would have you explain, please.'

'The person in question, is to be located within the walls of the Vatican. He is – was – a holy man. A cardinal.'

'You think this gracious man has been touched by the influence of evil?' Zanula asked morosely. 'Someone, whose faith has brought him through Hell.'

'Darling, if Dark Energy can corrupt celestial souls and turn angels from the light; trust me, faith is not a weapon to offer protection.'

'Jesus, Cole, this is madness. What has become of our beautiful world?'

'More importantly, why has the great ruling power of the universe not intervened to prevent this happening? This could have been quashed before it even began. Just an opinion. I suspect there is more to this than we will ever come to know.'

'Abigail would know. Not that she is sharing her knowledge.'

'We can ask her when we get our son back. Not that I'm expecting her to tell us everything. Some secrets are meant to remain so. Despite which, she is perhaps the only other angel I would trust our lives with, if you must know. Again, and it's only my considered opinion, it's my belief Abby is perhaps the most powerful of all the angels. We have witnessed her miraculous achievements, aside from her leadership and fighting skills during the war of angels. And I will never forget; it was Abby who gave us our son back. Damn, but she sank an island. Honey, there's no telling what she's capable of. I know in my heart; she will fight for the children of this world to preserve their future.'

'Okay, my darling. Let's get this over with, please. I wish to commit to our tasks so that we can go to our son.'

CHAPTER 4

CONFESSION . . .

> **To fall from grace**
>
> **And commit to evil,**
>
> **Is but one sin.**
>
> **To ask for mercy**
>
> **Having turned your back on the light**
>
> **Is, but another. . .**

'We're here, in this fine city, which literally takes my breath away,' said Zanula, the intimacy of holding her husband's hand instilling warmth to her heart and soul. 'It's so romantic, don't you think? As it once was.'

Despite the beaming smile slashing her face, she maintained an air of caution and continued to scan the people in the vicinity around the concourse they were on.

'Yet evil is lurking on the periphery of all which is beautiful and hopeful,' she added solemnly. 'Waiting to strike and remove all of hope which has been carefully created. The man we are to meet with, the holy man; is he now in his chambers at the Vatican? Is it there you propose to meet with him?'

'We do this together,' said Cole, preparing himself. 'You watch my back, I watch yours. All may appear quite innocent on the surface, as it frequently does. The fact remains; superior angels of light have fallen victim to the darkness already. Evil is insidious, clever, and incredibly powerful. We take nothing for granted. We cannot allow our conscience to get in the way of survival. Hesitation will destroy us, otherwise.'

'I'm ready,' she answered him as, hand in hand, they ducked away into a sheltered niche so as not to be seen teleporting away from their position. Zanula felt eternally grateful for the way Cole looked at her, smiled, and pulled her into a loving embrace, just before their forms faded to insignificance.

The corridors of power which was once a global beacon of hope and the beating heart of the old world, had visibly suffered the rigours of recent times. The Vatican City had met with the same destructive forces, as with any other city and town on the planet. Progress to rebuild the city was lacking purpose, in comparison to the speed in which the outer perimeters were experiencing rapid rejuvenation.

Within the hallowed walls of the Sistine Chapel and beyond, signs of neglect were clear, and remained as a reminder of the time the forces of nature combined with an unnatural course of events dispensed by the universe, taught a selfish and increasingly dark world to become humble. The message was clear among the ruins, one did not necessarily need a rich tapestry of possessions to be given automatic entry into a heavenly paradise beyond death.

LEGACY OF ANGELS

Most of the survivors understood there is a lesson in humility to be gained from this, where no single person should be burdened with the trappings of riches so easily taken for granted. Without wealth, there is a lessening of its power and potency to exert control.

What remained, was a stoic faith, all will be better.

Cole was of the impression however, that faith was merely a glorified mask to cover the truth of something else entirely.

Along with Zanula at his side, they materialised from teleporting within the confines of a cavernous chamber, where both picked up on a sequence of vibrations being transmitted from beyond the wide closed doors to the chapel interior. They detected a solitary deep voice, this punctuated by a continuous stream of moaning and quiet chanting.

Cole used telepathy to communicate with his wife.

'Seems to me, the person we seek is engaged in communion. I suppose, it's understandable, some will stay true to the old ways and will occasionally be called upon to renew their faith. What concerns me, is whether the preaching fermented by the Cardinal is sincere or has nefarious undertones. Are you ready for this?'

Cole moved to the flaking wood doors and Zanula stepped up beside him.

'Are we to enter in the traditional manner, or should we teleport, just to gain a reaction?'

'I imagine the doors are locked; not that they pose a problem. I think; materialising in full view of those inside will send out a clear message of intent. Always keep a protective shield around you, honey, just in case.'

'I'm picking up a mix of signals,' Zanula informed him. *'A combination of positive and negative influences, which surprises me, if you must know.'*

LEGACY OF ANGELS

'It's here, we are going to find our answers. At least, in part.'

'Let's get this over with,' she answered determinedly.

'If it comes to a fight, baby, we cannot be mindful or merciful. Evil has learned and adapted, can disguise itself behind the face of glory and light.'

'I'm ready.'

Cole gave a nod.

He would have liked to have kissed her at that moment. Instead, he grasped her hand and composed himself, channelling energy to his mind.

They emerged in the physical form in what was once the plush cloisters of the chapel. A congregation of more than thirty were receiving a sermon by the distinguished gentlemen Cole and Zanula recognised who, on this occasion was dressed in the full regalia of a Cardinal.

Cole saw the speaker pause briefly, then seemed to dismiss the unnatural arrival of two celestial beings materialising out of the ether, as if the occurrence was commonplace.

Cole and Zanula chose to remain at the rear of proceedings while sending out a scan on the huddle of people either side of a wide aisle. All were stood in rapt attention, hanging on the Cardinal's every word, as he quietly but firmly, reminisced on the importance of keeping faith. No one else, it appeared, was even aware of the new arrivals.

Zanula held her breath when she caught sight of children, ranging in age from five to nine years. Seeing them amid uncertainty made her increasingly uneasy, as she was remembering what befell her friend Naomi and her young daughter when confronted with the new face of evil, resulting in them both becoming infected with the darkness.

193

LEGACY OF ANGELS

She was pondering Cole's words, where he stated how evil had learned to conceal itself behind a mask of innocence.

The Cardinal chose the moment to interrupt his own sermon and acknowledge the otherworldly visitors.

'Welcome!' he called out, his voice powerful while exuding warmth. 'Everyone, it appears we have two more joining us this day. Please, let us give our arrivals a warm welcome.'

All heads turned, each of the children vying for a better position to gain a clearer perspective.

'Brethren of Rome, behold, for we are in the eternal embrace of two beautiful souls, those with a pure heart and spirit,' the Cardinal continued with a wry smile. 'I ask, that you state your purpose for coming here, as I am certain, you are not seeking salvation or have come to renew your faith.'

Cole telegraphed to Zanula she should remain at the rear by the doors as he glided effortlessly along the aisle, passing a sea of faces who showed no surprise at the feat he was displaying. Cole approached the central dais where the Cardinal was scrutinising him and moved to the right to put distance between them. Cole had observed how a few within the congregation had leaned away from the energy of his aura as he passed them, while others appeared not to be infected.

He was certain dark energy was residing within the chapel. Yet not all appeared to be infected, as others still retained their innocence and were content to walk in the path of positive light.

Cole spoke directly to the Cardinal, believing him to be exhibiting restraint, the man's placid mask of purity struggling to contain something dark lurking in the depths of his eyes.

'We recently observed the movement of a shipment of crates, from trucks to boats, and then taken to a fishing trawler out to sea. It is the content of the cargo which intrigues me.'

'And you believe there is something unnatural and nefarious in what you saw?' the Cardinal answered calmly. 'Is it to be considered a wrongdoing, providing for other nations who are struggling still to come to terms with the changes in our world; to offer them aid and in doing so, bolster flagging spirits?'

'You suggest to me, you were personally organising the movement of aid, yet I am aware of the cargo which was to leave these shores.'

'Enlighten me, my good man, and share your knowledge with us all. What is it you believe the vessel was to transport?'

The Cardinal had become sterner of expression, and rueful, like a fallow deer crossing the road and getting caught in the headlights of an approaching vehicle. He was aware all the power he had been granted and acquired in a short time, were no match against the supreme beings he was now facing.

It had come to this; he was thinking.

He'd been granted salvation, once, at another time not so long ago.

An angel had come to save him from evil. He wondered, even now, if this man and young woman who had followed him to the Holy City were as merciful.

Or indeed if his soul was worth saving.

'The ship has been sunk,' said Cole with ambivalence. 'Along with its crew and the cargo of dark crystal.'

'So many lives wasted, on a whim,' answered the Cardinal with a sigh of resignation as he lowered his bulk to a plush throne chair. 'You and your kind purport to be angels of mercy, beacons of light and goodness, yet you would let innocent souls perish.'

'No one, in this present climate can be considered completely innocent, as you're aware. Dark Energy has once again revealed itself and pursues a quest to seduce all in its path and have them walk in the shadow.'

'Please, will you allow these good people to return to their homes unharmed. They came specifically to receive guidance and salvation, knowing harmony and balance in the new world is being tested.'

'All are free to leave; but only if their souls remain pure.'

The Cardinal saw the ambiguities in Cole's statement, yet he reluctantly raised an arm to the congregation, signalling their dismissal. There came a gaggle of murmuring and shuffling feet as people began to herd themselves into the aisle and head towards the closed doors.

Zanula responded by casting a net of energy across the fabric of the exit, and by exerting her will, saw the wide doors creak open. Both she and Cole, from his forward position, observed those who approached and were oblivious and fearless of the trap which had been set. Others, including some of the children, became increasingly vocal and agitated, the pulsating waves of subtle energy making them hesitate.

Zanula was alert to signs of imminent danger and allowed her power to extend along her arm where a resourceful weapon of flaming energy emerged from her left hand. In her mind, she fervently hoped she would not have to wield the sword, especially in a Holy place.

The few who had balked, remained in a vacuum of confusion as those who remained innocent and free from infection, passed through the open doors without incident. They too were shrouded in confusion and mystified, as they had no idea what was happening, or the potential of what might happen should they linger.

They had much to talk about once they had vacated the Sistine Chapel, the sermon delivered by the Cardinal Rossini having already seeped away from their minds. The subject of their interest would centre on the ethereal beings who had appeared out of nowhere, who were not mortal as they were. There was a muttering, the good Lord had sent down his angels to show mankind the true path. Memories resurfaced, of how it had once been, before the great storms, quakes and floods. They spoke of crystal magic, the eco-friendly source of energy to replace all other fuels, and how it made for a better world, a better life. And angels had descended to continue lighting the path all should venture along. To banish the growing insidious threat of evil some were speaking of again.

For those who chose to remain and not confront the formidable power barring the exit, all gathered in a small huddle and turned to their leader for advice and guidance, and ultimately, protection.

Zanula vacated her position and approached, the weapon of light in her grasp, sporadically flaring as it reacted with obverse energy emanating off the group gathered in the centre of the aisle.

It was the moment the Cardinal chose to rise with arms extended to the side, and tilting his head back at an improbable angle, seemed to beseech the ornate gesso ceiling for divine inspiration.

'Forgive me, my Lord,' his voice boomed and resonating within the confines of the chapel, 'For I have shunned the merciful light and stumbled onto the path set out for me.'

He turned then to confront Cole, eyes dilating against the light of the celestial aura, with tears brimming in his lashes, lips quivering.

'I have witnessed beauty; I have embraced holiness. I received proof of all I believed in. I know not why I turned my back on all things good and just and holy. In my defence, I could not cope with so much joy and happiness when, all my life, I have fought to ease the burden of suffering in those who were struggling. You understand; my services were no longer required. I had become obsolete. Rejected. And yes; I renounced my faith for a taste of a life I had sworn to abstain from. I do not ask forgiveness, or mercy, as this insidious evil must be stopped.'

Rossini arched his frame and emitted a high-pitched keening sound as the front of his face split open and separated, to reveal the monstrous incarnation within. Cole threw him to the far wall with a single concentrated blast of energy, the ferocity of which tore a fist-sized hole in the Cardinal's sternum. And still he refused to buckle and fall, just as bedlam was unleashed within the confines of the chapel.

Zanula and Cole had correctly anticipated reprisals, both levitating and throwing themselves at the melange of people who had become transformed into the dreaded aquatic monsters. They struck at the flailing tentacles, cleaving, and decapitating the hoods, until all were in spasming heaps on the carpeted floor.

Zanula staggered away at sight of those who were once innocent children, and pangs of remorse had her almost dropping to her knees.

It was left to Cole to confront Cardinal Rossini's mutated transformation, where life continued, albeit weakly. Taking no chances and wishing only to end the evil, Cole slammed his mighty weapon down in the centre of the exposed domed hood and struck from the side to decapitate all which remained.

The deadly tentacles slumped in an oozing pile, some continuing to spasm, until eventually the creature's lifeforce was spent.

Zanula rushed to Cole's side and flung her arms around him, having first retracted her defences. He held and rocked her, giving her the necessary solace to appease a tortured conscience.

'I think I truly understand now,' he said within her mind *'Dark Energy is on a quest to corrupt the purity of any heart, soul and spirit, and deplete our numbers. If this does not end, we will no longer be a force of light able to withstand a full assault.'*

'I hate this, baby,' Zanula whimpered, and was again amazed at herself, she should so easily exhibit human emotions freely and easily.

She realised also, having these emotions made her vulnerable, and potentially a liability. Thoughts of their son brought things into perspective rapidly, and straightening her shoulders, she gave a commanding nod.

'Where too, next?' she asked resolutely. 'Have you received a sign?'

He kissed her amongst the carnage.

'As it happens, I'm no wiser than you, sweetheart.'

'Then I suggest we concentrate our resources, travel, and let the universe decide,' she said, and her smile was evidently strained.

'It would be nice, considering everything, we should be granted leave.'

'Yes, for I would like to go to our son.'

'No easy task there, honey. We can only get to our son when Abby approves it. Her home is a fortress, of necessity, to protect the children naturally. When the moment is upon us, we will use the coded language Abigail gave us, and hope she is receptive to us visiting.'

'Luka is our son. Our life. Please, I wish to leave this horrid place, that which was once a holy shrine to the world. Now, it has come to this. I wonder; how far has the evil spread, and can we hope to stem the tide?'

'We have to try, my darling,' he stated. 'It is our duty.'

He kissed her briefly, smiled pensively, as he prepared them for the next stage of their spiritual journey. Deep down, he believed time was running out.

CHAPTER 5

CHRONICLE'S OF A DISENCHANTED COMMUNITY...

The changes are evident,

Yet subtle.

It began with a frown,

When a reason to smile

Became lost.

As one remembers,

How it once was...

Byron Jones swung his legs off the bed and massaged both calves where the muscles had cramped.

Odd, he was thinking, as at no time in the past three years had he suffered aches or pains, of any description. At least, he was to convince himself, he had entered a new morning of a new day and

201

as with every day, he was grateful and felt blessed to have been given a lease on life when millions had not. From the time he'd met with the celestial forms on Snowdonia a few years past, he understood his purpose was aiding others to climb out of the pit of despair the devastated world had plunged them into.

Yet not a day passed without him conversing with his personal ghosts, despite the fact he'd drifted into a new relationship in recent months. He felt it was important to remain true to himself and retain the love he held for his deceased wife, Ellen, and two children.

His latest partner was supportive whenever he needed to talk about his past. She had a son, who he found adorable, and treated him as if he was his own flesh and blood.

Byron pondered the extent of progress made since he arrived on the fringes of what remained of the city of Chester.

The Atlantic had carved a destructive niche along swaths of the West coast, devouring numerous cities and towns and its inhabitants. The new coastline, with its own buried secrets and the memories of thousands upon thousands of ghosts, was less than a mile from the location of the stone cottage he dwelt in.

With the help of others, he'd rebuilt the home from the rubble, and it was the same for those who made up, what began as a small community, and had swelled considerably since.

Stretching and limbering his shoulder muscles, gave Byron an opportunity to once again, peruse all the artwork festooning the bedroom walls, all of which were drawn and painted by the young boy in his care. Byron believed them to be quite dark in their various subject matter, and perhaps understood why the boy would convey such an array of bleak imagery. He spoke little, and it was Byron's belief the boy was having a difficult time laying his own ghosts to rest.

LEGACY OF ANGELS

Most pictures depicted scenes of angels, predominantly male in subject. Byron always believed angels in art to be portrayed as messengers of hope, mercy and light. Mateo had darkened their souls by conveying an attitude of menace in the way their eyes seemed to bore into the observer, from their posture, and in the colouring of their wings. It had Byron wondering where the boy gained his inspiration from. He'd spoke of this to the mother on occasion, who merely shrugged with indifference, and the boy wasn't saying.

Whatever dark and dismal memories they carried with them, were to remain a secret.

He became distracted when the young woman in his bed gave a sleepy moan, and as he looked back and down on the beautiful recumbent figure, he found himself smiling. He voyeuristically observed the soft smooth tones of her bare back and the upper curve of her buttocks where the coverlet lay askew.

She was still asleep, locked within a private dream, yet appeared content.

Byron stepped away from the mattress and went to the window, peering across to the quiet street out front, and other properties opposite. It was early morning, the sun having barely risen, as it blinked in an out of scudding cloud. There was a sturdy breeze and it whipped up the bronzed autumn leaves to have fallen.

Hitching up his shorts, he went to the adjacent room to look in on Mateo. The boy was awake and sitting atop his single crib, eyes closed, posture relaxed. Mateo, as with his mother, was an advocate of meditation. It seemed to Byron the boy had immersed himself in a spiritual trance. Byron was aware also, the gifted boy could astral project. As to where his spiritual body travelled, the boy was reluctant to share.

Leandra and Mateo had arrived six months ago, chaperoned by a tall gaunt man of indeterminate age. He was another who seldom spoke and preferred his own company. He departed after only one week, never to return.

It was Byron who offered mother and child shelter, a temporary arrangement until they arrived at a decision on whether to stay or move on. Two days, and Leandra was sharing Byron's bed, a decision to stay having been made.

Life was good; Byron often told himself. The community he had gendered close to one of the ethereal and mysterious pyramids, was thriving, the inhabitants to have settled remaining positively upbeat despite all the hardships they had endured at the beginning.

Byron kept himself busy most days, tending to the farming outposts, employing his carpentry skills in renovating homes, and sometimes volunteering his services when the town's fishermen took to the sea.

There were occasions when he visited the two schools in the vicinity and assisted. There was also a mosque and a church, granting people who held to their faith an opportunity to reflect and give thanks.

The new town also boasted three renovated halls and a theatre, and these were used as venues for various entertainments, including bingo, indoor bowls, darts, snooker. A few musicians had formed bands. They were also a haven for social gatherings, and specialised groups offering yoga and meditation.

Normality out of chaos had returned.

The day ahead, was to be devoted to completing a census on the crystals in people's possession, and to ensure their selective energy continued at the capacity expected of them.

Byron had become an advocate of the magical properties the crystals revealed, as it had been discovered in recent times, the energy of the larger units was capable of driving machinery and transport, elevating progress rapidly and dramatically.

The rebuilding of roads was taking time, but they were getting there, as it was hoped they could link to other communities in the not-too-distant future.

Byron returned to the bedroom to get himself dressed, to find Leandra awake and sitting up in bed. Whatever itinerary Byron proposed for the day ahead, was instantly dismissed, the moment he saw the lascivious look she gave him. Leandra could be very demanding, as her appetite for sexual gratification was, at times, insatiable.

Byron believed she'd cast a spell on him. Not that he was complaining. After his wife, he always believed there could never be another to claim his heart, but physical allure could be very persuasive. Leandra had all those attributes in her locker, and more.

It came as no surprise, Leandra would keep him to the bed for much of the morning, and after, insisted they took Mateo out for a ramble and a picnic in the countryside. She let him know, it was important he gave up his time for them on occasion. *Family time,* she would state, *was especially important in the aftermath of the horrors the survivors had faced.*

Byron relented, and even helped prepare a makeshift hamper for their trip. He hoped the occasion might bring him closer to Mateo, even so far as to inveigle himself into the boy's heart.

It was to be a good choice, as the afternoon in the company of Leandra and an exuberant 4 - year - old was to have its rewards. He had missed these defining moments. Leandra was not Ellen, not that Byron would ever make the comparison. Leandra was simply someone who filled a gap where Ellen's passing had created a vacuum. Leandra was, in her own unique way, special to him.

LEGACY OF ANGELS

Sat side by side on the smooth flat bed of grass, each observed a robust Mateo expending energy. Byron noticed the way the boy would surreptitiously glance in their direction which was a little unsettling, as Byron believed the boy's interest was on him and not his mother. He was aware the infant could be very protective of his mother, and Byron could understand why he would feel possessive, as his mother had been his rock throughout.

When he wasn't running around, the boy would stare at them for a period, before simply closing his eyes. Leandra let Byron know there was nothing to be concerned about, as Mateo often behaved this way, prior to meditating. Leandra knew just how to mollify Byron if he hesitated whenever an explanation was given. She would give him physical attention, and would tease, aware Byron would submit to her wiles quickly. She knew how to play him. He just didn't know he was being played.

Byron was reserved, by nature, yet could be quite sociable at times. As with Leandra, who was not loquacious, and rarely spoke of her past. She never once regaled him on topics of Mateo's father, preferred to keep her past buried but not forgotten. At times, he would catch her reminiscing and become deeply pensive, bordering on anxious. Byron was of the opinion Leandra held a grudge against someone, not that she would say why.

Despite everything, their relationship suited both parties. Byron had a ready-made family and he worked hard at making it a happy one. Glancing off to the side occasionally to catch a profile of the devastatingly beautiful young woman to have entered his life, Byron was thankful he had someone to fill the vacuum left after losing Ellen and the children.

Leandra was a mysterious and unique individual, at times fun-loving, but most times she remained deeply reserved. She pandered to Mateo's every whim, and he was another who exhibited troubled behavioural characteristics, often, and Leandra sought to placate him by taking him on frequent nocturnal jaunts. Where they would go, Byron had no idea, and should he ask for details, all he would get was a poignant response and that was the end of it. Once, she proclaimed the open air could be a canvas of tranquillity and served to quieten her son's active imagination and pacify his soul.

It was safe for women and children to venture out unchaperoned, no matter the time of day or night, not like it once was. As this was a Utopian world, after all.

Byron was already planning to the next day; aware the fishermen of their community were set to venture onto the Atlantic and cast their nets. They were the hub of providing a sustainable income of fish to the eager patrons of their town, as it was still one of the main staple diets.

It would not be his first trip, as he was always eager to participate and play his part in helping others on the road to survival. Trawling was hard work, yet he found each experience enjoyable and rewarding. Especially as the haul they were to catch would be distributed to various locations where people would gather to choose what they wanted and needed to sustain them. There was no currency governing the edict of trade, as everything was shared. And it was a miracle, people only took what they needed, and at no time became enticed by greed and garnered more than their share. Which was a good thing, as it meant there was little waste.

There were a couple of restaurants in the main town, and these thrived on selfless hospitality while providing a social outlet for people to enjoy. The customers would thank the chefs and those waiting on them by assisting after, in washing down the plates and cutlery and cleaning all the surfaces and floor space, maintaining levels of hygiene were in place.

Byron was in awe of the way people responded, by repaying a giving community with kindness and compassion.

LEGACY OF ANGELS

Ellen would have loved the New World; he would often think to himself. She would have participated, and her own brand of jocularity and spiritual awareness would have captivated everyone.

That night, Byron had been restless since the moment Leandra and Mateo had sloped off on one of their nocturnal sojourns. Always, he was excluded from going with them.

Leandra and Mateo had yet to return by the time he was ready for a morning's fishing. He left a message on the white board in the kitchen, explaining his itinerary for the day ahead. He placed a small heart at the end and a couple of kisses.

It was time to make himself ready. The idea of a fishing trip was exhilarating, despite which, he had negative thoughts dampening his mood. This was a feeling he had not experienced since his time on Snowdonia soon after the tragic events to have destroyed a world, and his natural life, where he'd taken a few days to lay his ghosts to rest.

CHAPTER 6

A DAY LIKE NO OTHER...

Some events in life

Remain inexplicable.

What we sometimes see

Or what we hear,

Can be a figment of our imagination.

That, which is real,

And defies belief,

Is often,

Something which should be feared....

Despite the heavy woollen sweater and waterproof waders over denims, Byron was surprised by the inclement chill and light drizzle greeting the crew of eight at the shoreline.

Byron was always cordially welcomed, and had to suffer preliminary light-hearted taunts, suggesting he was not someone born for the sea even as the men were quick to praise his doggedness and commitment.

The captain on the scheduled trip was a seasoned veteran of the high seas, his wispy salt beard fanning a barrel chest, and his experience spanned fifty years. He started out as a lad of fourteen, following in the tradition of his father and grandfather. He was affectionately known as 'Old Larry,' and he was someone with a plethora of seafaring tales stored to memory, he often recited to an avid audience who hoped one day to compete with.

Before the world suffered and was thrown into turmoil, he would say; the seas were rougher and meaner, and claimed many lives. Every day was a challenge, leaving one wondering if they were to make it back to dry land; alive.

He had lost many close friends to the sea, not because they were clueless, careless or arrogant.

He would say, should the sea wish to claim a soul, it would take it, regardless, and without compromise.

It was different now, he claimed, as the sea was no longer hungry. The sea had been tamed.

A bloody miracle! he would proclaim.

And with his rheumy eyes awash with knowledge and mischief, and even sadness, would add; *I have witnessed many such miracles since the world went to Hell and back. All is good and wonderful at this present time, but take heed everyone, it cannot last. Never does.*

He'd leave his audience pondering, and he would chuckle warmly, slapping everyone affectionately on the back.

The crew of eight, plus one, trundled along a wide jetty to where 'The Neptune' was tethered to stanchions and anchored for added stability.

Another of the older generation with twenty years-experience on fishing boats was first to dampen the mood and spirit, when he stopped, gave the sign of the cross, and chuntered a short prayer in gruff tones.

'That,' he said, 'Are for all the lost souls the sea swallowed, who believed were safe in their homes, offices, and shops, having survived the climate changes and earthquakes. The sea, my friends, can play at God one moment; only to become the Devil in the blink of an eye.'

Byron answered by puffing out his cheeks and taking up the rear on the way to boarding The Neptune, thinking Bill Todd's words to be poignant, if not a little deep. He didn't want to dwell on the horrors of the past and of the millions of lives to have perished. He didn't want anything to cast a pall of gloom on this day. It was imperative, each and everyone looked ahead, and not back.

Despite which, Bill Todd's words left their mark and would not go away, as if there was something prophetic in all he'd said. A shadow of doubt was cast on his mood, and it was yet one more thing to unsettle him, as anything remotely negative to his way of thinking, was anathema in this new world.

Going back to the miracles Old Larry had expounded upon, The Neptune was powered by crystal energy, and not conventional fuel.

As the boat set out on its journey, it cut seamlessly and quietly through a gentle early morning swell.

The crew worked tirelessly preparing the nets and ensuring the galvanised winch was operational. Byron offered his services, with the captain 'Old Larry' at the helm in the wheel house.

They travelled several miles out to sea where a new dawn began to break, casting a gold, crimson and bronze sheen across the dull grey of the sea.

Old Larry gave the order to lower the vast trawling net, a separate crystal used for mechanically driving the sturdy crane. The metal struts gave a plaintive groan; it was the only sound.

Byron followed instructions as the other crew members barked commands to one another, their voices overlapping the cry of seagulls circling in the vicinity. Despite being treated as such, Byron was not exactly a novice, insofar as he'd made regular trips out on a variety of vessels under different captaincies, assisting in the hauling of fish to feed the town folk of the community.

It was the captain's duty to only return with sufficient haul to sustain the town for a short time, and any excess was returned to the sea. Although there was an abundance of marine life, no one wanted to deplete the waters, or encourage unnecessary wastage.

With the net submerged, and the trawler's momentum dragging it through the water, there came a moment of respite for the crew as the truly hard work was yet to come.

Old Larry even vacated the wheelhouse for a short intermission and joined the crew over a heady brew of locally grown coffee and participated in the ritual of reciting stories of past adventures each had enjoyed when there was not a crisis occurring.

The Neptune gave a sudden lurch, moaning heavily as it listed to the port side. All hands-on deck grabbed a solid purchase to prevent them plunging over the side into the sea. The Neptune righted itself and rocked unsteadily, just as the crystal motorising the vessel appeared to have suddenly become drained of its source, the boat labouring slowly until it settled.

Old Larry gave the order to drop anchor and haul in the net, knowing this was not to be an easy task he was asking of his crew, as without the winch operational, they would have to bring the net up by hand using two wheel-cranks, or cut the ropes and release their catch.

Byron tried not to think too deeply, as to why the crystals had become inactive, wanting to believe this was completely natural, and the net was perhaps over-ladened and putting too much strain on it.

Someone suggested they had caught a whale, or dolphins. Everyone was of the opinion the net would not cope.

All became alert to the crane signifying a protest as it miraculously powered back to life, the great net rising slowly and carefully to the surface.

There were a few nervous pats on the back as the crew gathered along the port gun-whale in anticipation.

'Jesus!' A comment which relaying shock from the youngest crew member, Nuno. He pointed. 'What is that?'

Revealed amongst the excessive haul captured within the net was a creature most had never seen, regarding its overall size and bulk.

It was Old Larry who offered an explanation based on his experience.

'That, my friends, is a jellyfish. A Portuguese Man O War is my guess, but never in my lifetime have I seen a specimen of this magnitude.'

'Has to be at least a hundred feet,' said Carl Rogers, another with a few decades experience on the open sea. 'Deadly, I would hasten to add.'

'We have to release it,' said Byron anxiously. 'Cut the ropes. Let it loose.'

'We can save the catch,' said Nuno. 'This will feed the town folk for a week.'

'Too risky,' remarked Old Larry, thoughtfully. 'Whether the monster is dead or not, contact with it can be fatal.'

'Byron's right,' said Karl. 'We don't need the hassle. We should release the catch and try again further out to sea.'

As if a decision had been relayed directly to the captured monster, it suddenly reacted, its wide sinuous tentacles thrashing amongst the dense haul of fish. Areas of the net fizzled away, The Neptune listing violently and all the crew were caught off-balance.

There came cries and a fearful scream as Nuno was struck by a loose, rogue lobster creel, and was pitched over the side. Some of the crew members were shuffling along the gun whale to release the life buoys, Old Larry crawling towards where a long sturdy pole with a hook was still tethered.

The monster had settled before thrashing around again, the strain on the net becoming too much, as the crane screeched and the boat rocked violently.

All the crew were thrown to the deck as it became a desperate struggle for survival. All were wondering if Nuno was alive, as his plaintive screams for help had ceased. Where the boat listed at a perilous angle, water surged over the bulwark onto the gunnels. Cries of panic outweighed Old Larry's faltering commands.

Byron slid along the groaning planks to where a metal trunk was lashed to other crates strapped to a stout mast. Byron knew the contents of the trunk consisted of a variety of sharp implements, primarily used for preparing the fish.

He ducked and only just in time, as a gigantic tentacle struck the floorspace, barely inches from where he was kneeling. He used the crates as cover, as the deadly whip flailed the air and flashed away.

The momentum of the boat listing further had Byron sliding to the bulwark, but not before he'd hefted the lid of the trunk and retrieved a machete from the stockpile within. Getting a thorough drenching and grabbing the looping ropes along the length of the bulwark for a purchase, Byron heaved himself over to where a taut rope strained against one end of the trawling net.

He hacked away and managed to throw himself down as the loose frayed end of the rope snapped the air with the ferocity of a hissing serpent. The sudden jolt as the boat righted itself, had everyone grabbing a support to prevent them going the way of Nuno.

There came a piercing scream as another tentacle whipped viciously across the gunnels and cut one of the men completely in half, the upper torso toppling overboard while the lower limbs slumped in a bloody, ungainly heap onto the planks.

At that moment, the prow of the boat was wrenched and turned sharply, the remaining crew thrown across the floorspace as scores of tentacles rained down on them. One of the gigantic whips demolished the roof and the side of the wheel house.

Byron realised he couldn't get to the other rope as he witnessed his friends becoming hideously cut down by the monstrous flailing tentacles. The Neptune was rocked and Byron was pitched from his position and thrown through the air to become swallowed up by a churning sea.

He was unable to react as he would have liked, becoming horrified and spellbound, at sight of two immense domed gelatinous hoods rising above the portside bulwark. The boat suffered a thunderous impact, was tipped over and began to roll. Byron let loose with a desperate scream as he kicked away into the path of fish carcases, churning clouds of blood, and dismembered human body parts. Old Larry's decapitated head bobbed and weaved as Byron

215

was sucked down, just as he was witness to the gigantic shadow of the Neptune poised to slam the water's surface.

Byron saw another threat as the current dragged him further into the ocean depths, that of several mutated jellyfish bobbing up and down around the boat as it struck the water.

CHAPTER 7

MIND GAMES . . .

That which is intimated at,

Or words left unspoken,

Has greater clarity.

As there is truth in lie

And lie, in truth...

Abigail excused herself from the confines of home where she'd become reunited with her mother and the twin souls of Gillian and Margaret O'Shaughnessy, following their travail around the United Kingdom.

Not all the reports they were to share reflected the harmonious beauty Abigail had envisaged for the new world. It was fortunate, they had not encountered evil in the flesh, even as they had been witness to pockets of degenerative behaviour where the influence of emerging dark energy had revealed itself.

Abigail had further concerns playing on her mind as she sought a private audience with Free Spirit who was out grazing in one of the fields. Her soul mate could always be relied upon as a source of spiritual comfort whenever she was troubled and in need of alignment.

The mare reacted instantly as it sensed the pull of Abigail's erratic signature and galloped across the smooth clipped grass to Abigail's position at the gate. Abigail greeted Free Spirit with open arms as the mare slowed at just the right moment to a gentle gait, telegraphing her love and smiling warmly. Dropping kisses along the mare's broad snout and petting its neck, Abigail let her know they were to ride, and then to fly.

Free Spirit would know they were on a mission, other than a time of pleasure, and prepared herself as Abigail rose with arms spread and dropped gently across the mare's back.

At first they went for a steady trot around the perimeter of the field at the rear, where the energy of the concealed pyramid beneath the circle of ancient oak thrummed a rhythm of suppressed power, as Abigail strived to smooth out the indents of a troubled conscience.

Chan's continued absence was foremost in her thoughts, as she'd received no message from him, and he was not responding to the coded sequence of communication she had relayed to him. Fearing the worst, she had even telegraphed a plea to the father of the universe, Genesis, and all she had received was a cryptic rebuttal, stating Chan was on a mission and his absence was inconsequential considering the troubles spreading across the globe.

Believing in her heart Genesis was not sharing his knowledge, for whatever reason, had Abigail angered and even remorseful. She would not forget the way she had greeted Chan Li when he followed her to the ice cave in the Antarctic region.

She had even thought about returning, so that even if he had departed and moved to another location, she could hopefully follow his auric trail. Except, and this was her underlying concern; Chan's signature was faint and without the necessary structure which could be followed easily.

There was something she could do; that which she'd been avoiding.

Until now.

Leaning low, she relayed her intent to Free Spirit, the mare instantly into a gallop, until both horse and rider became an indistinct blur. As with a solar flare, the verdant pasture was illuminated in a golden light, and when this dispersed horse and rider were gone.

Having traversed spiritual highways across parallel dimensions, Abigail descended with Free Spirit, where resplendent wings of a brilliant white were unfurled, coming to settle on the golden sands around the pyramids of Giza. The ancient monuments had withstood the ravages of destructive winds and earth tremors, as had the three smaller specimens offset against the larger trio.

Abigail embraced their collective power, aware the heart of the universe within each, was beating steadily. She had chosen the site specifically, as it was to offer her the necessary protection, should the invitation she had sent be met.

Abigail was of the belief Nemo's ego would not allow him to be deterred by all the positive energy rippling in the etheric currents.

Abigail floated down to the runnels in the sand and surveyed the environment she'd chosen for a confrontation, while sending out a scan to determine if there existed a threat.

The geographical vista was a daunting jolt to the senses. The Red Sea had joined with the Mediterranean, which had sliced across a great area of the Western Desert, the Qattara Depression serving as a vast lake.

Alexandria was gone, another coastal region to have found a ghostly grave beneath the water. A large portion of Cairo had also suffered from the ferocity of a relentless tsunami, the remainder of the city having been razed to the ground in the throes of periodic violent earthquakes.

It was an area more deprived than most she had encountered, with progress to develop seemingly lax, despite the great power of the pyramids nearby.

Abigail felt sure this was a region which should have benefitted beyond the devastation, with the guidance of guardian angels set in position to engineer regrowth and instil hope in the hearts of all who had survived.

Abigail turned her attention to Free Spirit who trotted over to nuzzle her mane of hair affectionately, and sensing the mare would have absorbed the negative pattern of her thoughts. Subtle threads of dark energy existed around the environs of the group of pyramids, yet mysteriously remained on the periphery of her auric scan. It was all around; like an elemental mist, which fluctuated and changed form, constantly.

Attention once again on the pyramidal monuments, Abigail was witness to centuries of archaeological digs and structural examination, that which had revealed many secrets.

Not all.

219

LEGACY OF ANGELS

The pyramid's reason for being had not been deciphered, although the message was more apparent now in recent times. Any archaeologists who were fortunate and survived the universal holocaust, were perhaps reluctant to travel or were no longer interested in unlocking the key to the past on the mysteries of the world. It was all about self-preservation, and, that was no easy task.

Abigail ambled over to the shoreline of the immense expanse of sea, another scan determining whether there existed mutated jellyfish in the waters. She hoped most fervently, the formidable power at the heart of each pyramid, served as a deterrent; which did not explain the etheric currents of dark energy drifting around at a respectful distance.

She knew it to be a reason why certain surviving civilisations had been plunged into a state of retreat and was directly responsible in slowing down progress in rebuilding and evolving, as was expected in a new world.

Free Spirit gave a snicker of warning, and without looking to the side, Abigail was alert to the approach of another celestial form. She felt an inimitable power tentatively probing her aura, that which she kept restrained, as she drew in a breath and held it.

Nemo stopped advancing, less than a hundred metres from the Angel he was seeking; she, who had summoned him to this meeting. He was naturally intrigued and cautious, knowing his adversary was capable of feats no other could employ.

Other than himself.

Nemo saw Abigail as his equal; neither superior nor inferior.

'Shall we sit, or conduct a conversation standing?' he taunted, his powerful voice carrying on the currents of a light breeze sweeping gently off the sea. 'Frankly, I'm easy, either way. Are you relaxed? As for myself, I am feeling – at peace, content. Beautiful horse; by the way.'

Nemo chose to sit and crossed his long legs, keeping his spine rigid as he gazed out across the tranquil water of the Red Sea. Abigail did likewise, while refusing to turn her head as a sign of acknowledgement.

'Do you propose to summon an army of mutants, to join the party?' she answered, as a clear taunt of her own devising.

'Ah, you suppose I need an army at my side. I thought, this was to be a meeting, conducted cordially, between two like souls, without the need of threats or a show of hostility.'

'You are wondering, why I have asked to meet with you?' Abigail continued, her tone less acerbic.

'It was inevitable,' he answered her, smiling, not that she saw him do so. She would have perceived his conviviality though. 'You are going to ask, that I desist from spreading discord across the globe. Why would I do that? It appears, I have acquired the upper hand, as it was meant to be as it has been written. However, for me to concede, there has to be an offering to appease all I am asked to relinquish. Your father and overlord; he occasionally speaks to me. Does that surprise you? I daresay, he communicates more with the enemy, than he does with his own daughter. Or is it, lover? I'm a little confused. Enlighten me.'

'I very much doubt my existence and how I choose to use my time and resources, is the architect of any confusion you might be feeling. We are not as mortals. Do not abide by their laws. As you know. Did you say, you communicate often with my father? Are you to make me privy to that which is being discussed, and what you hope to gain?'

'Naturally, as the conversation is being conducted cordially, almost intimately, I have no problem sharing my ambitions with my equal,' he replied, and realising he was enjoying the exchange, immensely. 'As I am being asked to desist from spreading chaos, I

221

require a sacrificial lamb as an offering. Let us say; that which can be used as a bargaining chip, should one not adhere to a promise.'

'This sacrificial lamb, you speak of; who or what is it you seek?'

'I'm open to offers,' and he chuckled warmly. 'Although, I have in mind someone who could make me content.'

'State your demands, and I will give my answer,' said Abigail, as she became uncomfortably drawn to the probability, Nemo was to ask that which she was unwilling to concede.

It was a moment Nemo hesitated, a ploy designed to add weight and substance, as he prepared to deliver an ultimatum; knowing in his cruel heart, his adversary would oppose the request he was to make.

'For a guarantee of peace, and for your world to exist in hope I ask, that you submit into my care; your son, or the child of the Chosen One.'

'I can never submit to your terms, with regards to the children. But you already know that.'

'And what then, will your answer be, if your father was to command to make that sacrifice?'

'He would not, knowing you are someone who cannot be trusted to keep their word. Neither the universe, nor I, will ever agree to your preposterous terms. I would willingly, sacrifice myself and position, to protect their future.'

'I thought, perhaps, you might not like my proposal,' he said good-humouredly, and taking an opportunity to study her side profile, wishing to absorb a visual perspective of the one entity who stood between him and immortalising his own father's ambitions and dreams. I do have an alternative proposition you might wish to consider.'

There came an expected pause, even as he was unable to clarify the First Angel's mood or her thoughts. She appeared totally calm, on the surface; assured and confident. He sought a reaction, so that he was to feed on it and exploit it to his advantage.

He became alert to the horse prodding at the sand with a hoof, positioned on his right and slightly to the rear.

'I propose this,' he persevered. 'A union, between myself and the First Angel of light. A union of the spirit and of the soul; of physical flesh. Before you declare your answer, think on this. A unification of two opposing forces of the universe can establish true peace and harmony, that which you seek. Imagine also; the offspring of our combined loins would one day rule, balancing all that is good, against all which is not.'

He flinched perceptibly as his adversary jumped effortlessly and unexpectedly to her feet, her slight frame thrumming with the energy she was absorbing from each of the pyramids.

'Or,' Nemo added nonchalantly, 'You could gift me your horse as a viable peace offering. As it is, I get quite peckish from time to time.'

'You have my answer,' said Abigail sternly, 'Without me having to explain myself in words. I will not consort with the enemy; at any cost.'

'Unlike the Oriental,' Nemo jeered. 'He is one to save his own skin, over those he proposes to care about. Even to love.'

'I know that you have met with Chan Li.'

'I ask this; would you save him? Or will you allow foolish pride to damn his soul to eternal oblivion?'

'It is not pride which governs my heart of purity. Let us just say; I abide by certain principals, those which are governed by faith. All that I have upheld since the moment of my conception.'

'Think of the children,' he said, and carefully, cautiously, getting to his feet to confront his nemesis.

'That's the thing; I am constantly thinking of the children.'

Nemo was caught unawares as Abigail's physical host form faded, and as he was to glance back, saw that she was astride the great white mare whose wings were slowly unfurling away from the bunched muscle at each flank and haunches.

'Do not attempt to follow on my trail,' Abigail warned Nemo.

He nodded, and watched as horse and rider rose, the immense wing span disturbing the currents of the ether, and in a blinding flash of energised light both soared to the heavens and were gone.

Nemo simply smiled and stroked his beard in cogitation.

In his mind, he was thinking; I will tame you, you haughty bitch! I will have you submit to my will as it will be written. Welcome to the new world. My world!

Nemo turned away from the shores of the Red Sea unhappily, knowing in his own heart, he desired retribution for having been disrespected. He would leave an everlasting mark on the world Abigail hoped to preserve, and by doing so, he will be sending a clear message of his intent.

CHAPTER 8

THE OCEANOGRAPHER...

Advancement of all things naturalistic,

The speed in which one evolves,

Is commendable.

Only, if it is achieved in a positive way.

Progress, at times,

Is not always acceptable or

Palatable.

For, there will always exist,

Abominations.

That, which should not be...

Matt Willis was at the helm of the *'Golden Chance,'* a sixty-metre motor yacht equipped throughout with high-spec technology. As an oceanographer with more than twenty-year's experience, Matt Willis believed he'd seen it all, from having personally filmed previously undiscovered species of marine life in the oceans and seas across the planet.

In his late forties, a confirmed bachelor by choice, he was someone who thoroughly enjoyed his work; to the point of obsession. Even now, following the devastating changes to have affected the geographical and geological landscape of the world, he wanted to persevere with his hobby and career, and record everything he was to witness for posterity.

He supposed he was fortunate, having been an only child to wealthy parents, and inheriting a vast fortune when mother and father perished on a skiing holiday in Austria. Matt had enjoyed several family jaunts, but he didn't like to ski. He always said; he might have been blessed in many ways but keeping his balance on steep hazardous ice and snow-packed slopes was not one of his gifts.

Breezing through exams and getting a degree, so he could realise his dream of becoming an oceanographer, was something he could do. Following which, he then had more money than he knew what to do with to exacerbate his dream.

He'd become fascinated with the sea and its secrets, the abundance of aquatic life to exist which most people had never seen. He learned quickly; the sea was a force of nature which could not be tamed. It was to be respected, always.

With patience and diligence, came rewards. He'd had to endure extreme and hazardous conditions over the years, but the fact he'd acquired knowledge, maintained dignity, and was a professional, made him a survivor.

He had been on The Golden Chance when the first climactic upheaval struck without too much warning, as to the severity one should expect. The dysfunctional climate changes had only been the beginning. Then came eruptions and earthquakes, causing the Earth to tilt. Matt was witness to the birth of a tsunami which defied belief;

that, which destroyed most of the Western seaboard of the United States of America.

It took time for Matt to overcome the shock of having witnessed the destruction of a huge swath of those states which had hugged the Western shores. They were memories which would stay with him indefinitely, he concluded. He could be thankful, he no longer suffered nightmares; not like before.

The first time Matt ventured onto dry land following the floods, it was to gather vital provisions and glean as much information as he could. All he witnessed, was enough to establish life was going to be slow to recover. The sea continued to beckon him, as it was now his permanent home.

The second occasion he returned to replenish waning supplies, he moored The Golden Chance close to what was once a cattle ranch, and which had been reduced to a ramshackle feature of the new coastline. After four days of scavenging, Matt came across the first signs of human and animal life he'd seen since the aftermath of the apocalypse, and the meeting with other folk didn't go as he'd hoped it might.

Naturally, any survivors would be desperate lost souls, and those he met were totally mistrusting of everyone. If there was something to be learned from the debacle and being given a second chance, people were not seeing it.

It was fortunate, Matt knew how to defend himself, even without firearms. He always carried a knife on shore, he never once expected to have to use it against his fellow man, after everything they had faced.

Wanting only to get back to his boat and head out to sea again, he was to face further obstacles in the manner of hostile natives, intent on stealing what was not theirs to take, and at any cost it would appear.

Two young men were attempting to steal his boat, not that they possessed the knowledge to get the craft started without the key, and Matt doubted either of them had ever driven a boat the size of The Golden Chance or knew how to operate its advanced navigational equipment.

Matt confronted them before they could damage anything, the situation turning hostile the moment the two young men realised Matt was the owner and their ticket to escape. There was no reasoning, not with two desperate individuals, who cared only about themselves and their own continued survival. Matt was outnumbered two to one, not that he saw it as a concern. As in the way he easily dispatched of them, and in a moment of angry delirium, pitched both bodies over the side.

No point reporting the incident as he doubted the existence of a functioning police force in any of the Western States.

Matt felt he should have been horrified by what he had done, as both men had suffered near-fatal wounds from his knife, and in the fact that he tossed them overboard and watched them slowly drown, without compunction or remorse. He was defending himself, protecting the boat and the recorded history stored as archives, and upholding his honour and existence from predators such as the two desperate men. It could have all been managed differently; he'd been thinking, had they a mind to be reasonable and shown courtesy.

Matt knew he would remain on his own, as the world was still at war; with itself and the people in it.

On the third occasion he dropped anchor and went ashore he was to be greeted by two women of indeterminate age, but striking of appearance, on his return to the Golden Chance. They stood side by side on the coarse rubble leading down to the water's edge, light robes flapping suggestively in a heightening breeze.

They waited for him to approach, and it even had him wondering if danger could be cloaked in the guise of sexy and tranquillity. There was something enchanting and soothing in the way they posed and studied him from afar. They didn't appear to be afraid of him, so Matt was able to relax, before initiating an exchange of greetings.

Something else which had Matt mesmerised was in the way their skin seemed to glow and radiate energy in subtle shifting waves. It was intoxicating and a lure. He was drawn to their eyes, as both women had irises the colour of deepest emerald, and they held him transfixed as the one on the left, whose long hair was a shade darker in brown than the other, was the first to speak.

She raised an arm and indicated an easterly direction, to where a large pyramid pointed to the sky in the distance. Until that moment, Matt was not familiar with the State of Arizona, but he never believed it boasted such a monument, and when he gave it further observation saw that the structure was composed of something dull and metallic and not necessarily of quarried stone.

It looked extra-terrestrial; was all he could think.

He was instructed to go there and meet with someone who would give him an insight into the future. Matt didn't want to leave the boat, and it was a considerable distance he would have to cover to reach the monument.

The thing is he felt compelled to go, not that he understood why.

When he turned his gaze back, he was further shocked, as he became a witness to the two women fading into insignificance, until nothing remained of them.

He believed, for a moment, he'd imagined them, the meeting and the short exchange. He even supposed the horrors he'd encountered and killing two men had made him a little crazy. Yet the pull on his senses to make the journey across a wilderness of devastation and desert grew stronger and dominated all reason.

229

Like he was given no choice.

No one would believe him, even if he had someone sharing his life and had not witnessed the exchange for themselves. He'd considered the imposing black pyramid in the distance might be an alien craft, so in all probability, the two women he'd met were extra-terrestrials. How else was he to explain how two people could miraculously disappear in plain view?

As if in a stupor, Matt stored away the provisions he'd collected, and it would have been an easy task, to fire up the engines and head out to sea where all he perceived was normality, whereas on land, there was so much he failed to understand.

So, it came as a surprise to him he should waken from a stupor, not to find himself on the deck of The Golden Chance, but steadily approaching the great black behemoth. How he'd achieved this feat went beyond his imagination, as with the two women on the shore. He wasn't fatigued, or even fearful. He felt more energised than at any other time.

Once he reached the designated site he was instructed to visit, Matt was at a loss, as to what he was meant to do. The woman with the darker hair had said he would meet with someone who would convey an insight into the future. *Whatever that meant.*

What surprised Matt further was witnessing the gathering of over one hundred survivors who had made the trek: men, women, and children of all ages. The atmosphere around the base of the pyramid where all appeared to be awaiting a sign or instruction, was convivial and friendly. There was an expectancy on the faces he observed, of hope, and there was laughter. And it was something beautiful, to Matt's way of thinking, because for a time he'd wondered if the world had forgotten how to laugh.

What didn't surprise Matt, was the numbers who had suffered quite debilitating injuries he assumed was a result of the earthquakes and falling debris. How they had managed to cross a devastated landscape and a desert, however, defied belief. It shouldn't have been feasible, or even necessary. Yet these people believed the pyramid was the source of hope, and the answers they were seeking, would be given to them.

Faith and determination had brought them to the pyramid, and everyone believed they were to be rewarded.

Matt joined the queue and found it easy to converse with those nearest to him. In time, Matt was to witness further miracles. As the line of people moved towards a man who stood in the distance where one edge of the pyramid sloped to the sand, Matt became aware of an incredible energy emanating off the smooth dull surface. *It had him wondering if it was the spaceship's engines or turbines which had been activated, and all the survivors were to be taken off into space.*

His aspirations were outlandish, as nothing sinister was going to happen to the 'happy folk' who had made the laborious trek to Arizona.

Matt felt only a moment's concern when a gaggle of cries went up, but it wasn't out of fear or harm. Matt was witness to people becoming healed as they passed along the base of the pyramid.

The people had a reason to laugh, for sure, and Matt had never felt happier. As now, he was a believer, in that there was hope for the new world.

As he approached the head of the line, Matt observed the man presiding over the situation he found himself a part of. He watched people skipping away from having met with the stranger, like he was the Messiah resurrected, as foretold in the Bible, and come to save the world.

The nearer he got, Matt saw that every person was to receive a gift; that of hope and given concise instruction on where to go and what they should do.

231

He already knew the man's name as Alexander when it was his turn to confront the ethereal person making miracles happen.

With Matt, the stranger appeared to treat him differently, in that he hesitated briefly even as Matt felt the man probing around his thoughts and easing a path deeper into his mind.

He wondered, if the man who was obviously telepathic, would judge him for what he had done. Would the stranger know Matt was given no choice?

Alexander spoke, not in verbal tones, but within Matt's mind. Matt was put at ease, and when Alexander passed him a quartz crystal for his personal well-being, Alexander gave an explanation. He was to be given one more possession, and Alexander moved to the side, stooped, and retrieved a large metallic box which was identical in composition as that of the pyramid. Alexander handed the chest to Matt with no effort whatsoever. It could have been an empty box, Matt was thinking.

It was only when Matt went to retrieve it, he knew differently in an instant, as the sheer weight of the contents almost drove him to his knees. Yet one more miracle was to transpire, as the box suddenly became completely weightless.

'I have given you the means to propel your craft and the equipment on the boat, as you have a part to play in the future. Inside is a larger crystal and a vital source of energy for when the liquid fuel and batteries run out. This gift is from the universe, and others like this one, are the future of mankind. We know of your research and its importance. Go, with faith, Matt Willis, and allow the crystals to guide and protect you.'

Alexander smiled and nodded, and it was a sign Matt was dismissed, as the ethereal stranger turned his attention to the next in line.

Matt felt distinctly light-headed, even joyous as he began the long trek back to shore.

He had been given a purpose.

He was to play a vital role in helping mankind survive, just from his research.

He failed to understood how, or who to show his findings to, supposing he was to make a life-changing discovery. Would he recognise it as such?

Matt felt sure he would. He'd been granted faith and he should employ that faith in the magic crystals he'd been given. He even believed for a moment he was on a mission, and he supposed he was.

Killing two desperate men in self-defence was forgotten. He would always remember the two women and Alexander.

And the Arizona pyramid would not be the only mysterious form he would encounter.

CHAPTER 9

BENEATH...

The ocean is a world beneath,

Separate from the one above.

Life underwater

Has its own laws.

It evolves differently.

It is world, untouched,

By all that has happened.

It thrives.

It evolves.

And where there is beauty,

There is ugliness.

Both, of which,

Are to be admired,

Respected,

And feared...

Four years had elapsed, and a tanned Matt Willis was enjoying some leisure time on the sundeck of his motor yacht, The Golden Chance.

It had become a lifestyle enriched with evolving optimism, and it was one he had come to fervently embrace. He had no one to share his experiences with, but he kept files of all his research, and backed them up on a hard drive.

The only occasions he returned to dry land was to re-stock supplies. No matter it had been difficult at the beginning, isolated communities, and even large townships, had developed rapidly. Everyone he met in that time was of a friendly disposition, and were eager to share their home grown produce, fresh water, and even home-distilled spirits.

The new world was growing and developing. The survivors of 'world's end' were imbued with enthusiastic hope and the same optimism Matt Willis was able to embrace.

Despite the wondrous community spirit to be enjoyed on land, Matt's heart was with the sea and the magical world which existed beneath the surface.

The giant crystal he'd been given by the ethereal stranger, Alexandra, had replaced fuel to power the boat and equipment on board, as it was explained to him after his visit to the Arizona pyramid.

With the crystal generating mystical power, there was no need for a satellite feed or internet facilities. He kept abreast of news around the states of America, and occasionally there were reports on other countries around the world, and this courtesy of a CB radio.

Matt had heard mention crystal energy was capable of operating smart and I-phones. Matt didn't possess a phone, as for so long, he had no one he needed to call. Any communications in the past, were done via email.

He was amazed a world could operate without a currency, as such, as there had always existed a means for bartering and trade. In the new world, it was apparent, people used kindness as a currency and everyone shared whatever they had with others. Matt hoped it would last. Somehow, he didn't think it would.

Rumour had it, there existed governing bodies across a few states, and those in charge were primarily responsible in assisting growth and prosperity, and miraculously not inveigling themselves in political wranglings. There were no democrats, republicans, or communists. All worked and served together, for the common good of all.

As he was lounging and enjoying the erotic kiss of a warm sun on his exposed skin and becoming soporific under the spell of circling gulls and their incessant squawking, he was alert suddenly to a distinctive shift in the air currents, causing his flesh to be pulled taut.

He opened his eyes and saw a young woman in jeans and a tee-shirt, observing him from the prow of the boat, almost nonchalantly it seemed.

Matt merely raised an eyebrow and smiled, as his brain endeavoured to compute how it was possible for the young woman to be on the boat. He dismissed the notion she was someone who had stowed during his latent period on land, sensing the person was so much more.

Her presence and overall demeanour reminded him of the two women he'd engaged with, as they prompted him to visit the pyramid and meet with Alexander.

LEGACY OF ANGELS

Despite the young woman's casual attire, Matt felt the power she exuded, even at distance. She was able to placate him as he watched her incredibly float across the polished deck to his position.

'Hey, miss,' he called out, and chuckled, but not from anxiety. 'Thought I'd seen it all these past few years, but it seems the miracles of life just keep piling up. It's my understanding, the mysteries of the universe are revealing themselves. I imagine, historians the world over are having a field-day, supposing anyone with a discerning intellect survived. I'm Matt; Matt Willis. Pleased I am to make your acquaintance.'

Abigail paused, her luminescent aura fluctuating, as she sent out a peripheral scan.

'I am Abigail. You may call me Abby. I am someone you need not fear.'

'I sense that about you, in that you're basically a decent person who means no harm. I'm not a stupid person and it's my belief you are perhaps other than mortal. I state this, based on my recent experiences. So, tell me Abby, how does your kind achieve the feats I have been witness to; like levitating, and floating to get from one place to another. One more thing; where did you come from? You didn't stow away; I think I would have known.'

'It's not important, where I have come from, or as to what we are,' she answered in warm tones to appease his growing curiosity, and to lessen his confusion. 'I am, however, a celestial entity and one of many. You have met with others; I am aware of. Our kind, a few of us, have existed since the dawn of time and were sent by the universe to assist mankind and Mother Earth in evolving beyond the tragic events to have decimated your planet and most of its population.'

'Okay,' said Matt, and leaning forward, as he became at a loss for words, if only briefly. He thought to offer the beautiful stranger a beverage, as it would be courteous to do so, and would prove to the young woman his intentions were honourable.

That was the moment she spoke within his mind, and he became momentarily flustered. She let him know in jocular tones, this was not a social visit.

Matt thought about getting off the padded sunbed, that was, until he felt a light pressure keeping him from rising.

'Why are you here on the deck of The Golden Chance?' he asked doggedly. 'I imagine celestials, as you call yourself, are therefore governed by purpose, if not to socialise. Is it the crystal generating power to the boat and equipment? Dear God: have you come to reclaim it? Was it something on loan?'

'Relax, my lovely. I have not come for the crystal. I am here, however, having acquired knowledge you are committed to meticulous research of our undersea world. I would like to peruse your archives of recent months, specifically. That is, if you don't mind.'

Matt gave a haughty laugh and slapped his thigh. 'I daresay, I don't have a choice. But as you asked so politely, and you seem enthusiastic, I would love to take you on a visual tour of a separate world beneath the sea. There's so much going on down there, which is, astounding and, baffling. It's my belief, the footage I'm about to reveal is your true reason for being here. May I please stand?'

Matt realised he was already standing, and he hadn't even known.

'If you follow me below deck, I'll get everything set up for you.'

Abigail nodded and allowed Matt to lead the way. Stepping into the galley, five steps descended into another level, which boasted state of the art equipment stretching along a solid surface on both sides. The hull space had been fitted with reinforced Perspex panels, and with a simple flick of a switch, Matt proudly activated banks of lights around the framework, illuminating a wide area and penetrating at a considerable depth. At either end were set cameras fitted with multiple lenses and infrared.

'Impressive,' said Abigail, using her voice on this occasion.

'The footage I'd like to show you,' he said eagerly, and he crouched to point off toward the stern, where a motorised mini-submarine shaped vessel was secured to two pincer clamps. 'That's my little baby that does most of the hard work. I can steer it via remote control. Hey; don't suppose you ever got to see the movie; 'The Abyss'? I have the equivalent to Little Geek, somewhat upgraded though, as there is no appendage attaching it to the boat. I call my baby; 'Cyclops.' Before the crystal was used to power the vessel, I could perhaps get up to two hours live feed. Now, is different, as the cameras and powerful searchlights on Cyclops can operate indefinitely. Just one of those miracles I was explaining about earlier.'

Her paused, just to get a sense of whether Abigail was genuinely motivated by his passion or was simply humouring him.

'Not meaning to get too technical, but Cyclops is fitted with one circumnavigating camera with six 360-degree rotational lenses. Fore and aft are housed search lights like the ones on the hull of The Golden Chance, and can throw out two multi-directional beams, both capable of penetrating to a length and depth of more than one hundred metres. Additional to the lights, are the high-density microphones. Extremely sensitive. Amazing as any footage comes with its own specific soundtrack. I have sonar, radar, and can record temperature readings, take measurements. So much more. Hey; I hope I'm not boring you. It's just that; I don't get an opportunity to share my work, passion if you like, with anyone. I've always been extremely fortunate, to be able to follow my dream; never more so, than now. With the crystal producing unbelievable energy,

239

everything operates without a glitch, is faster, quieter, and daresay; eco-friendly. But you'd know all about that; wouldn't you?'

He steered Abigail to a central area of the workspace along the port side, where an 80 -inch flat screen monitor was affixed to the panelled wall.

'Another thing, with this you will be able to review my studies in 3-dimensional splendour. Trust me, you'll be thinking you're a mermaid swimming around reef and coral and shoals of fish. Not just your normal, everyday fish.'

He gave a nervous chuckle and cleared his throat. Despite his excitement, he was in awe of his visitor, and wondering how a celestial would react to the film he was to relay to her.

'It's not only marine life I keep archives of. As you're aware, so much of the Eastern seaboard was swallowed by the ocean when the tsunami's struck. Thousands of miles of cities in ruins, lying in a watery grave, containing millions of ghosts, doesn't make easy viewing. I record it anyway, as I believe it's important a record exists, lest we forget.'

His guest was naturally and obviously becoming impatient, and when she raised a hand, the monitor blinked into life, and all the other panels of equipment lit-up or purred into action.

'You keep on impressing me, I'm going to think you're flirting with me,' and he added, 'Just kidding. Don't suppose celestials comingle with us mere mortals.'

'I'm not interested in the little *'fishes,'* Abigail remarked, and ignoring Matt's philandering comment. 'I am, however, intrigued by the evolving nature of a certain species of aquatic animal.'

'There are a few quite distinctive areas of marine evolving. I'll show you. It's not only about size you know, as a lot of marine life are exhibiting extreme behavioural patterns. Some passive examples have suddenly resorted to aggressive overload. There are several changing influences to consider. As an example; a few species have acquired movement and speed which simply, defies an immediate explanation. While others have combined these attributes with undeniable intelligence. You must understand, I have been studying ocean life and their habitats for more than twenty-years; and what I'm trying to say is, the program of evolving or mutating, has only begun in recent years. It is the rapid rate of it occurring which confounds me.'

He paused, to allow Abigail an opportunity to digest his words, before continuing his engrossing and exciting tirade.

'I imagine, your interest is in one particular species, and I bet I know what that is.'

'Jellyfish,' said Abigail patiently.'

'I knew it! Yes! Just one moment, while I access the supporting digital file.'

Abigail could easily have engineered access to the files, yet refrained doing so, so as not to have her host disgruntled or taking a defensive stance.

'I have located various schools, or shoals, of four separate species. *Covidarian Invertebrates.* The primary species is that of *Cubozoa Crideria,* generally known as *Medusazoa.* The box jellyfish. Now, consider this; the hood of the box jellyfish is predominantly twelve inches, with stalks or tentacles – the Pedalium's – numbering around eighty to an individual with a growth of ten metres. Multiply that by ten, upward of twenty, and you get an extreme example of rapid evolving, or mutating. Smaller in size, are the *Chirosalmus Quadrigatus, Alatina Alata,* which is perhaps the only species supposedly indigenous to the Pacific. And then there's the *Caruilia Barnesi.*

LEGACY OF ANGELS

The primary specimen is the *Chironex Flickeri;* or Sea Wasp. It has a faint blueish tinge, but at times, can appear invisible. Are you ready for the show? One specimen I forgot to mention, is the Pacific Man O War, not dissimilar to its counterpart, the Portuguese Man O War, a *Physalia Physalis.* I have recorded footage of these creatures in immense groups, but they lack the same propulsion exhibited by other species. As you examine the footage, I will give a rough explanation as to how these creatures have developed and changed in a truly short time.'

Abigail composed herself as the screen leapt into vivid technicolour imagery. Matt was not boasting, when he intonated one could be forgiven for thinking they were swimming in the mysterious and magical depths beneath the sea.

Matt did some tweaking on the timescale of the projected recording, to arrive at the first of several episodic timeframes he was eager to share with the celestial visitor at his side.

'What we have here, is my first discovery,' he stated, while becoming as engrossed as his guest was, no matter he'd lived this new life beneath the ocean's surface numerous times. It continued to fascinate him. He indicated with a finger, not that it was necessary to do so. 'What you are witnessing, is a group of twenty-two *Alatina Alata or Carybdea Alata,* a species normally indigenous to the Pacific and especially around Hawaii. I make mention of the fact, as there is nothing remotely normal in the image, as these evolving monsters measure upward of sixty-five feet, from head to the base of each Pedalium.'

Abigail absorbed everything; from the formidable size of each of the jellyfish, and in the way they collectively propelled themselves at a rapid rate of knots; most notably, against the flow of the current. She gave nothing away in her expression or the shimmer in her pupils, as to her thoughts, and what this discovery meant to the existing population of the world.

'I should warn you,' said Matt. 'Not all of what you are to see, will make for pleasant viewing.'

Abigail remained passively unresponsive, even as she became witness to a predatory instinct in the swarming group of giant jellyfish as they circled a school of porpoise, almost as if they were herding them, moments before they attacked as a collective unit.

Considering her love for all things living, Abigail raised her hand and skipped to another file.

'Awesome technique,' Matt interpolated good-humouredly, while nervously appraising the mysterious young woman beside him. The energy of her aura palpated his skin, and the sensation thrilled and enthralled him.

'What you are about to witness in this footage,' he added, 'Is something even more momentous on the face of everything you have seen so far. In recent months, I took The Golden Chance, to what remains of the island of Hawaii. The devastation; well, it's heart-breaking. I suppose, it's fair to say, I've become anaesthetized to all the horrors subjected to the planet and its population. The loss of life is unprecedented, along with the ruination of great cities. Only the Southern fringes of Hawaii remain. The peaks of the volcanoes; Kilauea and Mauna Loa, are seen jutting out of the ocean, as a reminder of the destructive part they played, as with the tsunami and quakes. The winds and the storms, baking temperatures. I was filming the lost world, now submerged, when I happened upon some extraordinary activity.'

He paused, only to brush a hand through his long hair and sweep it back, and to give himself a moment to compose himself.

'Predominantly, the images you are about to see, depict an area at the base of Kilauea.'

Matt drifted away on a sea of memories, and let his celestial visitor arrive at her own conclusions, having already watched the archive footage countless times.

Cyclops had been retrieving harrowing footage of a desolate grave beneath the surface of the Pacific, yet Abigail's fascination was on the numerous creatures who were some distance from the approaching vessel.

To Abigail's way of thinking, Matt would have been unaware he was filming the new wave of evil threatening the planet. What surprised Abigail was in the manner these monsters treated the intrusive machine arriving in their presence. The jellyfish, she supposed, might have reacted differently to the light, the vibrations and the crystal energy propelling the craft; had they not been single-minded and industrious in what they were doing.

As Cyclops was remotely steered closer, Abigail was awarded with a clear insight into the physical appearance and sheer enormity of the creatures. They were at least three times the size of the specimen she'd received at the pyramid on her estate.

They were beautiful, majestic, and grotesque all at the same time.

'It began,' said Matt, and interrupting the flow of her thoughts as he puffed out his cheeks, 'with twenty of the gigantic beasts, working in pairs it seems, excavating an area at the base of the volcano. After ten minutes or so, the next two Sea Wasps took the place of the pair in front and proceeded to remove great chunks of lava rock. Those Pedalium's of theirs can appear gangly and ungainly, yet in their suppleness lies extraordinary strength. They are quite capable of carrying loads hundreds of times their own body weight. I already explained, some species of aquatic animal has acquired a pronounced intelligence. *Chironex Flickeri* have it in abundance. It's feasible, the creatures have learned to communicate using electrical impulses or vibrations caused by the sporadic fluctuation of the velarium. I believe they have adapted an ethereal technology, not dissimilar to that which you celestials employ; that of telepathy. Just can't prove it; not yet, anyway.'

Matt noticed the avid luminosity in her eyes of rustic hazel, and in the way static enlivened the long trails of her light brown hair. The blue highlights on one side, seemed to have acquired a density and brightness.

'Are you aware,' he continued, 'This species has eyes? Not just the one set. Each has retinas, corneas, and lenses, set in clusters called Rhopalia. For every individual, they possess a total of twenty-four eyes, giving the creatures an ocelli advanced sensory system. I thought, initially, they would have been intrigued by Cyclops, even to attack it; but as you can see, they barely give Cyclops any consideration. Most probably, as it's a machine and not a warm-blooded entity. Just maybe, the energy field created by the crystal serves to repel them. Something else I'm working on.'

Abigail refused to offer an explanation, even as she was the one with the answers, and continued to study the industrious file of jellyfish diligently removing rocks from the base of the volcano. Abigail knew why, and what they were seeking. She hoped to understand the motivation driving them, at the same time, considering the likelihood the creatures were receiving signals from the universe, or a separate entity.

'The cameras continued to film,' said Matt, who could never tire of watching the miracle of nature unfolding on the screen, 'despite normally having a limited time to operate. Which, is a blessing of a kind, as the best is yet to come.'

Abigail was next to witness the mutant jellyfish emerging from a tunnel they had created in a short time, clutching clusters of the smoky quartz crystals in their scores of tentacles, propelling themselves away as others took their place to retrieve their horde.

'I would have liked to have followed the retreating jellyfish, just to know what they intended with their haul, or where they were going with it,' remarked Matt. 'Thing is; I had no idea how far they intended travelling, or even if Cyclops could keep up with them.'

Abigail moved from the screen to the viewing platform on the hull, where the lights around the perimeter appeared to dim momentarily. By exerting her will and projecting her inimitable powers, the beams of light strengthened and reached a wider area and greater depth.

As she'd expected, several of the giant jellyfish had approached, naturally inquisitive; and she suspected, were lured by her presence alone. The monsters kept to a respectful distance.

Matt stepped up to join her and gave an audible gasp of nervous wonderment.

'Shit! But this is a first. Until now, they've left me alone.'

Abigail considered telling him she was the reason and decided against it.

'You need not fear them,' she said quietly, 'the crystal is your protection. I must leave now, Matt. I would just like to say thank you, for your hospitality, and for sharing your amazing research with me. Take my advice; although you are quite safe, be always wary. Should the energy of the crystal fluctuate and appear not to have the strength it once possessed, head for the mainland instantly. While I can understand your fascination, and wish to persevere with your work, these predatory creatures surpass anything you have ever studied. Stay safe, Matt Willis. These monsters are evil incarnate, and should they perceive you as a threat, they will attack. Watch for signs. Study the crystal carefully, and if the jellyfish continue to remain inquisitive, leave for shore anyway.'

'Will they chase the boat if I head inland? You said, the crystal is my protection.'

'And as we have determined, this species has acquired a superior intelligence. It is conceivable, their bodies are imbued with electricity derived from a source of dark energy and could arguably drain the source of your crystal. Should that happen, you will be dead in the water, and helpless.'

'Wonderful. What you're saying, is that there are no guarantees the crystal can protect me against a concerted assault from these monsters?'

'There are factors which are an unknown quantity, at this moment in time. I can tell, just from your expression, I have made you fearful. That is not a bad thing, lovely. As another suggestion, why don't you take a break now and head to shore for an indeterminate time. You've earned it.'

'I might. Before you leave, I suppose, you already know what those monsters were excavating out of the tunnel? I did an analysis on the objects they were carrying away. My findings state they were making off with quartz crystal, not dissimilar to the example operating the yacht's propulsion and powering all the equipment.'

Abigail stroked his cheek affectionately to placate him. 'However, there is a difference. The ones in your possession are blessed with positive energy from the universe, while the specimens the jellyfish seek are imbued with dark matter; that which almost devastated the planet. It is for me and those of my kind to prevent dark energy from becoming all-powerful.'

'Oh, shit! I think you're trying to say; if you fail, it's going to happen all over again.'

'Not if I have a say in it,' she said; and with that, her physical form faded away and was gone.

CHAPTER 10

STONEHENGE...

At times,

When you can't control what's happening,

Challenge yourself,

By controlling how you react to it...

Scientologists and historians are given the auspicious task of seeking a means to unlock the mysteries of the past and the secrets of the universe. It has been learned over centuries, that an advanced technology once existed the world over. Other than speculation, supposition, and theorising, no one can say for certain why this supreme technology became suddenly lost and buried thousands of years ago.

LEGACY OF ANGELS

It has been suggested that entire civilisations and species of animal disappeared mysteriously, at a time when the geographical landscape underwent a cataclysmic change. Despite which, natural and unnatural features survived as a reminder.

The scientists and historians, the archaeologists, once chipped away at the fabric of each new and unexplained discovery; all theories never quite reaching a definitive answer.

As with ancient crystals, the answer remained elusive for a reason. Some things in creation had to stay a fortified secret; until the present time, when knowledge of the secrets was key to either the planet surviving, or its destruction.

The power generated by pyramids has been reactivated, providing a true source of energy, that which is governed and maintained by the universe. A legacy of symbols and pictograms carved into stone, etched on scrolls and painted on walls, even depicted in paintings and sculptures, intimated at the truth masquerading as mystery. These symbols and deities are the voice of a past long forgotten. Despite all the quakes and floods, landmarks remain which can only be viewed from an aerial position, and each serve as a message from the universe and early forms of celestial visitors.

Across the globe, ancient stone circles have instigated debates, as to their true purpose, how they came to be, and location in regard to strategic points in the galaxy of stars.

It is widely known; the stone monuments generate a source of energy; an electro-magnetic field. It's understanding them, which has proved elusive, as astronomers and historians can only resort to supposition, despite extensive research.

One such mystical circle of ancient megaliths, standing erect and proud on the plains around Salisbury in the United Kingdom, had drawn the First Angel Abigail, to visit.

She appeared from within a nucleus of brilliant golden light astride Free Spirit, the mare retracting her wings the moment her hooves set down on the hard sod around Stone Henge.

Gone, were the signs and indicators for the public to use. Since the quakes, the ancient site received few visitors, despite its calming ambience and tranquil beauty.

Abigail swung a leg to the side and dropped to the grass; her aura touched and kissed by the imposing shadow cast by the monument she confronted. As instructed, Free Spirit walked a wide circle around Stone Henge, planting the seeds of spiritual energy to create a gilded cage.

Abigail was using Free Spirit to deflect her own signature from the universe.

As with many of the existing stone circles, Abigail knew the origins of each, as they were a portal to the universe and beyond, where they were capable of breaching one to gain entry to another galaxy.

The energy garnered from the stones could be used to channel a precise path through dark matter and light energy.

Abigail saw this as a typical 'no man's land', a reference to those neutral areas separating opposing armies in trench warfare. These portals, rarely used in modern times, acted as a form of mediator. Only a limited number of celestials had the inaugural power to stimulate the universal vortex.

Abigail's purpose for visiting Stone Henge was to renege on the edict created by the opposing universal factions, and mastermind a unity of souls. She was set to travel a course dividing those conflicting energies in outer space, into what is generically known as a 'wormhole', a gateway to a parallel universe. Abigail hoped the message she meant to relay would be received, more specifically, to have her call reciprocated.

LEGACY OF ANGELS

Going against the edict of her father would undeniably have repercussions. She believed her father was spiting her, knowing she had consorted with another celestial entity. To avoid having her father speculate she was plotting without his permission and guidance, had to be conducted with precision.

It was not only her father and ruling overlord she was up against. There was his opposite, and greatest Nemesis. The enemy would not take kindly to all Abigail proposed to instigate.

Free Spirit continued to monotonously trek a wide circumference, with the purpose of laying down a deflective shield of protection, as Abigail approached the narrow arch between two of the upright stones. She removed her clothes and left them in a folded pile at the base of one.

She stepped naked within the circle and became instantly assailed with the reawakened energy drawn from a galactic source. She felt its ancient heritage, and knew to respect its exultant power, as she willed herself to embrace it wholly.

With hands crossed against her chest, Abigail closed her eyes, and channelled her own energy in a sequence of vibrations specifying a unique code. There came an intense auric illumination from a centrifugal point, enveloping Abigail in a spiritual vice, whereupon her soul was briskly sucked from the physical host body.

Free Spirit looked up briefly and continued to draw the elemental circle. Free Spirit understood his mistress had departed temporarily on a hazardous voyage, yet remained content and focussed, and driven by faith and love.

Abigail endured the intensity of electro-magnetic pressure as her soul became siphoned into a turbulent vortex. She concentrated her efforts on one set of sequential signals, having to temper her excitement and maintain composure. To have the link she'd established severed, could have devastating consequences, in that she might not be granted another opportunity.

LEGACY OF ANGELS

The signature she was seeking telegraphed a response, and Abigail's soul lit up.

Her propulsion was so rapid, there was no visual spectrum to enjoy, until the moment the signal she was approaching peaked, and Abigail had to concentrate on restraining the velocity of travel until her soul drifted to a lambent glide.

The signals telegraphed to her spiritual mind were stronger and explicit, and then she saw the orb of light approaching against a backdrop of a plethora of stars. The orb slowed, crept closer, and merged; and within their spiritual minds they could have been entwined in a physical union.

'*Sister!*' Abigail relayed with vivid intonations expounding joy.

'*Darling Abby; you found me.*' Seraphina answered. '*I knew you would.*'

'*I need you, my lovely. I would have you, once again, at my side.*'

'*It will not be easy.*'

'*I know; but it can be done. And I will guide you.*'

'*Genesis. . .*'

'*It's okay, sweet Sera. I know all of which my father is capable of. His spite is no different, as displayed by the enemy you defeated.*'

'*It has returned; has it not?*' Seraphina asked.

'*Evil has found a doorway into the mortal world, once again. My father, I presume, is the arbitrary keyholder who opened the door. He has his reasons.*'

'*We have so much to speak of. I must ask; how is my son, Daniel?*'

'*He is a wonder; just like his mother.*'

The light of their combined energy flared.

'*I have to leave now,*' Abigail telegraphed with a measure of remorse. '*You will know the path you are meant to follow when it is revealed to you. Sera, darling, what of the others you absorbed into your soul; Michael, your parents, the other ancients who sacrificed themselves, so that your powers could repel the Dark Lord?*'

'*They are gone,*' said Seraphina solemnly. '*We became separated.*'

'*I will give you a sequence of codes. Use them and recall the father of your son. If fortune favours us, you might locate your parents and the others. I need you, lovely. The children of the world need you.*'

'*Sweet Abby, soul sister; my heart. I am ready.*'

CHAPTER 11

UNCERTAIN FUTURE...

There is sadness in foreseeing,

Events unfolding,

Which will inevitably,

Decide the fate of mankind,

Once again.

For better, or worse

Nothing in life is constant,

Or definite...

Cole and Zanula were pulled along channels and highways, linked to a specific universal code assigned to them, and when eventually they materialised in physical form, it was not at a location they expected to be.

Zanula staggered and would have slumped to the hard unyielding sod beneath their feet, had Cole not anticipated the signs and stooped to catch her in his arms. He cradled her head to his bare chest where his shirt was open to the waist and flapping in a snappy breeze, like gull wings.

'Honey, what is it?' he asked, while ignoring the vista of panoramic fields all around.

'I wanted to tell you,' Zanula answered, smiling, despite the tear blossoms clinging precariously to long, dark lashes. 'Before we set out on our journey, I began receiving familiar signals. I am with child again, my handsome man.'

'Are you certain? I mean; how is it, I have not received the signals, as I did with our son Luka?'

He projected an inward scan, anyway, seeking proof Zanula was not imagining the pregnancy.

'I thought; had always believed, celestials were limited to the one child, as decreed by universal law,' and at that moment, Cole became witness to a heartbeat and delicate threads of energy emanating from within her womb. The foetus had no recognisable definition, as he suspected it was yet too early.

'I wanted it to remain a secret, and not let the news become a distraction on our journey,' she explained, both miserable and happy at the same time.

Cole lifted her with ease, and kissed her with passion, had her moaning against his mouth. He lowered her to the grass and cradled her face with both hands.

'I'm speechless,' he admitted. 'This news is the best, despite all the shit going down in the world.'

He noticed how she'd become distracted and was peering over his shoulder.

'Where are we, exactly? I thought; we were to be reunited with our son.'

'I don't know, in all honesty. But I can tell you this, an energy approaches. I believe it to be benign, but let's not take any chances. Stay alert, baby. Damn, but I'm going to be a daddy again!'

A shimmering light, ovate in form, heralded the arrival of another celestial a short distance from their position. It acquired form quickly, and Cole flashed Zanula a huge sigh of relief.

Abigail approached, tentatively it seemed, for she was another using a psychic scan on her visitors.

Cole saw the way in which she was scrutinising his wife and smiled inwardly. Abigail would know of Zanula's delicate condition, he was thinking. Abigail knew everything.

'Why are we to meet here in a field?' Zanula asked, without preamble. 'Where is our son?'

'Your son is quite safe,' Abigail answered sparingly. 'He is to be brought to you.'

'I thought…' said Cole, and the question tapered away. 'It doesn't matter.'

Abigail had however perceived the question he was to ask. 'I cannot allow visitors to the estate; it is a matter of self-preservation. Its location is protected from the one who means to engage with me. I must prepare for a confrontation, as it is inevitable. The evil sorcerer will come for me.'

'You are perhaps aware then, many of the protected sites around the crystals, have been compromised,' Cole added. 'We have not investigated all; have acquired proof the source of evil has become a rampant force across the planet.'

'Yes, I am aware of the spread of dark energy, as many beautiful souls have had their light extinguished.'

'How do we stop the infection spreading and defeat it?'

'I will know; in due course,' said Abigail, without submitting details she was unable to fully substantiate.

Cole noticed how she was entirely focussed on Zanula, and it unsettled him. There was a lack of warmth in her smile, her eyes, or in her posture.

'What happened in Abu Dhabi?' she further enquired.

'The pyramid,' offered Cole, 'was under siege when we arrived, the structure having suffered damage. Thing is Abby; I fail to understand how this can happen. When we approached the pyramid, it became obvious great slabs of stone had been removed to create a tunnel entrance. It would have taken a monumental feat of engineering to have achieved this. The source of energy the pyramid was protecting had been removed. We discovered this when we ventured inside, so that we had confirmation. It was while we were navigating the perfectly crafted tunnel complex which went deep underground, that we came face to face with evil; as it was in Rome, Moscow, and Oslo.'

'Thank the universe, you were able to overcome adversity at these times.' Abigail said, while reaching up to remove the braids from Zanula's downturned gaze. 'My lovely; you can tell me, if something is troubling you.'

'I fear for my son, and the child growing in my womb,' Zanula responded morosely. 'It is a miracle; yes? To conceive of another baby? And it has come at a most inauspicious time.'

Abigail stroked a tear from her cheek. 'Take Luka home, and rest. I will serve the children of the world, the best I can. And I wish

LEGACY OF ANGELS

to thank the both of you, for the crusade you have personally fought, and for your unswerving loyalty to the cause. We will prevail.'

'Maybe so,' said Cole, 'But at what cost? We have lost many wondrous souls already; how many more are to be sacrificed before this war is ended. And it is a war. Not like the last one. Somehow, this is worse, as evil has found a way to breach our defences. As with a sniper, we're being picked-off one at a time.'

'Yes; we will lose more before this ends. For those of us who survive, we are to face the rigours of great sacrifice, as it has always been. We do so, and continue to wield the sword of justice, so that the children of this world can survive and prosper.'

Attention was drawn to an effulgence greater than the sun's glare, and from the nucleus of this energy, glided the winged Free Spirit with Luka astride clutching the mare's fiery mane with one hand, while punching the air with the other. His excitable whooping had the adults smiling, and as Free Spirit dropped to the flat pasture, Cole went to her, thanked, and patted the mare's neck, before allowing his son to slip into his arms.

Cole carried him to a waiting yet pensive mother, who gathered Luka to her breast and hugged him with a fierce, unyielding passion.

Abigail levitated and came astride Free Spirit, waved farewell, and then horse and rider were inexorably sucked into a vortex of light energy.

'Time to return home,' said Cole happily, kissing the crown of his son's head and Zanula on the lips. Linking hands, they prepared themselves for the spiritual journey ahead.

On arriving at her estate and leaving Free Spirit to graze in the fields, Abigail utilised the next two hours giving quality time to the children.

Abigail's mother and Celestine were elsewhere tending to the rescue animals and taking the dogs for a ramble, the twin souls of Gillian and Margaret O'Shaughnessy having been given the onus to act as guardian of the boys in their absence. The one half of the host, Maggie, was astute enough to know her dear friend was embroiled in a battle; not only against the tide of emerging evil, was facing deeply ingrained emotional trauma also.

Aisha and Celestine were aware of Abigail's internal conflict, and knew not to interrogate, supposing Abigail would confide in them if she chose to do so. Maggie, on the other hand, could be quite bullish and confrontational, and it was apparent the beautiful soul to have taken her and Gillian to her bosom and grant them hope and purpose, was hurting. Maggie felt she should at least try and help, even to reciprocate comfort, whether it was to be gratefully received or not.

The older woman was rocking back and forth on an antique Windsor style chair, overseeing the frantic frolics on the lawn as Abigail came to join her and crouch beside her legs.

'Ah, bless my spiritual other half,' chuckled Maggie, with just a hint of mischief. 'Seems my dear-heart, Gillian, has fallen asleep.'

Maggie stopped rocking as Abigail scooped up one of her hands and grasped it gently, warmly, sensing this was Abigail's approach to reaching out. Maggie placed her other hand on the crown of Abigail's head, as if anointing her charge with a personal blessing.

'If I'm not mistaken,' said Maggie, and choosing her words carefully. 'You conceal great sadness behind the mask you have erected, my dear. You are concerned Mister Li has not returned from wherever he was assigned to go; am I right? You could recall him, you know as I believe it is within your powers to do so. Don't allow stubbornness to blind yourself to judgement and falter along the path to happiness. I know that you are happy around the children, and when you are with the animals. I have noticed also; the way you radiate great joy whenever you are in Mister Li's company.'

'I wish, Maggie, it was that easy,' Abigail duly answered, with her gaze cast thoughtfully to where their hands were interlaced, and realising she needed to confide to someone of her personal emotional conflict. 'I have tried on a few occasions to establish a link with Chan Li, using a specific language unique to the two of us.'

'And Mister Li is not responding; is what you're saying. I feel sure your man is perfectly okay, my dear. After all, he is a most capable individual; one of the great ancients notably and has faced many conflicts and proven victorious in each of them.'

Maggie gave a light-hearted chuckle, despite not knowing why. She was feeling an unnatural tension in the air around and between them.

'Chan has always proven his courage, and I daresay, there are few who can hope to challenge him in combat. Until now.'

'You, along with the Chosen One and a great and glorious army, defeated the enemy against all the odds in recent times. We will prevail again. And again, until the dark cur accepts it is beaten.'

'As you know, Maggie lovely, the new scourge of evil is rampant. Many wonderful souls have fallen; those who were ancients and powerful. The one who is on course to inflict the new world with his venom, has no equal. Except perhaps, for my good self. As I am First Angel and daughter to the universe of light; the one referred to as Nemo, is my opposite. As First Angel, son and Chosen One of the Dark Lord, Nemo is on a mission to avenge his father's ignominious defeat in the war of angels; and he is relentless.'

'Oh my! Oh, dear me! I imagine, you are thinking this monster will find his way to Spiritual Lodge? Can I assume; he wants you and the children? What to do? What to do? Oh, what a deplorable mess we find ourselves in, once again. And just when things were getting back on track.'

Abigail was able to smile, in response to Maggie's blustering concerns.

'I love you, Maggie. You truly are a wonderful soul, and an inspiration, even to me. The one I speak of though, will do all in his power to extinguish the glorious light we all possess. I cannot allow it, Maggie, for the sake of the children of the world, mankind in general, and Mother Earth. We have come too far, to fail now at this juncture.'

'If there is anything Gillian and I can do to assist, you only have to ask,' Maggie answered, in soft drear tones. 'We stand together, fight together, and if it should be written, we fall together.'

'Let us hope it doesn't come to that. As for helping, you are, lovely, just by being here and watching over the boys whenever I'm called to leave home on a mission.'

'For what it's worth, beautiful Abby; I believe in my heart, Mister Chan Li will find a way back to you. This is his home too.'

Abigail was unable to answer, and it took a monumental effort of willpower not to shed tears and fragment emotionally. It was not only Chan she was thinking about; there was Layla, Homer and Peter, the wonderful Joshu, and the impeccable Cardinal Rossini. There were others also, to have fallen into the abyss; others would follow. She knew this to be true.

Where would it end; she asked herself? Her own father and overlord of the universes was reluctant to answer her pleas in recent times and give an explanation to placate her. She wondered, not for the first time, if all was beyond repair and out of control.

LEGACY OF ANGELS

The eternal dream of a utopian existence was rapidly degenerating into dystopia. There would come chaos and disharmony. A pure spirit and heart will become cleaved. Kindness to one another, will dissipate in a short time, as with chaff in the wind.

The world was facing a pandemic, more deadly than any virus, and Abigail felt helpless to contain its course.

CHAPTER 12

DREAMING MONSTERS...

When all does not feel

As it should,

And leaves one floundering in a miasmic pool,

Of confusion,

I wonder if,

Those dreams I have,

Are the reason.

I hope not.

As I dream of monsters...

Byron Jones

Byron Jones was feeling grateful, on a morning which had turned inclement. Leandra had taken her son on an outdoor adventure. Whatever they chose to do on the occasions they left home without him, no longer fed Byron's interest. Leandra rarely talked about herself or shared her thoughts, or even participated in the things Byron liked to do.

She was attentive though, and could be fiercely passionate, and be relied upon to keep Byron believing he was special.

Three weeks had elapsed since the mysterious disappearance of the fishing crew. Byron had been discovered unconscious on the shore, and when he recovered, he had no recollection of events leading up to the moment he'd been washed up onto the pebbled beach.

Other boats went out for signs of wreckage, yet none were found, and neither were the bodies of the crew discovered.

The disaster had cast a dark drear cloud in the community; all the frivolity to have been nurtured since the apocalyptic carnage, having quickly dispersed to have gloom and uncertainty return.

Byron endured extensive questioning since his recovery, yet considering he had no recollection of events beyond meeting up with his fellow crew, he could not substantiate the facts to appease people's conscience.

Leandra was the only person to remain supportive, as surprisingly, most others were quick to shun him and make him into a virtual pariah.

Byron mooched around the kitchen in the absence of Leandra and Mateo, having no clear idea what he should do to pass the time of day.

For the first time since recuperating, he felt energised, and even positive. Having had coffee, even though he declined preparing himself a breakfast, Byron made up his mind to visit the coast at the exact location his unconscious body had been discovered, and where floral and handmade tributes were left in memory of those who had not returned.

He took a leisurely stroll to the location, unperturbed by the persistent drizzle or from the fact a few people he encountered along the way avoided him. By the time he reached the shoreline his shirt was stamped to his torso like an uncomfortable second skin. The rain trickled in runnels down his cheeks from his clipped hair. They might have been tears; had he been feeling any remorse.

Byron had become anaesthetised to most forms of emotions in the space of three long weeks, as with a veil to have slipped unexpectedly over his heart, there to shield him from grief and pain.

The shore dipped away on a silky bed of scree towards where the sea lapped gently, all the tributes erected for the missing fishermen, looking lost and forlorn and bedraggled beneath the elements.

Byron removed his trainers and stepped barefooted into the shallows, and liked the way the ocean caressed his skin, almost as if it had the power to lure him. He fought the urge to run and dive and swim, and to keep going until exhaustion left him floundering.

The sky had become a rare and turbulent bank of dark grey with whispers of white cloud, the sun having been swallowed, its brightness muted.

By coming to the place, he'd been found washed-up and barely alive, Byron hoped it might rekindle some vestige trace of all to have transpired on that fateful day he went fishing with a small crew of friends.

The gentle, undulating tide further out to sea, seemed to have acquired a voice, and he believed it was calling him and using a unique and specific language Byron was able to understand.

He was cast back to the moment he recovered consciousness, seeing numerous faces of gathered town-folk peering down at him without one assisting and giving him aid. The was something he only received when Leandra appeared, and it was she who took control of the situation and led him away, with a sullen Mateo keeping pace at her side.

Byron couldn't be sure yet felt he must have blacked out soon after they traversed the gradient away from the shore and gabbling people of the community, as he next woke up on their bed with Leandra mopping his brow and chest with a cool damp cloth.

He recalled the obvious way in which she telegraphed a smile, that which harnessed no concern or fear. It had, however, surprised him of her intent as she stood to undress, and then she was straddling him. He was cognisant, and physically willing to engage, in what was to deteriorate into a frenetic carnal battle.

He had always been a considerate and gentle lover, passionate and unselfish. Leandra had fed the flame at that time, to something which reached deep to awaken base and bestial desire. At the time, what dampened his ardour, came the moment he realised Mateo had entered the room to observe mother and the stranger wrestling on the bed.

Byron had protested, along the lines of having privacy, and that what they were doing was not suitable for a young boy to witness. Leandra showed nothing in the way of remorse, and apparently didn't think their situation was inappropriate viewing. She was in control and he was cajoled into complying with each of her insatiable demands. He became her chattel and plaything, and he let himself flow against her inimitable tide.

Byron was drawn out of his reverie, suddenly alert to otherworldly sounds reverberating in musical tones within his head. The interlinking pitch of varying decibels, the way in which notes were stretched and manipulated, gave Byron the impression he was receiving a specifically coded language.

What amazed him initially, was that he was able to understand their meaning and it was like several voices calling to him at once.

He was drawn to the horizon and a flicker of gold on the water's surface, where the cloud struggled to contain the persistent might of the sun.

The answer he was seeking was out there, somewhere. He closed his eyes, slowed his breathing, and took his mind back; hoping, he might remember something which could reveal the truth of what happened to the trawler and its crew.

The key to the door; that's what he was looking for.

Staccato images stabbed his conscience, and he saw himself running amok with a machete grasped in one hand. An instant of panic and horror had the visions disperse instantly. He took a moment to compose himself, closed his eyes and invited new memories. He was witness to a huge net and the monstrous thing squirming and thrashing around amid a haul of fish. The weight and angered movements of the giant caused the boat to list. There came a scream in his head as he relived a moment he had previously dispelled from his mind.

One of the crew was overboard.

Byron saw himself hacking at one of the thick ropes tethering the net to the crane. It was the moment he was witness to the beast breaking free of the net.

Next, he saw himself in the water, not that he was able to contemplate the images to which he was subjected. There were other such monsters, their enormous tentacles flailing the water and all the other remaining crew members were their target. Byron remembered body parts sinking to the sea bed, amongst crimson swirling concentrations of blood.

He still had the machete in his right hand.

All became a blank following the moment he saw the Lovecraftian monster's approach.

When he opened his eyes, the rain slipping down his cheeks, a scream hovering on his lips, he was intuitively forewarned he was not alone.

He turned and confronted an imperious looking woman alongside a man whose skin was the colour of polished mahogany. They were apparently observing him from a position atop the gradient composed of scree, and as he blinked the water from his eyes for greater clarity, believed they were people he recognised from another time.

He tried to smile, even as his lips remained pursed, as he recalled the man and woman on another occasion, presenting themselves while he was hiding out on Snowdonia. He knew them to be other than mortal. At that time, Georgina and Mazouma had granted him hope and had guided him on the path he should travel.

Their immediate arrival on the shore after all this time was disconcerting to Byron, as in the cool ambivalent stance both celestials had taken and in the way they were tentatively probing around his thoughts.

'Greetings!' he called to them. 'It has been a while. Have you come to assess the progress of our little town and its community? Or has something else brought you here?'

Byron became increasingly anxious as the man and woman refused to answer or even approach.

'Were you made aware of a recent tragedy? The entire crew of The Neptune perished as the fishing trawler came under attack from monstrous jellyfish. I have no idea how, but I managed to survive. Barely, I should add. It started to come back to me, hence the reason I returned to shore, in the hope it would trigger memories so that I can better understand what went down that day. As miracles would have it, I was washed ashore. I say miracle, as I'm surprised I didn't drown having escaped the creatures. You see, the incident occurred at least thirty miles out to sea, and no way can I swim that far. I'm just thankful, I didn't suffer the fate my friends were subjected to. Truth of the matter is I wished I'd not remembered, now it will haunt me always. And when I tell the townsfolk what I remember, no one is going to believe me. They will suspect I had something to do with their disappearance.'

It was Georgina who eventually answered, and her words trickled around his mind. They were not softly intoned words to placate him, as the intensity of her suggestions appalled him.

'You survived, only because you were chosen and have been changed,' she remarked. *'You are infected; by an insidious evil which has altered your DNA. It is possible you have infected others without knowing.'*

'What are you implying; exactly?' he blustered a response. 'I feel okay, in the physical sense. I'm feeling quite emotional at this moment, but I think that's considered understandable, now that I realise what happened to the crew of the Neptune. Did you say, I am infected? Has the virus returned? I'm referring to Covid. We all know it wiped out millions before the world went belly-up.'

'The evil masquerading as mutant jellyfish have chosen you as a harbinger of their own dark intent. It is a reason you cannot remember everything to have befallen you on that fateful day, and I'm surprised you are still able to recollect passages of the trauma you experienced. Dark energy has raped your body and claimed it, but not all your mind, it appears.'

'What exactly did they do to me?' and Byron sensed his tone had become strident, as he became fearful and desperate.

'One of the beasts merged with you,' Georgina answered, intonating sadness as she prepared to give an explanation. *'It became absorbed into your body.'*

'Bullshit!' Byron protested. 'Those fucking monsters were over one hundred feet in length. Do the math, as I'm pretty sure one of those creatures could not possibly find a home inside me.'

'I understand how it might be difficult for you to understand and accept. It is the way of it, so it appears. They liquidise the contents of a host body and use it, so that they can spread the tide of evil beyond these waters, their natural environment. Evil has found a way.'

Byron paced, flailing his arms, and shaking his head to remove the voice resonating disquiet within his mind. He felt pressure building, and there came a knifing pain to slice through his abdomen and chest.

'What you are telling me,' he said to his visitors, and dropping wearily to his knees, 'is preposterous.'

He cried out suddenly, as the pain he was enduring became an unbearable onslaught to his senses.

'The beast within you,' Georgina added, *'Feels threatened; knows, it is being challenged.'*

'What am I to do?' he cried, and lifted his face to the fine rain, as if to beseech the universe beyond the low banks of cloud, for salvation.

He gave another scream as his flesh erupted from sternum all the way down to his feet and was momentarily rendered mute at sight of the flailing tentacles to burst from his flesh, unravelling themselves and expanding.

He was able to stagger to his feet, his human mind no longer registering the pain or having the need to understand what was happening.

Concentrated streams of energy struck his host body, lifting Byron off the pebbles and scree, as the creature threatening to emerge was contained. Byron's face began to separate, a gelatinous hood revealing itself as it pulsed and grew. The frenetic power of energy vapourised both the host body and the monstrous incarnation, before the creature was able to fully define itself.

Georgina and Mazouma retracted their powers and bowed their heads in commiseration, in response to the action they were required to employ to stave off another source of evil.

They became instantly drawn to another's presence and saw the woman and child observing at distance. Even before they could react and initiate a confrontation, the mother and young boy teleported away from their position.

'Should we give chase?' Mazouma telegraphed to his companion.

'Not at this time, dear friend,' answered Georgina pensively. *'This has to be reported and await further instruction.'*

'I liked him,' said Mazouma. *'For one who was mortal, he gave so much of his heart to those in need of assurance and guidance.'*

'As with so many, in these difficult times,' said Georgina, and taking one of Mazouma's large hands in a soft grasp. *'I wish to visit the heart of the community our friend Byron has created and assess whether evil resides there.'*

'Who do you suppose the woman and child were? They had the power to teleport, which makes them celestial. Something tells me, their purpose here was not as guardians to the race of mortals.'

LEGACY OF ANGELS

'Emissaries of dark energy,' Georgina insinuated. *'And a possibility, they are a catalyst to the spread of evil in these environs. They are not our concern, of this moment, but I sense a day of reckoning will come, and our paths will cross once again. Let us leave now, good friend and dear heart, and hope we can spread a little love and light, and kindness to those of Byron's community who have lost direction. They have lost friends and loved ones in recent times, and they will never truly understand why. We need to maintain a course of hope and serve to protect those who are free from infection; if it is within our power.'*

'I concur,' Mazouma answered. *'Dark energy is a powerful influence in these waters. We need to assess whether that influence has been spread beyond these shores. We are at war once again, as it was claimed. We need to stay strong, and alert always.'*

'This latest evil has found a path to beautiful souls. It has been said, as you are aware, that many of our kind have fallen to the latest influx of dark energy. All-powerful ancients, whose inimitable powers were not enough to deflect the evil tide sweeping the globe. Come, my friend, let us finish this.'

CHAPTER 13

TRAUMA OF ANGELS...

When Angels feel emotion,

They run deeper,

And can impact,

With catastrophic consequence...

Cole hated being apart from his family, as this was a day Zanula was reluctant to accompany him on his daily ritual of visiting areas of the community, meeting with other guardians, and assessing all was going without incident.

It was to the detriment of the sprawling community, the social fun-inspired ritual of playing and bathing in the rock pool, lakes and rivers was practically non-existent. The attack on Naomi and her young daughter lived in the memories of most. Many refused to speak of the tragic and eventful day, while a few continued to remind everyone; monsters existed. Evil was still prevalent in their new Utopian world, and it reminded people of how it was like to live in fear and uncertainty.

Those who were witness to Cole dragging the carcase of a giant jellyfish from the waters of the rock pool, believed other such creatures existed. It was a reason why people avoided areas of water. Quite a few had reluctantly given up their homes and moved to a location further inland.

Not everyone fled their dwellings on the shores of two lakes, a river, and its tributaries. A few stayed, and defended themselves by carrying makeshift spears, always bows and arrows and long knives.

A few stalwart individuals continued to fish in the shallower waters, although food supplies were meagre compared to the way it was.

Since the attack on Naomi, and subsequent confrontation Cole had endured with the amphibious mother and daughter, not forgetting having to witness the tragic metamorphose of ancient celestial bodies into denizens of evil dark energy; there had been no reported incidents. Importantly, to Cole's mind, it was believed no person had mysteriously gone missing.

Cole wanted to believe it had been an isolated incident, as they were located hundreds of miles from the coast.

Despite which, he'd seen much in recent times, to make him think anything was possible.

Having recently witnessed the propensity of these mutant monsters existing out of water, Cole was not someone who could exhibit complacency. He wanted to ensure every person; man, woman and child, remained vigilant, as anything was to be expected.

It played on his mind often, as to whether the contagion of these mutant creatures, could be contained and eradicated.

Cole had stopped to assist a large family, tethering thatch to the roof over their dwelling, as inclement weather in recent weeks had caused a few unexpected problems.

One of the guardians approached and called to him. Cole knew him as Ankher, a tall man of almost seven feet and reed thin and was someone who was much respected in the community. The children, especially, loved him.

'Ankher!' Cole responded and wiping hands down his jeans. 'Judging by your expression, I sense something is troubling you.'

'Your dear wife,' he said, with caution and diplomacy.

'What about her? Is Zanula okay?'

'I have, this instant, come from your home. Something is troubling her, not that I was made privy to her thoughts. I have never seen her so distraught.'

Cole didn't wait for Ankher to elaborate, and instantly teleported away from his location to arrive outside their home. Zanula and Luka were nowhere around, and Cole established a wide scan of the surroundings. He was able to follow the threads of Zanula's auric trail and was further surprised he should find mother and son swimming in the rock pool.

He travelled there and was witness to a few of the older children in the vicinity, but they paid no heed and seemed to keep to a respectful distance from the pool.

Zanula stepped naked out of the water with Luka clutching one of her hands. She was smiling, and to Cole, she appeared radiantly happy and not distraught as Ankher had suggested.

Cole smiled at his son, even as his eyes were drawn to the advanced swelling of his wife's stomach.

'How are you feeling?' he asked and embracing both.

Without answering immediately, she moved away to reclaim her shorts and a tie-away blouse and proceeded to dress. Luka clung to his thigh, and he could feel his son trembling. Cole knelt, kissed him, and helped him onto his own shorts and tee shirt.

'You met with Ankher,' Zanula remarked then, interspersing her words with a light chuckle. 'He visited earlier when I was having a reflective moment. I can understand why he would think there was a problem. It's okay, honey, to be having the occasional mood swing, even for us celestials. Let's not forget; I am with child again, and it is a rare and momentous achievement.'

'Our baby grows quickly,' said Cole, drawing attention to the obvious swelling of her abdomen. 'Perhaps, too quickly.'

'Everything is fine and wonderful, my handsome considerate man. I would know, if there was something to concern us.'

'That's my problem. I should know. We both can create a psychic connection with our baby, as it was with Luka. I sense nothing, and I've tried to establish a link; trust me.'

'For the record; the baby is fine. It frequently speaks to me if you must know.'

'IT? Do you refer to our child as an 'IT'? Neither He nor She?'

'Sorry, that is not how I meant it to come out. Our baby is to be our second son.'

Cole was astounded by the news, yet unable to remove troubling thoughts. Zanula took his hand and led him away from the site of the rock pool and its memories. It was less than a half mile to their home, and they chose to take a leisurely walk.

Cole carried Luka on his shoulders, and any concerns he had laboured under for a time, had significantly faded by the time they reached their abode.

Zanula complained she was feeling tired and lethargic, and stated she needed to rest and take a lie down. Cole spent time playing with Luka and when his son grew tired, carried him to his cot in a separate room. He kissed his forehead, told him to sleep tight, and left to check on his wife.

From the open doorway, he observed her twitching and rocking her head on occasion, as if to rid her subconscious of a particularly unpleasant dream.

Removing his clothes, Cole slipped onto the bed beside her, drawing her naked body to his own hoping he could placate and dispel the anxiety she was subjected to. In time, he felt her relax, and she seemed to sense he was beside her, even suggestively moved her rump against him.

With a hand splayed against her swollen abdomen, Cole tried to establish a psychic link with the foetus, while at the same time, probing Zanula's mind to find a doorway into her thoughts.

Even though she slept, she gave a gasp and this was followed by a hungry growl, to feel him aroused against her.

Cole shook his head in frustration as once again, a passage into the mind of the unborn infant appeared to be blocked to him.

Zanula rolled into his arms and spread herself as a clear invitation. An intuitive warning had Cole not submit to his wife's sleep-driven demands, and he instantly wondered why the idea of making love to her was suddenly repugnant to him.

He touched her cheek, traced a digit around her mouth, and pulled back sharply. What he saw uncoiling between her teeth was not her soft moist tongue.

Instinct had him drawing on his own personal defences as Zanula pushed her head back and gave an orgasmic sigh. Her hands gripped his upper arms as she began to writhe beneath him and looking down to where she rubbed her smooth pubis against him, he was witness to undulating ripples across her swollen belly.

He forced himself to reach deeper into her mind and Zanula responded, revealing the reasons for her condition.

It began in Abu Dhabi, at the site of the plundered pyramid. A tunnel sloped away steeply and went underground; Cole and Zanula compelled to investigate.

Cole remembered all the mixed signals they were each bombarded with and recalled them both erecting a defensive perimeter as a precaution.

There came a violent subterranean tremor and the ceiling collapsed. They became separated as boulders and rubble and a thick cloud of dust kept them apart.

Cole had been alerted to a shift in the vibrational sequence around him, and instantly created a weapon. Out of the darkness and grainy particles came flailing tentacles, and he lashed out, telegraphing a warning to Zanula, it was a trap.

The monsters came as a flood from the deeper regions of the tunnel, two score and perhaps more. It took a monumental effort, but eventually, he'd established the enemy had been defeated. He hadn't wanted to expend his energy in rapid bursts, for fear of the pyramid collapsing completely on top of them.

He was alert to Zanula yelling and screaming in his mind, and he was given little choice. Using a concentrated beam of energy, he scoured a wide vent in the centre of the mound of rubble separating them. He hoped the weakened structure could withstand the weight of the pyramid but didn't think it could for long.

Cole had dived through the gap he'd made as the entire pyramidal complex gave a seismic groan. He caught sight of Zanula staggering blindly in the gloom. All around her were spasming segments and cleaved hoods of the creatures she had defeated.

Without hesitating, Cole had hauled her into his arms and teleported away from the carnage, just as the ceiling and walls seem to implode. The upper carcase of the pyramid fractured and began to dismantle, being sucked down in to the deep chasm the industrious creatures had created.

Zanula and Cole materialised quite a distance from the ruined city, where all around were untarnished sand dunes. Cole had set her down before slumping to his knees, and she rapidly came out of her stupor. His gaze had roamed in all directions, as if he'd been expecting the hideous mutations to be coming after them. He'd caught Zanula smiling down on him, and she moved silently and gratefully into his arms.

'We're going home,' he remembered saying. 'Once we have collected our son.'

That was three weeks ago, and Cole had missed the signs, or had simply ignored them.

Zanula's persistent claims she had fallen pregnant should have initiated caution over curiosity. He was recollecting Abigail's ambivalent response when they had met up, just before their son had been delivered to them.

It occurred to him; Abigail had known and chose not to say.

She fucking knew! his mind screamed, just as he felt Zanula's beautiful face distorting and separating in his tender grasp. He screamed; and this time, it was not in his mind, as he sought to prevent her flesh peeling away to reveal the venomous creature residing inside his wife.

As her body began to convulse, Cole summoned his energy and let it surge along his arms, just as her flesh erupted and writhing tentacles emerged, even as his energy restricted their metamorphic growth.

He screamed and wept within a tide of anguish, and believed he heard Zanula speak within his tortured mind.

'Forgive me, my love. You must end this; and now.'

Nooooooooooooooooooooooooooooooooooooooooooo!

His energy compressed her skull and the monstrous incarnation which had raped and extinguished a beautiful and glorious light.

He shuffled away from the gore and blood, and the shrivelled husk of his wife's host body, tears burning thick runnels down his cheeks and pooling off his chin to sear his chest.

Cole gave a start, the moment he realised Luka was standing in the doorway, a witness to the horrific scene of devastation to his mother.

How could he explain his actions to a boy of five?

Cole's nightmare had yet to reach its conclusion.

Luka's eyes had become sunken pits, his small robust body, spasming uncontrollably.

'Daddy!' Luka cried, just as a tentacle burst from his open mouth.

Cole was alert and rolled to the side, as the monstrous appendage snapped at the space he'd vacated. He launched a solid bolt of energy and watched in horrified fascination as the light force slowly devoured the monstrous incarnation fighting to escape the host body concealing it, until his son and the creature were vaporised.

Cole rocked himself, while unable to fully comprehend all he'd been forced to commit to, and of all which had become lost to him in a moment of deplorable madness.

His wife and son had been his life force; his reason for being.

And now evil had taken them.

He understood how Zanula must have truly felt when, at another time, she was the one to take the life of a teenaged son when dark energy had tainted his soul.

It had all become perfect and idyllic, to have their beautiful son returned to them.

Cole could feel all the pent-up rage spiralling out of control, threatening to erupt, as with the pyroclastic force of a volcano.

He rose slowly and shakily to his feet and let it out. Giant wings sprouted from his flanks and shoulders and burst through the walls and the ceiling. He soared skyward, shattering the thatched roof to tinder as his wings carried him upward, and where the stars seemed to blink and taunt him.

His resonating shrieks of emotional pain would be heard for miles around, and such was the raw power in each of his screams, the earth below gave a mighty groan and the trees to tremble.

Cole flew to the coastline and settled on the smooth sand; the vast ocean only perceived as a chaotic blur through eyes drowning in tears.

He heard someone chuckling, and wiping his eyes, saw the young girl observing him at distance. Cole recognised Naomi's daughter, who was other than mortal; was infected with evil, as had his wife and son.

Neither hesitant or appalled by his unswerving reaction, he fired gouts of searing energy at the monstrosity lurking in the host physical form of a young girl, saw the frail body launched and carried across the expanse of sea, where it became vaporised. The child's shrieks of agony were the last to disperse.

If not the child; the creature itself.

Cole dropped to his knees, his giant wings beating a symphony in the sand, as anguish ignited once more within his mind.

Dark energy had found a path into the new world and stolen something precious from him.

This, made it personal…

This, was to be war…

CHAPTER 14

THE VISITOR...

> **And when the rocks begin to sing,**
>
> **And there are butterflies by day,**
>
> **Fireflies by night**
>
> **Heralding,**
>
> **A wondrous miracle...**
>
> **Evil will once again tremble**
>
> **In the light of avenging angels...**

Mary Beth stepped out onto the lean-to of her modest ranch house, to be greeted by an early morning sunrise over the woodland copse in front, and where shadow was cast on the still pond and flagged the driveway all the way to the stone pillars and weathered gate.

It was a daily ritual she'd become used to in recent months, taking up residence in her faithful rocking chair, a Winchester rifle across her lap, and sucking on an empty meerschaum pipe as she kept vigil on the land around her.

Specifically, the woodland copse, and just as importantly, her attention would be on the pond.

Her scraggly hair, more in the way of grey than brown, fanned her shoulders from beneath a Stetson. The hat had been her husbands, not that he had a reason to wear it, as he'd passed away during the pandemic with the dreaded Coronavirus. He didn't hang around to witness the fireworks to follow, when the heavens could not make up its mind whether to vomit rain, snow, or fire on the sinners of the world.

They once had over three hundred sheep, the flock now sorely depleted to a mere thirty. More, during lambing season, but lamb had always been a local delicacy, so numbers in the flock remained low,

The pond was fed by the lakes at nearby Jackson Hole, and there had always been an abundance of Cutthroat Trout in the waters. Mary Beth had lost her appetite for fish, since she witnessed a sight no living person could possibly imagine. It was a reason she kept vigil on the pond.

Just in case, other unnatural and unearthly 'critters' returned.

She had a bottle of water beside her, and it would suffice for a time. Ordinarily, her chores would have begun, by tending to her flock and inspecting the two miles of fencing. Not that she feared trespassers or looters, as she rarely saw anyone come by the ranch in recent times.

As for her neighbours, they mysteriously disappeared a few weeks back.

She did go and investigate on the one occasion, taking some fresh-baked blueberry muffins as an offering, and as an excuse to socialise. Except, the family of four had fled their home, leaving everything. The doors were unlocked. There was half-eaten food on plates around the pine refectory table, an overturned chair and a broken mug. There were other signs, the Rampton's had left in a hurry. Their two dogs were missing: border collies and very friendly.

More importantly, their own livestock of sheep, a few cattle and chickens, were all gone.

Mary Beth had a notion, the family didn't leave by choice, and suspected foul play. They too had a pond on their land, not as large, and was fed by the same source as her own.

It had her wondering many things.

Unpleasant things.

Since that discovery close to her own estate, it was all the more reason she kept vigil, as there was no telling if the Devil would come calling on her once again.

She'd be ready, though.

Mary Beth sucked on the teat of her pipe vigorously, a sign she was anxious, and not as relaxed as she would have liked. The rosewood meerschaum gave a strident whistle, startling her.

She kept an index finger wrapped around the trigger guard of the rifle, as a precaution. The slim barrel rested across her dirty threadbare denims, her left leg juddering, cowboy boots beating a rhythmic tattoo on the creaky wooden boards.

She was thinking about her husband Roy, and what he would have made of all this kerfuffle. She was thinking also, of her one-time neighbours; Lou and Jessie, their son Brad and daughter, Chastity, who were both in their thirties with no desire to leave home.

LEGACY OF ANGELS

Mary Beth wanted to believe they made it out of their home alive, and often said a prayer for their souls.

There was no point reporting it to the authorities, she'd ascertained. She hadn't seen a cop swing by since – well, since the world suffered the wrath of God.

No one went to church anymore. Mary Beth had attended church on a few occasions; that was at the beginning, but she was the only one to ever grace the pews. Even the preacher deigned not to visit. She stopped going, knowing in her heart she didn't need a church as somewhere to repent or say her blessings. She missed the preacher though, as she'd liked him a lot, for he was someone who reminded her of a brother she'd not seen or heard from in two decades.

He was either alive or he was dead, and there was no way of telling; a fact she'd come to live with over time.

She was pulled from her reverie suddenly, and it took her mind a while to digest, as to why she was alerted to a strange anomaly. Beneath the foundations of her home came a steady stream of vibrations.

At first, she believed there was to be another earth tremor.

Then she was recalling a passage of time when she was barely six years old. At that time, she'd been playing in the wooded copse, and had been drawn to the ancient circle of stones residing there.

Her Pappy and Grandpappy told her they were fragments of history going back to the dawn of time. The stones themselves, each composed of granite, stood seven feet tall, and all were different in structure. Mary Beth had always believed the stones sprouted all the way up from the Earth's core as, no matter the elements, in times of warfare, or subsequent earthquakes, they still stood proud and unswerving.

LEGACY OF ANGELS

It was at that time, as a young impressionable girl, that she was witness to vibrations beneath her feet. She remembered going to her father, saying to him that she'd heard the stones singing to her. There was more; as she explained having seen a wondrous light in the centre of the circle, and it was full of magic.

She recited her tale with expedience, seeing that her father was not as receptive to her tale as she would have hoped, and was possibly thinking it was all to do with a fanciful imagination. Yet Mary Beth was witness with her own eyes, and they did not deceive her, of a figure emerging from the blinding source of light with glorious wings unfurled. She had not been able to determine the sex of the ethereal being, as the light bathing the angel had dazzled her. She did, however, notice how the angel had smiled at her, before rising, and was then gone in a flourish.

No one believed her story at that time, but it was a reason she went to church every Sunday and never missed a day, until recent weeks.

Now, the stones were singing again.

Mary Beth felt compelled to go investigate this re-emerging phenomenon and realised she couldn't raise herself out of her seat. Vibrational waves of subtle energy had the distant trees bowing and sighing. The surface of the pond was rippling, and there were swirls of dust eddying off the driveway.

After only a few minutes, all around appeared to settle again. Yet, it was not the only inexplicable phenomena to captivate her. Swarming, as a colourful cloud, came a thousand or more butterflies, to descend over the pond. They flitted, glided, and scurried, with no apparent direction. As with the stones singing their beautiful aria, five minutes elapsed, and then the resplendent flock of butterflies dispersed and were gone.

Mary Beth scooped away her Stetson and smoothed her hair down with a trembling hand, shaking her head in wonderment, and realising she was smiling. She couldn't remember the last time she was given good reason to smile or feel joyous.

Replacing the hat in position, she vigorously sucked on her meerschaum, hoping the simple act would alleviate some of the confusion she felt.

If it had been a miracle, with the stone's singing and sight of the congregation of beautiful butterflies, there was more to come. Mary Beth observed a figure staggering out of the trees, who seemed to hesitate, and perhaps coordinate bearings. The young woman was naked, and Mary Beth would have gone to assist, except she was still unable to move off the chair.

The index finger worryingly twitched around the trigger guard, and she quickly tugged her hand away to avoid an unfortunate accident.

From her position on the stoop, she supposed the young woman was beautiful, in an ethereal way, but from the young woman's posture and stuttering movements, Mary Beth sensed all was not quite right with her visitor.

The stranger approached, paused, before continuing; each step ungainly, almost as if she was drunk or learning to walk for the first time.

She was naturally distressed and looked quite forlorn and lost.

Mary Beth summoned a super human effort to stand and gave up; tutting with frustration. Something quite unnatural was occurring, as an unseen force kept her shackled to the rocking chair. Even her legs had stopped juddering, her boots no longer dancing a jig on the planks.

She kept a watchful eye on the figure approaching, as there was nothing remotely normal about her.

LEGACY OF ANGELS

Stood to reason; she was thinking. Mary Beth wondered if the young woman was an extra-terrestrial; an alien visitor come to assist the world and its problems. That much, she hoped. Inwardly, Mary Beth was chuckling wryly, as it had her further wondering what might be going through an alien's mind, visiting a vastly depleted world, of people, wildlife and natural resources.

The stranger was completely smooth all over, Mary Beth noted, the young woman's pale skin appearing almost luminescent. What she did find disconcerting, was the way in which the young woman's slim curvaceous form was constantly changing shape.

The visitor had difficulty engaging the three steps up onto the porch, but eventually and still tottering, the young woman let herself into Mary's home.

Mary Beth could only wait it out, and hope her instincts were right in that, there was no evident reason to fear the visitor.

A considerable time elapsed, and the young woman reappeared, having covered her modesty with a simple pink frock Mary hadn't worn in years, but didn't have the heart to dispose of. Too many good and naughty memories were attached to that little number; and the thought had her tittering.

The stranger's movements were more fluid, even graceful, the cumbersome uncertainty having been dispensed with. *That was one such miracle.* She no longer needed to contain the contortions of flesh and bone, and she had a sumptuous waterfall of golden blond hair, which fell in soft captivating ripples all the way past the curve of her buttocks.

The atypical luminous quality to her skin remained, as it cast a faint golden auric silhouette around her form.

Mary Beth was surprised, in that her voice hadn't been taken from her.

'Don't go getting many visitors these days,' she said, while appraising the stranger from her seat, whose eyes of a vivid aquatic blue were adjusting to the light. She was staring out across the pond, in a way which had Mary Beth wondering if she knew of its secrets. 'Gone back to the way it was after the last of the quakes. Don't travel far myself these days. Don't have a need to, as I grow everything on my homestead. And I have my lambs and a few chickens who are still laying eggs. I draw water from a well; so, all's good, you would think.'

She received no answer and was obliged to talk to dispel the creeping anxiety she felt.

'I don't suppose you're aware of what's going on. We don't have electricity or gas for the motor. What we have, is crystal energy. Who would have thought? The crystals operate all appliances, provide light, and powers the truck. Very eco-friendly, and about time too.'

She gave a haughty laugh, to cover her discomfort and realising she was babbling.

She removed her hat and lay the Winchester down, out of harm's way, and it occurred to her she had fluidity in her limbs. She chose to remain seated, so as not to startle or intimidate her visitor, who had yet to acknowledge Mary Beth, or speak, if she was able.

'Have to ask and I don't mean to come across as rude or nosy,' Mary Beth continued. 'You an angel from the heavens, or did you crawl out of the ground? Thing is I've seen a lot of crazy stuff in recent weeks, most of which defies belief, so it has me wondering if the Devil's own is upon us.'

Without turning to acknowledge her host, the young woman chose to answer Mary Beth telepathically.

'You have nothing to fear from me, Mary. I know that my unexpected arrival and appearance must seem quite strange and yes,

I am not a mortal, as you are. You may call me an angel, if you wish, for I am a descendent of the stars. Our purpose has always been to assist mankind and Mother Earth in various stages of awakening and evolving. There exists, our opposite, who would have it otherwise; a despicable foulness who strives to remove all of hope and reap chaos. As it has always been.'

'Phewee! Is that a fact?' said Mary Beth with a gruff snort. 'I got no time or patience with any of that foulness, as you put it. I sense you are a good person, young lady. So, tell me, how are you feeling now? It's just that, when you staggered out of the trees, you didn't look too good, if I'm honest.'

'My spiritual soul was adjusting to the transition of travelling from the stars as an energy form.'

Mary Beth nodded, as if she understood completely.

'You planning to stay around these parts long, missy? I mean; you're more than welcome. I have plenty of vacant rooms, food, and beverage.'

'Thank you, Mary. I am to receive visitors, and then our purpose is to relocate.'

'These visitors you're expecting, are they also descendent from the heavens, honey?'

'Yes.'

'Well, that's something, at least. I should inform you, missy, but it isn't always safe to go wandering these parts without protection, you know. There's something in the pond, and it don't figure, rightly. Thing is, until the quakes, never once had us a pond on the land. My guess is, the water's gone and flowed down from Jackson Hole yonder, and brought with it something quite unspeakable. Something mean, ugly, and monstrous. It's okay though; I have myself my trusty Winchester repeating rifle. Got it working after a time. Barrel got all jammed-up and warped. There's nothing I don't know about guns, honey. Well, praise the Lord I do, as I would have no means to protect myself. The critters in the pond, I tell you, aren't too partial to a bullet.'

Relating her story had Mary cackling and rocking in her chair.

She took a moment to study the celestial being leaning against the rails, who appeared to be keeping vigil on the copse. She noticed her feet were bare.

'Think I may have a spare set of boots that will fit your dainty feet, if you're of a mind. Don't suppose there's anyone left to make quality boots anymore, not like it used to be. Had these twenty years, and more, and they're still going strong. Are you hungry, missy? Would you like a drink? I have fruit juice, water, even coffee.'

'No, thank you.'

'Well, you got to look after yourself, is all I'm saying. Got to keep your strength up, and your wits about you. Don't suppose you have a voice; it's just, you talking in my head, well it takes some getting used to. You got a name, missy?'

The stranger paused before submitting her answer.

'Seraphina…'

LEGACY OF ANGELS

PART THREE

MAELSTROM

THERE
IS HELL IN HEAVEN
AS THERE
IS
ON EARTH

CHAPTER 1

A PLEA TO REASON...

You can recite an argument,

And spout it from the roof tops,

But if no one is listening,

They become wasted words...

Abigail was of the belief she needed to go to the source directly, just to gain a perspective and understanding of the present situation. For a time now, she had become dissatisfied with the cryptic responses delivered to her; of that which is omitted causing her the greater consternation.

Having prepared herself mentally and spiritually, traversing the concourse of spiritual highways, across a medium of parallel dimensions, was a convoluted and hazardous process, even for the First Angel.

It was of necessity, as it was important her destination was not compromised.

At that moment in time, Abigail had no idea the haven she sought, had been discovered in advance of her arrival.

She materialised within the small pyramid on the remote island the Chosen One, Seraphina, received her *'Awakening'* and would conceive of Luke.

Abigail remained suspended at a midway point, her host physical body adjusting to the astral punishment it had endured on a harrowing journey. She was aware, the source she was seeking was not evident, and sent out a clear message to the Divine Power; her father – Genesis.

Accepting the situation, Abigail removed herself from the confines of the pyramid and ventured outside, instantly breathing in the familiar view and its atypical beauty.

Her initial intent was to visit the library where Genesis established a continuous link, expecting to be greeted by its custodian, Francis Peabody. The library was void of inhabitants, and having done a careful inspection, Abigail was assured nothing was out of place or had been tampered with.

The suspended console, almost to be perceived as the beating heart to Genesis, glowed faintly and periodically changed shape as it was wont to do.

Even here, Genesis remained mute and did not respond to Abigail's presence.

Next, Abigail approached the main residence, sending out a preliminary scan, as to her mind, all did not bode well or appear as she expected.

The atmosphere, normally imbued with positive vibrations, seemed tainted; almost to the point, where those who had remained, continued to grieve the loss of so many beautiful light souls who perished in the War of Angels.

Abigail emerged in the grand foyer, startling the permanent resident and matriarch, Myra. The imperious 'angel' was seated facing the panoramic windows and was pulled from a state of meditation to be greeted by her unexpected visitor.

'Are my eyes deceiving me?' she queried and rising to her feet slowly. 'What brings you to the island, Abby, for I was not forewarned you were coming.'

'Genesis did not invite me,' Abigail responded with a smile and taking Myra's hands with affection. 'So much is happening in the new world, that which had not been foreseen, and it has become apparent, Genesis is being frugal with an explanation.'

'The situation is dire, I admit,' Myra interjected. 'We receive regular reports, despite which, it has become obvious even to me, not all the information is filtering through. I have been reliably informed; this new scourge of evil has found a way to infiltrate beautiful souls and extinguish their light. As with the war, we continue to lose many of our celestial ancients to the rise of dark energy. I received news; we have lost Joshu. Can you verify this?'

Abigail's smile faded quickly, and simply nodded without submitting details. Abigail would always live with the memory she was the one, who had eternally extinguished the once beautiful light Joshu had maintained throughout eons.

'When was the last time you connected with Genesis?' she asked Myra.

'Unusually; four days ago, was the last time we received a communication, as we all wait an edict to signify the course we should take.'

Abigail turned away and paced the expanse of floor, trying desperately to establish some sense out of the disorder she was confronted with.

'Will you be staying long?' Myra asked.

'For as long as it takes,' Abigail responded firmly. 'My father has a duty to this planet; to all the wonderful souls who made the new world credible, and of those who were sacrificed for the cause. I demand answers and make it my vow to get them. Our duty, if not to the planet; is to the children.'

'Would you like me to summon refreshments, dearest Abby?'

'I will decline your offer this once, my lovely, as I wish to reacquaint myself with an old friend.'

Myra cast her gaze to the floor, feeling unusually dejected, knowing all was not as it had once been.

Abigail teleported away from the residence, leaving Myra to ponder what was to transpire from the First Angel's undeclared presence on the island.

A parakeet with predominantly white plumage, having tinges of orange, red and black to the tips of the feathers crowning its head, alighted on a branch of a tree and gave a squawk which resonated wide and far. It settled, to observe a view of the ocean, blue sky and overhead sun. The bird appeared content, outwardly.

Inwardly, as the parakeet was not entirely as appearances showed, was attuned to a distinct vibrational change in the atoms in the vicinity. It was a signature the bird was accustomed to, and it was unexpected.

The subject of interest emerged on the narrow strip of golden sand and seemed intent just to gaze out on the horizon.

The parakeet became aligned with the source of energy exhibited by the unexpected visitor who, it appeared, was using a coded sequence of symbols interwoven with tones the parakeet knew to be a language devised by ancients to communicate.

It had the bird intrigued, yet it knew not to divulge its own source of energy by employing a scan, or further attempting to reach into the thoughts of the young woman. It only became restless, the moment he was witness to the First Angel of Light energy removing her clothes and stepping naked into the sea.

There came a response from the depths of the ocean, which went deeper than the craggy rock bed, of several intertwining signals. Whatever was responding, was also rising at a rapid pace, and the parakeet could only wait and observe.

The mind within the exotic bird was firmly fixated on the young woman, the smoothness of bare skin and in the way the dense fronds of her light brown hair tinged with an iridescent blue, seemed to acquire a life all its own.

She was like the mythical Medusa.

From the depths of the ocean rose six bulbous heads supported by thick sinuous tentacles, and they bobbed and weaved as they extended outward to meet with the young woman.

The parakeet remained transfixed, as it was to witness a union of ancient souls, aware this was not a first occasion.

For all its cumbersome bulk and grotesqueness, the monster moved with balletic grace, and Abigail became swept up in a formidable embrace of intertwining necks.

LEGACY OF ANGELS

The parakeet was unflinching as the person to captivate him was conducted to sea and became aware of an intimate pact to be shared with the great behemoth.

It was also established, four others resided as sentinels, forming a perimeter around the island.

The moment it became evident one of the heads had become spooked and attention was on the cluster of trees around the shore, the parakeet took flight, only to return a short time later having metamorphosed as an adult marmoset.

The monkey took up vigil and watched the scenario played out over the calm sea, somewhat frustrated by the fact it dare not expose himself by projecting a scan to dissect the coded language the group were conversing in.

The energy using the marmoset as a host became desperate to elevate himself and conclude his purpose for coming to the island. Abigail's untimely arrival changed everything, albeit temporarily.

It gave Nemo an advantage, if he were to remain anonymous and an insignificant bystander, as it afforded him an opportunity to assess his nemesis from an alternate perspective. There was much about the First Angel he had yet to understand, and his goal was to break her and have her become obsequious; stripped of her powers.

The marmoset observed the shenanigans to be played between beauty and the beast for a short while and chose to leave the moment it experienced a conflict of emotions; those, which had it becoming unreasonably agitated. As a witness to the aberrant intimacy shared between the First Angel and the ancient creature, Nemo sensed a powerful merging of souls through physical contact.

He turned his back as pulsating waves of harmful light energy stippled the ether, and then he was skipping from branch to branch to be away from them. Eventually taking flight, as once again he transformed himself into a parakeet.

He needed time to initiate his plan and came to realise it would take unnerving courage and fortitude to see it through to completion. For him to succeed, it was imperative he remained incognito. Not that his presence on the island was a secret entirely. The ruling power of the universe would know its defences had been breached. As to how the mighty Genesis would react, was not Nemo's primary concern.

He understood, certain laws existed within the universe, which could not be broken. Nemo was one part of a complex universal design which afforded stability in the composition of gases, molecules and energy. This alone, made him invincible; as with his opposite – the Yang to his Ying.

CHAPTER 2

INCENSED

Facing obstacles, is mandatory.

How we overcome them,

Is the achievement.

The act of trying, is key,

And to keep trying,

To believe,

And not to quit…

Following her reunion with the great beast of the ocean, Abigail transported herself to specific locations on the island, intent on determining its defences were wholly intact. She lingered for a time when she emerged on the edges of the tiny inlet, which was home to memories she at once, found regrettable, as it was her belief a moment of madness when she allowed human emotions and a physical bonding with the celestial Chan Li, to take precedence over universal law. She sensed that a moment of human weakness was the root cause of everything which had become discordant in the universe.

Genesis was conspicuous by his unnerving absence, and silence. Chan Li was missing. Joshu, along with other beautiful ancient souls, had fallen to the latest pandemic of evil. Abigail was even thinking about her friends; Cole, Zanula, and their son Luka.

When last she met with them, she was given a glimpse of the future, and she'd been helpless to change its course, no matter the extent of her powers. She already knew the outcome; having connected with Cole's signature and endured his overwhelming grief in the aftermath of what he had had to commit to. And it was not only his grief she'd felt, for his anger was festering and out of control, and it was his emotional state of mind causing Abigail concern. If he was unable to contain the rage rampant in his aura, he could become lost in the spiritual sense.

She would have to go to him, even as she feared he might cast blame on her. She hoped, at least, to pacify his damaged soul and broken heart.

Abigail grieved too, and her own rage should she ever release it, would be greater than Cole's, and the consequences would be catastrophic and irreparable. Control was key.

Abigail joined the residents for a simple banquet that evening, in preparation for what she had to do to get the planet back on a harmonious balance and breathe hope back into the ruptured veins of a beleaguered world.

Only nineteen celestials currently resided on the island she was to discover, a few of whom, were regarded as permanent fixtures and were responsible for the island's upkeep.

Abigail was greeted fervently by everyone, as all knew the role she'd played in the war of angels, and of the mantle she'd carried into the new world. Except for one individual, as he was the only person not to express excitement, and even went out of his way to keep a low profile.

By segregating himself, Francis Peabody made himself conspicuous.

Abigail took Myra to one side, having assured everyone the prodigal children were safe and progressing steadily. She came straight to the point, having already projected a discreet scan to ascertain a reason for the librarian's unusually reserved disposition.

'Myra,' she said succinctly, 'Why did Francis Peabody leave the island? He is not someone who gets to travel beyond the perimeter of the island as with other earth angels. His powers are not as pronounced, and he is not one of the senior ancients.'

'Genesis recently sent our dear Francis on a mission,' Myra answered studiously, 'To procure a specific tome thought to be hidden in the mountains around Tibet. He returned two days ago, without the book he was sent to retrieve, and has been unable to speak of his travail or his reasons for having failed to locate the subject of Genesis's interest.'

'The tome he was sent to uncover and return with; did Genesis reveal its source or content?'

'The mission was clandestine. No one knows, other than Francis, and he has been sworn to secrecy. As you're aware, Abby, Genesis has been very quiet in recent times. Everyone; me included, have become susceptible to the changes occurring, and it's our fervent hope your presence on the island will make a difference and restore the faith.'

'It is my aim, also. Our kind sacrificed so much in the war of angels, to restore hope to the survivors of the new world. The Chosen

One; my soul sister, Seraphina, was perhaps the greatest sacrifice and I will not have dark energy spurn that legacy, or have my father weaken in the face of my own failings.'

'My dear, as First Angel, you have not failed mankind or the children of the future. You have remained true, against all the odds, and you continue the battle; regardless. It is, because your heart, spirit and soul are pure, no matter the personal cost you have endured.'

Abigail felt close to tears and apologised, saying she needed to go out and breathe fresh air.

She was pacing the lawns out front when Francis Peabody confronted her on his way to the library. It became apparent he had no wish to engage with her yet was obliged to when Abigail approached.

'Francis, my lovely,' Abigail said around a vivacious smile of greeting. 'I did notice at the banquet, you seemed quite withdrawn, preoccupied even. I was informed, that you were sent on a secret mission. I imagine, it took you out of your comfort zone. I must ask though; did you locate the tome you were sent to uncover and retrieve it from the mountains of Tibet?'

His eyes flitted side to side, and he even turned his head to cover his fear and shame, or that he believed they were being observed.

'I failed,' he uttered meekly. 'Sorry, my dear, I did however try.'

'Why do you suppose you failed? I need to know if you located the source; or were you misled?'

'Abigail, upon my soul, I had the tome in my hands for a brief time. And it was another which had been scribed in elements of energy, and not with ink or dye. I felt its power, and it was not good, my dear Abby. I had my instructions though; to return with it. Except…'

He hesitated, his grim expression denoting he was close to genuine tears of remorse, and Abigail saw from his posture that he was afraid.

'A man appeared out of nowhere,' he continued. 'He was not a mortal, naturally. And I daresay, he was not of the light. Despite which, his manner was genial and convivial. I had no choice but to hand him the tome. He ordered me to leave.'

Abigail was certain Francis had met with their nemesis, Nemo. For Nemo to have allowed Francis to return unharmed, Abigail was of the impression Nemo would be able to follow his passage back by tracing the librarian's spiritual signature. Which would mean, Nemo could have located the island retreat. As to whether he had the power to breach its defences, Abigail was assured it was feasible, and she saw it as her duty to determine if the island and its residents were facing a formidable threat from the enemy.

Abigail was prepared for a confrontation, and she would do so brazenly, with or without her father's support.

Abigail bid Francis a pleasant night, and as he made his passage to the library, Abigail instantly threw out a wide scan of the island and beyond.

She allowed herself time to determine whether the slightest anomaly or discordant vibration was prevalent in what had always been an impregnable fortress and haven. Only when she was completely satisfied there was no immediate threat in the area, did she retract the scan and prepared herself mentally and emotionally for a confrontation, of another kind.

She teleported herself into the interior of the pyramid, removed her clothes, and ascended naked to a midway point. She instantly sent out a clear message of intent, and composing herself, could only wait and hope her plea was met.

Eventually, she was greeted with the emergence of the familiar helix of spiralling energy at the apex of the pyramid. It appeared to hesitate and then it expanded and drifted down to encapsulate her, its exultant power palpating flesh and immersing her.

'Finally,' she proclaimed within her mind, and in the coded language devised between daughter and father, *'You heed my call.'*

'Why are you here, and not at home protecting the children?' the lilting voice of Genesis responded, and Abigail noted in the sequential tone of symbols and notes, an inflection of ambiguity.

He would know why, without the preamble. Abigail countered with a reply, Genesis would understand, and was designed to throw her father off his guard; should it be feasible.

'It would have been Chan Li's duty, had he not mysteriously disappeared. As it is, Chan is not responding to any of my calls, and his signature is - how can I put this? – non-existent. Can you give me an explanation?'

'Chan Li was given a mission of great importance and was instructed not to convene with anyone; even yourself.'

'And that is simply an untruth. Please, father, do not patronise me. I know, in my heart and in my soul, Chan Li is suffering. Perhaps, worse. It is my belief; he has been taken by dark energy. But you would know this, naturally. Tell me father, lover, and sire to Luke; is this my punishment? Your way of getting back at me?'

'Why have you come to the island; in truth?'

'To find out why you are not confiding in me, as to the meteoric rise of Dark Energy sweeping the planet. Will you have your universal design, your creation, discredited out of jealousy?'

The Great Power, as a languid spiral of green energy, seemed to pause, indicating a careful choice of answer to placate the First Angel.

It was aware Abigail had chosen to reveal herself in the physical host flesh, as she hoped to rekindle a spiritual connection, and was reluctant to express any emotional attachment Abigail had hoped for.

'As you are aware,' the phonetic vowels, symbols and tones were relayed to her mind, *'Dark Energy has unleashed its primary weapon; your equal. He is not someone, or thing, who can be destroyed. It is your task to seek a means to appease him; or to contain him.'*

'Why did you not inform me, Nemo was to infiltrate the protective powers of our own celestial angels? He is depleting our resources at a formidable rate.'

'And you must act quickly to stem the tide.'

'Where is your support? Why can you not intervene?'

'You know, I cannot directly, as my own intervention will herald total destruction; not only of the planet we serve to protect, but of the universe as a whole.'

'We both know; Nemo is not someone who can be appeased,' Abigail reacted defiantly. *'He is not to be trusted. Will you be honest with me, father, as even though I can perceive the future in episodes; are you able to divulge more so that I know to make the right decisions.'*

'Child of my loins; bearer of my son, I have never known you to commit otherwise. I trust you to make the right decisions and redress the balance of power. Before, it is too late.'

The spiralling helix retracted with a sudden flourish, the extensive pull on the energy flowing around and within Abigail causing her to scream as she was made to feel a violent orgasm.

Genesis had telegraphed its intent and formidable power, establishing his role of puppeteer and was the one manipulating the strings.

Abigail lowered herself to the floor and wept, feeling as if she had been abused and treated as nothing less than a chattel; an act designed and committed to undermine her position of power.

CHAPTER 3

INVASION...

>Power corrupts,

>Destroys,

>Is merciless.

>When exploited,

>With no compunction

>Or conscience given.

>The power is real,

>An emerging presence of evil

>As with a virus,

>Will spread until

>All in its path

>Is infected...Or Dead...

Abigail said her farewells and departed the island, having once again scanned the area within the perimeter defences. She had to be sure, as intuitive powers of perception let her know all was not as it should be. And she had no answer.

She let Myra know, this was not a time for lassitude and complacency, and all should remain alert to changing vibrational patterns in the ether; to have everyone expend their energy in protecting the island.

Myra became defensive, and eventually accepted the message of caution was delivered to them by the First Angel, and not someone prone to theatrical displays of pessimism.

'These are dark times,' Abigail had expounded, 'The present situation is more dire than it was before the war of angels. Evil has found a way to infiltrate our defences. I have witnessed the fall of great and powerful ancients. The tide of Dark Energy is relentless, and it is for me to find an Achille's Heel and repel its formidable charge.'

Abigail was not to know; the island fortress was to receive visitors after she'd vacated it to return home.

With the children in her auric circle and the animals and wonderful guardians on the estate, Abigail needed to focus on implementing a plan and to prepare herself for that which was still to come.

The island's first visitor on departing was to herald the return of the parakeet, who settled on the branch of a tree overlooking the residence, both domed structures adjacent to the immense mansion, and the pyramid situated at the farthest point.

It ruffled and fanned its feathers to discard the residual traces of the light energy it had again circumnavigated to find a pathway onto the island, having used Francis Peabody's signature as a beacon and focal point to achieve the feat.

It swept down, metamorphosing mid-flight into a naked Nemo, as he continued in a languorous gait towards the pyramid.

A scowl changed into a contented smile when the coded Sanskrit appeared, and with a nonchalant sweep of a hand, an aperture opened to allow him entrance. He was unconcerned the doorway should become sealed again, plunging him into an impenetrable darkness. His powers allowed him to see, without the use of optics. He sensed dust crawling over his host flesh, as a faint thrum of energy palpated along his veins.

His smile became richer and broader as he was to envision traces of the First Angel's recent visit. He was able to perceive the exchange between daughter and the light power of the universe, and recognised elements of disharmony, those he hoped to exploit to his advantage.

Nemo sent out a message to the universe and waited, knowing any response would be diluted as a reaction to opposing energies in a confined space would have a devastating impact on the environment.

He became instantly aware of a vibrational pattern of impulses attacking his host flesh, despite which, the universal great power seemed reluctant to reveal itself.

Nemo telegraphed his disdain in an archaic ancient code.

'I can end the chaos!' he relayed. *'But it comes with a price. As ruling father of the universe, you make it happen. You know what I want, as does your First Angel. Yet she fights me, without considering the benefits of my proposal. I am from the loins of the Dark Lord and will be perceived as untrustworthy. Yet, it is my sworn duty to assist in harmonising opposing forces, where both have a say in mankind's evolving and keeping the planet alive. As it*

once was, it can be so again. With your First Angel at my side and the offspring nurtured from a union of opposing forces, there can be a guaranteed balance of energy. The children will have to be stripped of their powers, so that your First Angel and I can exist as equals, with neither side granted superiority. Think on my words; as until my demands are met, the chaos will continue.'

Nemo was loathe to linger longer than was necessary to do so and teleported away from the pyramid to appear on the shoreline.

The large assuming sun was on the wane, dipping towards the horizon where a vast bank of grey mist approached. Its span was more than one mile and continued to extend in a short time.

Beneath the ocean calm, the mysterious fog bank reflected itself as hundreds of monstrous jellyfish teemed towards the lone figure calling to them from the thin belt of sand. Between the dense mass and the shore came a spiralling vortex of energy as the great ancient relic was awakened to the threat.

All around the island, other sentinels were beginning to rise as a warning signal was relayed.

The grey mist had stretched and completed a full circle around the island, converging on land at a formidable pace, as with the unnatural army of mutant jellyfish beneath it.

Nemo saw everything; his encroaching army, the rising of the ancient beasts with their multiple heads aloft tentacled columns. The creatures under his control followed the signature he relayed to them, having assessed a safe channel to approach the island from.

The grey mist itself, was a potent mass of energy and was cover to those creatures who adapted to propulsion out of the water, monstrous tentacles employed as powerful limbs to carry them forward.

Nemo's smile broadened as the encroaching scenario played in his mind. The assault he had organised was another clear message of intent, one designed to be of greater significance and more devastating than all which had transpired to the present time.

Following which, Abigail would know she was in a battle she could not hope to win.

It was Nemo's belief, the loss of so many she had deigned to love would have her cow to her knees and submit to his demands. As First Angel, she had allowed human emotions to conflict with those of a supreme celestial entity, and each was her Achille's Heel.

Nemo was someone who did not allow baggage to cripple his focus and goals, as he was without the capacity to feel, to regret, or to love. He harnessed desire, in that his goal was to assume control over all living things and to have the universe concede to each of his whims.

The great ancient beast the First Angel had an unnatural and intimate affinity with, burst into the open, throwing out erratic streamers of energy at the jellyfish amassed within the grey mist.

The kinetic tide was overwhelming, the tentacled creatures circling their prey and attacking. Scores of the incarnate mutations, latched onto the immense body and individual columns supporting their heads. Tentacles lashed and throttled the ancient flesh, their own deadly potent venom eating through its formidable defences.

Its cumulative roar and screeches of agony were met with others around the island, as the grey mist concealing Nemo's army poured over the beach, swallowing up the trees and undergrowth and arriving at the residence. The sheer weight of numbers caved in the roof and windows, the library and adjacent annexe suffering the same.

The onslaught was brutal and brief, even as the residents fought to repel the insidious tide sent to destroy them. Their collective power was not enough, as Nemo had predicted, and all the celestial angels were eventually overwhelmed; the universal life-force within, extinguished. As with the ancient guardians who dwelt in the ocean depths.

Nemo laughed raucously and changed into a parakeet; his immediate task concluded but knowing there was more to come.

He considered the First Angel's reaction to the news and the impact it would have. He sensed victory, could taste it, as all was within his power.

Where his father had failed, he was set to succeed.

CHAPTER 4

WHEN THE STONES ARE SINGING...

There comes a time,

When miracles exist

To bring hope,

Where hope is lost...

Mary Beth had taken up her routine vigil on the porch, keeping a wary eye on the pond lying to the left of her property. The pond had a history, and even though all had been quiet in recent times, Mary Beth was not someone who left anything to chance. She had witnessed and battled with monsters which had no place in the real world. And it was fortunate for her, she had her trusty Winchester repeating rifle working just fine when she needed it, and her aim was true.

The one who called herself Seraphina, explained; weapons could only be activated against evil energy, and would not function if used against an innocent soul.

Mary had chuckled, thinking government security forces, marines, Navy Seals and the National Guard are probably wondering why their weapons are ineffective.

'Without their weapons, they goin' to be lost and I daresay, there will be a lot of weepin' if they can't fire a gun,' she'd cackled.

Seraphina explained; that it was not the same in the new world. Leaders existed in every country, but without all the political furore attached to individual governments. The military was primarily defunct, as with policing. Those who served and survived, are employed to oversee the growth of towns and cities, and ensure all needs are met.

Mary Beth had taken time to digest Seraphina's statement, before remarking, 'And you believe that, missy? You been away from the real world way too long, is what I'm saying. Admittedly, there have been plenty of changes. Aside from which, not all in this world is good and God-faring. I have seen bad stuff. You know it. Evil is everywhere, honey, and it never went away. Never will. Without the military and the police, how are we supposed to defend ourselves?'

'It is not your fight, Mary Beth,' Seraphina had answered. 'It never was or will be.'

Pondering the young woman's answer, Mary Beth had sucked deeply on the stem of her pipe, feeling a little indignant, as she recalled previous exchanges with the stranger.

'Not our fight, you say?' she'd chuntered. 'Never was, or will be, you say? That's plain bull-crap. Where you been with your head in the sand, girl? Our boys fought wars to protect their nation from the enemy, and given the opportunity, will continue to fight. For our flag. And for freedom. Yessiree.'

Mary Beth raised her head as she was brought out of her reverie, cocked an ear, and smiled to herself, finally.

LEGACY OF ANGELS

The stones were singing once again.

Her visitor was nowhere around; had taken herself off to Jackson Hole and Yellowstone National Park – or what remained of it.

Had something to do with those jellyfish critters; Mary was thinking.

The vibrations beneath her were getting stronger, and there came a blanket of butterflies over the pond. And as before, when Seraphina first appeared, Mary Beth was unable to move out of the rocking chair.

She recalled Seraphina saying she was to receive visitors, and later, would be relocating.

Mary Beth was excited at the prospect of another person sharing her ranch home. She'd missed having company. So, it came as a pleasant and quite shocking surprise to her, when a naked man stepped cautiously out of the trees and hesitated.

As with Seraphina, his gait was ungainly and his muscular body went through similar contortions as it sought to establish physical form.

Mary Beth supposed it would have been respectful and good-mannered and a Christian thing, to have averted her eyes from seeing the man's 'privates.' The thought had her tittering mischievously.

No harm looking; she told herself. *And darn it; he was a handsome looking fella. Yessiree! Even if he did walk like a man in his cups.*

The new visitor was smooth all over and as he approached, his stride became more assured.

Mary raised an eyebrow and pushed her Stetson higher, so as not have it obscure her view as the stranger lumbered onto the porch.

He nodded a greeting, smiled warmly, and she was witness to a bright twinkling in his piercing blue eyes.

'Upstairs, second room to the right,' said Mary Beth. 'You'll find clothes that just might fit. Or not. Don't matter to me if you wear duds, or not.'

She laughed raucously as the stranger entered her home.

A while later and the latest visitor reappeared, and without acknowledging his host on this occasion, stepped up to the rails and cast his gaze in all directions.

'Is there more of your kind coming, or you the last of them?' Mary Beth enquired. 'Not that your being here is an imposition. Already have a young lady come stay; sweet little thing, she is. You got a name, young man?'

'You may call me Michael.'

'Praise the Lord, but the good gent has a voice, and not forcing words around my head.'

'Who has arrived ahead of me?' Michael asked, and Mary Beth was quick to note anticipation and excitement in his tone.

'Calls herself Seraphina. And she's a natural with the animals, I hasten to add. She sings and talks to them, that she does. She's been going about the estate, putting up defences; that's what she said, not that I notice any defences in place.'

'Be assured, they are there, for your protection Mary Beth.'

'And how would you be knowing my name? Just like your compatriot, Seraphina. Holy; but is nothing about me sacred?'

'My apologies for reaching into your mind, Mary.'

She cackled good-humouredly. 'No need to apologise, young man.'

LEGACY OF ANGELS

'There will be two more arriving,' Michael added. 'We will not be imposing on you for long. However, I wish to thank you for your hospitality. These clothes are a good fit.'

'Yes, I can see they fit just perfectly. You are all welcome to stay for as long as you want. Don't get to see many folk these days. Has me wondering, what in all creation is going on in the world. I used to travel around a lot, following the last of the quakes. I wanted to help folk, as I imagined a lot would have fallen on hard times. And I was curious, if you must know, as I wanted to see for myself what God had done to our fair land.'

'Not your God,' said Michael softly.

'The Devil, then.'

'Seraphina returns.'

Mary Beth was looking beyond the rails, unsure of the direction she would come.

'You see the fair one?' she asked.

'I feel her, deeply. Seraphina is a part of me, as I am to her.'

'If you say so, young man. Does that mean, the two of you are married, or something?'

'Not in the conventional sense as it is with mortals. We do have a son together, Daniel. One day soon, we will become reunited.'

'That's real nice. Your son; how old will he be?'

'Almost five; in your calendar years. And before you ask, we became separated of necessity; not by choice.'

'Will he remember you?'

'He will know.'

LEGACY OF ANGELS

Michael turned his gaze to the long sweeping drive where a dense cloud of butterflies had accumulated, and from within the colourful spectacle emerged a beaming, luminescent Seraphina.

She hesitated momentarily and was then running to greet the new arrival.

Mary Beth sighed and rolled her head as the one called Michael levitated and sped the short distance towards the oncoming young woman. He caught her in a powerful embrace, swung her round effortlessly, and was then kissing her.

Mary Beth was remembering how it had once felt to be desired and kissed, as with her visitors.

Yup, she was thinking, *those two love birds are so in synch. Hope they don't go making a lot of noise in the night, if they can wait that long. There's only so many memories this old gal can cope with.*

The stones were no longer singing, so she supposed it was enough excitement for one day. And supposing, the pond wasn't about to give up some more of its secrets.

The butterflies had dispersed; as before.

Hand in hand, the lovers approached and Mary Beth was able to ease herself out of the chair to greet them, trying to remain imperious considering she was playing host to two angels, or extra-terrestrials. She didn't mind either way, as they made her feel useful, and safe.

She offered them a beverage and they accepted, both staying back and then following her into the home.

Michael and Seraphina had a lot of catching up, it appeared, and most of their conversation was conducted telepathically. Mary Beth didn't mind being excluded, sensing some things had to be private, especially amongst celestial beings. Just having them close and being friendly, was enough; she surmised, as their presence was a balm against the loneliness she'd endured for a time.

It saddened her, to think they would be leaving once they received other visitors. She'd be alone again, in this strange new and hostile world, and it would feel different. Mary Beth knew it was going to be difficult making adjustments once again.

They had to have been reading her mind, as both turned to engage her in conversation. She wanted to ask them; what it was like to be descendants of the stars and not mortal, as she was. She wondered if they possessed potent powers, which surpassed telepathy and teleporting, to defeat the spread of evil. Dark Energy: Michael had explained.

Whatever that entailed. Evil was evil, no matter how you dressed it up. Evil was ever-present, had always been the way, turning man against man, man against nature. And when nature fights back, man is helpless.'

Mary Beth asked Seraphina how her trip to Jackson Hole went, and whether she'd discovered anything. She added the Yellowstone National Park as an afterthought. She was desperate to know if she'd met anyone else on her travels. The idea that everyone was gone, and she was the only one left, was deplorable.

Seraphina had quickly put her mind at ease, stating she had encountered several groups, all of whom appeared to be safe and thriving and had set up small communities.

It was Michael who suggested Mary Beth vacate her home for a time and visit. He'd added she wouldn't be alone anymore.

'Have my babies in the field, and there's the chickens,' she'd countered, without too much conviction. 'Would like to have myself a dog for a companion. I do simply fine. This is my home. I can't just leave. I have some wonderful memories, going back to my childhood. I'm not going anywhere, but it sure is nice and heart-warming, knowing there's other folk around. Not just me.'

As dusk approached, Mary Beth excused herself and assumed her routine vigil on the porch, a habit she couldn't seem to break, even if she did feel safe. As much as she craved company, she still hankered for occasions to be on her own.

The evenings were her favourite time of day, as insects came to visit in swarms, not that she paid any mind to their peskiness or irritating hum. Frogs began a chorus of croaking, and birds noisily settled for the night. The sheep were bleating and the hens were a constant gabbling.

This was home.

Mary Beth chose these moments to recapture elements of her youth, interspersing these with memories of her dear departed parents and husband.

Her attention was drawn to a vibrant display over the calm pond, of huge swarms of fireflies and only came out of her reverie with the emergence of Michael and Seraphina.

That was the precise moment, the stones in the distance began to sing once again.

'The visitors you have been expecting; I presume?' Mary Beth stated with a smile. 'You said, the circle of ancient stones are a portal between this world and the universe, allowing energies to travel between dimensions. What's to stop others using it, those with black hearts and souls?'

Michael favoured her a beautiful smile. 'Evil has its own doorways,' he said, even as he returned attention to the copse in the distance.

'That's a relief,' she answered with a nervous chuckle. 'Now that your visitors are arriving; how long will you be staying? I mean;

I have plenty of room and I can provide for you all. I don't want you to think you're imposing.'

'We will stay only one week,' said Seraphina. 'We have work to complete, before we must relocate from necessity. Thank you, Mary Beth.'

'Might I ask, what this work entails, and can I assist in any way?'

'Our task is to ensure your safety. That is primary,' said Seraphina, as she turned to meet with the deep sepia of Mary's eyes. 'You may not know this, Mary Beth, but you have always been guardian of the stones, and will continue in the role. We will assist in re-establishing your powers.'

'Baloney, child,' Mary chuckled. 'I'm mortal, and not like your kind. I bleed, I swear, I fart; and put one foot in front of the other to get about. I don't go around floating on cushions of air, or fly, or read people's private thoughts, I hasten to add. Sure, you're not mistaking me for someone else?'

'We will help you understand; and reveal a past which has been suppressed.'

Michael interrupted the exchange. 'They are here. Your parents, Seraphina, are to join us.'

CHAPTER 5

ULTIMATUM...

> **I will flow in your veins,**
>
> **I will be the subject of your thoughts.**
>
> **I will be the dream from which you cannot wake.**
>
> **I will have you want me,**
>
> **Breathe me,**
>
> **And crave the sustenance I give.**
>
> **And you will know,**
>
> **ME!!**

There can never exist a quiet, uneventful time for reflection, as the evil tide of chaos continues to sweep across the globe as an irrepressible and unstoppable tsunami.

LEGACY OF ANGELS

Abigail was enjoying a family meal with the children in the garden at their home. Gillian and Margaret were humorously at odds with one another, as neither could agree on a topic or share the same opinion. Mostly, they were discussing the situation the new world was facing. Abigail's mother, Aisha, not wishing to get involved on their friend's debate, could only expound on the meal Celestine had prepared for them.

Abigail was first to react, upsetting her plate and going ashen, as images of the slaughter on the island retreat she'd recently vacated, impacted with her senses.

Then the children cried out in unison, as they too felt and witnessed the aftermath of carnage wrought to the haven which had for them, a store of wonderful memories.

'What is it?' Aisha asked, astounded and confused by the sudden outpouring of calamitous grief and looking to Celestine for support.

'Abby? Children?' Celestine cajoled.

A tearful Abigail raised her arms to the side and the children were quickly out of their seats to receive comfort. Luke clung tightly, trembling uncontrollably. Daniel was more reserved and was able to shield his thoughts.

'Mummy?' Luke implored. 'The island? All the people and our friend of the ocean? What does it mean? How could this have happened?'

'It's a clear message, honey,' said Abigail softly, and fighting the tears as best she could. 'Letting us know, there is no place on earth or beyond, which is truly safe. We must prepare ourselves, for we are at the heart of what has become, a personal war.'

She caught the women and Daniel staring at her.

'It's him!' snapped Daniel, his expression denoting anger and shame. 'The one who calls himself Nemo. He destroyed the island, and now he is coming here.'

Abigail conceded and nodded, while marvelling at the boy's advanced intellect and growing powers.

'Yes,' she admitted finally. 'Nemo intends to advance to here, our home, and he will come with a set of proposals. I must warn you now, children, under no circumstances must you let his presence provoke you into revealing your powers. Now, is not the time. I know that you are both hurting and grieving, but you must trust me to manage Nemo and make a decision which will benefit everyone.'

Daniel broke away, barely able to contain himself, and ran into the house. As Celestine went to rise, Abigail said to give him time and space.

She was not at liberty to share the truth, as the fate of the future was finely balanced.

That, which defined survival or extinction, of all life.

Luke ducked his head round the frame of the patio doors, stating his need to be alone, and asked permission to go to the stables. Daniel asked to go with his soul-brother, saying they would be quite safe.

Abigail broke protocol for the first time and granted the children leave without a guardian to watch over them, perse. With the children's departure, Abigail telegraphed a message to Free Spirit, to go to the stables and be their keeper. She let the mare know, that dark energy was approaching.

Luke had not said as much, but when his mind became cluttered with images of the carnage wrought on the island and to the ancient beasts who were sentinels, he'd also been thinking about his

327

friend and mentor, Chan Li. Luke was certain, something bad had happened to him, so it was a surprise he should experience a flood of unexpected emotions.

Abigail believed she owed the women sat around the table, a concise explanation of all occurring in the world. It was no easy task, relaying an inventory of the tragic events she was aware of.

She warned them of the evil presence to have unleashed dark energy on the new world and gave a representation of the Dark Angel they were to face, and the monstrous army he had spawned to assist him.

Silence around the table was palpable as the celestials ruminated the prospect of another war, if it should come to it. So many of their kind, including Joshu, had fallen to the new tide of evil in recent times and gave perspective to their predicament.

Abigail found herself apologising, and the women would know Abigail was blaming herself, since she was the one who strayed from the edict the universe passed down, by consorting with Chan Li under the watchful gaze of the great power of the universe.

Chan's continued absence and silence was naturally a very deep wound, and all hoped it would not affect Abigail's leadership. As with the Chosen One at another time, not so long ago, they believed Abigail was their one hope of salvation.

Aisha, Gillian and Margaret, along with Celestine and the children, were all potential targets. Celestine sensed this, perhaps more than the others, and she was also thinking about Free Spirit, as another the face of evil might seek to remove from Abigail's life.

As Abigail rose to leave and go to the children, she had access to all their thoughts. She understood why her mother would fear for her. Abigail's disappointment was directed at her own father, in that he should turn his back on her at a time when she needed him most.

She failed to understand, that petty spite could be the reason their Utopian existence was dismantling at a startling pace, and beautiful souls were having their light extinguished.

Abigail met with the children at the stables. Daniel was outside the gated entrance and was studiously watching Caleb munching on hay. Luke was out on the drive embracing a spiritual connection with the mare, Free Spirit.

Daniel turned, having sensed Abigail's approach, and waited. His expression gave nothing away, and as Abigail crouched to give him a hug, Daniel placed a forefinger to her temple. He telegraphed a sequence of images to her mind, proving a maturity in one so young, as he was letting her know the content of his thoughts must not be revealed or discussed. Using a coded language, he was able to explain his feelings.

'My parents have returned,' he informed her around a beautiful smile. *'I hoped they might find their way back. I know you are the architect behind their return, and I can't thank you enough.'*

Abigail felt hot tears brimming on her lashes as she pulled him tight to her breast.

She already knew, without having to be told; she was linked to her soul sister, and that of Michael and Seraphina's parents, their return ostensibly tenuous and cloaked in secrecy.

She was excited and thankful, knowing Seraphina and her close friends had found their way back. Their combined presence, she understood, had to remain guarded. It was imperative, their arrival remained undisclosed, even to her father. *Especially, to her father.*

LEGACY OF ANGELS

It would be no easy feat, as very little escaped the Great Universal Power's attention. Her only hope: was that her father was licking his wounds following the devastating assault on the island haven. It had always existed as the primary portal from the universe to the planet.

Genesis had a secondary option, which was the pyramid situated beneath the circle of ancient oak in the field at rear of the estate.

Abigail's priority over all things, was to protect the children, until such time as their collective powers unified and matured. The waiting would be difficult, as it had been for the Chosen One in the years leading up to her *Awakening*. It was at a time, when focus from the universe was on the emergence of the Chosen One, deflecting attention away from Abigail as First Angel; as she presumed it was, with Nemo.

With the Dark Lord defeated and forced to retreat, Nemo had been unleashed and was to seek revenge. Nemo could not be killed, as First Angels existed as the balance keeping the energies of the universe stable. Removing one of those elements would cause catastrophic instability, resulting in the universe imploding; and subsequently bringing an end to all life forms, the complete destruction of all planets and stars, instigating a chain reaction of discord throughout the galaxies for billions of years.

For planet Earth to survive, Abigail had to devise a way of containing Nemo, and prevent him from using his powers of destruction, death and mayhem.

Taking Daniel's hand, she led him to where Luke continued to hug the mare's snout, where a spiritual connection had been forged to placate the trauma he was experiencing.

Luke became aware of their approach and turned on his heels, a fire blazing in his eyes behind a shimmer of tears.

'Is my friend, Chan Li, lost to us mummy? I wish to know, as I am unable to connect with him,' he spluttered, which served to enhance his agitation.

'He is not lost, lovely. I too, cannot reach him as I would like, although periodically I perceive his signature. However, it is too faint, and is constantly fluctuating, so that I am unable to grasp his energy trail and go to him.'

'But what does that mean exactly, mummy?' Luke stubbornly enquired, and not have his mother's explanation placate him. 'What of father? He must know. So why doesn't he help, and bring Chan Li home?'

'I will be honest with you; the both of you.' Abigail crouched, so that she could conduct her appeal at eye-level. 'I have done things which have disappointed your father.'

'Why would he be disappointed?' Daniel interrupted.

'Why?' she answered and paused. 'Because our father knows I gave my heart to another, that which is not decreed by universal law.'

'But mummy!' blurted Luke. 'Father needs you to be strong. With Chan Li at your side, you had that strength which is needed now.'

'Sweetie; sadly, father sees it quite differently. I have broken a universal law, and it is seen as a cardinal sin. I can only hope, he will forgive me in time. Before it's too late.'

Luke moved quickly to embrace his mother. Daniel's attention was elsewhere, his gaze penetrating beyond the gate and perimeter force-field, as a small deer loped past the stone pillars at the end of a small drive and stopped. Daniel believed the deer was watching him, perhaps studying them all as a collective, and then it skipped away to be swallowed by the undergrowth and trees on the opposite side of the road.

Daniel sent out a scan, as something in the way the deer had looked at him, had him curious and cautious.

'What is it, Daniel?' Abigail asked, as she locked onto the boy's scan and pushed further. She saw the deer Daniel was perceiving, and the way it was hugging the shrubbery for cover. She also sensed; it was seeking ways to penetrate the defences with its own extraordinary powers.

Abigail tensed and ordered the boys inside the house and to go to the spare room. They were to protect themselves within the circle of crystals.

'I wish to meet with this Nemo,' said Daniel, his answer quite unexpected, and shocking Abigail momentarily.

'As I do,' mimicked Luke.

The children sounded so grown-up; Abigail was thinking. And perhaps they were as they were both descendants of ancient lineage.

'It's not wise; not at this present time,' said Abigail, as she tried to come to terms with the fact Nemo had found them and had arrived in the guise of a fawn.

'I'm not afraid of the enemy,' said Luke with a strong pout.

'I'm not afraid of him,' said Daniel, and was first to approach the iron gates.

Abigail grabbed Luke's hand before he could protest and followed quickly after Daniel.

It became apparent to Abigail; Nemo could have acquired knowledge as to the location of the estate from a few sources. She was thinking of Joshu, even Chan. There was also her one-time friend, Leandra who had been succoured by dark energy. She doubted Nemo would have been able to follow her own signature.

She also knew it was a matter of time only, before Nemo would reveal himself at the location she felt most protected, as a way of proving a point and his intent.

Abigail telegraphed a command to the children in the coded sequence they often used to communicate and known only to them.

'At no time reveal your powers to the enemy,' she said. *'The time to express your full potential will come; but it is not for the present. Do you understand?'*

Both boys let her know they understood as they formed a line at the gate.

Abigail called to the enemy.

'Will you show yourself?' she taunted. *'Whatever you need to say, state it, and then leave. Never to return.'*

The fawn stepped out of the undergrowth and paused on the road, at a safe distance beyond the perimeter defences. Nemo responded telepathically, even as he chose to remain in the guise of a deer.

'Thought I should come and visit, in person,' he said to Abigail directly., who was attempting to keep the exchange singularly channelled to her mind, even as she sensed the children were tentatively probing at her thoughts.

'You were warned never to come here,' Abigail responded sternly.

'And what can you possibly do? You can threaten me, but we both know, you cannot function as you might against other energies.'

Abigail tested him, by pushing the defences further out, to meet with her adversary, and saw the deer flinch away and retreat a short distance.

'I cannot end this, as I would like; but I can hurt you.'

'Sadly, yes, and as you know; I can hurt you too,' Nemo countered, in a tone which vibrated caution and contempt.

'Do not test me,' Abigail warned.

'Will you approach me; to better converse, as equals?'

'We have nothing to say to one another, so I suggest you give up on your quest and crawl back to your lowly place in the universe and assist your father in licking his wounds.'

She sensed him growl, knowing the barb had struck.

'Know this, for I will have you feel me flow in your veins, First Angel,' he retorted. *'I will forever, be the subject of your thoughts. I will become the dream from which you cannot wake. I will, have you desire me, to breathe me, and crave the sustenance I can give. And you will come to know; ME!'*

Abigail responded, and not in a way Nemo would have expected, as pushing the fortified boundaries further, she cast a net of energy around the trees behind her foe, and poured her power into the road beneath him, so that he jumped. As she'd expected; he changed form and became a tawny owl. With a wild, frantic hoot, it went to fly away and came up against a wall of energy. Diverting course, the owl faltered, as it couldn't prevent its feathers becoming singed.

Smiling triumphantly, Abigail released him, and the owl flew away above the tree tops, anger fuelling its speed and determination to flee.

Luke gave Abigail's arm a tug.

'Why did you let him go?' he enquired. 'You found a way to ensnare him.'

'Yes; but now was not the moment. My powers alone, are not enough, sweetie. Nemo would have found a way, the consequences of which might have been dire. The important thing to remember, is that I have proven to him; that he cannot take, which I choose not to give freely. He miscalculated.'

'It has made him angry,' Daniel snarled in response. 'And it will spell disaster for others. My brother is right; you had him and could have ended it right now.'

'As I said, my powers alone, are not enough. All I did, was contain him for a short time.'

'What now?' Luke asked.

'We wait,' Abigail answered. 'Now, boys, do you wish to assist in feeding the animals? It will be good for our souls.'

The boys nodded in unison, even as Abigail was aware of their reluctance.

'Followed by home-made ice cream,' she added, and was grateful to receive two beautiful smiles in response to her suggestion.

CHAPTER 6

HIRAETH...

(Meaning) A spiritual longing for home,

Which maybe never was.

Nostalgia, for ancient places

To which one is unable to return to.

It is the echo of the lost realms.

Of our soul's past,

And our grief for them.

It is in the wind,

And the waves.

It is nowhere,

And it is everywhere...

LEGACY OF ANGELS

Seraphina knew a time was approaching for them to leave Mary Beth and her wonderfully eccentric hospitality. Mary loved her home, the open spaces, the scenery, the lambs, and chickens.

In the conversations they had shared in a short time, Seraphina had become fascinated with Mary's rendition of all the exciting and fulfilling memories she had procured over time. Seraphina also admired Mary's courage whenever she had faced adversity and overcame it.

She would have liked to have stayed longer.

She had Michael back, and he was going nowhere without her. Her parents, Aurora and Dolmati who had recently joined them, both knew they had returned for a reason, and knowing in their heart the family was not complete.

And could never be, until they were reunited with Daniel.

It grieved Seraphina, in that she was forbidden to reach out to her son. She supposed; she would give just about anything to see him in the flesh, to hold him, and be able to give him motherly kisses.

There was one other, to tug at her heartstrings. Her soul sister, Abby, had shown her the way back. She was remembering all the wonderful occasions she'd shared with Abigail in the past. There had been frequent liaisons of an intimate nature, in the physical and spiritual sense. All were moments which had them bonded, conjoined of the heart, soul and mind.

She understood, patience was required, something which had been asked in the years leading to her time of Awakening; as the Chosen One.

She would not have to wait as long, as the crux of evil was on the rampage, and a confrontation of opposing forces was imminent and unavoidable.

Nemo, she knew, was not someone who could be repelled, or destroyed. Containment was the only viable course to maintain an equilibrium and continue mankind and Earth's survival. It would be no easy feat, as Nemo was the Chosen One and First Angel to the Lord of Dark Energy, and this made him formidable and omnipotent in the extreme.

They had to try.

Otherwise, all was lost; and every soul to have been sacrificed, would be in vain. It was a concept both deplorable and unacceptable.

Seraphina excused herself from Mary's home, as she needed to be alone with her thoughts and memories for company. Even as her desperate yearning to be reunited with her son and meet with her soul sister was to take precedence and torment her.

She levitated around the outer reaches of Mary's ranch estate, only pausing to give comfort and assurance to the flock which had trebled in size since she arrived. Following which, she circumnavigated the pond, and still felt the necessity to scan its depths, should evil have found a way back.

Mary had encountered Dark Energy's monstrous centurions on the one occasion, drawn perhaps to the ancient memories the stone circle in the wooded copse evoked.

The ranch was remote, of little significance and no immediate threat, on the surface.

It was conceivable to Seraphina, the stone circle had acted as a beacon; as with light energy, it could attract elementals of dark energy also. It was uncommon, yet feasible.

As with the spiritual highways traversing parallel dimensions, opposing forces travelled them and oftentimes a brutal confrontation between good and evil transpired.

LEGACY OF ANGELS

Michael had assured Seraphina the ranch was adequately protected. The portal had been the perfect choice for the celestials to return safely and undetected. Their presence in the new world had to remain a secret, until such time as they were called to reveal themselves.

As decreed, by their First Angel.

Even Michael had private moments when he could reflect on the nature of those meetings he had had with the First Angel, Abigail, as all had awaited the emergence of the Chosen One.

Abigail had been another of the guardians assigned to protect Seraphina from the forces of evil, and from their first unexpected meeting when Abigail herself was in the guise of a child, Michael had recognised a great power she adeptly suppressed.

Years later, he'd come to suspect Abigail was more than she appeared, and knew she was the only one he and Seraphina could entrust their son to, beyond the war of angels.

As it was written.

Aurora met up with Seraphina on the periphery of the stone circle, her sudden arrival pulling her daughter out of a meditative state of mind and spirit.

'Darling,' she spoke within her daughter's mind. 'I hope, most fervently, you are not trying to connect outside your circle of protection.'

'No, mother,' Seraphina answered with a strained smile. 'I am not so foolish, as to risk everything to appease my own selfish needs. You taught me patience, and it seems, I am required to maintain forbearance for a while longer.'

'I know how difficult this must be for you,' said Aurora, and taking Seraphina's hands in an affectionate grasp. *'Thanks to Abigail, we have been shown a way back. We can do this, Seraphina. We may not be an army; but we are, an exceptional and powerful force.'*

'It's sad, to think we fought and sacrificed so much, yet saved so little, as billions perished beneath the wrath of Dark Energy.'

'Think on this; of the billions who survived and have risen in the embrace of hope. Nature rebuilds and thrives. The sacrifices you speak of, were not in vain, darling. It may not be apparent, but our victory gave the people of the world a second chance.'

'And now evil has returned, to finish all that was started. As First Angel to the Dark Lord, you know that he cannot be destroyed. Nemo can be repelled, but he will find a way back. He must be contained indefinitely, not that I am to foresee how this can be possible.'

'It will all become apparent, when the time comes,' and Aurora cajoled a smile when she briskly pulled her daughter into an embrace and kissed her cheek. *'I couldn't bear to lose you a second time,'* came the whispering words to Seraphina's mind. *'We have so much more to fight for.'*

'Will you walk with me, mother; just for a little while?'

They returned to the house as dusk approached, and a swarm of fireflies congregated over the pond.

Michael was in a telepathic discussion with Dolmati, with Mary having taken herself off to the kitchen to prepare drinks for everyone. The women received warm smiles as Michael extended a hand for Seraphina to join him on the sofa.

'We leave tomorrow,' Dolmati telegraphed. *'There is a safe and viable location in the Amazon forest. It is there, we are to*

prepare and await a sign. The journey will not be as traumatic as our previous travail. Other than the process of teleportation, it is imperative we conceal our powers within the protective energy field around a lost ancient temple, which is our location. I know that you have been tempted, daughter, but you have to understand the importance of secrecy, even from the overlord of universal light. It is my belief; Genesis cannot be trusted at this time.'

'We are not only at war with evil,' Michael interrupted. *'It appears that we cannot wholly trust everyone who walks in the mantle of light. Too much is at stake, and a reason we cannot reveal ourselves. Our return, naturally, was not in the Grand Design.'*

'Who do you suppose, dictates the course of the future?' Seraphina enquired. *'I have the distinct feeling, opposing forces of the universe have worked towards an accord, and all which has been sacrificed to preserve life on the planet, has been in vain. What of the children? Are they simply pawns in the ridiculous game the Universe contemptuously plays.'*

'We will find a way,' said Aurora. *'That, which is beneficial to all who serve, and for the children to develop their powers.'*

'I trust Abby to do the right thing,' Seraphina responded firmly. *'She will not let us down, nor the children. She will fight on two fronts, against her father and the enemy, and I will willingly stand at her side and commit to her.'*

'As we each pledge to do,' said Aurora, and smiled.

CHAPTER 7

GRIEF...

To grieve with intensity

Can be a dominant emotion,

To allay all reason.

In grief, one is changed,

Into someone who is nothing

Or becomes, an uncontrollable tide,

Of great, and unrelenting power.

There will come,

Abominable rage...

Cole had been travelling the spiritual highways and when he materialised, he staggered and fell headlong across a carpet of burnt grass. He gave himself a moment to adjust to the change, as his journey had been arduous and erratic.

Through a coruscation of tears, he somehow found a reason to laugh. Except, the laughter was manic and seemed not to be his own. If he were to analyse all the permutations for the way he was feeling, he would have a thousand and more reasons to celebrate. For he had survived a great battle and was victorious. And he was miraculously unscathed. He fought with no army at his side or at his back. He had defeated evil, with a rage borne of grief, and knew he could and would not stop until he found the source.

Cole was aware there was one supreme being who controlled the swelling tide of dark energy, that which infected all who stood in its path, of those who had been granted hope following the war of angels. The one he sought, was the same entity responsible for turning his beloved Zanula, and for the second time, his beautiful son, Luka.

He made a vow, not to rest, until there came a day of reckoning. Should he survive a confrontation, or not, he was compelled to try.

Vengeance was all which motivated him.

Cole rolled onto his back, the warm grass sensually reacting to his skin and the energy he had yet to retract.

He watched the flight of a Kite circling overhead, a majestic creature gliding on silken currents of air, and Cole likened the great bird of prey to an angel.

The analogy made, he abruptly sat up and surveyed the area around him. He had no idea why his spiritual travels brought him to an open pasture with coarse hedgerow on all sides. The nearest trees were a considerable distance away. He saw no inhabitants in the vicinity, no vehicles or farm implements, just a blank canvas of exquisite tranquillity. He could have been just about anywhere in the world, not that it concerned him.

LEGACY OF ANGELS

For as long as the influence of evil existed, Cole would wage a private war and seek to destroy it, no matter the form it chose to take.

His recent travels had taken him into towns, villages, and cities, where he'd discovered emerging pockets of infected inhabitants. Men, women and children had fallen to the resurgent tide of dark energy as mankind became hosts to its abomination.

Cole had no compunction when faced with the enemy; for each victim was already lost, their souls having been blighted with the foulness to have taken control of them, and all with no exception, became fodder to his avenging wrath. Cole had dispatched without remorse.

Latterly, he had waged a monumental war against all the odds, on the banks of the Saragossa Sea, where the enemy; numbering in the hundreds, had converged on his position undercover of great swaths of seaweed and dark mist.

Cole had defiantly summoned evil to him, not knowing or caring as to the numbers who rallied to meet his taunting cry. The box jellyfish mutations were legion and operated as a singular cell.

Unperturbed in the face of danger, Cole had watched as a great stretching wall of grey leaden mist rolled over the surface of a quiet sea. He had sensed the sheer intensity of accumulated power within the mist and beneath it.

The only thing in life Cole had ever feared, was to lose his wife and his son. Now they were gone. It was neither arrogance nor machismo ignorance governing his emotions. He believed totally in the power coursing around his spiritual form, and it was this, which made him omnipotent.

At the time he faced the enemy might by the sea, Cole had kept his powers restrained and honed, until it was the moment to unleash its full force. Cole had eerily felt each presence the mist cloaked, long before he saw the enemy he was to face.

As the grey mist rolled towards him, Cole levitated and unleashed his formidable weapon. He rotated his body, having witnessed the mist stretching on two sides to create a horseshoe effect, the intention naturally to encircle him.

He was reminded of the legendary story of Custer's Last Stand at the Battle of Little Big Horn. Custer had not survived his battle with Chief Sitting Bull, and Cole was not thinking he would be defeated, despite the vast numbers opposing him.

As energy extended from both wrists, Cole was taken back to the War of Angels, when he had fought alongside his wife, Zanula. He was reminded not only of her beauty; he'd been inspired by her focus and determination, and unswerving courage.

Cole had felt the ecstatic pull on his senses the moment he let his energy erupt as lethal darts and lasers. The great swords of flame he wielded lashed in a frenzy at the dense morass of lethal tentacled monsters.

All had become a blur to his mind as the deadly jellyfish pummelled him from all sides. Only his instinct and desire to win, drove him to discover greater heights of determination.

Always, there was Zanula and Luka in his mind, as he sensed them urging him on. The battle had lasted less than an hour, and at the end, he had repelled the mist and slaughtered close to a thousand of Dark Energy's soldiers.

Cole had no idea how many of the foul beasts existed to prey on the earth and beneath the seas and oceans. Even if they numbered in their millions, Cole's duty to his departed wife and son, was to destroy everyone, should it be within his scope to do so.

LEGACY OF ANGELS

He was sending out a private message to the One who spawned the evil tide, and it was Cole's belief, the creature he sought would know of him and his personal vendetta.

Having sent out a scan of the pasture and beyond, Cole began a leisurely amble over to where he'd espied a small gap in the hedgerow. He could have teleported once again, except he was tired, and needed a generous moment to recharge and regroup.

He wanted more than anything to simply connect with memories and to sleep for a time, before continuing his mission, hunting the enemy.

Cole believed he'd been given a moment's respite from the torment afflicting him, when he thought Zanula was speaking to him. There followed laughter, and he could swear his son was a part of the reverberating memory in his head. An overwhelming and debilitating surge of raw emotion had him weep and clutching his stomach. There followed a scream and a flood of hot tears he had no control over and had no wish to stem.

He regained consciousness and caught himself staring up at the 'angel' circling and sweeping overhead, against a sheer blanket of vivid azure. He had no idea how he came to be lying in the middle of a narrow country lane, its warm tarmac surface stippling the bare flesh on his upper torso.

He came alert the moment he sensed the presence of two individuals and rolled over to better observe. He saw them then, a short distance from his prone position. One was a young woman of a rare beauty, with a flood of reddish-brown hair fanning around her arms and hips. She was clutching the hand of a boy child, whose mop of unruly hair was the colour of jet.

He became intrigued, sensing they were other than mortal. They were scanning him, their combined distribution of power insinuating a path into his thoughts. Cole encouraged them to continue, feeling the trickle of energy seeping along his veins. He welcomed the intrusion as it established their intent. He would know if their influence was spiritually benign, or otherwise.

It was the boy's signature which had Cole scrambling to his knees, and not the young woman's. She was apparently more adept concealing her true feelings behind a carefully erected mask.

As with Cole, the boy was full of anger and frustration. His thoughts conflicted with those of his mother, was understandably precocious and had yet to learn restraint.

It was the boy who, in effect, let Cole know they were other than benign entities. He felt a disruptive flow of evil energy, that which was mirrored in the coal-black of the child's eyes.

Cole rose to his full height, more steadily and acquiring greater focus, as he pulled an untenable wrench around the inquisitive trails mother and child had inflicted on him. Letting his own powers evolve, Cole established an instant of confusion in the young woman, as she'd not expected to confront a celestial entity who walked within the power of light.

Cole received a melange of intent, the woman believing him to be one of the guardians of the estate. Not that Cole had an inkling as to why she would think this, or as to its importance. There was mention of two children, as Cole detected elements of hatred. He didn't think the children were the main reason.

Grappling their trails and not relinquishing them, had Cole feeding on their emotions and telegraphed thoughts from the mother to the boy. There came anguish and admonishment, and it was the woman who revealed their purpose for being on the road, and of their ultimate destination.

Cole determined she was on a quest for revenge, having intimated the loss of her lover and father to her child. She'd been warned, to desist from ever taking revenge on the person responsible. A name: the subject of the young woman's degenerative hate, began to spiral around her thoughts, not that Cole was able to comprehend.

At mention of Abigail, Cole had to wonder if his close friend resided nearby. The young woman he confronted, and he'd determined she was called Leandra, seemed to think so.

The fact this dark scourge was seeking retribution against Abigail, incensed Cole, and he telegraphed a message; stating their quest was futile.

The woman tempered her emotions and was mature enough to know she was facing a great power and would have to employ a different tact. Cole's eyes widened; the moment the boy revealed an image of the creature cocooned within his stout body.

Consumed with the rage he felt when faced with evil, Cole let the energy of his spirit flow from his arms, and sensed the woman meant to teleport away from their position to a safe location. Cole would have followed their trail with relentless determination, but the boy had pulled away from his mother's connection and was preparing to unleash a charge.

Cole was aware the mother had been thrown in a panic, and he seized the moment without hesitating. He was facing a great evil and knew his dear friend Abigail was in peril.

It was Cole, who in fact, teleported away from his position, only to reappear immediately behind the threat he'd faced. He instinctively swept his arms side to side, the fizzling weapon he wielded, slicing through the woman's body, and decapitating the boy.

The creatures within them were endeavouring to burst free of their hosts, yet Cole was relentless and maintaining focus. He hacked furiously at the hideous incarnations revealing themselves, until only scattered mounds of gore remained to stain the tarmac.

Cole backed away as the weight of his achievements, that which had been fuelled by his obsessive hatred of evil, slammed his senses and drove him to his knees once again. He had yet to retract his powers, and the ferocity exuding off his aura caused him to convulse. He pitched forward onto his face and lay still, his powers spent, incapacitating him.

He had only his memories to comfort him as he wept afresh.

It was conceivable he lost consciousness for a time, when next he felt, or imagined, a hand soothing the back of his neck and pouring energy into his soul.

He expelled sour air in a burst and eased onto his back, the figure kneeling beside him appearing nebulous behind a veil of tears.

A voice trilled with soothing tenderness into his mind and feverish confusion had him believe his beloved Zanula was present and tending to him.

'Take your time, Cole,' the voice spoke to him. 'Deep breaths. Slow, deep breaths.'

The person administering care acquired definition, and he was surprised and thankful, it was Abigail who had discovered him.

He was unperturbed she should be feeding on his thoughts to glean information. She would become a witness to his terrible anger and would know he had unleashed his fury against a young woman and her son.

Not that they were innocent, as the new breed of dark energy had infected both. They had been vessels and carriers of an insidious parasite.

It had been the same; with his wife and son.

Cole was again taken by surprise when Abigail took his hand and teleported him away from the carnage he'd wrought on the country lane, not to her home, but somewhere isolated, peaceful, and picturesque.

Cole found himself gazing across an area of unsurpassed beauty, and realised he was smiling. There was a vista of dense undergrowth, and trees enclosed a smallish lake, where a waning sun reflected burnished gold and red on the smooth undisturbed surface of the water.

He looked to the side and caught Abigail studying him.

'Thank you,' he said. And it felt good to have been released from all the tension. Even the confusion within his mind had abated.

'I understand why you acted as you did,' she remarked. 'I cannot and will not judge you for expressing your feelings in the manner you were to commit to. I am so deeply sorry for your painful loss, my lovely. As you know, we are in a desperate war, and many wonderful souls have fallen to the new wave of evil. I feel the depth of your pain, as if it is my own.'

'You say, you do not cast judgement on me as a result of my actions,' he answered her, while feeling an irrational urge to pull her into an embrace, as her calmness and complete understanding were a balm to his tortured conscience. 'No matter, for I will be my own judge. I am on a personal vendetta, and will not desist, not until I have rid the planet of this evil scourge. Or, until I am dead.'

'I will not stop you,' said Abigail succinctly. 'I can only pray and hope, you will come to know when it is time to remove yourself from grief, and to be able to live once more. You are a wonderful inspiration, Cole, a great leader. More importantly, you are a beautiful soul. Your anger motivates you now, and your feats against a common enemy will not go unnoticed. You will not have to seek the source of dark energy, for it will find you. You must take care. Please. For me, and for the planet.'

'I cannot rest, Abby. As I have vowed to confront the arbitrator of evil and destroy it. I know that the one I seek must be your equal, but I have to try.'

'Please, Cole, you cannot defeat him; or come close.'

'That is your understanding, knowing I do not possess the same powers. I know that I am seen as a lesser echelon in the hierarchal calendar and cannot possibly win a personal battle. In the Bible, there is the story of David and Goliath, and David smote the giant with a stone and slingshot, and guile. The moral of the story; no matter the odds, the minnow can win.'

'I ask this the once; that you desist now in your vendetta,' Abigail pleaded, and saw the answer in his thoughts, before it reached his eyes and curled the corner of his mouth in a wry smile.

She reached up and kissed him on the lips and was then gone.

Not for the first time, Cole was taken by surprise. He fervently hoped he'd not disappointed or hurt his friend with his words and the need to continue a determined quest.

Following a moment of pondering, Cole went to leave the idyllic area Abigail had brought him too and discovered he could not teleport.

He tried several times, to no avail, and had to wonder if Abigail had set him a test. It was obvious to him; she didn't think he was the Biblical David to Nemo's Goliath.

As an alternative, Cole endeavoured to summon wings of energy and felt an instant of exultant pull on his host flesh.

Yet he was unable to rise.

He could have forgiven himself, had he resorted to frustration and become further angered, except he was neither.

She had ensnared him; of this he no longer had any doubts, and Abigail was the arbitrator, only in that she was trying to protect him. She cared, ultimately.

Cole threw out a panoramic scan and instantly saw the reason why he was unable to leave, as Abigail had incarcerated him within a gilded cage of her inimitable positive energy, that which he was unable to penetrate. She had employed the same tactics when imprisoning the nest of dark crystals, he'd discovered with his wife and son on the atoll in the Sea of Crete.

Cole laughed at his enforced predicament, and it felt wonderful to do so, as on this occasion it was delivered with genuine good humour, and not so manic as in previous episodes.

He sat on the verdant grass around the silky perimeter of the lake, crossed his legs, and induced a state of meditation; in the hope he could find a solution to the dilemma he was placed in.

Abigail's power was supreme, as he would expect from the exalted First Angel, and it was up to him to attempt to break and dissect the coded sequence of energy she'd erected around him, as a fortress to protect and contain him.

What surprised Cole, was his uniquely positive attitude to his plight, believing he could win. And in finding the key to unlocking the gilded cage he found himself in, would prove to Abby, he was more than capable.

His underlying grief was temporarily forgotten, as Abigail had hoped to achieve.

Cole chuckled. He liked a challenge, that which could push him to his limits, and beyond. Of all he'd encountered up to the present moment, this was perhaps his greatest hurdle and conundrum. His self-belief, astounded him, as he was quietly convinced nothing could stop him from achieving his goal. Not even the formidable power of the First Angel.

CHAPTER 8

THE REEKING TIDE OF EVIL...

And there will come,

Hell on Earth,

To obliterate

All hope...

Matt Willis was standing at the gun-whale, observing a view of an endless line of fog on the horizon, as it seemed to stretch to infinity. Its dark-grey colouring was in stark contrast to the blue of the morning sky. Its symmetry suggested to Matt, it was other than a natural phenomenon.

What began as a thin sliver, acquired greater definition, as it became apparent the grey mist was approaching at a rapid rate of speed.

Matt became animated and hurried to the wheelhouse, firing the engines in one fluid motion. It was fortunate he was facing shore, as time was of the essence, and was thankful the yacht had speed. He hoped it had enough to outrun the nebulous fog bank, as he had a premonition all was not natural with the encroaching mist and it filled him with a sense of foreboding.

The Golden Chance cut a clean swath through the Pacific waters on full throttle, a glimpse at the screen on the customised dashboard, showing the fogbank was gaining.

That which he feared the most, occurred, when the crystal powering the craft began to fluctuate. Matt was expecting the yacht to stall and become stranded, as tension tightened his chest and dried his mouth.

He was recalling words of advice given to him when he'd received a celestial visitor, who introduced herself as Abigail, should the crystal fail him at any time.

Matt believed the crystal was being drained, and supposed it came as result of the approaching mist, that which was drenched in dark energy.

Matt willed the crystal to fight for him and his yacht, just as he glimpsed fronds of mist cutting across the view on port and starboard.

The Golden Chance gave a sudden capitulating whine, as it drifted to a steady halt. All the electrical circuitry blinked once, the screens going black.

Matt only tapped the steering column, as much as he wanted to punch it. It was now, all about self-preservation. He had no idea what to expect once his yacht was overwhelmed with the energised fog.

What concerned him, was whether the effects would prove fatal if he were exposed to it. Much like radiation; he surmised.

He hurried to the lower deck where all his equipment had died. He was floundering in darkness, with only a soft glow from the steps he'd descended, illuminating a possible hiding place.

The largest cupboard space housed all the cabling, with much of the boarded area remaining uncluttered. Throwing back the doors, he lost balance as something struck the hull of the boat with enough force to rock the vessel.

Matt dragged himself into the crawl space, taking meticulous care around the cables. He lay down with his knees drawn to his stomach as he pulled both doors shut. It plunged him into complete darkness, not that it mattered, as he had his eyes closed.

He realised he was praying; despite the fact he was not religious. He was a scientist, whose faith was governed by material findings and visual proof submitted by the universe.

Abigail's otherworldly visit had proved to him, his alternate faith was just.

The Golden Chance gave another fearful lurch, and Matt gasped as the hull gave a petulant whine. He was in the hull, and if it had been breached, Matt was certain he would drown in a matter of moments.

He opened his eyes as the rocking motion of the yacht threw him to the side and both doors slammed open. In a panic, he reached out to close them, and hesitated at sound of heavy thuds on the roof and decking. There came the brittle tone of glass shattering, and Matt understood all the panels of windows along the sides and at front were being pummelled.

He shut himself away again and was thankful he'd not seen water flooding the hull area. All he could do under the circumstances, was brazen out the horrific assault on his yacht, and pray it would soon be over.

Matt endured unspeakable terror for close to an hour, when all became steadily quiet, the Golden Chance finally settling. Matt waited a considerable time before he dared venture out of his closet prison.

He rolled and tried to stand, grabbing at the surface of the overhead unit to steady himself, until the cramping subsided. Casting his gaze around the gloom, he didn't notice any structural damage or to his expensive equipment.

Shambling over to the steps leading up to the galley, he paused and listened before making the short ascent, establishing all was quiet and with nothing moving around. He sucked down a breath as he became witness to the carnage, where all the windows were broken, and where the panelled ceiling was buckled and split open in several places. The floor space was littered with debris.

Beyond the windows, Matt noticed the sky was clear, with the sun flaring off the ocean swell. More importantly to Matt, there was no visible sign of the mysterious fog bank to have overtaken his yacht.

He wondered if the phenomenon had simply dissipated, even though he was of the opinion, the fog had unnatural substance to its structure. The speed with which it covered the mass of water, without wind currents to drive it, suggested the grey mist was the ultimate project of evil. It even had Matt wondering if the fog bank had been given a purpose.

Ahead lay the mainland of the United States of America, and Matt was thinking the fog meant to target land and its inhabitants. He didn't want to think beyond that.

Matt stepped through the gap a leaning door left so that he could inspect the deck for damage. He was at a midway point when the vessel suddenly pitched left and right, and he instinctively spun on his heels having perceived a threat.

'Fuck me!' he mumbled in shock, as he wondered if his legs would fail him.

The gigantic box jellyfish, coiled and crouched on the upper storey, seemed to be observing the mortal looking up yet not making any sudden movements.

The monster began to laboriously raise itself, just as Matt dived for the doorway, narrowly avoiding one of the enormous Pedalium's as it whipped through the air.

Matt went to a shelf beneath the sonar equipment, dragging out a metal box and prising back the lid, as the yacht bucked under the weight of the monster jumping down onto the deck. Several its tentacles had slammed through the planks and became caught, the domed hood descending so that it was able to peek between the trembling columns supporting it.

Matt faced the beast, and smiled, raising the loaded distress signal flare gun, and firing; the projectile striking dead centre of the immense fluctuating hood.

The creature let cry a piercing screech as the intense phosphorescent ball of fire ate into its gelatinous flesh. Matt calmly reloaded the gun with a second flare, aimed and fired, the flare ripping across the underside of the hood and dismembering several of the bunched tentacles.

He had one more flare, and Matt stayed composed as he loaded and for the third time, took careful aim.

'For mankind and wrecking my boat; you piece of shit!'

The missile decapitated the monster, its deflating hood pitched over the prow into the sea, the flare continuing to ignite the remaining flailing tentacles.

Matt stayed calm as he retrieved an extinguisher from an internal housing, prepped it, and moments before the deck threatened to burst into flame, released a thick jet of foam.

357

Minutes later, he was leaning against the doorframe, the cylinder dropping noisily and heavily onto the step as he appraised the aftermath of his personal battle.

There was still the problem of the spindly Pedalium's jutting out from the ruptured decking. Matt knew from experience the Pedalium's could deliver a fatal sting, despite the fact the monster was very dead. More so, as these were the product of a seriously *'fucked-up'* mutation.

He suddenly chuckled, the moment he felt The Golden Chance give another lurch and began to move forward. From the quiet blipping sounds at his rear, he was aware also, his equipment above and below deck was stuttering back to life.

The crystal's energy had returned to give the yacht back its power, and if fate decreed, Matt believed the yacht would make it back to shore. Ignoring the remnants of the creature on deck, Matt stepped down and took the wheel, intent on steering a course to shore.

The only thing weighing on his mind, was the possibility he might confront the fogbank retreating away from the mainland. Added to this, he also had to wonder what might be awaiting him on his return to dry land.

CHAPTER 9

A WAY OUT...

A doorway is an entrance and exit.

Finding a way out

Must mean,

There can be a way in...

Cole suspected he'd spent a period of incarceration within a net of powerful energy for more than three days, and he was still no nearer to unlocking the ancient code devised to contain him.

Cole was of the belief, energy was composed of a specific and generic code, or several as each controlled the purpose of energy and in the way it could be manipulated. As with the way a celestial could erect a personal shield, wield a formidable weapon of destruction, or to teleport across dimensions and along spiritual highways.

Cole remained undeterred by failure and would keep trying.

Whatever force Abigail had used to imprison him, negated most of his own powers. He was still unable to teleport or use his wings. He could levitate, even summon his energy as a force; not that it was effective when trying to rupture the shield around him. Positive energy could not be used against positive energy, as it opposed itself.

The cage created to keep him incarcerated stretched to a diameter of half a mile and was similar in height. He'd walked the entire perimeter numerous times, using a scan to verify its density, and if a weakness could be established.

The architect of his prison had been thorough. She'd succeeded in suffusing his rage; only in that he was given no purpose to wield it. As he would have liked.

On the fourth day, Cole saw the lake as an invitation. He waded out a short distance, until he felt the hard bed beneath his bare feet slope away. He kicked out and dived and swam across to the other side in next to no time.

He congratulated himself for having achieved the feat, easily and quickly, and pushed away to continue the swim back to the other side, intent on swimming until he became exhausted or bored.

After a few crossings, he deviated from the course he'd set himself, and chose to swim underwater. It would establish the depth of the lake and what life forms existed. All he'd seen was a derivative species of shrimp, and algae. A lake without fish, just didn't seem right.

Cole discovered the lake bed was significantly uneven, with deep depressions and rough-hewn raised areas, he surmised was a result from the geological trauma the planet had suffered.

He came across a particular depression which gained his interest and sparked curiosity, as the water appeared agitated and was kicking-up pockets of cloudy silt. On closer inspection, he saw a small, hollowed area, which might have been a pipeline for drainage, or quite possibly an inlet from another source of water.

Easing away clumps of rock and clay, he saw the black hole slipping to infinity and was fathomless.

It had Cole intrigued enough to summon a steady flow of energy, which he applied directly at the mouth of the deep depression and carefully plough away at the bed, widening it so that he was able to push down and ahead with his upper torso.

Burrowing to any great depth was nigh impossible as the wet sod being clawed away began to smother him, and Cole knew; should he proceed without applying a safe strategy, there was every likelihood the walls and ceiling of the tunnel he'd created, would invariably collapse.

He slowly eased himself back and was witness to the inlet folding in on itself, and when he eventually emerged at the entrance, an alternative ploy played on his thoughts. Cole had to wonder, if there was every possibility, he could blast a path downward and under the erected force-field. He was certain the net of energy did not penetrate too deeply, as the vibrations the net created would have disturbed the water greatly.

The idea grew from seed and Cole set about the task of excavating clay and rock and create a passage he could work with safely.

He toiled for more than two days, using tree branches and twigs to shore-up the weaker areas of the tunnel he was fashioning beneath the surface of the lake. He used his energy sparingly to chisel and carve a passage, relying on manual labour to disperse the sod he'd removed.

On the third day since he began the task of excavating the lake bed, as the sun began to wane, and following a period of relaxation, Cole made a determined quest to bring his efforts to a conclusion. He eased himself along the tube he'd fashioned, anticipating whether the glutinous slimy walls would hold, or collapse around him.

He slowed, the moment he approached the location where the net of erected energy was almost directly above his position, and where its vibrations thrummed rhythmically, stirring up thick clouds of silt to obliterate his vision.

Not that Cole had to rely on his physical eyes, as his third eye was his guide. He was motivated to continue; in the hope he had achieved the miraculous.

Cole continued to claw away the soft clay ahead of him, pushing it down along his body to his rear. The moment he sensed the waves of energy on the surface were fainter, Cole changed tact and pummelled the thick silt ahead of him with his own energy, releasing thicker, larger clumps of clay.

Cole rolled and began tearing away at the ceiling, the hideous slime pouring over his head and torso as he sought to continue the tunnel upward. Despite being a celestial with inaugural powers, in that he could breathe underwater indefinitely, he began to tire and his movements were becoming increasingly laboured.

He persevered, because going back was no longer an option, and was rewarded when he made a concerted lunge and was met by a glorious vista of clear sky and a bright sun.

Cole dragged his weary body out of the confined space and slumped headlong across a bed of lush verdant grass.

And laughed.

The sound was expounded as a cry of victory, as he came to realise he had succeeded in breaking free of his prison. He felt elated, and at the same time, felt at peace.

He waited awhile so that he was able to recover from his exertions and regenerate, and the moment he was ready, he teleported himself away from the location and let the universe act as his guide.

Cole, not for the first time, was of the belief another force dictated his passage and assisted him on his relentless quest for revenge against evil.

He was not about to stop. He would do so only, when he was satisfied he'd avenged the loss of his wife and son.

CHAPTER 10

WARRIORS AND GODS...

Angels await a sign,

As they prepare

For war, once again...

Life on Earth hangs in the balance,

And it is for a chosen few,

To ensure victory against

A great evil...

AS IT WILL BE WRITTEN

Deep within the Northern reaches of the Amazon Basin, one hundred kilometres from the extensive River Amazon, the four celestials were gathered in unified spiritual repose, at the apex of a small stepped ancient pyramidal temple, originally built by one race of the Aztecs.

LEGACY OF ANGELS

It had been the ancient portal used for the travellers to leave the Wyoming ranch and Mary Beth and was a designated focal point for each to hone their energy in preparation for what was to come.

It was hoped, a plan was to be contrived and implemented which would concurrently end the rapid tsunami of Dark Energy sweeping across the globe, and effectively avoid a recurrence of cataclysmic events of a few years ago.

The stone blocks forming a platform under a columned feature at the apex of the pyramid, was weathered smooth, so that seated in a four-pronged group was not uncomfortable, as a meditative state was required and could conceivably take hours.

A unified aura of energy created the semblance of a low-rising sun within the four sturdy pillars and flat overhang.

The apex of the temple was considerably lower than the tree tops which formed an expansive green sea of foliage in all directions.

By late afternoon of the fifth day, the group descended and gathered at the base. The chatter of wildlife in the branches of the trees was vibrant and discordant.

Aurora and Dolmati offered to traverse the perimeter defences and scan for a threat, leaving Michael and Seraphina to enjoy some free time together.

Michael was even able to chuckle as they walked hand in hand, where the undergrowth was less dense and made passage easier.

'You are easy to read at times,' he remarked in a jocular mood. 'You want a quick end to all this, as it is difficult for you to remain patient.'

'Understandably; don't you think?' Seraphina countered, herself smiling in response to his remark, and to be granted a precious moment away from celestial duties. 'I wish to become reunited with our son and meet with Abby and Luke.'

'It all augurs well, darling, and it's my belief your wishes will be granted, and soon.'

'Once again, we are required to confront the might of evil, defeat and banish it for an eternity,' she responded with passion. 'We cannot have it return.'

'The force we are to confront, is the Dark Lord's son and First Angel. As with his opposite, Abigail. It's my understanding, the evil cannot be defeated in the physical sense, as their purpose for being is to maintain a balance in the universe. They are untouchable and cannot be destroyed. To remove the one, you must remove the other.'

'What exactly are you implying, Michael?' Seraphina queried and calling a halt to their travail so that she was able to face him with her concerns. 'If the enemy cannot be defeated, what are we to do, to effectively put an end to this?'

'It's my understanding, evil must be contained, and our unified power is the key.

'Containment?' and Seraphina gave a rueful shake of the head. 'And you believe this is the only course to be taken, to ensure Dark Energy does not lay waste to the planet once again?'

'I am assured it can be done,' said Michael, and tilting her chin up so that the vivid blue of his eyes could connect with her own, binding them spiritually. 'We hold to faith, and trust Abigail to find a solution.'

'I have the faith and know that Abby will put the safety of the children ahead of everything. Now, my handsome man and father to our son, I will have you kiss me.'

'I was about to, my darling; and more.'

LEGACY OF ANGELS

Seraphina raised an eyebrow in query, and Michael stopped a sudden peal of laughter with a kiss steeped in desire.

The next morning, having each taken turns throughout the night to establish the perimeter force-field remained intact, Dolmati awoke ahead of everyone and went to stir Michael from repose. Aurora had been alerted from her guardian duties as Seraphina was gently awoken from a peaceful slumber.

'I wanted you all to be aware, I am feeling an atmospheric disturbance,' Dolmati explained in hushed tones. 'Let me just add, that I am not perceiving a possible threat from this anomaly. I think it would be prudent, at this time, if we all prepare ourselves for any eventuality.'

He caught his daughter smiling at him, and it was one of radiance. It had him wondering if, perhaps, she knew something of which he was not aware.

'Everyone can relax, for she is coming to meet with us,' Seraphina informed the small group. 'My soul sister has come to visit. She was the sign we have all been waiting for.'

'Are you certain, darling?' Aurora asked. 'Abigail would be taking a monumental risk by coming in person.'

'She risked a perilous journey through the heart of the universe to free us. Abigail knows what she is doing, and I would know her signature anywhere, so deeply enmeshed are we. As to be one soul, at times.'

Michael indicated the ancient pyramid. 'Look to the temple,' he said. 'The summit glows with a powerful concentration of electro-magnetic currents.'

LEGACY OF ANGELS

Attention was on the monument, and it was Seraphina who approached ahead of the group. She chose to levitate to reach the top, ahead of climbing the steep steps which would have taken longer.

At the apex of the monument, the interfolding waves of effulgence began to dissipate around the solitary form of the First Angel, Abigail; and her smile of greeting was effervescent.

Seraphina held out her arms, while appraising the fine sequinned second skin of miniature white feathers hugging areas of her flesh. Unable to wait, Seraphina grasped the hands of her friend and soul sister, pulled her close and kissed her on the mouth.

'I have missed you so much,' Seraphina cooed softly, just to feel this much joy once again. 'I feel I am blessed, even during these difficult times.'

Michael arrived ahead of Seraphina's parents, and each greeted their exalted guest with affectionate hugs.

'We've all been expecting a sign,' said Michael. 'I never imagined for a moment; you would deign to come to us in person.'

'We have much to discuss,' said Abigail, and as she sat she pulled Seraphina down beside her, not wishing to relinquish the grasp of her hand. The others followed and formed a small circle. 'First on the agenda; I wish to impart news with regards to Daniel. Just to say; he is a remarkable boy, whose powers have matured in a short time. He is truly a prodigal son, who is set to rule over a new world beyond this one.'

'It is your belief then,' Dolmati interrupted, 'the evil power, that of the Dark Lord's First Angel, can be contained indefinitely?'

'It can be done,' said Abigail calmly. 'Not that it will be easy.'

368

'We all hold to faith,' announced Aurora proudly, 'As I, for one, cannot wait to embrace peace once again, and to spend time with our grandson.'

Abigail telegraphed an image of Daniel to each mind and became witness to the rapture on their faces.

'I stated, just how his powers have matured for one so young. He is aware of your presence yet knows he must put a restraint on his emotions.'

'Forgive me for asking; but what of your father, Genesis?' Seraphina begged the all-important question Michael and her parents were thinking. 'I think it would be foolish to believe the great power is unaware of our arrival, despite our best efforts to keep our presence clandestine.'

'My father is licking his wounds,' said Abigail wryly. 'As he recently suffered a humiliating defeat. Which leads me to impart some incredibly sad news, and it's my hope, this will serve to make us stronger and more determined.'

CHAPTER 11

NO MERCY...

An Angel's wrath can be a terrible thing...

Cole materialised on the ruptured aft deck of The Golden Chance as it drifted lazily on an ocean swell.

He wondered why a motor yacht was a location for him to arrive at, and as he threw out an initial scan, he perceived no immediate signs of life. As if the boat was dead in the water.

Judging by those areas of visible structural damage, Cole believed the yacht had suffered an attack; either from adverse elements, or something else entirely.

Intensifying the scan as a precaution, Cole received a weirdly confused set of signatures, each of them revealing dark connotations.

Cole stepped to the port side and looked along to the prow. The boat creaked in response to the rocking motion of the waves, not because of old age, but where damage to the structure was exposed and had become dislodged.

Threading his way carefully and avoiding clutter and debris, Cole widened the scope of his scan, to determine whether a threat existed in the waters around the yacht.

He paused to gaze up at the immense shimmering spectacle of stars and a half moon. Looking up at the sky had Cole thinking about his wife and son and wondered if their souls had been returned to the universe.

Would they sense him; was a thought which was always prevalent? Not that he felt the connection he once shared.

Dark Energy had severed the cord which had bound them as a unified source of love and light. The pain of his loss continued, and would not abate for a moment, to grant him solace.

He'd rediscover it again, one day; in that, he had no doubts.

In the interim, he was on a mission of vengeance, and would not desist until he faced and defeated his nemesis.

Cole proceeded to the front of the luxury cabin and wheelhouse, taking mental stock of all the broken windows, and what appeared to be scorch marks and scrapes in the paint and woodwork.

Arriving at the prow end, Cole stopped himself, at sight of the decaying tendrils strewn on the splintered decking.

Not storm damage; he realised.

Each of the tentacles gleamed in the lambent light cast by the moon, and Cole became wary, as he felt energised signatures emanating off the putrefying flesh.

He stepped closer to the preponderance of decaying Pedalium's, only hesitating when his aura brushed them, and saw the way they reacted to his energy.

He didn't suppose there remained life in the severed limbs, but an inherent memory which existed within the membranes of each appendage, and Cole's energy was breathing substance to each of the latent signatures still harnessed within the remains.

Cole came alert to a presence and turned on his heels to greet the person leaning in the doorway to the galley.

A naked, surprised Matt Willis ran fingers lazily through his long lank hair, scooping it down to cover a lesion above the right nipple.

'Fuck, man!' he guffawed, using laughter to cover his anxiety. 'You people; whatever you are, must love my research.'

Cole was still pondering a reason why he should be drawn to a useless yacht bobbing serenely on the waves.

'Are you another, who has come to witness one of life's miracles?' Matt continued, seemingly unperturbed he should be naked in front of a stranger. 'It's apparent, you must be one of those celestial entities, like your predecessor; Abigail.'

At mention of his good friend's name, Cole's interest and expectations heightened.

'You received a visit from Abigail?' Cole enquired curtly. 'What was her purpose for meeting with you on your boat?'

'Same as yours, I daresay,' Matt answered, and out of necessity, hanging resolutely on the door frame to support himself. 'She came seeking proof of a mutated species of jellyfish. I say mutation, but it's gone beyond rapid growth; we're talking about the incredible evolving intelligence of an aquatic animal, over a noticeably short period.'

'I know of the jellyfish,' said Cole, alert to a stream of erratic signals in his mind. 'And know exactly what they're capable of.'

'I take it; you've come from the mainland? Man, it's a warzone. Something out of a horror movie, with aliens taking over humanity. I've been witness to unbelievable and inexplicable atrocity. As you can see, from the remains on my deck, the yacht came under siege. The one who called herself Abigail, said the crystal was my protection. Hey, you obviously possess similar powers, so maybe you could get my crystal energised again. As you can see; the yacht's pretty much useless now.'

'The crystal has been drained, for a reason,' said Cole sternly, and without warning; even a glimmer of conscience, he projected a lance of pure energy outward. The ferocity of his power punched a fist-sized hole in Matt's face, to exit out back of his head and continue, smashing through the interior on a path one half mile out to sea.

The body of Matt Willis went rigid and spasmed violently, as tentacles attempted to burst out of his anatomy.

Cole's energy contained the creature within, without completely severing the head from its deadly Pedalium's.

'Your evil stench cannot be disguised,' Cole spat venomously. 'I know; you are all connected to the one source I am seeking, and I will have you reveal the monster to me! Before I send you and the rest of your fucking kind, to Hell!'

The interior fabric of the cabins ignited, with flames and smoke finding an outlet through the window frames, the ceiling quickly yielding to the inferno.

Cole telegraphed his intent.

'You murdered my wife and son! I dare you to face me! Hear my call to arms; or are you a coward, who must hide behind an army of misfits?'

Cole teleported away from his precarious position, an instant before scores of jellyfish reared out of the sea and launched themselves onto the vessel. They weaved and floundered, seeking their prey as the Golden Chance exploded and incinerated most of the invading army of mutants.

Cole's astral energy became greatly constricted, as he was propelled along spiritual highways, at a speed faster than light and sound. As before, the control was not his own to make. All he could do to alleviate the depths of pain to which his spirit was subjected to, was keep an image of his wife and son in his mind.

CHAPTER 12

A LEGACY OF ANGELS...

The secrets of the universe

Were always meant to be revealed.

AS IT HAS BEEN WRITTEN...

Abigail sensed; a confrontation with her nemesis was increasingly imminent, and she had to be ready. All that she had fought to preserve since the planet's conception and the emergence of life, hinged on a plan she'd devised to contain the tide of Dark Energy at its source.

She had faced the might of greatest evil on numerous occasions, culminating in the Chosen One's dedicated sacrifice to repel the wrath of the Dark Lord.

Abigail recognised the fact, Nemo was her equal; a twin-flame, who reflected all which Abigail was capable of. If he possessed a weakness, Abigail needed to discover, understand and exploit it to her advantage.

LEGACY OF ANGELS

She would only have the one opportunity, and if she was fortuitous, she had to effectively make it count or all of existence would be lost.

In the early hours, while all were sleeping and with only the five guardian sentinels out in the fields, Abigail relayed a message they were to maintain vigil at the perimeter while she prepared for a possible, final confrontation.

So as not to disturb the horses, all of which had been taken to their stalls, except for Free Spirit who was another acting sentinel in the fields; and not to alert the other animals in her menagerie, Abigail teleported to the circle of ancient oak trees situated in the field at rear.

As it was prudent and pertinent to do, despite the stringent defences in place and constant monitoring of events outside of these, Abigail projected a wide scan of the area around and above.

Satisfied, all was relatively peaceful and was not being observed, Abigail stepped within the circle where she immediately felt the formidable embrace of ancient energy. She once again teleported, only a short distance, to emerge within the pyramid under the sod.

Abigail's long wavy tresses immediately swept into a radiant fan around her slight frame as she became assailed with the energy of the giant quartz crystal.

Composing herself and drawing on the crystal's energy to connect with her own, she willed the great obelisk to rise from the earth, where she had it levitate so that she could manipulate its position. The point slotted perfectly against the apex of the pyramid to create a vertical column of iridescent splendour.

376

The crystal was in direct alignment with the universe, feeding on its unequivocal power so that a spiralling helix swept down to caress its majestic form.

The crystal's inimitable glow flared sharply and briefly, and Abigail had to close her eyes to create a shield against the surge of power ignited within the crystal.

Content, Abigail returned to the surface, and spoke to each of the seven mighty ancient oak trees, in a language and universal code the trees would understand.

Leaves of burnt red and copper shook, as energy was stirred, Abigail raising her arms to the side as the earth trembled. Each tree was fed by the crystal beneath them, and there came small eruptions of the sod at the base of each of the seven sentinels. Immense intertwined roots became exposed and these began to yawn and separate with a plaintive groan and a creaking of limbs, to reveal seven sister crystal obelisks: each, two metres in length and breadth.

Abigail thanked the ancient oaks and as she levitated, the seven quartz prisms rose in a shimmering circle and travelled with her to the field adjacent to the cottages, and with the road at front.

Abigail drifted as a leaf to settle on the grass, the crystals aligning in a perfect circle, emulating the exact circumference and positioning of the oak trees in the field at rear. Their flat base hugged the ground briefly, as Abigail concentrated her powers, willing each to seep into the earth. When they were completely submerged, the grass and sod magically repaired itself, Abigail finalising her achievements by ensuring all sources of energy were primarily deactivated.

As she turned away to amble across the rising and dipping field, Free Spirit cantered across to join her.

Judging the mare's momentum and positioning herself, she rose and leapt astride the horse, urging her into a relentless gallop.

LEGACY OF ANGELS

She was smiling, she was free; knowing she had implemented the only course of action open to her.

Genesis would know, naturally; yet she hoped most fervently his attention would be elsewhere, dismissing her attempts to instigate a new universal design, as futile. It was within his power to interfere and eradicate all she meant to achieve, and to do so, negate any chance of saving humanity from the evil scourge sweeping the globe. Genesis could support her or challenge her powers. She would have her answer, in due course.

By the time Abigail returned to the cottage, everyone was awake and enjoying breakfast and beverages. All ceased what they were doing as eyes were drawn to Abigail standing in the doorway.

All knew, Abigail was to impart startling news, that which could determine the outcome of the war against evil.

'Would you like a water, juice or coffee, darling?' Aisha queried, while attempting to keep the family gathering as close to normal, under the circumstances.

'A coffee would be nice,' said Abigail, compelled to join the boys and kneel between the rustic chairs they were seated on.

They each responded by hugging her, while astutely keeping their eager thoughts private.

Abigail raised her head to confront all around the table, and her mother who came to join their group.

'As you all know, I mean to instigate a confrontation with the enemy, and doing so I have to employ certain measures. I have called upon ancient magical and mystical tradition for my plan to conceivably work.'

'The alignment of the moon in respect of the constellation of stars,' said Celestine. 'An event which only takes place sporadically throughout time.'

378

'And this is to occur; when?' Aisha interposed.

'Two days from now,' Celestine submitted. 'Ancient energies, of those lying dormant, will awaken once again. It could conceivably change the course of nature, as respective elements within the universe converge at this time. It is, from my understanding, not without its problems; as a balance must be maintained to ensure a unified equilibrium.'

'And should the balance, you speak of, become disrupted, my dear?' interjected Maggie.

'The end of the world,' Gillian countered, and tittered, to have been able to add her observations to the conversation.

'The maelstrom effect,' said Celestine, with all seriousness.

'What is the maelstrom effect?' Aisha responded and forgetting for a moment she was making her daughter coffee.

Luke had become overtly agitated by all the remarks shared around the table, unlinking his arms from his mother's neck, slapping the surface of the table to vent his frustration, and succeeding in getting everyone's attention.

'Mummy knows what's required to end this war,' he stated defiantly. 'I trust mummy to do the right thing.'

Turning to gaze directly into his mother's eyes and placing hands either side of her face, he was unable to prevent his lower lip trembling.

'I know this is the only way,' he remarked softly.

'How do you propose to initiate a confrontation with that monster, Nemo?' Aisha asked.

'All is in place and in readiness,' said Abigail, her heart swelling with pride, and allowing her love for her son to channel a path to his mind. 'We all have a part to play; more so, for some of

379

us. For my plan to work in our favour, seven celestial elements are required to contain the source of evil, so that his powers are negated and made ineffective.'

'What is this containment you speak of?' asked the elemental, Gillian. 'If you are to capture the beast, would it not be wise to remove him completely? Destroy him?'

'Wisdom is not in the obvious,' said Abigail. 'Wisdom is knowing, some things cannot be eradicated indefinitely, as with the universal might of Dark Energy in the war of angels. Evil can be repelled and deflected; or it can be contained.'

'To destroy the source of one or the other of the opposing energies,' Celestine continued the explanation, 'Would result in the maelstrom effect I mentioned.'

'Precisely,' said Abigail. 'Containing dark energy, will ensure a balance of power within the universe continues. To eliminate one faction, the other must be sacrificed, to ensure the balance continues.'

'And if and when you contain this evil,' queried Aisha, still not convinced as to the planning of a proposed confrontation, 'What do you mean to do with your prisoner? Is he to be banished to the far reaches of a distant galaxy? And can you hope to contain him indefinitely? Has this even been done before? Honey, I'm not trying to denigrate any decision you make, but it seems to me; this is a plan based purely on wishful thinking.'

Heads turned as Daniel added to the debate, having remained silent all this time.

'It is the only way; as it will be written,' he stated, in a tone which was ethereally succinct and etched with maturity and knowledge, 'The seven elements will act as an unbreakable bond, and a means to create a prison within the pyramid.'

'Oh my!' ejaculated an exasperated Maggie. 'You mean to keep the Lord of Evil on the estate?'

''That is my intention,' Abigail answered, 'For I will remain the gatekeeper, and be the one responsible for overseeing Nemo's incarceration indefinitely.'

'The seven elements you speak of?' Celestine queried.

'So that you all know,' Abigail responded, 'The seven elements I speak of, comprise the most powerful and ancient influences in existence. Each will be fed and governed, by the forces of light derived from the most ancient and powerful crystals. Their energy is linked directly to the universe and will become effective at the time of the alignment of planets and stars in the constellation. The source of power, which connects to that which the pyramid provides, will act as a conduit. The crystals I speak of; are now in position.'

'What role are we to play in the forthcoming events?' Maggie asked.

'You have a choice; mother, Gillian, and Maggie, to leave or to stay. Should you choose to stay you must, under no circumstances, interfere in the proceedings I will have implemented. Celestine will oversee the protection of the children in the interim, until such time as they are called to assist me.'

Aisha gasped her dismay and feeling as if her legs would give way and have her sprawling on the floor.

'You mean to use the children as bait?' she threw at her daughter, before she could retract her words and relent. She was remembering another time, when her daughter had faced a great evil, the Dark Angel Azinor, and Luke was used as a pawn at that time to ensnare the demon.

'We are not to be used as bait,' said Daniel calmly. 'We are to be employed, out of necessity. Abby is aware of our powers, of a pure strain from the universe. Luke and I, are the future, and despite the fact we are not full grown and reached our capacity; we are ready.'

'This is crazy!' recoiled Aisha and diverting attention to making her daughter coffee. 'This does not bode well.'

'And your negativity will put our plans in jeopardy,' Abigail countered churlishly. 'Think I would personally endanger the children if I believed my plan was doomed to fail? The children will always have the ultimate protection. In the past, I have committed to deeds I wished I had not had to, had I been given a choice to solve issues differently. It is for me, to restore hope to a dying planet. And I mean to do so; whatever it takes.'

'So, what exactly do you propose?' Celestine queried. 'You have stated we are to be given a part to play in the unfolding of events to ensnare the enemy. What is the protocol required to ensure all goes smoothly and accordingly?'

CHAPTER 13

THE WAIT...

Anticipation, can result in

Overthinking a planned situation,

So that reality is not how one,

Perceives it should be...

Abigail had sent her message to her nemesis, purporting she had considered all of Nemo's previous proposals and had arrived at a decision which would benefit and satisfy both parties involved, while ensuring peace across the planet.

She offered to meet with him in person on her estate and specified she would be alone. She even gave him the option to attend a meeting alone or having a guard for support if he believed she could not be trusted.

She let him know in the message she telegraphed, to prove her sincerity, that all defences in and around the estate would be relaxed, and all the guardians will have been released from their duties.

Abigail made no reference to the children.

The message was telegraphed along a specific channel in the multi-faceted and complex network of spiritual airwaves. Abigail knew not to expect an immediate response.

She had a slender window of opportunity, of only two days, for her plan to be implemented and gain the required impact, in conjunction with the alignment of certain stars and the moon in the cosmos.

Should Nemo suspect, or believe she could not be trusted, it was conceivable Nemo would delay a meeting or even to suggest another location.

It was her most fervent hope, the carefully devised message she'd telegraphed to him, carried enough conviction of her intent to engage his curiosity and for it to feed his ego.

In the meantime, it was to become a torrid waiting game, as tensions were set to rise.

Abigail used her time sparingly, separating attention between family and the animals. The herd of horses had been brought in from the fields and were stalled in the stables, except for Free Spirit, who had been given the freedom to roam and was assigned as another of the guardians.

The mare had her own role of importance to play in the ensuing confrontation, her own specific and unique ancient powers to be employed to erect a shield around the elements Abigail meant to use against her adversary.

If all failed, the children were to be taken by Free Spirit across dimensions, where they could not be followed or captured.

Abigail hoped it did not come to that, as it would mean the children spending an eternity alone and forever fleeing; and it was not a life she would choose for anyone who were blessed with a beautiful soul. As it would mean; having the brightest flames extinguished.

On the evening of the first day, Abigail's mother let her anxiety get the better of her; where she protested vociferously, Abigail should want to use the children as pawns when luring Dark Energy into a trap.

In response to her mother's tirade, Abigail rose from the sofa where she'd been entertaining the boys with a story, and all within the room felt her composure slipping away and were witness to a disruptive flare of energy in her eyes which caused ornamental possessions and pictures to tremble.

'Mother, you are dismissed from my home until further notice,' she ordered, while delivering the retort in measured controlled tones. 'Your continued attitude and negativity puts us all in jeopardy, and I cannot allow it to continue, not when the moment is almost upon us. Leave, mother, and return to your home. You will know when it's time to return.'

Aisha looked mortified at her daughter and the cold disdain Abigail was displaying.

Not for the first time, Aisha knew she had crossed a line, and it was an occasion when forgiveness would not be granted.

She went to the boys, hugged, and kissed them stiffly, and when she tried to embrace her daughter, felt her daughter's disappointment wafting in waves.

Under the circumstances, she could only nod her farewells to the others, feeling defeated and forlorn, an outcast.

As Aisha headed for the front door, the twin souls stood up.

LEGACY OF ANGELS

'If it's okay with you, my dear,' said Maggie to Abigail, 'We will go with your mother, as it's not right she should have to face this difficult time alone.'

Abigail said nothing and did not respond as the old woman gave her a hug, kissed her forehead, and went to follow Aisha outside.

Celestine could only cast her gaze to her lap, knowing in her heart Abigail was doing the right thing, yet wondering if the human emotional response Abigail displayed as she conflicted with her mother, did not linger, and have Abigail lose focus.

Luke went to his mother and embraced her, even though her attention was on Daniel, and seeing the way he was appraising her.

'It was the correct and sensible course,' he said in soft tones. 'The negativity your mother was displaying would have conflicted with everything you mean to do. Understandably, it's the difference, between defeat and success.'

Abigail beckoned him to join the huddle where she clung to the boys in desperation, letting her love wash over and through them.

Come the morning, when the sun peeked over the crest of the stone wall, with Abigail sat on the patio at rear of the cottage; she was enticed from her reverie by Nemo's curt response.

She was both thankful and surprised, Nemo cordially agreed to her terms and would conduct a meeting in person, and without the necessity of a guard to support him. Nemo would have realised, Abigail would be true to her word, and know in advance if the guardians were deployed around the estate waiting on an ambush.

Despite which, his ego would lead him to believe he had already triumphed. For, like Abigail;, he was untouchable.

Abigail desired only peace on Earth, while it had been Nemo's task to create disharmony and further his father's bidding, by delivering chaos.

The only compromise he sought, was in taming the opposition First Angel, and make her his chattel.

Abigail still had several hours in which to prepare before her encounter with the enemy. It was imperative she kept the children safe, and in readiness for when they were to receive a cryptic signal for them to engage with her.

Celestine's specific role was to maintain calm and to initiate defences around the children within the crystals aligned in a circle in the spare room.

Every time she entered that room, she couldn't help transporting herself back to the time she'd returned with Chan Li, having taken a foray into a possible future. One of Nemo's despicable monsters had followed them back, only to become ensnared in the energised trap within the portal created by the seven crystals.

Abigail and Chan had been consummating their love for one another on the floor of the room beyond the circle of energy, and it was Abigail who witnessed a looming threat.

It seemed like a lifetime ago, and the memory only served to enhance her despondency, regarding what had befallen her celestial lover.

It was her intention, to confront Nemo and demand an answer; as to whether Chan was alive or dead, and she would seek proof one way or the other.

During the day, Abigail employed her time keeping the children occupied in normal playful activities, and not dwelling on anxious issues with regards to the anticipated confrontation to come.

On other occasions, she spent time in the field at rear of the estate, interacting with Free Spirit and going for a therapeutic canter.

Come the afternoon, with the sky remaining clear, Abigail took herself off to the pyramid where it was necessary to have her energy commune with the giant crystal obelisk and install sequential patterns of signals so that when the precise moment arrived, the portal above ground could be activated.

Following which, she meditated within the comforting and spiritual embrace of the oak trees, where she telegraphed further sequential codes along a protected highway to yet another of her designated sources.

Abigail could do no more. The wait was almost at its conclusion.

What will be, will be; she silently acknowledged.

CHAPTER 14

EQUILIBRIUM...

> **Not all is set in stone,**
>
> **Not all, is an exact science.**
>
> **Opposing forces dictate**
>
> **The level of balance in the universe.**
>
> **Should the scales be tipped,**
>
> **There will come that, which cannot be realigned.**
>
> **There will come,**
>
> **CHAOS...**

Abigail entered the adjacent field, as the sun dipped away, and the blue of the sky became leaden with the most prominent stars winking a greeting in the early evening tranquillity.

She chose to meet with Nemo as an angel, her fine costume of small silvery white feathers barely covering her modesty and employed specifically to entice and distract. Each feather gleamed as a fairy light beneath the rise of a full moon.

LEGACY OF ANGELS

Abigail levitated across the field in a leisurely manner, as she had no wish to allow anxiety precedence. She had to remain in control of the situation she was architect of, to ensure a smooth transition.

Her bare feet welcomed the cool of the grass as she set down and flexed her toes to grip and massage the dew-stamped blades beneath her tread.

Her mind was periodically on the children, as ensuring their safety and future was paramount to everything else. It was to be her legacy to the world, and to all she coveted within her soul.

A light breeze occasionally raised itself to whisper around her fan of hair. It caressed exposed flesh and murmured a sensual aria within the thin cloak of feathers.

Abigail crossed to where the seven crystals had been planted deep within the earth, awaiting a signal to become activated once again.

And it was there she waited, aware of the time by the ascension of the moon and position of the stars. She had given Nemo a time, and he was late, which she'd expected from him. He would decide when to make an appearance, as it would give him false security and the belief, he was in control.

Abigail ascertained he was close, as she was able to feel his presence, almost as if he flowed in her veins. His signature was at a respectful distance, and he seemed to have hesitated before making a final approach. She suspected, he had stopped to engage a scan, to determine the level of defences around the estate's perimeter; just to be sure Abigail was being true to her word.

She believed he was observing her, not that he was trying to reach into her mind. She would have known.

Nemo was no fool, and as his equal, would know Abigail had the capacity to change a specific scenario in the blink of an eye. He would be alert to any shift, no matter how slight, in the etheric patterns around her.

She was of the belief also, Nemo would suspect a trap, and it was her task to accommodate a feeling of trust between them, and to have him lower his defences.

She needed him to understand, she would go to any lengths to reach a compromise and end the bloodshed, and for both celestial forces to exist side by side.

Abigail would not be aware of one consideration he was to make; in that his purpose was not only to make Abigail his chattel, but he also had to remove the children from the equation, and thus eliminate their collective powers. The children were Abigail's lifeblood. If they were to cease to exist, Abigail would become nothing. Her spiritual powers will have weakened sufficient for him to exert his control.

From his position, Nemo was able to smile around a particular thought he was entertaining; believing they could have children of their own. It was an idea which appealed to his ego, as any offspring of two First Angels would be a mix of opposing energies. They were destined to be the future.

Nemo was certain in his own mind, should he gain control over his intended slave-wife, he could manipulate the future to his personal advantage and by doing so, tipping the scales unfairly.

Abigail remained within the hidden circle of crystals, her posture denoting calm, as she composed those thoughts she needed to focus on. She had her eyes closed, even though she was able to see clearly with her mind's-eye.

She became aware of an etheric shift in the air currents around her and felt a concentration of energy emerge a short distance in front. She hoped Nemo would approach, as she determined his position was outside the invisible circle. It was for her to encourage Nemo to enter the circle of his own free will.

Within her mind, Abigail saw a shimmering effulgence, having a distinctive orb of light at its nucleus.

Abigail knew patience, and believed also, she had the wiles to seduce her prey when the moment was right to do so.

She opened her eyes and saw that he was facing her. Instinctively, her brows were raised, as she was pleasantly surprised by the way he formally introduced himself.

Nemo had come to the meeting alone, and she perceived there was no threat in the vicinity. What surprised her most, was the effort he'd made to engage with her. Gone was the long scraggly salt and pepper beard, and his hair was shorter, neater. His face was perfectly smooth, as if he had been sculpted from a flawless section of marble. His pale brown smock coat was open to the waist, revealing a broad smooth chest.

He was devastatingly handsome; she was thinking, and he would have read her mind easily as she was able to do, while noticing the way his gaze surreptitiously danced over areas of her slight frame.

He genuinely liked what he was seeing; she noted.

Despite everything, he remained cautious, as she had expected him to. Nemo was no fool.

'Finally,' he said within her mind, *'We get to have a cordial meeting, without all the trappings expressing a level of mistrust.'*

Abigail refrained answering, and her posture remained relaxed.

'You have had the time to consider my proposals,' he said, and even smiling as he delivered his words. *'It would make perfect sense, should we compromise now and arrive at a decision which benefits both parties.'*

'Thank you,' Abigail replied, herself smiling, without restraint and neither was it forced, *'For answering my call and agreeing to meet with me. The reason I chose my home as a location, was to offer proof of sincerity, and to show I am willing to concede to certain demands. You know that I ask for peace and harmony across the planet, for mankind to be granted another opportunity to exist without fear, and nurture hope for the future.'*

'For me to arrive at an accord, you are aware; I will ask for much. However, I am also willing to concede ground to reach a harmonious agreement we can each exist by. I think; I will be asking more of you, than you can ever ask of me.'

'I am aware, sacrifices have to be made,' Abigail remarked with an element of caution, as she didn't want to appear over-eager and state only that which he hoped to hear. Nemo would see through the charade with ease.

There came a distinct pause, with neither offering more to the exchange, Abigail remaining passive, and keeping her personal defences at a low ebb. As with Nemo, who made no significant attempt to exert his own formidable power.

'I have to ask,' he finally submitted, *'As to where you have placed the children?'*

'The children are not the subject of any agreement we are to make,' Abigail answered, and used mortal feminine wiles to ingratiate her adversary's evident interest, in that she was able to control the ebb and flow of a visual aspect regarding her scant

costume of feathers. Where they faded to insignificance, she was able to reveal herself naked, only to again cover her modesty.

She repeated the necessary flirtatious tease a few times, and had Nemo approach, as she'd hoped.

Finally, she had him within the circle of dormant crystals, and from his posture and expression, he perceived no threat to himself.

'What have you decided?' he asked, both intrigued and intoxicated with Abigail's blatant display of wantonness.

'Is it not apparent?' she remarked, and found she was smiling, to have read his mind so easily. *'The deal is this: you get to have me as your concubine and equal. This depends, however, on you delivering proof the celestial, Chan Li, is alive or dead. Either way, my terms are genuine. I desire peace, hope and harmony, to reign supreme. I will stand at your side.'*

'And what of the children?' he countered.

'They are to remain in obscurity.'

'Ah; but their continuing survival will always pose a threat, as you could recall them at any time.'

'Any compromise made between us, must be based on trust. You cannot ask or expect me to remove the children permanently; for I will fight you. I can, however, offer an assurance, in that their powers will never be used to influence the future. I think you know; I am the only one who can make it happen.'

'There is another. Your father could also determine their fate,' he said, levelly. *'Or are you of the misguided belief, you are stronger and more powerful than the one-part universe?'*

'We both know, my father is licking his wounds; as with your own. And I think we both know, we cannot be destroyed, for it would

impact on the cosmos. Our fathers can play their petty games, but the truth is I too, can play, and will do so to win.'

'If I am to accept your terms?'

'It's what you want,' she stated calmly, and had her glistening feathers once again fade to insignificance.

She noted the way his porcine lips had parted, to allow the tip of his tongue to moisten them. It was something a mere mortal would do.

She covered herself once again.

'You tease, as part of your game,' he said, the tone within her mind, having grown husky with desire.

'I will ask once more; what has become of Chan Li?' she threw at him and noticed the way in which his pupils suddenly darkened.

'The proof you seek, may not be to your liking.'

'Alive or dead,' Abigail responded, *'Is of no consequence, and does not challenge my decision to concede to your demands. I wish to know; that is all.'*

CHAPTER 15

MASTERPLAN...

Even the greatest minds,

Wielding inexhaustive power,

Can falter.

And fail...

Celestine and the children received a brief coded signal, alerting them to prepare for the execution of Abigail's masterplan.

The boys were already ensconced within the inimitable protective force of the seven crystals situated in the spare room of the cottage. Hours of inertia had not deterred them from losing focus and following the guide lines set down by Abigail.

Celestine had utilised the time of waiting and minimise tensions, by constantly involving the children in conversation. She was able to paint an idyllic picture, of what it would be like to exist beyond the night.

Her eternal optimism was unwavering and kept the boy's encouraged and fuelled with determination.

Not that he was sharing, but Daniel had personal reasons he should be feeling inwardly excited and needed the plan to succeed.

Elsewhere, in the field at rear of the stables and kennels, Free Spirit was alert to the command she had received from her mistress and continued to pace around the exterior perimeter of the circle of ancient oak.

It was the mare's task to ensure the portal remained sealed, while laying the foundations of a shield which was hoped, Nemo could not detect.

Free Spirit's connection to Abigail, meant that the mare was able to see beyond the hedgerow and trees. She was also attuned to each of her mistress's thoughts and could establish a pattern of emotions Abigail was exhibiting.

Many thousands of miles away and deep within the Northern reaches of the Amazon Basin; Seraphina, along with Michael and her parents Aurora and Dolmati, all perceived their signal at the same time and for them to finalise preparations.

Despite the enormity of their mission and the potential hazardous travelling to their designated portal, it was important the group maintain single-minded focus, and not become distracted.

It was no easy task for Seraphina, knowing she was close to becoming reunited with her son and to once again, fight alongside her soul sister, Abigail. For the sake of freedom, and a chance for the world to again, embrace hope.

The four celestials gathered at the apex of the ancient Aztec pyramid, interlocking hands to create a positive circle of energy, and channelling their collective powers to meet with the helix flow descending from the universe and beyond to substantiate a portal.

LEGACY OF ANGELS

On the estate, with Abigail facing her adversary with undisguised nonchalance, Nemo was pondering all which was required of him.

The First Angel of light demanded she was given proof; Chan Li was alive or dead; and he was intrigued to know how she might respond.

He let his powers develop and sent out a signal, and he too was required to remain patient.

Nemo focussed his attention firmly on his adversary, expecting her to renege on her promise of commitment, at any time. He sporadically sent out a scan, and despite coming across anomalies of concentrated light energy, they were at a considerable distance and at no time had they fluctuated to pose a threat.

'We have spoken of mutual trust,' Abigail remarked, to steer his concentration back to her, and once again allowed the fine covering of feathers to slowly evaporate and re-emerge. *'The sacrifices I am to make are greater, and still you are wondering if I can stand at your side without plotting a different path. How will it be for you, having me as your equal and cementing a future of harmony together? Does it not conflict with all your principals? Will it content you, sufficient, as you will not be spreading evil across the world and instigating chaos in every realm?'*

'It is your belief, Dark Energy exists to permeate discord, and I can understand why you would not think differently. You have been given no reason, throughout time, to consider an alternate path where a measure of discord with that of harmony can exist as a necessary balance. Everything has its opposite; we both know that. You cannot have one without the other. Together, we can create a world of opposites which, unified, can work to prosperity.'

'It makes sense.'

'*On a personal level,*' Nemo added, while carefully outlining his intentions with the right choice of words, '*When we eventually unite as one, will I detect a certain amount of repugnance within you, knowing that you commit to it unwillingly?*'

Abigail responded with a vocal chuckle, and Nemo was surprised by her reaction.

'*Bless you,*' she answered, *but am I detecting a small measure of uncertainty and lack of confidence?*'

'*Why would you think that?*'

'*Let me just say this; whether you choose to believe me, or not. Keep to your promise and leave the children alone, and I will prove my worth, beyond your expectations. It makes perfect sense; it has finally come to this. We are First Angels, and a result of the loins of both opposing forces in the universe. Just maybe, we've been viewing this all differently, and this is how it was always meant to be. You have come this day, having made time and effort to change your appearance. I'd just like to add, that you look younger; by a few million years at least.*'

The intimate exchange had her smiling, and the smile turned to ripples of gentle and genuine laughter.

'*Know this, in my heart, I do find you handsome, and more besides,*' she said, and retracted her costume of feathers so that she was naked, without being vulnerable. '*What turns me on; is honesty. That which turns me off; is someone who purports to say one thing, while thinking something else entirely.*'

The feathered features returned and she detected his breathing was heavier, his pupils lightening to a pale grey, yet his attention was firmly on Abigail and no place else.

'Then let me just say this, in all honesty; in that I find you immeasurably enticing and most pleasing to the eye,' he admitted, and Abigail believed he was being sincere.

Thoughts of Chan Li were not her only consideration, knowing that the teleporting of individuals could take time. She had time.

She was also curious.

'What you see, and what you feel, is a physical response,' she delivered to him in sensual tones. *'But what of a spiritual connection? Are you willing to participate, Nemo? As a test of trust and unity?'*

To prepare herself implementing a course which had not been considered within the realms of her masterplan, and was ultimately taking a monumental risk, Abigail revealed herself naked once again and allowed the physical image to linger.

At the same time, she created an aura of energy around her and had a sinuous column of her signature extend away from the position of her third eye.

Completely enamoured, yet not wholly convinced of Abigail's sincerity, Nemo responded likewise and extended a tendril of his own energy towards Abigail.

Abigail had already determined Nemo had remained a pure spirit and was not self-inflicted with one of his own monstrous creations.

The sinuous effulgent tentacles tentatively approached one another, and as with magnetic poles of resistance, the adverse energies conflicted initially. Slowly and insistently, the field of adversity was broken down, each tip of energy spasming before slowly settling. The opposing tendrils exhibited curiosity laced with caution. Yet both were eager to explore the boundaries they were to breach, to know how it would feel; how the other would respond.

The tips oscillated, a moment before a connection was made, and there came a brief blinding flash. The opposing trails coiled around one another and Abigail was the first to gasp and close her eyes.

The intensity of emotions was far greater than she'd anticipated, and for one disheartening moment, believed she might regret her decision to test Nemo's integrity.

Feeling Nemo exerting his will and attempting to control her, she repelled him with a surge of energy. They remained connected, and each began to levitate. Their physical host bodies began to convulse, and neither one was able to break the link.

It was only as another glowing orb approached, Abigail and Nemo were able to sever the spiritual alignment they had created for each other and settle on the ground once again.

Abigail's eyes blazed fire, which was not an indication of anger. It was taking a considerable effort to have her energy recoil, even as she pulled around a fine cloak of feathers, the sensual feel of them fluttering like small moths on her host skin, had her endure continuous orgasms.

She was able to assess; Nemo was experiencing similar emotions, and she was gratified to know the effects of their spiritual unity had astounded him in a way neither of them had foreseen.

A bright effulgence appeared between them and as the glare slowly dissipated, a grovelling Chan Li was revealed. He suddenly seemed to sense where he was and looked up to Abigail's position with red-rimmed eye sockets. He was muttering without speaking, and Abigail was reminded of the guardian Panea, when she had discovered him in the ice cave in Antarctica.

She didn't react as Nemo would have expected her to and saw that he was intrigued by her cool ambivalent façade.

Abigail responded in a different way, by relaying a sequence of codes to the crystals hidden beneath them.

Abigail remained unflinching and stood her ground, as her lover scrabbled around the grass on hands and knees, pawing at the blades like he had found his salvation, even as he knew his plight was a hopeless one.

Abigail tried not to concentrate on the limb with the missing foot, or dwell on his empty sockets, or the fact he had no tongue.

It was his plaintive cry for mercy which slammed into her mind.

'Kill me!' Chan pleaded with her. 'I am lost to you. Lost to myself. I am no longer Chan Li as you knew him, warrior elite and crusader for justice. I am infected.'

Abigail ignored his plea, on the surface and did not reply in the verbal sense. It was within her power to relay a code to what was left of his mind, in the hope he would understand.

'Sorry,' she said. 'This is all my fault.'

'No! Never think that!'

In the field at rear, the crystal within the pyramid, became activated on a different frequency, and drew energy from the universe.

The portal within the circle of oak thrummed and began to glow.

LEGACY OF ANGELS

Free Spirit broke into a canter to ensure the perimeter defences acted as an impregnable shield to the intensifying vibrations emanating from the stellar portal.

It was imperative Nemo remained oblivious to the change and looming threat.

There came a formidable column of effulgence from within the circle's spectrum, its intensity waning quickly to reveal the four celestials who had travelled from the Amazon Basin.

From the moment they arrived, they were to embark on another, shorter travail, and timing and precision in the execution of the signals given to them, was of the essence.

The children, standing side by side within the smaller cluster of crystals in the spare room of the cottage, knew the moment was upon them, and each gave an audacious wink to the watchful Celestine who was unable to completely mask her anxiety.

She released the children at the same time the circle of ancient oak released the four celestials.

Out in the field, Nemo was unapologetically satisfied his adversary was cowed at sight of the stricken Chan Li she'd deigned to commune with in the mortal sense, seen as an abuse of her powers and position in the hierarchy of angels.

He noticed her posture had stiffened, yet she hadn't moved to go to the pathetic creature scrabbling on the grass between them. Nemo sensed she was hurting deeply though.

He believed; this was a battle he could win and do so with ease.

LEGACY OF ANGELS

Nemo flinched the moment he felt the rising circle of energy all around them and was trying to understand what was occurring. He came to realise Abigail was not outwardly motivating the unwelcome surge to palpate his host flesh and seep into his pores.

He stood aghast, as all around, bright columns of energised light oozed up from the earth and he became witness to identifiable forms within them. Six, in total, merged with the brutal aura swelling around the First Angel, making seven. When definition could be identified, Nemo was astounded by those he was to confront.

He didn't react, as he was unable to; the circle of energy – a unified ring of power – superior even to his own, contained him.

'You conniving bitch!' he sneered and growled within Abigail's mind. *'You talk about trust, and this is how you deceive me!'*

'I can be trusted; to maintain a harmonious balance. I cannot imagine for one moment, you are someone who can exist, without chaos. It ends here.'

'You think; it will be this easy?'

Nemo had surmised his physical and spiritual form had been incarcerated, not that he understood how they meant to preserve the fortress they had created for him, over a specific framework of time.

He might not have his physical prowess; but his mind was free.

Nemo relayed a command, and doing so, smiled wickedly; triumphantly.

Now, he was thinking, they would know CHAOS.

AS IT HAS BEEN WRITTEN.

CHAPTER 16

UNLEASHED...CHAOS...

And there came,

A nightmarish vision

No one can wake from...

It began; as a dense grey mist, roiling off the seas and oceans, hugging ponds and lakes, rivers, and streams.

Wherever there existed water, so the ethereal mist embraced it. And it moved, at a relentless pace, drawn to dry land and its unsuspecting inhabitants.

Across the planet and the new Eastern hemisphere, families numbering in their thousands who resided along coastal regions of countries and depleted islands, had ceased whatever they were doing to observe the encroaching phenomenon.

There was excitement and boisterous comments, murmurings of uncertainty and even lamentable sobbing. While some viewed the immense folds of mist as a divine miracle; a sign from the heavens, others were inclined to think they were facing impending doom.

All the positive energy permeating the atmosphere became quickly tainted.

And it was felt, as even the most optimistic of souls clung to vestige traces of how it once was, when the world suffered extremes of climate as a prelude to the destructive quakes and tsunamis, volcanic eruptions, and thunderous winds,

As the fog banks bore down on these exposed regions, people of all races were witness to sporadic lightning flashes within its vast roiling tent.

Some ran away, and there came fearful screams and panic. Some stayed to pray. While others stood to face the onslaught, mesmerised, and unsure how to react.

The Western hemisphere, enjoying the tranquillity of night under clear skies, a coruscating miasma of stars, and a magical full moon, the inhabitants of these areas were oblivious to the encroaching phenomena.

Only the fishermen; out on the waters from Alaska to the far Southern reaches of Africa; and of those who loved to camp on the beaches at night-time, and of those who could not sleep for one reason or another, were alert to change in the etheric patterns and were witness to the immense black curtain steadily moving inland, its unnatural course highlighted by lunar rays.

Violent electrical flashes lit up the horizon, illuminating the roiling fog further, as it swallowed up the surface of seas and oceans on a relentless path to the mainland.

Those towns and villages which had been developed around lakes or sprawled the banks of rivers, had residents observing a grey misty wall rising from the depths of the tranquil water's surface, creating a vast dividing wall which obliterated a view of the opposite side.

All who saw this, waited apprehensively and hoped to understand.

The attack on inhabitants across the entire planet was synchronised to occur at precisely the same time.

It was another occasion; the whole world screamed in unison.

Abigail saw everything, as Nemo intended her too. She was unable to react, as world domination was in its infancy.

She was torn into making a radicle decision, while at the same time, was alert to her son's anxiety and despair. It was only natural, as Luke was a witness to his great friend's horrific and pitiful predicament, and an enormous welter of anguish built within him.

Nemo was clearly enjoying the plight of the seven sentinels as he telegraphed images of catastrophic horror taking place on the coastal regions of the planet and inland areas around bodies of accumulated water. All became witness to a world under siege, its population helpless and hopelessly defenceless.

Every warm-blooded individual came under attack from the marauding mutant jellyfish, some of the species more than two hundred feet. The predators were not intent absorbing themselves into host bodies, for they had been instructed to kill everyone.

The monstrous incarnations poured out of the mist, tentacles raging and lashing at unsuspecting crowds, panic having people run amok, yet there was no safe place to flee.

As thousands of the creations in every locale gambolled onto land and, as a tide, swept into inhabited areas, they crashed through doors and windows to get to those who believed they were safe inside their homes or shops.

The creatures scaled the taller buildings to get to anyone cowering on the upper floors, and there came despicable carnage.

Everywhere, on every continent, there was incessant screaming, as people were mercilessly ripped apart or incinerated by the lashing electrically charged tentacles flailing in their thousands out of the mist.

People were blind, unable to see where they were going, until it was too late.

Children cried lamentably, calling to their mothers and fathers, and every cry was a beacon for the rampaging monsters.

Abigail could only grit her teeth in despair as she was witness to the horrific slaughter of innocents, and momentarily believed she was helpless to bring an end to the genocide, as much of her attention was on restraining Luke and stopping him from doing anything rash.

It was Nemo's braying laugh which severed the untenable link.

Luke launched himself away from his designated position of power, and Abigail along with the others, could only watch in stupefied horror, as Luke threw streamers of energy at his one-time friend grovelling helplessly and forlornly on the ground.

Chan screamed, or it could have been the creature using his host body, even as Abigail heard him within her mind, saying; *'Thank you.'*

Luke stepped back and was unable to stem the flow of tears which sprung ingloriously to his eyes, his energy continuing to gnaw away at Chan's host flesh and the creature trying to emerge.

LEGACY OF ANGELS

Nemo could have taken advantage of the sudden breach to the fortress ensnaring him, with Luke having broken the powerful circle of energy. He could have teleported away from his position and waged a war of revenge at a great distance.

It was, however, Luke's reaction and emotional pain which had Nemo hesitate, as he saw humour in the boy's plight and pain.

Abigail reacted instinctively and urged Luke to take up position once again; and miserably, Luke complied.

Even before she could unscramble her thoughts and salvage something from the impending debacle, something unexpected and inexplicable at the time, occurred.

From behind Nemo's position, along with Aurora and Dolmati, hurtled a bright orb from the night sky having burst forth from another dimension.

Abigail wanted to cry out; *'NO!'* the moment she recognised the signature arriving.

She briefly caught Nemo studying her, while his attention was on the wholesale slaughter of already depleted civilisations he had engineered to avenge his father's defeat in the war of angels, and for Abigail reneging on a promise.

Even for one so powerful, he was slow to react, as the energised anomaly slammed into the earth at his heels, a lance of energy penetrating his back at the same time, protruding from his chest.

CHAPTER 17

MAELSTROM

And there will come,

HELL ON EARTH...

The unexpected visiting celestial thrust a second and third time with a shortened flaming blade of energy, Nemo finally slumping to knees he no longer felt, while wondering how it had come to this.

The group of celestials were reduced to shock yet maintained a circle of confinement. None, more so, than Nemo; whose black heart had been pierced. He instantly felt the surge of light energy absorbing his host organs and flesh.

At no time did Nemo remove his gaze from Abigail's stricken face, and even believed, he was witness to genuine remorse.

He failed to understand why, in that moment, the First Angel had not acted to prevent the calamitous assault, supposing she had not instigated it as part of the plan to nullify his powers. She would know the consequences of destroying one of the powerful energies which created balance in the universe.

The consequences of her folly, had him believing he was the victor in their private war.

The flaming weapon used against him was retracted, the glowing orb having descended from the universe to implement the assault, changing form and extending vertically as it acquired human form and definition.

Cole stepped to the side, ignoring everyone, as it was imperative he had an opportunity to gaze into Nemo's eyes before the enemy's life-force expired.

As the flesh, bones and organs of the host body became quickly devoured, Nemo's soul spiralled frenetically, with no place to escape to.

The shield created to confine him continued to keep him restrained and trapped.

Cole stepped back, the moment he sensed the evil soul studying him. He thought about again summoning his weapon of power, and relented, believing his powers alone were not sufficient to kill Nemo's spirit.

Having existed in a stupor for a moment, he flinched as Abigail reached out to grasp his arm and looking at her, he felt the depths of her pain and anguish.

Cole understood instantly; in that his rage had damned them all for an eternity.

It came as a surprise to him, Abigail should raise a hand and stroke his cheek, to get him to focus through his tears.

411

LEGACY OF ANGELS

At the precise moment Cole had thrust home with his formidable lance of energy, the monstrous hell-spawn jellyfish in their thousands across the globe suddenly froze, as each one absorbed the impact of the attack on their master. They each endured the consequences through a spiritual connection with him.

They were seen to tremble and to sway, before collapsing in a gelid heap. The heavy pall of grey mist quickly dissipated as immense hooded domes squelched to the ground on the floors of apartments, homes, shops and offices; on tarmac, sand and grass. Their enormous tentacles juddered briefly and became lifeless.

Human survivors of every coastal region had no time to overcome their shock and fear, and even to understand what had occurred. As the jellyfish attack, was only the beginning.

Worse was to come.

For those who were blissfully unaware there had been a vicious attack on vast populations all over the globe, those who dwelt further inland away from lakes, rivers, and streams, where large communities inhabited caves and cabins and had been content for a time.

They would come to know; there was no escaping the wrath of the universe.

Abigail felt the first tremors, before anyone else, and knew would follow.

She felt Cole's tremulous digits tease a path of affection down one side of her face, removing traces of her own tears.

'I know that I have damned us all,' he sighed remorsefully. 'In truth, I had no idea. It always felt, like something was pushing me; feeding my rage, and governing my course.'

'Lovely; this is no fault of yours,' Abigail responded. 'I confess; it is I who has been the architect of this moment. It is apparent, my father cannot forgive me; that much I feel, even as I fail to understand why he would let it happen. He knows the consequences of having the universal balance severed.'

'What am I to do, Abby? There must be something, to make amends for this debacle. You have been a wonderful friend, throughout, and wish to recompense.'

'I ask, that you take my position in the circle, and to stay for a time beyond the moment. The children are in capable hands, but it's my belief, you have an important role to play in their future. It would please me, should you accept, and it's the only recompense I seek from you.'

'I do so, willingly; dearest Abby.'

She raised herself up and kissed the corner of his mouth, before stepping across to confront the spiralling energy form of Nemo, which had everyone entranced.

Abigail telegraphed her intent to him, before turning to gather the children to her, crouching, so that she was level with their downcast gaze.

It was the moment there came a deep rumbling from the depths of the earth, a wind strengthening, as dark clouds gathered across a wide area of the sky.

Abigail knew then, time was of the essence.

'You are leaving us,' said Daniel morosely.

'Mummy!' Luke pleaded. 'Do you have to go?'

'Sweetie, I have no choice. It is the only way.'

'Will you ever return?' Luke asked hopefully, a stream of tears free flowing, to pool at his quivering chin.

'I cannot make any promises, darling. I would like to say, yes. I will try, baby. If it is within my power and is meant to be, I will return.'

'I love you so much, mummy.'

'Oh baby, I love you too. I never wanted it to end like this. I ask, that you watch over the herd and other animals. Free Spirit belongs to you now.'

Luke's sobs quashed any other words, as Abigail hugged, rocked, and kissed him.

Time was running out, as the adults looked to the sky, and were witness to a phenomenon they hoped never to see. As with the survivors of every race across the globe.

Blacker than the night sky, emerged a cavernous black hole which seemed to extend and yawn, resembling a hungry mouth, as those who were witness to it would swear the great hole was swallowing the stars.

Immense electro-magnetic and plasma-fuelled lightning bolts slammed to earth, annihilating everything beneath, buildings, mountains, rivers and lakes, and people. The ferocity of the onslaught incinerated huge swaths of forest, and bodies of water were boiled dry, stamping craters in the earth a hundred metres across.

Then came the destructive and poisonous radioactive winds. They struck with relentless momentum, flaying flesh from bone, hurling debris at a velocity which demolished vulnerable dwellings with ease, uprooting trees, and launching boulders as missiles.

Abigail crossed to Seraphina with a little more urgency, knowing in her heart, she did not have the luxury of delaying her farewells. They embraced and kissed and shared a deluge of tears – so much more, as their souls were inextricably entwined.

'You know what you have to do,' Abigail telegraphed to her mind. *'You are all guardians to the children, of mankind and Mother Earth. It is now my time to be the one given as a sacrifice, to save all that we have fought to save.'*

With a last kiss, Abigail moved to Michael and embraced him. She went to Aurora, and then to Dolmati.

'You will be forever in our hearts and minds,' he said to her. *'Find your path back to us. We will be here; waiting.'*

Before saying a final farewell to her son, Abigail was witness to Free Spirit cantering towards the group.

Abigail went quickly to the mare and hugged her broad neck, lavishing kisses on her snout. She gave instructions to her greatest companion and kindred spirit, and let Free Spirit know; there would come a time when they will connect again and ride like the wind.

Abigail went to Luke and dropped to her knees, tugging him to her breast as everything became an indistinct haze with the onslaught of fresh tears.

'Be brave and wise,' she said to him in a feathery whisper.

With her emotions threatening to have her crumple and concede, she gave a nod to Cole who had taken up her position over the crystal embedded deep within the earth, and approached the tranquil spiral of energy, that which was Nemo's trapped soul.

LEGACY OF ANGELS

The energy of the pyramid fought to repel the destructive forces unleashed by the maelstrom, where its hungry maw continued to stretch and sucked up all beneath it.

Abigail raised a hand and let the spiralling energy encapsulate her, sensing her host flesh was slowly evaporating, until only a glowing orb remained, and this became a gyrating helix of a light green hue.

The two souls melded, interlocking, and became as one. And then they rose; slowly at the beginning and were then catapulted skyward into the eye of the gargantuan black cavity.

A great blinding light flared and illuminated the entire sky.

It was a matter of moments only, before the vortex began to retreat, the force of the maelstrom weakening, and the electro-magnetic winds abating.

CHAPTER 18

A NEW BEGINNING...

The legacy of angels

And war with the universe

Has, once again,

Caused carnage and suffering.

Mankind will rise from the ashes,

More resolute,

As with nature and Mother Earth.

The planet has been saved.

It is a new beginning...

All was not calm, even as the climate settled, and for every mortal who miraculously survived the maelstrom, there existed lamentable screams. For they were afraid and confused, desperate, and lost.

LEGACY OF ANGELS

The animal and avian population across a devastated planet remained in hiding for a time, as even nature's creatures were fearful and uncertain.

It was for the universal energy of every surviving pyramid, of those not to have been ransacked by dark energy's army, to remove deadly traces of radiation from the atmosphere and create a positive balance.

As it was for every celestial guardian, whose task was to embark on a mission of mercy once again and restore hope to beleaguered civilisations.

On the Spiritual Lodge estate, all who had gathered to implement Abigail's masterplan before Cole's unknowing calamitous intervention, became a witness to the unbelievable carnage beyond their perimeter defences.

Luke's unrelenting misery had him scamper away, as he had no wish to engage with anyone. He wanted only to be with Free Spirit, who was an integral link to his mother.

Celestine had vacated the cottage and was floating across the grass to meet with the formidable group of angels who were gathered within the circle of energy.

Even angels can suffer human frailties, and all it appears, were in shock and endeavouring to console one another.

Celestine understood why as she shared a spiritual link with them, and she too was saddened Abigail was given no option but to leave with the enemy and maintain balance in the universe.

One in the group, stood apart and seemed like a lost soul. His sadness was two-fold, as aside from guilt, he was mourning the loss of a wife and son. And he wore his grief as a badge.

Celestine was required to remain strong and buoyant, having received a plea and instruction from Abigail before she allowed herself to be a sacrifice, to extend a message to her mother Aisha and have her return to the estate.

She'd watched Luke levitating and launching himself astride Free Spirit, where he grabbed a fistful of mane and dug in his heels to spur the mare into a canter.

Celestine was satisfied Luke was in no danger, as he could have no better companion or guardian, than his mother's faithful Free Spirit. She understood also, his need to be alone to grieve his losses.

Celestine was also aware of Luke's courageous decision to release his good friend, Chan Li, from the grip of dark energy and defeat the creature which had taken him over.

As she reached the circle, Seraphina and Michael were embracing their son, Daniel, when his grandmother Aurora joined the reunion. They were all fighting to create an element of joy. It was a beginning.

Dolmati stood to one side and was observing Luke and Free Spirit cantering around the field. He understood, no matter how much Luke pleaded, Free Spirit would not take him from the sight of the adults. The mare was another, to have received instructions.

Dolmati wanted entry into the boy's mind and thoughts and was quietly pleased at the way Luke was dealing with his grief and in such a short time. He was showing commendable maturity, as he'd convinced himself his mother leaving was only a temporary aberration. His faith was unbreakable.

As Free Spirit fed the boy hope, Dolmati was of the opinion, there could be no way back for the First Angel; not without the other.

LEGACY OF ANGELS

It was all about maintaining an equilibrium and was a reason Abigail had to leave with a defeated Nemo. Nemo's soul could be repaired, as it was imperative it remained united with Abigail's as a singular entity.

Celestine concentrated her energy and time on the figure who stood apart and was gazing up at the sky, as if all his answers could be read in the correlation of stars.

Cole didn't, at first, acknowledge the arrival of another, as his mind was deeply enmeshed with the events he had created; the pain he'd caused. He came out of his reverie the moment she audaciously took one of his hands in her own and fed him her energy.

He became instantly captivated with Celestine's gracious smile and the smouldering unjudgmental lustre of her pale eyes.

'I can help rebuild your life,' she spoke within his mind. *'You have been chosen to stand with us and help repair the world, once again. You are also, Chan Li's replacement, and guardian protector of the children. I sense, our First Angel Abigail, knew more than she let on, and recognised your strengths and purity of spirit. You were given no choice, Cole, and no one casts blame on you. Abigail stores great faith in your abilities, and it is not for I or anyone, to question her reasons for choosing you. I think Abigail knew, all along, you were the perfect choice.'*

'I owe Abby so much, and will do all that is required of me,' Cole responded.

'I can help you in other ways,' Celestine continued, and hoped to cajole a smile from the stricken warrior whose hand she clasped with fervour. She raised her free hand and stroked his temple and cheek. *'Your grief is relentless and can weaken you. I make no promises, Cole, can only try. If you will allow me. Together, we can traverse the spiritual highways across dimensions, as it will now be safe to do so, Wherever we travel, we telegraph a coded sequence along these channels, to the universe. It is possible, not definite, the*

lost souls of your wife and son will respond to an echo of your own. Abigail taught me many things. She helped me expand my own powers. You must hold on to hope, Cole.'

'*Thank you, Celestine,*' and he'd plucked her name from a pattern within her thoughts. '*If I am to connect with my family, I will do all in my power to bring them home. That is a promise I make to myself.*'

'*As you know, the universe is a great store of secrets and unquestionable power. Anything is possible.*'

They came alert to Daniel's strident laughter and that of his jubilant parents.

Aurora had joined Dolmati, and she liked that he observed a mortal tradition, as he slipped an arm around her slender waist.

It was romantic; she was thinking.

Attention was drawn to a row of shimmering orbs to appear at the site of the solitary horse chestnut tree in the field. Each took on the form of the estate's esteemed guardians, having been recalled. There was also Aisha and the twin souls of Gillian and Margaret O'Shaughnessy.

A shooting star fizzed across the sky, and then another.

Following a brief lull there came sporadic bursts of interstellar activity.

'Beautiful,' Cole stated simply. 'It is something which never ceases to amaze me.'

Celestine was surreptitiously studying his handsome profile.

When he added, 'There will always exist beauty amidst all the ugliness.'

Celestine smiled; looked up.

Seraphina gave a chuckle and waved to the sky. Turning, she stated what she believed was fact. 'Darling Abby, is letting us all know; all will be just fine for the future of our new world.'

Luke was laughing also as he was feeling carefree and remembering all the wonderful occasions he'd enjoyed riding with his mother. And to fly. As angels.

Free Spirit had no intention of spreading her wings, and Luke understood why, knowing a time would come when he would have wings of his own; and greater power, to exceed that which he had already.

He vowed to learn how to be a great warrior, and emulate his wonderful friend and mentor, Chan Li.

The one who was named Cole, who had single-handedly defeated the source of Dark Energy, had his mother's total trust. She chose Cole as guardian protector.

Until she returned.

Luke believed his mother would find a way back.

He also felt, he could learn much from Cole.

His mother had sensed the man's potential, and Luke felt it too. Cole was so much more than he appeared.

Luke steered Free Spirit to join with the swelling group of honourable angels, who were gathering in the field where the crystals beneath the ground were singing a sweet ancient aria.

A sudden flurry of shooting stars in the firmament had everyone gasping in wonder.

The tragic state of the world beyond the perimeter of the Spiritual Lodge estate, was temporarily forgotten.

Dark Energy was forgotten.

No one was imagining a recurrence of evil.

Despite the fact, dark forces had always found a way to inflict its poison and chaos, since the dawn of time.

It was insidious.

And it was inevitable.

EVIL – WOULD – RETURN.

It was a matter of, when. . .

THE END

IT IS NEVER THE END

AS THERE WILL COME

THE ANGEL WARS CONTINUUM

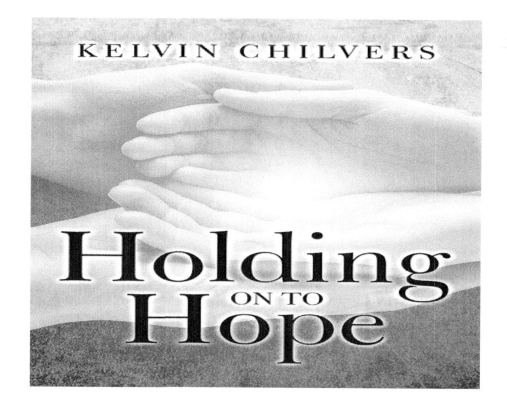

KELVIN CHILVERS

Holding ON TO **Hope**

Victim of abuse, Rebecca 17, finds love with Nick and his canine companion Max. Having witnessed the death of her alcoholic and abusive father in a car accident, aged thirteen, Rebecca carries a terrible secret which, at that time, stole her voice. Rebecca's mother is the only person who knows the truth and will go to any lengths to ensure her daughter suffers. Rebecca must battle her ghosts, a jealous and embittered mother, the unwanted attentions of her mother's latest boyfriend and the narcissistic obsession of a school tutor, in the hope love can be her salvation.

LEGACY OF ANGELS

DREAMING ANGELS: Volume One ANGEL WARS TRILOGY

A MODERN DAY FANTASY

As the two opposing forces of the universe conflict, all await the Chosen One's 'AWAKENING,' a force of hope in a War Of Angels, to save the world from extinction.

THE TIME IS NOW

Seraphina has been groomed since the dawn of time to lead a battle against Dark Energy, as evil challenges the Angels of Light. Mankind and Mother Earth faces its greatest test and all will witness, HELL ON EARTH!

FIRST ANGEL: THE PREQUEL Volume Two ANGEL WARS TRILOGY

First Angel Abigail and daughter to the universe, has come to Earth periodically since the beginning of time and waged war against dominant evil so that mankind and Mother Earth can evolve.

At this present time, she enters our world in human guise so that her secret is preserved, her duty to the Chosen One and the planet's survival. She is the future beyond a War of Angels, as evil can never be defeated. It will come again.

Printed in Great Britain
by Amazon

18060718R00246